# Praise for Anne Stuart

'Anne Stuart delivers exciting stuff for those of us
who like our romantic suspense dark and dangerous.'
—Jayne Ann Krentz

'THE HOUSE OF ROHAN series begins with a
scintillating, titillating, wickedly dark and sensual tale as
Stuart brilliantly draws you in like a black widow spider.
Intelligent characters swirl around a beautifully rendered,
complex plot. The erotic overtones—one masterful scene
after another—and dark hero simply add to the delicious
story that captures the heart and soul.'
—*RT Book Reviews* on *Ruthless*, Top Pick!
*RT Book Reviews* Reviewer's Choice Award winner for
Best Sensual Historical Romance

'Powerful'
—*Publishers Weekly* on *Ruthless*

'The strong plotline and marvellously crafted characters
flesh out a love story that's a feast for those who prefer
lots of heat and depth of plot.'
—*RT Book Reviews* on *Reckless*, Top Pick!

'Anne Stuart proves once again why she is one of the
most beloved and reliably entertaining authors in the
genre. Every book she writes is witty, inventive, dark and
sexy—a wild adventure for the mind…and the heart.'
—Susan Wiggs on *The House of Rohan*

'For dark, triumphant romance…Anne Stuart
can't be beaten.'
—Elizabeth Lowell

'Stuart crafts a heated romance with a glimpse into
the darkness of passion and the humour of love while
maintaining a strong plotline and a powerful secondary
love story. These are marks of a grand mistress
of the genre!'
—*RT Book Re*

D1513067

# PROLOGUE

He was packing when he heard the first scream. He shouldn't have been doing his own packing—there were servants enough for menial labor such as that. But Phelan Romney was unconventional, a private, cynical man who had little need of servants, and Hannigan, the only man he trusted with his possessions, had disappeared on some obscure errand. Phelan had no intention of staying in the small, drafty manor that housed his parents for even one more night.

He should never have come home. He hadn't wanted to—the open warfare between his drunken, philandering bully of a father and his hysterical mother had made Romney Hall a battlefield, and Phelan had had enough of battles during the past few years to last him a lifetime. All he had to show for his seven-year stint in the army was a knife scar damnably near his heart and a passion for exotic climates. He'd already developed a healthy distaste for life in England, particularly on the cold, remote moors of Yorkshire that his reckless younger brother loved so well.

He'd sold out his commission years before, the one he'd

bought over his parents' furious objections. He'd finally come home, not for the sake of his father, whose health after a lifetime of dedicated debauchery was finally failing; not for the sake of his mother, whose clinging possessiveness and shrill temper seemed to have increased with age, something he wouldn't have thought possible. He'd come home for the sake of his half brother, Valerian, one of the very few people he'd ever dared let himself care for.

But not even for Valerian would he stay one day longer. The dark, cold Yorkshire nights made him feel as if he were suffocating. God willing, his father would live another twoscore years, and he himself would be allowed to roam the world at will. By the time he inherited his unwanted duties, perhaps his wanderlust would be slaked.

He heard the screams from a distance, and an unnamed horror swept over him. He knew the sound of his mother's voice—it was raised often enough in rage or misery. No one else would be shrieking through the drafty halls of Romney Hall. And the word sounded eerily like "murder."

He found her in the tower room, the cold stone bedchamber she'd never shared with Lord Harry. She was kneeling over her husband's body, the pool of blood beneath him soaking into her skirts. "Murderer!" she screeched, her eyes dark and mad within her pale face, her long gray hair hanging witchlike around her. "You've killed your own father!"

Phelan followed his mother's stare, to the sight of his half brother. Valerian was as motionless as the body of their father. Only Lady Margery moved, moaning, wringing her long thin hands, rocking back and forth over the body of the husband she'd despised.

"He's murdered your father," Margery screamed, her

shrill voice bordering on madness. "I saw him, Phelan! He stabbed the poor man, who always loved his filthy little bastard more than you, his true son. He—"

"Enough!" Phelan thundered. He took a step toward his younger brother, and he could see the pain in his eyes, the anguish in his soul. Just as he could see the blood on his shirt, and on the knife in his hands. Of the three Romneys left alive in the room, only Valerian, the wild, reckless one, the one with no legal claim to the name, had actually loved Lord Harry. Only Valerian would truly grieve his passing. "Give me the knife, Val."

Valerian moved across the room numbly, placing the knife in Phelan's large, outstretched hand. It was warm, and wet with their father's blood. Valerian raised his eyes to meet his brother's, and for once his pretty face, the one Phelan had always teased him about, was pale and ugly with grief. "I didn't, Phelan," he said. "I heard your mother screaming and I—"

"Liar!" Margery shrieked. "I saw you, you vicious little killer! I saw you plunge the knife into his heart."

There was no dismissing the shock on Valerian's face as he looked at Lady Margery. "She's lying," he said desperately. "She's mad, Phelan. You know I couldn't have—"

"I saw you!" Margery screamed again. "And I'll tell everyone. They'll hang you. I'll make certain they do. Patricide is a crime against nature. You'll be hunted down like a dog if you try to run. You'll be dragged through the streets in chains. Stop him before he tries to run, Phelan. Kill him if you must!"

"No!" Valerian cried. "I won't run. I'll stay right here, and find out who killed him. I'll prove it..."

Lady Margery had risen to her knees, and Phelan

watched in numb shock as her blood-streaked skirts flowed against her thin body. "Do something, Phelan!" she hissed. "Or they might not believe the truth. They might think you did it. Kill him before he runs away. If you don't, I will. I won't rest until he dies!"

Phelan moved then, grabbing his brother's arm. "We're leaving here," he said. "Come along."

"I won't run," Valerian said again, stubbornly.

It took Phelan only a moment to decide. In the distance he could hear the servants, coming to investigate Margery's screams.

"Yes, you will," he said. "And I'm going with you."

up with something to last a few days. You look as if you haven't eaten in a while."

Julian's smile was faint, charming. "The truth is, I haven't, sir," he said.

For a moment Mowbray didn't move, shocked by the beauty of the boy's smile. It was up to the lad, of course. If he'd a mind to, there were a great many easier ways to earn a living than mucking out a stable or carrying water for the kitchens, both of which required hard work and not much pay. Sir Neville Pinworth was known for his odd tastes, and he had more blunt than almost the entire town of Hampton Regis. If Julian Smith were to catch his eye, a comfortable future for the lad would be ensured. If he liked that sort of thing.

Somehow, Mowbray didn't think he would. He made it his duty not to pass judgment, particularly on men like Pinworth who could buy and sell him five times over, whose goodwill was almost a requirement for those doing business in Hampton Regis. What Sir Neville found to warm his bed was his own concern. Mowbray just didn't think Julian Smith would find the notion more appealing than shoveling horse droppings.

And he wasn't going to put him in Sir Neville's way if he could help it. The Fowl and Feathers was a prosperous enough business; surely it could afford another pair of hands and a strong back, even if the lad looked a bit frail.

air and good Exeter food to fatten you up. You look like a strong breeze could blow you away."

Once more Julian produced that faint, enchanting smile. "I'm stronger than I look, sir."

"Mowbray," he corrected. "And we'll see how strong you are, once you finish the stables."

It took Julian Smith three and a half hours to muck out the old hay and manure, replace it with fresh bedding, and feed and curry the horses. They were prime horseflesh, Julian could recognize that, even though they were a far cry from the graceful Arabian stallions he'd ridden in Egypt.

He shoved a hand through his hair, grimacing to himself as he felt the short-cropped ends. It was undoubtedly cooler this way, he thought, rubbing an arm across his sweating forehead. If only he dared remove his jacket.

"You've done a fine job, lad." Mowbray appeared at his elbow. "You can have a wash over there in the trough, and then come in for some supper. My Bessie's wanting to meet you, and she says to tell you another pair of hands is always welcome, even if it comes with a mouth to feed. I don't suppose you have a place to stay?"

"Not yet," Julian said, shaking his head.

"Well, we've a spare room over the kitchen. You're welcome to bed down there for a night or two."

"You're very kind," Julian said shyly.

Mowbray looked embarrassed, his bluff, hearty face

"No need to worry, lad. You'll be in the kitchens." Mowbray gave him a reassuring cuff on the shoulder, and Julian reeled backward beneath the impact. "My Bessie will see to it that you're well fed and safe."

*Safe,* Julian thought, keeping his face determinedly cheerful. If only it were so easy. Even someone as warm and matronly as Bessie couldn't accomplish that feat, he thought several hours later, sitting in the corner of the overwarm kitchen, sweat forming beneath his jacket, his stomach comfortably full, his eyes drifting closed from exhaustion. If only he could have just a few days of rest, of decent food, of freedom from having to look over his shoulder to see whether he was being followed.

Agnes, one of the overfed serving wenches, breezed through the kitchen door, her plump cheeks red with excitement, her massive bosom heaving. Her eyes immediately went to Julian, and he controlled his instinctive discomfort with an effort.

"Sir Neville's here," she said breathlessly. "Came with those two from Sutter's Head. The three of them are wanting supper, and French brandy, and God knows what else. Dorrie's busy in the taproom, and I'm going to need some help."

Julian didn't move. Bessie glanced up from the hearth, her broad face troubled. "Mowbray said as how the lad wasn't to go into the common room," she said.

"They're not in the common room, they're in the private parlor," Agnes said impatiently. "And you know how the quality is—I should be back there right now. Send the boy up with the brandy."

"I don't know as I should." Bessie looked torn by indecision. She'd been kind to him, immeasurably so, and it was a small enough thing to repay her. It wasn't as if he stood in any danger from the local gentry of Hampton Regis. He'd faced far worse and managed to survive.

"I'll do it," he said, rising from the bench, glad to be away from the soporific fire.

"Why don't you take off your coat?" Bessie suggested kindly, not for the first time. "You must be terribly warm."

Julian shook his head, hoping no one would notice the beads of sweat on his forehead. "I was in the warmer climates for too long," he said. "Even this weather feels chilly."

Bessie shrugged, handing him a tray with brandy and three fine crystal glasses. "Mind the stairs. If anything happens to those glasses, Mowbray would have your hide. Mine as well."

Within a matter of moments Julian had seen through Mowbray's bluster to the essentially kind man beneath. He grinned. "For certain he would," he said.

Bessie gave him a playful swat with her beefy hand. "No sass from you, lad. And keep an eye out for Sir Neville."

"Why?"

Bessie looked perturbed. "You are a young one, aren't you, lad?"

"Seventeen last October," he said, subtracting five years off his actual age.

"Time enough to learn about such things. Just be polite and keep your distance. He's a wondrous sight, is our Sir Neville, but he's got a way about him... Never mind," Bessie ended with a sigh. "Just do as I say."

Sir Neville was a wondrous sight indeed, Julian thought when Agnes let him into the upstairs parlor. He entered unobserved, his large eyes taking in the full glory of Sir Neville and his elegant guest, clearly in the midst of a flirtation.

Sir Neville was dressed in puce. Lace cascaded from his sleeves, adorned his neckcloth, dripped from his fingers. His thinning hair was brushed into a windswept style and faintly tinged with pink, and his complexion owed more to artifice than to nature, with a dead-white pallor offset by several cleverly placed beauty marks. He held a gold quizzing glass in one hand and a chicken-skin fan in the other, which he was languidly waving in the direction of a quite spectacularly attractive young woman.

Oddly enough, Julian thought, the woman, beautiful though she undoubtedly was, was far more masculine than the gentleman was. She was large-boned, healthy-looking, and her golden-blond hair was curled around her broad, creamy white shoulders. Her face was lovely, with huge gray eyes, high cheekbones, a large, sensual mouth, and a chin perhaps a trifle stronger than fashion might decree perfection. She was dressed in pale blue, and if her waist were a bit wide and her satin-slippered foot a bit large, such small inadequacies were more than made up for in the charm of her smile.

They both spied Julian at the same time, and their laughing banter stopped abruptly as they stared at him. He wished he had a hand free to tug at his collar, but had to content himself with keeping his face modestly downcast, hoping he'd be able to escape without further notice.

"And who's this pretty young creature?" a soft, feminine voice crooned. Julian looked toward the lady, then realized with a shock that it was the gentleman who'd spoken.

"He's new, Sir Neville," Agnes offered nervously.

Sir Neville didn't even glance in the maid's direction,

his faintly protruding blue eyes fastening on Julian's face with an almost hungry expression. "I'm aware of that, girl," he snapped, closing his fan and advancing on the hapless Julian. "What's your name, lad?" he continued in that gentle, mincing voice. Julian set the tray on the table, in hopes of making a fast escape, but Sir Neville forestalled him, putting one skinny white finger beneath his chin and tilting his face upward.

"Leave him alone, you wretch," the lady chided in a mocking voice that was a husky drawl, deeper than her gentleman escort's. "Can't you see the boy's an innocent? Not your type at all."

"Oh, I like them innocent," Sir Neville murmured, his finger caressing Julian's chin, his flesh cold against Julian's skin. "It's so much fun debauching them."

There was a third guest in the room. Julian hadn't even noticed as he stood trapped by Sir Neville's basilisk eyes and the lady's amusement, until he felt a presence behind him. An exceedingly large presence, towering over him.

"You heard her, Neville." The deep voice sent unexpected chills down Julian's spine. "Leave the boy alone. Not everyone shares your perverse tastes."

"But how does he know unless he's tried them?" Sir Neville was undaunted. "How would you like to come with me, boy? Live in a beautiful house, wear lovely, silken clothes, have all you want to eat? You'd never have to work, and you'd sleep in a soft feather bed."

"Maybe you'd better explain to him that he wouldn't be sleeping alone," that sardonic voice behind Julian continued.

Julian could feel the blush mount his face. He'd heard of certain tendencies during the time he'd spent in Araby.

Despite Bessie's warning, he hadn't realized the English shared such proclivities.

He backed away from the encroaching white hand, the avid eyes, forgetting for a moment the presence behind him. He came up against someone very large, very solid, very warm, and the hands that came down on his arms were hard and strong and steadying. "If I were you, lad," the voice behind him said in a pleasant drawl, "I'd run like a rabbit from here. Away from dangerous wolves like Sir Neville."

Julian turned, to stare up, way up, into the face of his captor. For a moment, transfixed, he couldn't move.

If the lady was lovely, the other gentleman exquisite, this man was something else entirely. He was tall, maybe not the tallest man Julian had ever seen, but close to it. He was lean, almost gaunt, but there was a steely strength to his body, one Julian had felt in his hands. His hair was black and unfashionably long, and his face was very different from the lady's. It was a narrow, mocking face, with a cynical twist to his somewhat thin mouth, a cool intelligence in his eyes. And those eyes were extraordinary. Gray, like the woman's, yet with an odd silver light to them. Julian had the strange, unnerving feeling that the man could see through to the very center of one's soul. And his need to escape grew even stronger. He had too many secrets to risk sharing them with this clear-eyed stranger.

"You know, Philip," the woman said in her husky voice, "I think he's far more taken with you than with Neville here. Maybe you should consider changing your interests."

The man called Philip paid her no heed, staring down at Julian with an arrested expression on his face. "I don't think so," he said enigmatically.

The door to the private parlor opened, breaking the odd impasse, as the second serving girl rushed in, breathless. "You're needed in the kitchen, Julian," she said importantly. "I'll help out here."

"But I want the lad to wait on us," Sir Neville announced in a peevish voice.

"Let him go, Neville," the lady murmured. "You don't need to debauch anyone today. Concentrate on me instead."

"Lovely though you are, Valerie, you're not my type," Neville said, still casting a longing look at Julian.

"You might be surprised, dear Neville," the lady cooed.

For a moment Julian couldn't move. He had the strange notion that each person in the room, from the two serving girls who'd flirted with him mercilessly earlier in the evening to the lovely lady and the two disparate gentlemen, was viewing him with an unexpectedly sexual curiosity.

It was an absurd, irrational thought. The two gentlemen couldn't be further apart, in looks, in temperament, and presumably in amatory interests. Nevertheless, Julian backed away, completely unnerved. No one made any move to stop him, but as he closed the door quietly behind him, he heard the young lady's husky voice drawl in amusement:

"You know, Philip, maybe we should keep him instead of Neville."

The door closed before Julian could hear the tall man's reply. Only the sardonic tone of his voice carried through the thick oak door. Just as well, Julian told himself, moving down the narrow back stairs to the kitchen. Things were already getting too complicated.

Bessie took one look at him and shooed him upstairs to the loft over the kitchen. It was a hot, airless place, with a small, sagging bed near a window. Someone, probably

Bessie, had made an effort to make the place more home-like, and Julian stared at it in numb surprise, the soft coverlet on the thin mattress, the jug of water for washing. Even his small satchel had been left, untouched, at the foot of the bed.

At least he hoped it was untouched. He hated to think how people would react if they peeked inside at his only possessions.

They were little enough. A change of clothes, this one even more threadbare than the outfit he was wearing. Lace-trimmed, fine lawn undergarments. Another swath of linen. And a pair of diamond-and-pearl drop earrings worth a small fortune.

Julian glanced toward the window, at his reflection in the moonlight. The village of Hampton Regis was still on such a warm summer night, though he could hear the trill of laughter from the tavern below, the sound of the ocean in the distance. And he still marveled that it was Sir Neville who owned that light, feminine voice, not the lady.

He unfastened his jacket and leather waistcoat and took them off, folding them in a neat pile. He stepped out of his breeches and stockings, wiggling his toes in the evening air. Reaching up under the voluminous white shirt, he unwrapped the linen, breathing a sigh of relief.

And then Julian Smith, better known as Juliette MacGowan, daughter of the infamous Black Jack MacGowan, lay down on the pallet and fell into a deep, exhausted sleep.

"What do you mean, we'll keep him instead of Neville?" the man called Philip asked.

"Now don't quarrel," Neville drawled. "You know I detest arguments that aren't of my own making. Besides, I saw him first."

"But my interests in him aren't perverse," Valerie cooed.

"He's about half your age, and doubtless a virgin," Neville replied. "That's perverse enough."

"Oh, I thought I'd get him for Philip."

"The two of you are giving me the headache," the tall man said, dropping down into a chair with lazy elegance and reaching for the glass of brandy Agnes had already poured. "Leave the boy alone."

"I suppose I should," Valerie said with an exaggerated pout. "Still, he tickles my sense of the absurd."

"Why?" Neville inquired, mystified.

Valerie shot him a naughty smile. "I'll tell you when you're older, darling."

Sir Neville reached for her surprisingly strong hand, bringing it to his lips. "If I could ever love a woman," he murmured, "you would be the one."

"I'm immensely flattered," she replied, batting her eyelashes. "I don't know how my husband feels about it."

"Follow your heart, dearest," Philip said in a sardonic voice. "Don't let me interfere with your little pleasures."

Neville dropped her hand with unbecoming swiftness. "I said 'if,'" he said hastily. "But, alas, we'll simply have to stay friends. And speaking of friendship, I might suggest the most wonderful skin cream, made of champagne and sow's milk. It will do wonders for your rough hands."

"Too kind," Valerie murmured.

And Philip only snorted, downing his glass of brandy.

Two hours later Sir Neville's guests were safely ensconced in their carriage, heading back over the moonlit road to their comfortable lodgings at Sutter's Head. They traveled in silence for the most part, until the lady broke it.

"There are times, Phelan, when you have absolutely no sense of humor."

"All I have to do is look at you, brother mine, and my sense of humor reasserts itself," he replied with a mocking drawl.

Valerian kicked at his skirts. "God, did you see the way that little sodomite ogled me? I'm sure he'd be far happier if he knew what I really had under my skirts. As it is, he's totally disgusted with himself for being attracted to a woman."

"I'm pleased you find it amusing," Phelan James Murdock Romney replied.

"Lord knows there's little enough to keep me entertained," Valerian said. "How much longer do I have to be cooped up in these damned skirts? Why in heaven's name did we have to choose this of all masquerades? Couldn't we have been sailors, or tradesmen, or even gypsies? I'm actually beginning to mince," he said, his voice rich with disgust. "And do you realize how long it's been since I've had even a mild flirtation? Not to mention a real flesh-and-blood woman?"

"You were flirting quite effectively tonight."

Valerian shuddered. "That doesn't count. I'm tired of this. Tired of being cooped up in that house, tired of wearing skirts, tired of celibacy and inaction. I tell you, Phelan, I'm going mad."

"I doubt it," Phelan drawled. "I hate to tell you this, Valerian, but with your blond hair you'd never pass for a gypsy."

"You would have, curse your black soul," Valerian muttered without any real rancor. "If we had to go as man and wife, why couldn't you have been the girl?"

"Not fitting for my dignity," Phelan said. "Besides, it's your own fault for being so bloody pretty."

"I don't know how much more of this I can stand. Lord Harry was killed more than a month ago, and what's happened?"

"My mother is enjoying a very public mourning," Phelan said in a bland voice.

"All the while accusing me of cold-blooded murder. Damn it, we need to go back."

"You know as well as I do we can't. My esteemed mother might be half mad, but she's managed to convince a magistrate and the Bow Street runners that you're a cold-blooded murderer. Our safest chance is to leave the country until this blows over."

"I'm not going anywhere," Valerian said mutinously. "Who do you think killed him, Phelan?" he asked in a more subdued voice.

"If we knew that, we wouldn't be hundreds of miles from Yorkshire. We'd be tracking the bloody bastard down and bringing him to justice."

"And that's my only hope, isn't it? Finding who really killed him."

"Our only hope. You're forgetting, I'm in this, too. According to Hannigan, opinion is divided as to which of us actually did the old man in. Most people seem to think I'm the logical culprit and my mother's lying to protect me. They know Lord Harry and I always hated each other, while you, in more ways than one, were his fair-haired boy. I didn't even want to visit Yorkshire, much less step into an inheritance I've always despised."

"No one would be daft enough to believe you could kill him."

"No one would be daft enough to believe you're a woman," Phelan countered. "People believe what they want to believe. They'd rather believe the obvious than look beneath the surface."

Valerian shrugged. "At least you're allowing us out into society a bit. Even playacting is preferable to the damned solitude. Particularly when you won't even let me ride in public. I never knew my black-sheep brother had such a repressive streak."

"You may consider yourself to be completely convincing as a female," Phelan said. "I, for one, am not so certain. We're much better off keeping to ourselves."

"Don't you think people will question why we're such recluses?"

"I simply put it about that you were in an interesting condition."

Valerian stared at him blankly from beneath his long golden eyelashes. "What do you mean by that?"

"I mean that I told people you were expecting. In a family way. Smocked. Pregnant."

"Oh, God," Valerian moaned. "Was that strictly necessary? Surely I could have been spared that indignity!"

"It was very effective. It explained our keeping to ourselves. It also provided a good excuse for your less-than-dainty waist."

"But will it explain my less-than-dainty feet?" Valerian countered, casting a frustrated glance out at the moonlit road. He shook his head. "Damnation," he said wearily. "And that reminds me. What are we going to do about her, Phelan?"

"About whom? Margery? I don't think there's much we can do at this point."

"Don't be deliberately obtuse. I'm talking about the girl."

Phelan leaned back and sighed, remembering. She'd had the most extraordinary eyes, set in that tanned face. Maybe she would have fooled most people, but not the Romney brothers. In the midst of their own absurd masquerade, it was child's play to see through another, less polished one. "She's not our concern, Val. We have our own heads to think about."

"She's only a child, Phelan. She must be in terrible trouble, to be out on her own…"

"She's older than you think. Probably her early twenties. And I doubt her troubles are any worse than our own. We don't need another lost soul, Val. We have too much to deal with as it is."

Val shook his head, yanking at his artfully arranged ringlets. "I suppose you're right. We might just make things worse. Still, did you notice those eyes, Phelan?"

Phelan Romney stared out at the moon-silvered landscape, keeping his face deliberately expressionless. "I noticed," he said. And silence once more filled the carriage as the two brothers were left with their own troubled thoughts.

# SHADOW
## Dance

# ANNE
# STUART

Published in Great Britain 2013
Mills & Boon, an imprint of Harlequin (UK) Limited,
Eton House, 18-24 Paradise Road, Richmond, Surrey TW9 1SR

© Anne Kristine Stuart Ohlrogge 1993

ISBN: 978 0 263 90250 1

012-0613

Harlequin (UK) policy is to use papers that are natural, renewable and recyclable products and made from wood grown in sustainable forests. The logging and manufacturing processes conform to the legal environmental regulations of the country of origin.

Printed and bound
by CPI Group (UK) Ltd, Croydon, CR0 4YY

# CHAPTER TWO

Juliette was dreaming again. On her third night in the old attic above the Fowl and Feathers, she lay beneath the scratchy wool cover, the fresh salt breeze dancing across her skin, and dreamed of her father. Black Jack MacGowan had been unconventional, a gruff, bluff charmer of a man, who'd loved his only daughter dearly. Loved her enough to take her with him during his travels, through wondrously strange climates and war-torn countries, on adventures that were both dangerous and fascinating. She'd been passionately devoted to him, following him everywhere, sharing in his enthusiasms, being a mother to his childlike nature, adoring him. Until he'd committed the ultimate betrayal, and died of a heart attack beneath the hot Egyptian sun, leaving her in the hands of Mark-David Lemur.

But she didn't want to dream about that. About her father's death, or the weeks and months afterward. That portion of her life was over, forever, and nothing would make her return to that existence. Or even relive it through dreams and memories.

Not that she wouldn't have given anything to return to Egypt. Or Greece, or any of the warm, sunny countries where she'd lived with her rapscallion father, clambering over ruins as soon as she could walk, drinking goat's milk, and wearing boy's clothes from the time she was four. She could still remember the first time she'd worn a dress. She'd been all of sixteen, and her father had traded for it with an ancient Syrian.

It had been made of silk, much too big for her slender, boyish frame, hot and stifling and decades out of fashion. And she'd put it on, and felt like a queen, like a creature out of a fairy story, listening to Black Jack's extravagant and utterly sincere flattery. Until she'd looked up, into the eyes of MacGowan's old friend Mark-David Lemur, and known the first tricklings of uneasiness.

She should have trusted her judgement. Black Jack should have trusted it as well. She'd tried to explain her misgivings to him, but her father had brushed off her concerns with his characteristic lightheartedness. He didn't want to think his daughter was less than safe at his side. He didn't want to consider the possibility that his good friend and cohort couldn't be trusted.

Assuming people couldn't look down from heaven and see the mess they had left behind, Black Jack MacGowan would never know what his actions had wrought. And Juliette, who still loved him dearly and missed him just as much, nine months after his death, as she had missed him the day he died, was content. As long as she never had to see Mark-David Lemur again.

She sat upright in bed, pulling the rough blanket around her, cold and sweating at the same time. The rope bed sagged beneath her weight, but she paid it no notice. She'd slept in more uncomfortable places than this hot, airless attic on the south coast of England. Doubtless she'd sleep in worse places still.

She didn't want to dream about the other man either. The tall, cynical man with the still face, the silver eyes, and the thin, sensual mouth. She didn't like men, didn't like their animal appetites and savage disregard of others. The fact that something completely irrational drew her to that man frightened her even more than the transparent threat of Sir Neville Pinworth, or the memory of Mark-David Lemur.

Juliette climbed out of bed, padding barefoot to the open window. She could see the sea from that vantage point, and she stared at it longingly. England was the land of her birth, yet she felt more of an alien here than she had in any of the diverse foreign countries she'd lived in with Black Jack. If she could, she would stow away on the next ship bound for the warmer climates and never look back.

But she didn't dare. Her masquerade was already fraught with danger. On land she could find enough privacy to keep her secret intact. On board a ship it would be impossible. From what she remembered of the nightmarish journey back from Portugal with Lemur, there was no such thing as solitude or modesty. And a woman masquerading as a boy definitely counted both of those commodities essential.

She needed to wait until she'd found enough money to book passage to France. At least that would ensure a certain amount of privacy, and once out of the country, she could wear skirts again. If she wanted to. She'd miss the blessed freedom of breeches.

For the time being, she was better off staying where she was. The past three days had been full of hard work, but she was strong, stronger even than the two strapping serving maids who kept ogling her. Bessie was a motherly soul and a wonderful cook, Mowbray was gruff and kind, and even the two silly girls usually found better things to chase after. In all, she was content to stay on in Hampton Regis until the proper opportunity came along.

But right now she couldn't stand another moment in this stuffy attic. She wanted to run along the beach, barefoot, and feel the salt spray in her hair. She wanted to breathe in the air, lie in the sand, listen to the sound of the night birds. For a few short hours she wanted to feel free again.

She pulled on the brown breeches beneath her voluminous shirt, not bothering with the linen binding that flattened her small breasts. She left her hose and her shoes behind, rolling up the modestly laced sleeves to her tanned elbows and letting her hair flow free.

She'd learned to move silently in her years away from England. No one heard her as she tiptoed down the narrow, winding back stairs. The kitchen fire was banked, still sending out waves of stifling heat, and she paused long enough to cut herself a hunk of bread before she headed out into the moonlit night.

There were stars overhead in the inky-black sky, the same stars that looked down over Egypt. When she reached the sandy beach she shoved the bread into her pocket and took off at a run, racing barefoot along the wet sand, the wind tugging at her hair, plastering the white cambric shirt against her body. She leapt over rocks, danced along the edge of the water, took deep, cleansing breaths of the clear salt air, so intent on the sheer, mindless pleasure that she didn't realize she wasn't alone on the beach until she slammed full force into a tall, unyielding figure.

The tiny scream of shock that erupted from her throat was definitely girlish. She choked it back as hard, strong hands caught her arms, holding tight, and she looked up, way up in the darkness, into the face of the man she'd been afraid to dream about.

She didn't even know his name. Mowbray hadn't mentioned it, and she'd been unwilling to ask. It didn't matter. He was a member of the quality, and obviously not interested in a serving lad. Which didn't explain why he held her arms so tightly, why his fingers seemed to caress her skin through the thin cambric shirt, why he stared down into her face so searchingly.

"What are you doing out here at this hour?" he demanded abruptly, his voice harsh in the still night air.

She didn't bother to wonder why her comings and goings should interest him. "It was too hot to sleep," she said, consciously deepening her voice. "Sir," she added as an afterthought.

A ghost of a smile flitted across his face, but his grip on her arms didn't loosen. "That's a proper lad," he said, his voice mocking. "Remember to do the pretty to your betters."

Juliette wasn't in the habit of considering anyone, particularly a man, her better, but she swallowed back her instinctive retort. She tried to squirm away, but his hands tightened painfully. "Might I go back to the inn?" She made her voice properly deferential, lowering her defiant gaze.

"I don't think that would be a particularly wise idea."

She glanced up at him again, not bothering to mask her surprise. "Why not?"

"I've just come from the Fowl and Feathers," he said in a reasonable voice. "I've spent the past three hours trying to drink Sir Neville under the table, and so far I've had absolutely no success. I was hoping a walk on the beach might clear my head so that I could approach my task with renewed energy."

"Why were you trying to drink him under the table?" she asked, forgetting for a moment that a proper young lad wouldn't presume to question the quality. By the time she remembered, he was already answering her artless question.

"Because, my dear boy, he needed distraction from his primary goal."

"And what was that? Sir," she added hastily, wishing he'd release her arms.

He did, but the result was even more unnerving. He touched her face, pushing her dark brown hair back from her brow. "You, Julian Smith."

She held herself very still beneath his suddenly gentle hand and his mocking gaze. He must have asked Mowbray her name, but why should he have bothered? And why should he want to protect her from a frivolous creature like Sir Neville?

"I believe I'm capable of looking after myself," she said. "I've been on my own for the past five years."

"Have you, indeed? And have you had much experience with gentlemen such as Sir Neville? Gentlemen with a preference for pretty young boys?"

She glanced up at him, taking a deliberate step backward. "Not until tonight."

It took him a moment to realize what she was saying. She half expected rage to darken that cool, mocking face. Instead, he laughed. "Not me, lad. I find women to be vastly more entertaining. I just happen to have a soft spot in my heart for stray lambs."

"I'm hardly a stray lamb," she said frostily. "And I can protect myself from the likes of Sir Neville."

The dark man didn't deny it. He just looked at her from those mocking silver eyes, his thin mouth curved in a faintly derisive smile. "Such a brave soul," he said softly, and she shivered in the warm night air. "Sir Neville could make mincemeat out of you if he wanted to. He's not quite as frivolous as he seems."

"I can take care of myself."

"I wouldn't count on it." His voice was low, and curiously beguiling. Until Juliette remembered that she wasn't the sort to be beguiled by a mysterious man on a moonlit beach.

She turned then and ran. She was half afraid he'd reach out those strong hands and capture her again, but he let her go, standing motionless in the moonlight, watching her as she ran up the strand. She didn't dare glance behind her. For some reason, the man unnerved her with his cool, steady glance. She didn't trust any man, including this dark, nameless one who'd deemed himself her savior.

She didn't know what idiocy made her enter the front of the building, rather than sneaking in through the kitchen. She wanted to get back to the safety of her attic room, away from eyes that could see too clearly in the darkness, away from hands that were hard and gentle at the same time.

She'd forgotten whom he'd left behind. She no sooner had reached the stairs than she saw Sir Neville lounging near the fireplace, a dazed, bleary expression on his pale, powdered face. If the other man had planned to outdrink Sir Neville, it was clear he'd had more success than he'd realized. Pinworth seemed barely conscious. Until he looked up and saw her.

Sir Neville rose on unsteady feet, mincing toward Juliette as she paused at the foot of the stairs, momentarily transfixed. "There you are, lad," he said in his soft, slurred voice. "Been looking for you. Came here hoping to find

you, but then Ramsey got in the way. Got a"—he hic-
cupped loudly—"a little proposition for you. Come back
to Pinworth Manor with me. You'll like it, I know you will.
A pretty lad like you shouldn't waste your time carrying
slops and mucking out the stables. You'll ruin your soft
little hands." He captured one of those hands in his, and
his grip was surprisingly strong.

"Please, Sir Neville," she said, trying to break free and
squash down the desperation that filled her. She'd been too
rash when she'd told the other man she could take care of
herself. She was finding she was far from able to handle
the amorous attentions of one drunken aristocrat.

"Oh, I do please, boy," he said, reaching his other hand
to pull her against him. "I do, indeed."

"Take your hands off the boy, Pinworth." The voice
was low and chillingly pleasant. The dark man stood in
the doorway, calm, unruffled, and absolutely implacable.

Sir Neville pouted, still clutching at her. "Why should
I, Ramsey? I saw him first. It's not as if I'm suggesting
anything so unusual, and I know for a fact that you don't
share my tastes. Leave us alone and I'll convince the lad."

"I don't think so." Ramsey stepped into the room, and
Sir Neville wasn't so sotted that he didn't recognize a threat
when confronted with one. He released Juliette, albeit reluctantly, and she sank back against the stairs, rubbing
her bruised wrist, wrapping her arms protectively around
herself.

"Don't be a spoilsport, Ramsey. He won't be so hard to
convince. I've seen the way he looks at you. He could be
persuaded to shower that attention on someone who'd be
more appreciative of it." Sir Neville's voice had deterio-
rated into a slurred whine.

Ramsey's mouth curved in a sardonic smile, but he didn't even glance over at Juliette's huddled figure. "You see what you want to see. As a matter of fact, Valerie was asking about the boy, and I promised to bring him back to Sutter's Head. We could use the extra help."

"So could I!" Sir Neville protested.

"Here now, what's all this?" Mowbray appeared at the top of the stairs, his grizzled gray hair going every which way. "Oh, begging your pardon, Mr. Ramsey. I didn't realize you and his lordship were still here. Where is that Agnes? I'll give her a hiding..."

"We sent her off," Ramsey said easily. "We had need of a bit of privacy."

Mowbray looked startled. "You, Mr. Ramsey? I...er... hadn't realized..." His glance fell on Juliette, and he looked even more troubled. "What's the lad been up to?"

"I'm stealing him, Mowbray," Ramsey said. "We have need of a young lad to help around the house, and Julian here seemed a likely sort. I assume you have no objections."

"But I want him!" Sir Neville wailed.

Mowbray took all this in, a disturbed look on his face as he slowly descended the stairs until he came even with Juliette. She kept her arms wrapped around her, acutely aware that her breasts were unbound beneath the thin shirt. "What do you want to do, lad?" he asked kindly. "There's no denying that Sir Neville would be generous, and a lad sometimes can't afford to be too picky about how he's to make his way in the world. But you've got choices. You can stay on here—we'll find work for you somehow. Or you can go with Mr. Ramsey."

Juliette looked up at him. She knew as well as he did

that the Fowl and Feathers couldn't support another mouth to feed for long. And Sir Neville's intentions were painfully obvious. If she went with him, he'd be doomed to a major disappointment in no time whatsoever. And she'd be unmasked.

Which left Mr. Ramsey. She glanced at him beneath her heavy lashes, hoping he wouldn't read the expression on her face. He frightened her, in ways no man had ever managed to do. Mark-David Lemur had hurt her. Sir Neville's intentions were far from pristine. She'd been in fear for her life on any number of occasions, running from bandits in Egypt, hiding from white slavers in Morocco, with only her father and her own wits to protect her. This dark man, who neither desired her body nor her pain, could hurt her far more than any of them.

"I'll go with Mr. Ramsey, sir," she said quietly.

Mowbray sighed. "Are you certain, lad?"

She nodded, wishing her hair were still tied back in a queue. Even at its current short length, it was too girlish falling around her face. "Certain."

If she expected Mr. Ramsey to be pleased, her expectations were dashed. He simply nodded, as if it was no less than he expected. "Get your things," he said.

"Now? Tonight?" Her voice shook slightly. She'd made her decision. She just wasn't ready to act on it.

"I'm leaving for home in the next ten minutes. It's a long walk out to Sutter's Head, Julian."

"You can always change your mind," Sir Neville said, swaying slightly.

"I'll be ready in five minutes," Juliette said, scampering barefoot up the stairs.

There was no sign of Sir Neville when she walked out

into the moonlit stable yard. She'd dressed quickly, pulling on her hose and jacket, lacing the stout brogues. She hadn't dared risk taking time to bind her breasts, hoping the loose coat and the darkness would cover any betraying curves. At least her figure was conveniently boyish to begin with. If she'd been shaped like Agnes, there would have been no way she could ever carry off such a masquerade.

Ramsey was standing next to his midnight-black gelding, waiting with deceptive patience. "Is that all you have?" he asked, glancing at the small parcel that held her extra clothing and all her worldly possessions.

"It is. Sir," she added, cursing herself. She had no difficulty in being properly deferential to everyone else. What was there about this man that made her risk everything for the sake of petty defiance?

The lines bracketing his mouth deepened faintly as he smiled. "Do you want to ride in front or behind?"

Juliette looked up at the horse. It had been months since she'd ridden, and Ramsey's gelding was a high-strung beauty. "I'd rather walk."

"Not your choice, lad. I'm due back at Sutter's Head, and I'm taking you with me. Can't disappoint a lady."

"But I don't…" Her protest was in vain as he reached out with his hard, strong hands and lifted her up, way up, and plopped her down on the horse's back.

"Steady, Sable," he soothed, vaulting up behind her, settling his body tight against hers. She tried to sit forward, to keep her back ramrod-stiff, but it was a losing battle.

He caught the reins, his arms threading around her, and though he didn't embrace her, she could feel their enveloping presence as surely as she could feel his legs at the backs of her thighs. She shivered in the hot night air.

Mowbray came racing out into the stable yard, a knotted kerchief in his hand. "You forgot this, Julian," he said, thrusting it into her hand. "Your wages."

She could feel the solid weight of good English coin beneath the thin linen. "But I haven't earned…"

"Keep it," Mowbray said, wrapping her fingers around the little parcel. "It gives you a choice."

She forgot who she was. Tears of gratitude filled her eyes, and she leaned down from the horse and kissed him on his grizzled cheek. Mowbray looked startled for a moment, and then he grinned. "You look out for yourself, laddie. And if you need a place to stay, there's always room at the Fowl and Feathers for you."

A moment later they were off, riding in silence toward the end of town, the horse's hooves making a quiet ringing sound on the cobbled roadway. Juliette kept her back straight, trying to ignore the sudden weariness that swept over her, trying to ignore the warmth of the body pressed up close behind her, the strength in the arms that surrounded but didn't touch her, the muscles in the long thighs behind her.

"You might want to watch who you go about kissing, young Julian," Ramsey said after a few minutes, when the road had turned to dusty ruts and the town had receded into the distance. "Some might misunderstand."

She could feel her face flush, and once more she thanked God for the dark night and the fact that she rode ahead of him. "I was brought up to show affection," she said stiffly.

"Were you, now? I'd suggest you be careful where you bestow that affection. People might take advantage of you."

"I can look after myself."

"So you've said. You have yet to convince me."

She swiveled around in the saddle to face him, and immediately she knew she'd made a mistake. She was better off not looking at him. Better off not moving any closer. But now that she'd made such a rash move, she was determined not to show him how he affected her.

"Is that why you're taking me back to your house, Mr. Ramsey?" she demanded boldly. "Are you still under the mistaken notion that I'm a young boy who needs rescuing?"

He looked down at her for a moment, and his gray eyes shone silver in the moonlight. "No," he said.

It wasn't much of an answer, but she had enough sense not to press him for an explanation. She turned back, trying to shrink within the oversize clothes she'd traded with a banker's son who'd traveled on the same boat from Portugal.

"Does your sister really expect you to bring me back?" she asked, staring down at the horse's silky black mane, trying not to look at the well-shaped hands that held the reins.

"My sister?" He sounded startled. "You mean Valerie? I'm sorry to say she's my wife."

There was no logical reason why Juliette found that information distressing. But then, she'd grown accustomed to illogic. She turned to glance up at him again, ignoring the danger. "Why are you sorry?" she asked.

"Forgetting your place again, Julian?"

She jerked her head around again, staring straight ahead. "Beg pardon, sir," she muttered.

"Why don't you pull your forelock while you're at it?" he mocked. "I'm sorry she's my wife because she's a completely ramshackle female, wild and reckless, always getting herself into trouble, and I'm a very staid gentleman indeed. It's all I can do to keep her in line."

Juliette had met a great many gentlemen in her travels, both staid and otherwise, and the man sitting behind her, his long, strong arms lightly around her, was the furthest thing from those respectable and unexciting men she'd come to regard as staid. As a matter of fact, a little staidness, a little solemnity, would be welcome at the moment. Life had been far too harum-scarum in the past few months. Juliette would have given anything to be bored.

"Odd," she said. "I would have sworn you were related. You have the same eyes."

"Very observant. As a matter of fact, we are related, by blood as well as by the bonds of marriage. Valerie happens to be my second cousin. Most people don't notice any resemblance. But then, you're not most people, are you, my boy?"

She didn't like the faint drawl in his voice when he called her "my boy." Not for a moment did she believe he could see through her disguise. She'd spent enough of her unorthodox lifetime in breeches to have become accustomed to them, and she knew she walked with just the right sort of diffident swagger. In the weeks since she'd landed in this benighted country and run away from Lemur, not one person had seen through her disguise. This tall gentleman with the mocking smile and the cool silver eyes would hardly be the first.

"I try to keep my wits about me," she said, pleased at the faint trace of London accent she was able to insert in her husky contralto. That was the one area where her years abroad had failed her. She could walk and act like no proper young lady, but her voice constantly gave away her genteel background. And she wasn't conversant enough with her fellow countrymen to pick up the proper working-class accent. The few times she'd attempted it, she'd almost risked exposure.

"You *do* manage," Ramsey drawled. "You might want to lean back against me. It's a long ride, and a boy your age needs his rest. What is your age, by the way?"

"Seventeen," she lied, knowing full well she looked even younger. In fact, she was twenty-two.

"Such a youth," he murmured. "And where is your family, young Julian?"

"Don't got any." She was getting quite adept with the accent, she thought. "Sir," she added hastily.

"You 'don't got any'?" he echoed, mocking. "Charming. Lean against me. Unlike our friend Pinworth, I promise I have no interest in molesting innocent young boys."

"You prefer jaded young boys?" she asked before she could control her unruly tongue. Her own gasp of horror followed her artless question, and she waited, holding herself very still, for him to dump her off the horse and into a nearby ditch.

Instead, he laughed. It was a disturbing sound, soft, oddly sensual on the sea-laden breeze. "It's a good thing you're coming out to Sutter's Head, Julian. With a tongue like that on you, you'd be bound to run into more trouble than you could deal with." He took the reins in one hand, slid his arm around her waist, just beneath her breasts, and pulled her back against him, not gently. "And no, don't tell me again how you've taken care of yourself. You were about to get yourself into a great deal of trouble with Pinworth, and even Mowbray couldn't have helped you. Accept it, my child. You'll be a lot safer and happier at Sutter's Head."

He was very hard and strong behind her, and hot as well. The man must have been made of solid bone and muscle— there didn't seem to be a soft spot at all in his lean body. She didn't bother fighting the restraining arm. If she did, he might accidentally touch her breasts, and that was the last thing she could risk. She had no choice but to lean back against him.

She didn't have to like it. A soft breeze had picked up, blowing the loose tendrils of hair about her face. They were following the edge of the sea, and the steady hush of the waves mingled with the gait of the horse, the heartbeat of the man pressed against her. She could close her eyes and feel safe for the first time in months. Surely it wasn't wicked of her to give in to that momentary temptation?

"That's the lad," Ramsey murmured in her ear as she relaxed against him, and she was suddenly too tired to resent the amusement in his voice. "Come tomorrow, Valerie will keep you hopping. Best get what rest you can. Trust me. I won't let you fall."

"Trust you?" Juliette murmured sleepily, wishing she had the energy to drag herself out of the delicious torpor she was floating in. "I don't trust anyone."

"Very wise, lad," he said, his breath tickling her ear. "But just for now you can relax. No one's going to hurt you. Not while I'm around."

Perhaps not, Juliette thought, unable to fight the mists of sleep any longer.

*But who's going to protect me from you?*

# CHAPTER THREE

Val glared up at his older brother. "You don't have to be such a brute about it," he snapped.

It was the next morning. The two brothers were in the largest bedroom of the house at Sutter's Head, and Phelan was assisting the recalcitrant Valerian with the rigors of his daily toilette.

"Hold still." Phelan yanked at the lacing of Valerian's corset, then cursed as one of the strings snapped. "Why don't you do without this instrument of torture? Those dresses Hannigan found for you were made for a mountainous female. No one will notice if your waist is several inches larger than it was yesterday."

"Especially since you put it about that I was in an interesting condition," Val grumbled. "I expect you find it amusing."

"A bit."

"Then why are you glaring at me? I would have thought you'd be in a delightful mood now that you've got your little waif safely out of Pinworth's clutches. Though it almost might have been worth it to see his reaction once he managed to strip her clothes off."

"We wouldn't have been there to see it," Phelan said in a reproving voice. "And I doubt it would have been a pretty sight."

"Really?" Val looked at him curiously. "Now, I happen to find young Julian, or whoever she is, quite enticing. I suppose you prefer 'em well rounded, but I wouldn't mind seeing her..."

"I'm talking about Pinworth," Phelan said tightly, retying the broken corset string.

"You've got a point there. Still, once he discovered Julian was a girl, he might have been persuaded to change his proclivities."

"You are a naive one, aren't you, Val?" Phelan said, yanking the strings mercilessly tight. "He'd simply use her as a boy. Something she wouldn't have found pleasant at all."

Val looked a trifle pale. "Fortunately, I haven't your breadth of knowledge. This is the first time I've even been out of Yorkshire, and the habits of pederasts aren't part of my experience."

"I try to avoid 'em myself," Phelan said, giving his brother a shove. "Try to behave yourself, brat. Young Julian has already noticed a family resemblance, and once she gets settled in here, I'd wager she'll see through your little disguise in no time."

"She's hardly likely to give us away. She has her own secrets. What do you suppose she is—a runaway heiress? Maybe she's the answer to my problems. After all, you're the heir. I don't have a feather to fly with."

Phelan glared at him. "Don't count on it. She's older than she looks, probably in her early twenties. And if she had some convenient fortune, she'd hardly be racketing around Exeter, wearing someone's castoffs."

Valerian yanked the dress over his head, glaring at his reflection. "Then who do you think she is?" he demanded, flinging himself down in front of his dressing table and staring at his reflection. He'd already shaved himself very smoothly indeed, and the careful application of makeup covered any incipient beard growth.

"I don't know," his brother said. "But I mean to find out."

Valerian glanced up at him as he whisked a hare's foot full of powder across his chin. "Are you planning to bed her?" he asked bluntly. "Is that why you brought her here? Because you wanted her for yourself?"

Lesser men would have quailed before Phelan's cold glare, but Valerian had never been afraid of his older brother. "Just because you're wearing skirts doesn't mean I won't thrash you if you deserve it," Phelan said in an even voice.

"You could always try." Valerian's response was equally pleasant. "All right, so you acted out of the purest motives. What are you going to do about her?"

"I haven't decided. You refuse to leave England, and short of coshing you over the head and carrying you off, I'm stuck here as well. Without me, you'll be staring the hangman in the face in no time."

"I can take care of myself!" Valerian shot back.

"Why do people keep telling me that?" Phelan asked wearily. "With your hot temper you'd end up challenging someone to a duel, or something equally outrageous. I can imagine you storming back to Yorkshire and insisting that

Lady Margery tell the truth. Something with which she has little acquaintance. If you refuse to leave England, so do I."

"I don't want to stay forever," Val said in a more conciliatory tone. "Lord knows I can't wait to get out of these damned skirts. But running is so blasted cowardly!"

"We'll have to leave eventually," Phelan said, apparently unmoved by his brother's bitterness. "You'll be expected to produce an offspring sooner or later, and that's beyond even *your* acting abilities." He leaned forward and tugged one of Valerian's flaxen strands of hair. "Though you do make a lovely girl, brother," he teased.

Valerian batted his hand away. "A diamond of the first water," he said wryly. "My nose is too aquiline, my mouth too big, my chin too stubborn, my chest too flat—"

"And your feet too big. At least you're fully as vain as any woman I've ever met," Phelan said smoothly, and ducked when Valerian sent a perfume bottle hurtling in his direction.

"You're still avoiding the subject. What are you going to do with the girl now that you've brought her here?" Valerian persisted.

Phelan shrugged. "Not what you'd do in my place, obviously."

"The more fool you, then. I wish you joy of her, though you don't seem very appreciative of her subtle charms. I have better things to do today than watch you waste a lovely woman. I'm off for a round of morning visits."

Phelan frowned, but Valerian was unmoved. "Whom do you plan on visiting?"

"Oh, I thought I might stop in at the Fowl and Feathers and see if Mowbray has some of that excellent brandy he'd be willing to part with."

"I imagined he does. The free traders are active in these parts, and I have no doubt Mowbray's cellar is filled with finer French wine than we've seen in a decade."

"And then I thought I might stop in at Hackett's Library and see if they have any new gothic romances."

"You don't really have to read that trash, Valerian. Lord knows no one would realize the difference if you simply pretended."

"You're wrong, brother mine. I pick up a great deal of invaluable information from those terrifying love stories. I've learned more about the convolutions of the female mind than I ever thought possible."

"Such diligence in the pursuit of your role is admirable," Phelan murmured.

Valerian smiled wickedly, a very smug, masculine smile. "Don't fool yourself, brother. I intend to apply my new-found knowledge in far more profitable areas."

"Oh, God," Phelan muttered. "Not the bluestocking?"

"But such a lovely bluestocking," Valerian said, patting his silken blond hair. "And I can tell she is quite fascinated with me."

"Val…" Phelan warned. "We're playing a dangerous game. You know as well as I do the Bow Street runners are after you, and there's a limit to what I can do to protect you. Don't endanger yourself for the sake of a passing fancy. Let us leave."

Val's smile was rueful. "That's the trouble, Phelan. I'm not certain that it is. A simple fancy. Or the slightest bit passing."

Phelan's expression was nothing short of grim. "You've spent your entire twenty-five years falling in love with every presentable female in sight. You can't choose an impossible time like this to finally conceive an eternal passion."

"I don't think one can be logical about these things, old man," Valerian said. "Trust me, I'm fighting it. Manfully, I might add." He kicked at his yellow-flowered skirts, then glanced up at his older brother. "I suggest you do the same. Young Julian has already needlessly complicated our lives. Don't make things worse by bedding her."

"She's pretending to be a boy, Valerian. I'm hardly likely to convince her I share Pinworth's oddities."

"You could always persuade her to give up her masquerade."

"I'm not ruled by my appetites. Your safety and clearing our name come ahead of any stray attraction I might feel. If we find out who really killed Lord Harry, well and good. He and I always despised each other, and he probably deserved his fate. I just don't wish to see you pay the price for someone else's crime. As for the girl, we've already discussed the fact that she's not my type. I like buxom, feminine blondes."

"After all," said Val with a pronounced simper, "you married one."

A quiet knock on the door stopped Phelan just as he was about to give his brother a less-than-gentle punch on his shoulder. Hannigan opened the door without waiting, and his expression as he gazed on Valerian was, as usual, doleful and amused. "I thought you might like to know, your lordship, that the girl's awake."

"Did you tell Hannigan about her gender, or did he guess?" Val wrested himself from Phelan's bruising grip.

"Hannigan knows everything," Phelan said.

"Except how to get out of this current tangle, my lord," Hannigan said heavily.

"I thought he was going to stop with the 'my lords' and 'your lordships,'" Val said. "It wouldn't do for anyone to overhear plain Mr. Ramsey being addressed so grandly."

"Jealous, brat?" Phelan inquired coolly. "I'd gladly give you the blasted title if I could."

"Go to hell," Valerian shot back, deeply offended.

"Hannigan has a head on his shoulders, which is more than I can say for you most of the time," Phelan continued. "He knows when he needs to be discreet. Where's the girl right now, Hannigan?"

"In the kitchen with Dulcie, eating enough to feed an army. Can't imagine that Bessie Mowbray would let the girl starve."

"I imagine her hunger goes back further than the few days she's been in Hampton Regis," Phelan said absently. He turned back to look at his unrepentant brother. "Are you certain it's a wise idea to pursue your bluestocking, Val? She's not a fool. I suspect if it weren't for her presence here, you'd be far more amenable to leaving."

Valerian smiled ruefully. Phelan knew him far too well for him to deny it. "She's not my bluestocking," he said instead. "Her name's Sophie, remember? And if I don't have something to distract me from these damnable skirts, I'll end up strangling someone, and they'll hang me for that murder, and all this will have been for nothing."

"It depends on whom you'd strangle," Phelan said with a ghost of a smile.

"I wish your mother were within arm's reach," Val grumbled.

"I'm not certain I blame you."

"I'm only looking for a little distraction, Phelan. You don't have to worry that I'll be indiscreet. And for all that Miss de Quincey has a lively, intelligent mind, she's also quite naive. She probably wouldn't realize I'm a man if I stripped to the buff to convince her."

"And I can count on you not putting it to the test, can't I?" Phelan said mildly enough.

Val gave him a bewitching smile. "As much as you trust yourself with your little waif, brother mine." He scooped up a lace shawl and draped it artfully around his arms, disguising some of the muscled strength. "Don't expect me back at any particular time. I'm hoping to be invited to the de Quinceys' for dinner."

"Have a care, Val," Phelan warned in a somber voice.

"I always do," Val replied, striding toward the door, at the last moment remembering to moderate his walk to a more discreet pace.

Phelan's only response was a disbelieving smile.

Miss Sophie de Quincey, beloved and only daughter of Mr. and Mrs. Percival de Quincey, was not in the best of moods. The latest novel by Mrs. Radcliffe was a dead bore; her bosom bow, Miss Prunella Styles, had decided to be totally tedious and fall in love with a very handsome young man of her parents' choosing; and even the weather refused to cooperate. It was raining this morning, a cold, soaking rain, when she most particularly wanted to go for a solitary stroll on the beach and daydream about pirates. She sat in the window seat of the library in her family's home on the outskirts of Hampton Regis and stared out at the rain disconsolately.

Sophie was in general a sweet-tempered girl, a little too

smart and a little too pretty for her own good, but with a generous heart. Today, however, she felt like an absolute fishwife, and only the knowledge that the sophisticated and fascinating Mrs. Ramsey had presented her card enabled Sophie to rouse herself from an incipient fit of sulks.

She'd never been one for crushes on older women, unlike Prunella or her other schoolmates, but there was something about Valerie Ramsey that absolutely enthralled Sophie. Perhaps it was the way she carried herself, as if she had no nagging self-doubts, her creamy white shoulders thrown back, her strong chin thrust forward, her silky blond hair tied back in a casual bundle of curls. Perhaps it was the deep drawl in her voice, or the unexpected strength one suspected lay beneath her overlarge hands. She was a woman who hadn't been enslaved by the rigors of marriage, a woman with a mind and a will of her own, and Sophie wanted to be just like her.

"Mrs. Ramsey," she cried, rising from the window seat and rushing across the room to embrace the tall woman. She kissed the air beside Mrs. Ramsey's cheek, and found herself caught in those strong hands as she smiled shyly up at her new friend. "I was about to die from boredom, and here you've come to save me!"

"Surely not," Mrs. Ramsey said in her husky voice. "A young girl with your intellect could never be bored. What's wrong with all the young men in this town, that you have to sit alone on a rainy day?"

"I'm not interested in young men," Sophie said frankly. "I'd much rather spend my time with an intelligent woman like you."

A faint smile played around her companion's well-molded lips. "Would you, now? I must say I'm flattered.

But sooner or later you're going to have to develop a taste for the gentlemen. How old are you?"

"Eighteen," Sophie said, drawing her guest back to the window seat and pulling her down beside her for a comfortable coze. The large area was surprisingly crowded with the two of them sitting there, but Sophie simply moved closer to her idol. "Old enough to know whether I like men or not. I don't know if I wish to marry."

"Never?"

"Not if I can help it," she said artlessly. "You've been extremely lucky—you and Mr. Ramsey barely seem to notice each other. Most marriages I've witnessed haven't been nearly so fortunate."

Her companion reached over and patted her hand, covering it. "Surely that's extreme?"

"Not in the slightest. Most women are slaves to their parents until they marry, and then they become slaves to their husbands."

"You don't seem enslaved by your parents."

"That's the problem. Both of my parents are exceedingly broad-minded. They've brought me up to think for myself, to be independent. They taught me I was any man's equal. I'm worried that I might not find a suitable husband who'd agree with that."

"You might be surprised," Mrs. Ramsey murmured, her strong hand warming Sophie's smaller one.

"How do you manage to keep Mr. Ramsey in line? I must confess, I find him rather frightening. He's so tall, and forbidding, and so very cynical."

Mrs. Ramsey shrugged. "He's quite charming once you get to know him. Besides, I can get him to do just what I want if I go about it the right way. We rub along very well together. I don't interfere in his life and he doesn't interfere in mine."

"As long as you obey certain rules of society," Sophie said. "Rules dictated by men."

"Actually I don't obey any rules I don't care to." Her companion said carelessly, leaning back against the enclosure and stretching her astonishingly long legs out in front of her.

Sophie glanced at her. "I do envy you your height," she said wistfully. "Perhaps I might be more self-assured if I weren't such a little dab of a thing."

"Believe me, Miss de Quincey, I don't beat Ramsey into submission."

Sophie giggled. "I didn't imagine you did. And please, call me Sophie."

"Only if you can me Val. After all, addressing me as Mrs. Ramsey only serves to remind both of us that I'm a man's chattel."

"Never that," Sophie said. She screwed up all her courage. "I do admire you enormously. You're different from any woman I've ever met. I do so wish to be your friend."

Mrs. Ramsey had the most shimmering gray eyes. She looked down at Sophie, and for a moment Sophie couldn't read their expression. There was something both tender and faintly predatory in the glance, something that warmed and alarmed her. "You're a very sweet child," Mrs. Ramsey said in her deep voice. "But perhaps a bit too trusting. You know nothing about me or my husband. Who knows, we might be something quite different from who we say we are."

Sophie pulled herself upright. "I'm not as naive as you think. I imagine you have some dark secrets in your life—

you've clearly led a life that's a great deal more adventurous than most. I hope I can be your confidante."

"Share my secrets?" A faintly mocking smile played around Mrs. Ramsey's wide mouth, and for a moment she looked startlingly like her sardonic husband. "Sometimes secrets are better left alone."

Sophie wasn't quite sure whether or not she was being rebuffed. "Have I offended?" she asked miserably.

The mockery left her companion, and the large hand that still covered hers tightened. "Never, dear child," she said. "You only remind me how very jaded I am."

"Not jaded," Sophie said loyally. "Just more experienced. I wish you would give me the benefit of your wisdom."

"I don't know what you mean."

"I wish to know everything. Everything you care to impart," she amended.

"It would shock you."

"I'm difficult to shock. My parents have seen to it that I have a very liberal upbringing. I've been allowed to read anything I cared to."

"I see." Mrs. Ramsey's voice was a deep purr, rather like a jungle beast's. "And what about more, shall we say, practical matters? Have you learned about what goes on between men and women?"

Again Sophie felt that strange tickling inside her, half pleasure, half alarm. "Of course," she said.

"Really?"

"My mother explained it in scientific detail. She was very clinical."

"Having met your formidable mother, I have no doubt

whatsoever that she was. It's astonishing to me you were ever conceived."

Sophie giggled. "It's true Mama is a bit…intellectual," she conceded. "But then, I've been taught that one should always use one's brain to the best of one's ability."

"To be sure," Mrs. Ramsey agreed. "But you should also learn to use your body as well."

"But the body is simply for animalistic urges."

"Nonsense. You live in your body. It behooves you to take care of it and give it pleasure. Unless you're interested in becoming a nun. I know all sorts of repressive orders where you can wear sackcloth and ashes and beat yourself with a little whip all day long."

"You're making that up."

"Not at all. I haven't seen it for myself, but my brother has told me about them."

"I didn't realize you had a brother."

Mrs. Ramsey looked momentarily disturbed. "Did I fail to mention it? Dear Phelan spends most of his time abroad. He has an absolute longing for exotic climates—I'm afraid he finds England sadly tame."

"Phelan. That's an unusual name. You must find it confusing to have a brother named Phelan and a husband named Philip."

"Not particularly," she said. "If I have to refer to my husband by name, I usually make do with 'Mr. Ramsey.' Or, failing that, 'you there.' It seems to suffice."

"I'd like to meet your brother. Perhaps I might change my mind about men."

"You wouldn't like Phelan," Mrs. Ramsey said sharply. "But you might like my other brother. Valerian."

"Two brothers? You are lucky. I always wished I had siblings," Sophie said enviously.

"You might change your mind if you were as blessed as I was," her companion said wryly. "Particularly with a twin."

"Valerian's your twin? How wonderful! Are you identical?"

"Not entirely," she drawled.

Sophie blushed. "How absurd of me. Of course you— That is, I mean…" she floundered.

Mrs. Ramsey shook her head. "I see how it is, my dear. For all your prodigious learning, the practical part of your education has been neglected. I see I shall have to do something about it."

"Would you?" Sophie asked, her eyes alight with anticipation.

"It would be my pleasure," Mrs. Ramsey replied. And once more Sophie was reminded of the wolf.

Juliette was alone in the modest kitchen of Sutter's Head when her rescuer walked in. It was the first time she'd seen him in the full light of day, even such a rainy day as the one they were enjoying. If he'd been overwhelming before in the darkness, with his towering height, his sardonic face, his silvery eyes that saw far too much, in the daylight his subtle threat wasn't even slightly diminished. And all Juliette's temporary equanimity vanished.

She'd felt peaceful for the first time in months, sitting at the well-scrubbed kitchen table, devouring Dulcie's delicious food. Even the attic over the Fowl and Feathers had been merely a way station, a place to hide and to catch her breath.

This place felt different. It felt like home.

And yet there was nothing familiar about it. It was an old country cottage perched at the tip of the headland that jutted out into the sea, a huge, rambling old place, in benign disrepair, kept in reasonable shape by a pair of middle-aged servants who looked after their master and mistress with possessive pride. While Dulcie had been kindness personified, sharing the need of all cooks to fatten Juliette up, it was obvious her first concern was to her employers, with the kind of loyalty that went generations deep.

There was something oddly appealing about those kinds of roots. While she relished her freedom, she wished she had more of it, wished she were back by the Aegean Sea or the River Nile, exploring some new and exciting place. There were times when she wished she could taste just a moment of security. Of connection. Of belonging.

But she did belong. To Mark-David Lemur. And the memory sent waves of remembered disgust through her, just as Philip Ramsey strolled into the kitchen.

Masters of the house usually didn't enter the kitchens, particularly in search of a new servant. They ordered them to present themselves. But then, Mr. Ramsey was different from most men Juliette had met. He had a certain elegance in his tall, lean body that suggested he'd be at home in the Court of St. James's or in a cow byre. She liked that about him, despite her wariness.

"Dulcie said you're going to eat us out of house and home," he said, pulling out a chair and dropping down opposite her.

Suddenly she remembered she ought to scramble to her feet in the presence of her employer. It was rather late for that, so she stayed where she was, one slender hand still cradled around a thick, chipped mug of the best coffee she'd tasted outside Italy.

"I'll work for my keep," she said.

"No need to be defensive, lad," he said, a sardonic gleam in his cool gray eyes. "I imagine we can afford to feed you. The question is, what are we going to do with you now that we've got you?"

"I'm good with horses," she said.

"Hannigan's more than capable of taking care of the stable," he said.

"I can carry wood, water, any kind of rough work. I'm very strong."

Her new employer looked frankly skeptical. "A stiff breeze would blow you over."

"Then why did you bring me here if you don't think I'm up to the work?" she demanded, uneasiness bringing forth her defensiveness.

"Maybe I share Pinworth's interest in you?" he suggested blandly.

For a moment she almost believed him. There was something about the way he looked at her, something she couldn't quite define. But then she dismissed it. "No," she said. "You're not that kind of man."

"Perhaps not," he allowed. "Perhaps I just wanted to save you from such a sordid fate." He reached over and picked up her slender hand, surveying it with seemingly idle curiosity, and the absent caress of his thumb sent shock waves through her body.

She jumped up, pushing herself away from the table, away from him. "I've told you, I can take care of myself," she said fiercely, wishing she believed it. "I'm quite capable of defending myself. I don't need anyone's pity or charity. It won't take me long to walk back to town. I can find other work if Mowbray has no use for me."

She made it halfway to the kitchen door. She wasn't expecting it, otherwise she would have had more of a fighting chance. Or so she told herself.

He caught her wrist, spinning her around and pushing her up against the rough stucco wall, holding her there. His hands were as strong as steel, and there was absolutely no way she could escape.

"I don't think so, young Julian," he murmured in her ear. "You're not going anywhere, at least for the time being. You're no more self-sufficient than a day-old kitten. No one's going to harm you here—you won't need to defend yourself."

"No one's going to harm me?" she countered in a muffled voice. "Then what are you doing?"

"Not hurting you in the slightest."

She realized *it* was true. Immobilized as she was, helpless as she was, she was in no pain at all.

He released her then, stepping back, and when she turned to look up at him, she hoped to read something in his eyes. But they were cool and enigmatic as always. "What do you want from me?" she asked, her voice husky.

He raised his hand for a moment, and she flinched, afraid he might touch her. He dropped his arm. "The damnable thing about it, young Julian," he murmured, "is that I haven't the faintest idea. When I do, I promise to inform you."

Juliette looked up into the unreadable face of the man who towered over her, and she shivered. For some cowardly reason, she simply didn't want to know the answer to her question. She could only hope that by the time he decided, she'd be long gone.

# CHAPTER FOUR

It was a beautiful day on the south coast of England. Even Phelan Romney had to admit it. Much as he disliked the provincial feel of his native land, on a warm summer day such as this one, with the fresh salt breeze from the ocean and the brightness of the sun overhead, he could almost pretend he was back in the south of Italy, or Egypt, or Greece, where there were no rules, no strict social order, no responsibilities. At least, not for a willing vagabond.

Not that he was paying much attention to any of those things nowadays, he reminded himself wryly as he strode down the narrow path to Dead Man's Cove. Being on the run from a murder definitely had its advantages. At least he didn't have to worry about matchmaking mamas or the problems of Lord Harry's far-flung estates. He didn't even have to waste his time brooding about his mother's instability. He much preferred to have his concerns on more elemental levels. Such as how to preserve his half brother from his mother's bloody but misguided vengeance. How to keep Valerian from rushing back to Yorkshire in a hotheaded fury, determined to ferret out the truth and clear his name, only to find himself at the end of a gallows rope.

And what to do about the slender, game little creature struggling along behind him, carrying a picnic basket, his sketching supplies, and a bottle of claret he had no intention of drinking.

He'd planned to carry the heavier things, but young Julian was having none of it. Her damned stubbornness would be her undoing, and he longed to tell her just that. She was pale and sweating beneath her heavy jacket, but he doubted he could get her to remove it. Much as he longed to do so. He wanted to see whether she had breasts beneath that loose white shirt.

Not that it mattered, he reminded himself sternly. He hadn't brought her into his house to seduce her. God only knew why he'd done so. As a whim. A capricious gesture, one more masquerader joining the family of deceivers. Or perhaps it was simply to alleviate his god-awful boredom, which surpassed his brother's. At least Val had the sly pleasure of plying his wiles on the unwitting folk of Hampton Regis. Phelan didn't even have that distraction.

He hadn't stayed in one place for so long since he'd reached his majority, at least not in England. Almost four weeks in Hampton Regis, with nothing for distraction except his sketches. And there was bugger-all to sketch around here. The flowers were pale and civilized compared with tropical blooms, the ocean a dull gray compared with the bright azure of the Mediterranean. To top it off, he hadn't had a woman since he'd left Greece. He had never been a man to allow his desires to overwhelm him, but right now a willing female body would provide a welcome distraction indeed.

Julian Smith, or whatever she called herself, wasn't the answer. She was unwilling to admit she was even female—

she'd hardly be likely to strip off her disguise in order to alleviate his boredom. Phelan simply had to make do with fantasies, wondering if she was flat-chested and thick-waisted beneath the loose-fitting boys' clothes. He was horribly afraid that she wasn't.

He glanced back at her. She was huffing and puffing, shifting her heavy parcels back and forth, and he took pity on her. "You're carrying too much, lad," he said, letting the term slide mockingly off his tongue.

She glared at him, with that singular lack of subser-vience that would have unmasked her sooner or later if she'd stayed on at the inn. "I'm fine," she said, hoisting her bundles up higher. "Sir," she added with only a faint shimmer of contempt.

He considered taking the parcels from her. He suspected that might engender a tug-of-war, and while he would ap-preciate the chance to put his hands on her, he decided the time was far from opportune. "Suit yourself," he said with a shrug. "It isn't much farther."

"It better not be," she muttered under her breath, mis-takenly assuming he wouldn't hear.

He smiled to himself. He had unnaturally sharp hear-ing, a leftover from his days in Arabia, where the faintest sound might make a difference between life and death, and there was very little he missed.

She wasn't happy about being dragged away from the house and loaded down with paraphernalia. He knew that by the disgruntled little sniffs she emitted every now and then, by the occasional growl, by the way her ill-shod feet slipped on the narrow, pebble-strewn path down to the beach. She probably wouldn't be feeling any more cheer-ful once they reached their remote destination.

The path grew sharply steeper, and he heard her intake of breath as she stumbled once more. He slowed his pace deliberately, wondering if she was going to take a headlong plunge toward the sea.

"Where are we going?" she finally demanded in what she probably considered a subservient voice. It simply sounded irritable to Phelan's ears.

"To a very remote, peaceful spot of seaside. It's called Dead Man's Cove," Phelan said, slowing his pace still further in deference to the faintly breathless sound of her voice.

"Charming," she replied, once more forgetting her place.

He smiled to himself again. "This part of the coast used to be populated by wreckers. You've heard of them, no doubt. Most of the English coast has been plagued with their sort at one time or another. When times are bad, people do what they must to survive, and to feed their children."

"Even if it includes luring a ship onto the rocks and drowning other people's children to line their own pockets?" Julian said sharply.

"Even so. I doubt anyone particularly wanted to commit cold-blooded murder. They were interested in the cargo of the ship, not the lives of the passengers." He allowed himself to stop and glance back at her, slightly higher up on the steeply descending path.

"And did they save those passengers' lives once they'd lured their ships to their doom?" she asked, clutching the heavy picnic basket in hands that looked too delicate for such rough work.

"I gather that in this particular corner of the world they

simply clubbed them on the head to make sure there were no witnesses."

She shivered in the warm sunlight, and she glanced past him with faint anxiety, as if she expected the wreckers to suddenly reappear.

"Don't worry," Phelan said. "The wreckers stopped their profession more than half a century ago. If any of their descendants live on, they doubtless are as law-abiding and God-fearing as you and I."

"That's not necessarily a recommendation," she muttered.

"True enough for me. I expect you're far more conventional than you first appear."

She lifted her head to stare at him in unguarded surprise. "I don't appear conventional?" she asked.

"Not particularly."

"Well," she said briskly, "you'd be greatly surprised."

He turned and continued down the narrow pathway. "I am seldom surprised, young Julian. I am jaded beyond belief, and it takes a very great deal to amaze me. How do you intend to do it? By proving that you really do appear conventional? Or that beneath your slightly odd demeanor you're an absolute madcap?"

"Neither. I am exactly what I seem to be."

"Of course you are, lad," he said, enjoying himself. "I never doubted you for a moment."

He heard her slip half a second before she shrieked. The scatter of pebbles beneath her feet, the quick, panicked intake of breath, and he'd whirled around to catch her as her burden went flying in all directions.

She landed in his arms with a solid thud, and he decided she must have breasts, if she had to take the trouble to bind them. She was soft in his arms, and damn it, she smelled like a woman. Faintly flowery, faintly musky, and just slightly like Dulcie's best cinnamon rolls. He wondered what she'd taste like.

She was trembling. He didn't release her, though he knew he ought to. He was never a man who did something simply because it was what he ought to do.

Her waist was damnably small beneath the thick jacket, and her hips flared sweetly beneath his hands. She was well past the seventeen years she claimed—in the bright sunlight he could see too much knowledge in her wary brown eyes, and he had a sudden desire to wash that sad knowledge away.

As if he could. He released her, so abruptly that she stumbled for a moment before righting herself. "I'll carry the things the rest of the way," he said in a cool voice, gathering up the fallen parcels.

She tried to protest. "It's my duty…"

"You are the least dutiful serving lad it has been my misfortune to meet," Phelan said flatly. "I don't wish to have my luncheon mixed with sand, or my art supplies crushed, or my—" He picked up the shattered bottle of claret and stared at it mournfully. "Or my wine shattered," he added heavily.

If he expected her to be cowed, he was in for a disappointment. "You could always beat me," she suggested, her coolness matching his own.

He glanced at her, his eyes narrowed in the sunlight, giving her a look that had intimidated many a grown man. She didn't even flinch. "Don't tempt me," he growled.

Dead Man's Cove was a deceptively peaceful half-moon of a beach, with the still, gray water masking dangerous shoals. One might think it a perfect little harbor, until one saw the ghostly hulk of a ship listing on its side, its broken masts eerie against the bright blue sky. Once Phelan reached the sand, he dumped his burden down and began to strip off his jacket. He glanced back at the girl, but she was standing a few feet away from him, staring at the wreck with troubled eyes.

"How long ago did that ship founder?" she asked.

"I'm not certain. She's still fairly solid—I would guess no more than fifty years ago. The salt water tends to preserve the wood for a bit. She probably won't fall apart for at least another fifty years." He dropped his coat onto the sand, sat on it, and proceeded to pull off his boots. "You might consider stripping down yourself, lad," he said in a silken voice. "It's damnably hot today, and those shoes are too big for you. You'd do better barefoot."

She looked torn, as well she might. "I prefer to keep my jacket on," she said.

He rose, moving toward her, his bare feet reveling in the feel of the sand. "And I prefer you remove it," he said. "Since you're my servant, it would behoove you to do as I say."

He could see by the expression in her eyes that it took all her self-control not to retreat in the face of his steady advance. "And if I refuse?"

He smiled. She was not reassured. "Then I'll remove it for you."

She stripped off the coat, hurriedly. The cambric shirt beneath was too big for her, of course, and successfully masked any curves that might have escaped whatever she used to bind herself.

"And the shoes," he said, very gently.

She glared at him, but she was wise enough not to argue. She dropped down onto the sand and began to remove the oversize brogues.

Satisfied, Phelan retrieved his sketchbook and pencils and started away from her. "I don't like to be disturbed while I'm working," he called back over his shoulder. "Find something to amuse yourself with while I sketch this old wreck."

"If you don't like to be disturbed, then why did you bring me?" she asked stubbornly, sitting there with her small, delicate bare feet stretched out.

"Julian, my lad," Phelan said sadly, "you must learn proper deference if you're going to remain in your current role."

"Current role?" she echoed, trying to disguise her nervousness.

"As a servant, my lad," he said in a soothing voice, amused. "Servants are supposed to be silent and subservient. Never challenging. While I work you might take a walk along the water's edge and meditate on the error of your ways."

"You're very generous, sir," she said in a dulcet voice, staring angrily at him beneath lowered lids.

He smiled. "You really have no idea, my boy."

He knew. There was no reason why he should have guessed, and Juliette told herself she was panicking over nothing, but she couldn't rid herself of the belief that her mysterious new employer, Mr. Philip Ramsey, knew she was unquestionably female.

She'd done nothing to give herself away, of that she was certain. She'd perfected a boy's walk, part swagger, part stride. She held her narrow shoulders back, even whistled when she remembered to, and kept her small chin stuck out at a faintly pugnacious angle.

Indeed, she didn't really know how to be a woman, at least not the kind of woman he would be used to. She was uncomfortable in dresses, ignorant of most social minutiae, and totally incapable of flirting. After her enforced sojourn with Mark-David Lemur, she found proximity to the majority of the male sex distasteful. She did her best to look and think and act like a boy, and there was no way her new master could guess her secret.

Once more she contemplated leaving. She had come to the port of Hampton Regis for one reason and one reason only. To earn enough money and then book passage on the next ship bound for sunnier climates. She didn't particularly care where—Greece, Arabia, Egypt, even Italy were all acceptable to her. Some place where she could live on the pittance her diamond-and-pearl earbobs would bring her, some place where she wouldn't run into the man who called himself her husband.

She put her toes in the icy water, shivering slightly. Even in this heat, the chilly Atlantic waters didn't warm. Not the way the Mediterranean, the Aegean, the Nile did. She wanted to see those waters again. Only there would she be safe from the man who hunted her. She could disappear into the countryside, blend in with the people, and a starched-up Englishman like Mark-David would be helpless to track her down. Here in England she was far more vulnerable, and each passing day was a danger.

She glanced back at the man who had brought her to this desolate, beautiful stretch of coast. He was leaning against an outcropping of rock, his sketchbook propped on one knee, and he was totally absorbed in his work. His dark hair had fallen around his face, and his slightly thin mouth was taut with concentration. Surely if he had any inkling of her secret, he'd hardly bring her to such a secluded spot and then proceed to ignore her.

No, she was getting fanciful. The strain of the past weeks was taking its toll on her. Too much hiding, too much hard work, and not enough food or sleep. And worrying, always worrying, that Lemur would pop out from behind a rock and claim her.

He wouldn't, of course. He could have no earthly idea where she was. After she'd disappeared from the hotel in London, he'd probably tried to track her to the nearest major port. That was the primary reason she'd chosen Hampton Regis. It was small enough to be relatively unknown, large enough for some of the more modest ships bound for the Mediterranean. If Lemur were to search for her, and undoubtedly he would, he'd concentrate his efforts in Dover and Plymouth, and not waste his time on the tiny ports dotting the British seacoast.

And, of course, he wouldn't be looking for a boy.

He knew of her predilection for boys' clothes—after all, he'd known her for most of her twenty-two years. But he would assume, with typical male arrogance, that she would never willingly don trousers when presented with the sumptuous dresses he'd had made for her.

She hated every one of those dresses, with their high, strangling necklines, heavy skirts, and muddy colors. She hated the tight lacing underneath, the layers of petticoats, the uncomfortable shoes. But most of all, she hated anything that came from Mark-David Lemur.

The tide was coming in, bubbling along the sand with cheerful insouciance, and Juliette leaned down to roll up the legs of her trousers. Even icy British seawater was welcome.

She wondered if she'd made a very grave mistake in leaving the Fowl and Feathers, in coming with Philip Ramsey in the first place. Surely she would have found her way out of Pinworth's clutches—if she'd managed to escape Lemur, she could get away from anyone. She glanced over at her employer, still rapt in his work. Ramsey might prove a bit more difficult to get away from. His silver-gray eyes were a great deal more far-seeing than Sir Neville's protuberant orbs, or even Lemur's colorless gaze. It would take a fair amount of thought and daring to outwit the strong, powerful man who lounged on the beach nearby.

Juliette had little doubt that she had the brains and the determination to do so. She simply had to decide her course. At her current level of employment, she'd earn enough for passage to the south of Italy by the time she was thirty. Not a happy proposition. She couldn't sell her earbobs. For one thing, the MacGowan diamonds were well-known—if she tried to pawn them in this provincial country, she could bring her nemesis to her doorstep. Besides, she'd need that money to live on once she found a place to settle down.

No, in order to get out of the country, she would simply have to steal. The lady of the house had jewels littering her dressing table in a haphazard fashion—Juliette had already ascertained that. She could take one of the more modest pieces and hope she could trade it with some unscrupulous captain for a berth. Or she could keep her eye out for cash. If Ramsey irritated her enough, she'd take it all.

On second thought, it was just as well she'd accepted his offer. Mowbray and Bessie had been too kind to steal from. Philip Ramsey, with his sardonic air and veiled comments, deserved whatever was coming to him.

The sun was high overhead, and doubtless a proper young serving lad would set about his duties. Dulcie had packed a mountain of food; Juliette knew that because her shoulders still ached from the weight of the basket. She wondered if she was supposed to share the meal, or wait until her lord and master was finished and then retire behind a rock to finish the leftovers. Or even wait until they made the long climb back up that twisting trail to the house at Sutter's Head.

She glanced up to the top of the headland, and a stray shiver danced across her backbone. She could almost see them, the wreckers of old, with their false promise of safety, luring ship after ship to a rocky doom on the shoals of Dead Man's Cove. She wondered if they'd ever paid for their crimes. Whether the ghosts of their victims haunted that derelict ship, and the cove itself.

Juliette refused to believe in ghosts. Nevertheless, it suddenly seemed a wise idea to move closer to her irritating employer. She strolled toward him, glancing idly over his shoulder at the sketch he was working on.

He slapped the pad facedown on his knees and grimaced at her. "I don't like an audience for my work," he said.

"It's very good," she said, surprised. The rough sketch was more than an accurate compilation of details. It conveyed the sense of eerie desolation, of loss and sorrow and conscienceless crime.

"An art critic, my boy?" he drawled, gazing up at her out of those perceptive silver eyes. "I merely dabble at it. Something to help me remember my travels."

It was a thick sketch pad, well worn. Without considering the consequences, she held out her hand for it. To her surprise, he handed it to her, watching as she sank down in the sand beside him and began leafing through it.

He was more than good. He was astonishing. The depth and detail, the emotion and wit, in his pen-and-ink drawings brought each scene to life, from a bazaar in some Arabian city to a goatherd in what looked like Greece. She turned page after page, overcome with nostalgia, stopping with surprise at the drawing of a spectacularly naked woman.

"Sarita," she said, her voice rich with amusement.

She'd managed to shock her companion. He stared at her. "How in God's name would you know the most famous courtesan in Alexandria?" he demanded.

Juliette smiled, a smug, boyish smile. "I've traveled a bit in me time," she said. "I've even been in her house on El-Babeer Street."

His dark eyebrows drew together in blatant disapproval. "You shouldn't have been," he said flatly. "Who was fool enough to take you there?"

"My f-friend." She'd been about to say her father. Indeed, she'd been all of twelve at the time, dressed as a boy as usual, and Sarita had fed her sugared grapes and sweetmeats before she disappeared with Black Jack MacGowan, leaving the young Juliette to entertain herself with Sarita's pet monkey. "When I was fifteen," she continued, embroidering the tale. "M'friend and I saved up our money and went to see her for an initiation, so to speak."

"I doubt it," he said wryly. "She doesn't waste her time with scrubby schoolboys."

"Am not!"

"Then what are you, young Julian?" he asked in a voice that barely disguised its menace.

Damn him, Juliette thought. He couldn't know the truth, but he was certainly perceptive enough to know there was more to her than met the eye.

She drew her knees up, clasping her hands around them and turning to look at him. She hadn't realized she was sitting so close. He was lounging against the rock in a comfortable enough posture, but she couldn't rid herself of the notion that all that graceful energy lay curled beneath the surface, ready to leap into action. He was not a restful man.

"What do you think I am?" she countered boldly.

He smiled then, that small, taunting smile that made her want to slap him. "I'm not quite sure. Perhaps it would be easier to tell you what I *don't* think you are."

Juliette could feel the chill of fear in the pit of her stomach, but she refused to give in to it. "All right," she said. "What don't you think I am?"

"I don't think you're a serving lad. Apparently you told Dulcie your mother was a serving maid and your father was a sailor. I doubt that very much. Someone in your parentage comes from the upper classes. I imagine you might be some minor aristocrat's bastard. The serving-maid mother might be accurate enough. I know of a likely lad with just such a parentage."

"Not me, sir," Juliette denied it. "My father was a sailor. Took me with him, he did, when my mother passed away. Then he died aboard ship, and I was stranded in Egypt with no one to look after me. I learned how to take care of myself early on."

"Indeed," he murmured. "And what made you return

to England? Homesickness? Patriotism? Longing for your native land?"

She tried to keep the grimace from her face. "It was a mistake," she said. "I thought I ought to come back and see if I could find some of my mother's people. But they'd all died out, and there was no one. So I'm off for sunny climates again, as soon as I can earn passage."

"You could always sign on as cabin boy," Ramsey suggested, mockery dancing in his gray eyes. "You're a pretty enough lad, and I wouldn't imagine you'd have any trouble getting a position."

"Considering the trouble you went to to save me from Sir Neville's attentions, that would be somewhat of a waste, wouldn't it?" Juliette countered.

"No trouble at all, my boy," he murmured. "Think nothing of it. But if you think you're going to earn passage to Egypt on the salary I'm planning to pay you, then you greatly overestimate my affection for you."

Juliette bit her lip. She shouldn't have been so frank about her plans, but in truth, he had a way of getting inside her guard. "I intend to look for the right opportunity."

"I'm certain you do. Remind me to tell Hannigan to lock up all our valuables."

"Sir!" Juliette protested. "I wouldn't think of repaying your kindness by stealing."

"Julian!" he mocked in an identical tone of voice. "I believe you're capable of just about anything. Why don't you see what delights Dulcie has packed for us? I, for one, am famished."

She started to rise with unconscious grace, then quickly remembered her role. "Right-o, guv'nor," she said, giving him a little salute.

His mocking voice drifted over to her as she rummaged through the picnic basket. "You and I have something in common, my boy."

"What's that, sir?" She was getting adept at remembering the "sirs," Juliette thought, proud of herself.

"A dislike for 'this blessed plot, this earth, this realm, this England,'" he said.

"It's not that I dislike it," she said earnestly. "Indeed, for some it is a 'demi-paradise, a scepter'd isle.' I just don't feel at home here."

"A boy who knows his Shakespeare," Ramsey said. "Astonishing. Did you pick that up from your visit with Sarita?"

She met his gaze with commendable boldness. "Since you knew her well enough to sketch that picture, I imagine you know the answer to that. She's not one to waste much time on intellectual conversation."

He responded with a shout of laughter. "True enough. But her physical communication is beyond compare."

She could feel the involuntary blush rise to her face, and could only hope the remnants of her exposure to the sun would disguise her reaction. "I wouldn't know," she said stiffly, detesting the idea of the tall man with the leanly elegant body wrapped in Sarita's plump, talented arms.

"I thought you and your friend enjoyed her favors one night," he said.

Hell and damnation, the man was tenacious. She considered brazening it out, then dismissed the notion. He could start asking detailed questions, ones for which she had no answers.

"I lied," she said.

"I know you did, my boy. I just wonder what else you're lying about."

"Not a bloomin' thing," she protested, summoning all her earnestness.

"Really? I suppose I'll have to take you at your word," he said pleasantly enough. "For now," he added.

Juliette held herself very still, watching him from across the small stretch of sand. "If you don't trust me..." she began, affronted.

"Not in the least. But then, I trust no one. Except for Val, of course. I might offer you a bit of advice, Julian—a helpful hint or two if you want to go on in this world."

Juliette controlled her very strong desire to tell him to stuff it. "I'd be honored."

"You might try to remember to keep your accents straight," he said.

She stared at him, making no effort to disguise her hostility. "I don't know what you're talking about," she said frostily.

He laughed, rising to his full, overpowering height and starting toward her across the narrow spit of sand. "I'm sure you don't," he mocked. "Maybe I'll have to explain in detail."

He reached for her, his long arms stretched out, and Juliette very calmly wondered whether she was going to have to swim to safety.

Instead, he took the basket, moving away from her without touching her. It was relief, not disappointment, that swept over her, making her almost dizzy. She watched him stroll back to the sunny spot by the rock and sink down. He patted the sand beside him invitingly. "Come have some lunch, my boy."

And Juliette decided there and then that she would leave Hampton Regis at the first opportunity and take her chances in one of the larger ports. She was beginning to have the very lowering suspicion that Philip Ramsey might be a great deal more dangerous than Mark-David Lemur himself.

At least with Lemur, her feelings were uncomplicated. She hated him, pure and simple.

With Philip Ramsey, her feelings were a great deal less clear. And right now she didn't have room for uncertainty in her life.

She would run. First chance she got. Before she found she wanted to stay.

# CHAPTER FIVE

Phelan had never known a creature like her. Granted, women dressing as boys were not part of his general acquaintance, but he'd seen a great many things during his travels, and yet no one came close to the girl who called herself Julian Smith.

Her eyes, for one thing. They weren't the calculatedly bewitching, kohl-accented eyes of a professional seducer like Sarita. They weren't the demure, shyly flirtatious ones of the proper young ladies paraded in front of him whenever he held still long enough for the matchmakers to catch wind of him. And they weren't the cool, disinterested gaze of the women he'd known who'd been far more involved with their lovers or with other passions in their lives, and had none to spare for him.

Her eyes were alive with emotions: wariness, hostility, defensiveness, boldness. She watched him when she didn't think he was aware of it, and he recognized the unwilling fascination in her warm brown gaze, the rampant curiosity mixed with a healthy fear.

She was making her way through a goodly portion of the food Dulcie had packed, and he watched her surreptitiously. He'd seldom seen women eat as much, and according to Hannigan, she'd put away a similar amount at her previous meals. He wondered idly whether she was pregnant.

It would explain a great deal. She could be the daughter of the bourgeoisie, seduced by some lecher and thrown out of the house by a stern father. Or perhaps she'd run before she could be ejected.

But he didn't think so. There was a certain purity in her curious brown gaze. He wanted to satisfy that curiosity. For all the unconventional aspect of her current life, he was convinced she was an innocent. Or perhaps not innocent in the way proper young English ladies were— anyone who recognized the legendary Sarita knew far more about matters of the flesh than many women of her class learned in their entire lifetimes. And he had no interest in whether she still possessed her virginity. As far as he was concerned, chastity in a female was a greatly overrated commodity—an inconvenience to be disposed of as swiftly as possible. He wasn't possessed of any romantic illusions about being the first one.

But she was emotionally untouched, of that he was fairly certain. Virginal in a way that was more complete than Valerian's beloved Sophie. Julian Smith's innocence went deeper than mere flesh. There was a certain childlike quality about her that she tried to fight, and only made stronger. What in God's name had made her embark on this ridiculous masquerade? What in God's name made her think she could get away with it?

"It's actually hot," she said in her husky voice, pushing her brown curls away from her slender neck.

He turned his gaze out to sea. He'd never been aroused

by the nape of a woman's neck before, but apparently there was a first time for anything. "I suppose even England gets hot occasionally," he said, tossing an apple core into the bushes. "Why don't you go swimming?" he suggested, waiting to see her reaction.

She was getting used to him. She cocked her head to one side, considering it. "I might," she said, and he knew she had no intention of stripping off her disguising clothes to do any such thing. "Though I expect the water's too cold."

"Not for such a stalwart little thing as yourself."

"Why don't you join me?" she countered.

Obviously he hadn't managed to cow her. He should have found that knowledge annoying. Instead, he found it faintly exhilarating. "I'll consider it. You strip off your clothes and go first."

To his surprise she rose, graceful as always, and reached for the bone buttons at her throat. She undid first one, then a second, exposing a small portion of her skin. It was as golden as the rest of her skin, the result of whatever time she'd spent away from England, and he wondered how far that pale golden color extended. And how far she was going to carry her bluff.

He stretched out in the sand. "Go ahead," he said cheerfully. "I'll watch to make certain you don't drown."

She didn't even hesitate, damn her. She walked straight to the edge of the sea, her narrow back to him, and a moment later the white shirt descended to her shoulders. Long enough for him to stare at the delicious shape of her upper spine, before she yanked the shirt back up again and stepped away from the incoming tide. By the time she turned back to face him, the shirt was carefully fastened most of the way to her neck, and he was so damned hard he had to put his sketch pad across his lap to disguise his condition.

"It's too cold," she said, obviously feeling triumphant that she'd managed to fool him. Little did she know that no boy had ever had such beautiful, delicate shoulders.

He surged to his feet, grimacing in discomfort. "I'm going for a walk," he said. "Wait here for me."

"Aren't you going to swim?" she asked innocently.

He almost snarled. On the one hand, the icy British water would take care of his pressing problem. On the other, one look at his body unclothed and she'd think he was as dedicated a pervert as Sir Neville Pinworth. If she was brave enough to look.

He was almost tempted to do it, just to pay her back. He could think of a lot more pleasant ways to teach her a lesson about teasing the male of the species, but he'd already decided now wasn't the time. Hadn't he?

"I'll be back," he said, walking away from her before she noticed his interesting condition. The sand was hot beneath his bare feet, the sun was blazing overhead, and the ghostly wreck of the doomed ship cast a dark shadow across the beach. It suited his mood perfectly.

Juliette dropped down to the ground, well pleased with herself. She'd managed to wipe out any possible doubts, of that she was certain. If by any chance he suspected she might be female, she had now put those suspicions to rest. She was just as glad he hadn't taken her up on her suggestion, however. She didn't want to see him strip off his clothes and dive into the water. She found his body too disturbing fully dressed.

It *was* hot. She would have been more than willing to cool off in the icy Atlantic waters if she hadn't had a witness. As it was, she would let the exhaustion of the past few weeks take over, let the hot sun bake into her bones, warming her for the first time since she'd been back in this shadowed land. She lay back in the sand, feeling the hot grains through the thin cotton of her shirt, and she stretched, letting her toes dig into the ground, reaching her arms out over her head, blessedly alone and unobserved.

She felt oddly, femininely sensual, despite her trousers and her short-cropped hair. Languishing there in the bright afternoon sun, she felt like a sleek, contented cat: graceful, self-absorbed, and slightly wicked. It was a good thing her new employer had decided to make himself scarce. If he saw her stretching out on the ground, he'd probably decide she was even odder than he already suspected.

She closed her eyes and watched the colors and patterns the sunlight played against her lids. She smelled the sea, the earth, the distant drift of roses on the air. And then, content, she thought about the events that had brought her to this time and place.

She could see it happening all over again. Mark-David Lemur, his soft white hand holding hers, forcing the wedding ring down over her finger, his grip hot and damp and painful. She'd been too numb with grief over Black Jack's death to think clearly. The fever had come upon him so quickly, turning his vibrant, robust body into a skeletal frame, leaving him only enough strength for a dying request. She was to marry his good friend Lemur and travel back to England with him.

She'd done so, of course. How could she deny her beloved father anything, particularly his final request? Indeed, for the first week it had made little difference. She'd spent the time packing up all her father's belongings, a long and varied lifetime filtering down into a few trunks and boxes.

It wasn't until they were aboard the ship that was to take them to England that she discovered she had made a very grave mistake. Mark-David's feelings for her were far from avuncular, and far from affectionate. His notion of a long-delayed wedding night left his bride bruised, debased, and degraded. And still a virgin.

He'd raged at her, blaming her for his inability to complete his acts. He'd demanded her assistance, something she'd been too angry and too ignorant to provide. And then he'd hurt her, deliberately, taking pleasure in administering the pain.

The trip to England had been endless. For days on end she would see no one, locked in the small, stuffy cabin. And then Mark-David would come to her again. And once again fail.

There was no escape from a ship at sea, except over the side, and Juliette wasn't ready to do that. Her father had taught her that cowardice was the greatest sin of all, and she wouldn't take the easy way out. She lowered her hateful glances, spoke in a soft, pleasant voice, and bided her time.

It had come soon enough. They'd been in London a scant three days, and Lemur was planning to take her out to Chichester, to the dark and dank old house that had been in the MacGowan family for centuries. Black Jack had always said it was the house that had driven him to foreign climes, that and the bloody English weather.

Juliette had planned well. She'd managed to trade the diamond stickpin that had belonged to her father for a set of boy's clothes. She had no access to most of the famous MacGowan diamonds, but Mark-David had insisted she wear the earbobs to the opera that night, and he'd forgotten to retrieve them. They were her hedge against total disaster.

She had no foolish doubts that anyone would help her. She was Lemur's wife, his chattel. Her money and possessions now belonged to him, as did her body and soul. Her mind and heart she could still call her own, and she was unwilling to deed her body over to him any longer. Chopping off her long dark hair, she'd dressed in the clothes she'd bought, pulled on the too-large shoes, and taken off into the predawn light.

There was always the possibility that Lemur might let her go. He had what he wanted most—control of the money her father had left her. For all her practicality, Juliette had little idea as to whether it was a fortune or a competence, and she didn't care. It had brought Mark-David Lemur down upon her head, and for that she cursed it. Besides, since it was no longer her own, the amount involved hardly mattered.

But it wouldn't do to underestimate Lemur. He was a greedy man, an insatiable man, one who wouldn't relinquish what was his, no matter how worthless he considered it to be. And he had unfinished business with her.

A stray shiver swept over her body as she reclined in the sand. Sooner or later he would have killed her, she knew that with an instinct both irrational and absolutely certain. Each time he came to her, his rage grew, and the look in his pale eyes had bordered on murderous. If he found her, after she'd run, then there'd be no hope for her at all.

But he wouldn't find her. He wouldn't comb the tiny seaside villages, looking for his runaway bride. And he'd never think that the new serving lad out at Sutter's Head had any connection with Juliette MacGowan. Juliette Mac-

Gowan Lemur, she corrected herself truthfully, with a hateful shudder.

Better not to think about it, brood on it. Better to revel in the warmth of the sun baking into her bones, ridding them of a month-old chill that she'd been afraid would never leave her.

Philip Ramsey's gaze was another source of heat. She wasn't sure why; there was none of the wet-eyed, slack-jawed lust she recognized in Lemur's pale face. But there was a warmth, an intensity that burned her hotter than the sun, and like a moth drawn to a flame, she wanted to drift closer.

What if she'd married a man like Ramsey? What if he'd been the one touching her body, forcing her to do degrading things? Would she have fought so hard?

Though he didn't strike her as the sort who wouldn't enjoy the more natural forms of mating. And even some of Lemur's odd desires might not seem so odd if practiced by someone of Ramsey's attractions.

She put her hands up to her cheeks, wondering if she was getting feverish in the hot sun. What a bizarre, indecent thought! She never wanted a man to touch her again, particularly not in that way. She certainly didn't want someone with Philip Ramsey's hard, beautiful hands and thin, sensual mouth touching her.

But she could dream of the perfect lover. Someone gentle, sweet, undemanding, someone to protect and cherish her. Someone to slay the dragons and keep her safe.

There was only one problem with knight-errants. They kept their damsels safe behind a locked wall. They'd slay the dragons, all right, but then keep her chained to the life they decreed. Perhaps she might even prefer the fiery death a dragon might provide. But was Philip Ramsey a knight-errant or a dragon?

It didn't matter. She wanted nothing from him but his money. And a safe place to hide before she could book passage away from this cold green land. This demi-hell, this England.

She must have drifted off to sleep. The dreams were vague, shifting, erotic, soft as a sea breeze, damp as the rough surf. She couldn't remember details, didn't even recognize them. All she knew was the warmth and nervy frustration that filtered through her body as she arched against the hand that slid over her cheek, under her tumbled mop of hair, and she turned her face into that hand, nuzzling against it, her lips soft on the callused palm, tasting the sea-salt taste of him.

And then her eyes flew open, to meet her companion's ironic gaze, and she jerked away, slamming her head against the outcropping of rock and letting out an anguished howl.

He sat back on his heels, watching her. His shirt was unfastened, exposing his chest, and she saw with utter fascination that he had hair. Dark hair, not too much. She wondered what it would feel like beneath her fingers. Beneath her mouth.

"I was trying to wake you gently," he said, his cool silver eyes seeing too much. "You looked as if you were having such a pleasant dream."

"I don't remember it," she said, edging away from him. It was only half a lie. She didn't remember all of it. She just knew it had something to do with his mouth.

"Pity," he murmured. "You look quite flushed. Do you want to change your mind about swimming?"

She put her hand to her throat, pulling her shirt together. "Not me, sir," she said, remembering his stricture about keeping her accents straight. "You go ahead if you like."

"Generous of you," he said, and his smile held more amusement than mockery. It was a devastatingly attractive smile, and for a moment Juliette simply stared at him, enchanted.

And then she pushed herself to her feet. She must have hit her head too hard on the rock, to be thinking such thoughts about a member of that class of people she considered to be her direst enemy. Man.

"It's time to get back," he said abruptly, moving away from her. "The climb up the path is going to be worse than the descent. If I were you, I'd dispense with those ill-fitting shoes until we reach the top. I don't fancy having you land on me."

"Yes, sir," she said with what she hoped was suitable deference as she began to gather the remnants of their picnic lunch together. His sketch pad was a few feet away, and she reached it just as he did, her hands touching the worn leather cover before he could snatch it away from her.

"I'll take that," he said sharply, yanking.

She still had a problem with obedience. She held on, and the resistance, slight though it was, was unexpected enough to make him let go. The sketch pad fell in the sand, opening to a rough drawing of a beautiful woman sleeping.

Juliette stared at it in shock. Of course it wasn't a woman. It was the person Ramsey thought of as Julian Smith. And she wasn't beautiful at all, never had been. Except that in the brief, clever lines of his pencil she looked quite lovely and surprisingly sensual. Like an enchanted creature in a fairy tale, waiting to be awakened. Except that a man usually did the job, and he did it with a kiss. And probably more as well. She preferred to sleep on, untouched.

It unnerved her to think he'd sat there watching her while she slept, sketching her. There were certain primitive people who felt that if you sketched their likeness you captured their soul, and she couldn't rid herself of the strange, superstitious thought that while he'd captured her on paper he'd taken part of her into him. A part she could never recapture. The thought was infinitely troubling.

"Not bad," she blustered, picking up the drawing and looking at it with a critical eye. "But you made me look too much like a girl." It was a bold move, and she waited for his response.

"Julian, my boy," he said, taking the pad out of her hand, "you quite astonish me."

"How so, sir?"

Ramsey put his hand under her chin, and once more the touch of his flesh against hers sent flashes of heat through her veins. And she was already too hot. "You are totally fearless, aren't you?" His voice was oddly gentle.

It was a strange thing to say. Juliette didn't move away from his mesmerizing touch; indeed, she couldn't even break his gaze. She was far from fearless—she was terrified of snakes and rats and Mark-David Lemur. Surely someone who could see through her defenses so ruthlessly would know that.

But she wasn't about to say so. She wet her dry lips. "What's to be afraid of?" she said, her voice slightly raspy, but she told herself it simply made her appear more boyish, not unaccountably nervous.

He smiled, and this time there was no mockery at all. It

was a sweet, beguiling smile, and a part of Juliette's hard heart began to melt. "Sometime I'll tell you," he murmured. "But not now." He released her chin, took the sketch pad from her nerveless hands, and turned away.

It was a good thing he did. She needed a moment or two to collect herself. She watched him move across the sand, and she shivered. There had been more eroticism in the gentle touch of his hand on her face than she'd experienced in all of Lemur's assaults on her body. And suddenly she was very frightened indeed.

They made the climb back up the narrow path in silence. She went ahead of him, not particularly wanting to, but he gave her no choice. He carried everything—her protests about that had been in vain also. It was just as well. She scampered up the steep path, agile as a mountain goat, and hoped he wasn't paying too much attention to her backside. She suspected, though of course she couldn't be certain, that her derriere was nothing like a boy's.

If she'd hoped he'd be too burdened down to be distracted, she'd greatly underestimated his strength. By the time they reached the bluff, he looked cool and collected, not the slightest bit winded by the steep climb and the heavy pack. Juliette found that deceptive strength disturbing. But then, she found everything about Philip Ramsey disturbing.

"Come along, lad," he said, striding across the headland. "If I know you, you're probably ready to eat again. You've already proven to have a bottomless pit for a stomach."

Juliette scampered after him, feeling curiously lighthearted. For now she was stuck with him, in the comfortable old house at Sutter's Head, overlooking the sea. She might as well accept it, and enjoy it. "I expect I will grow sadly fat," she said cheerfully.

"You could do with a bit more padding."

"I'm still a growing lad," she protested.

"Are you, now?" The question was lightly spoken, and Juliette refused to allow herself to react.

"Indeed," she said, catching up with him. "Haven't even reached my full height yet. Not that I'll be as tall as you, sir," she continued, warming to the theme as she glanced up at his impressive height. "Me father was not above average height, nor me mother either. But I shouldn't stay such a tiny mite of a thing."

"Ah, yes. Your father, the sailor," Ramsey said. "And when do you think you'll reach your full height, Julian?"

She shrugged, shoving her hands into her pockets in what she hoped was a typically boyish gesture. "There's no telling," she said carelessly. "I haven't yet reached manhood."

"No," he said, his voice rich with amusement. "You're not even close."

The house at Sutter's Head was a sprawling affair on a spit of land jutting out into the sea. It was surrounded by a low stone wall, and sitting on that wall was Hannigan, waiting for them, a disapproving expression on his rough, reddened face.

Juliette wasn't the slightest bit cowed. Here was a man she trusted completely, understood, and approved of. Hannigan had one main purpose in life, and that was the well-being of his master and mistress. Once that was taken care of, his goodwill extended toward those with the same purpose, and he accounted Juliette to be one of them. He wouldn't take too kindly to the notion that she intended to rob his master, but he'd probably put a stop to it with kind efficiency, giving her a lecture about the error of her ways before sending her off to the kitchens to fill her belly once more.

"You look as if you'd swallowed a sour apple, old friend," Ramsey remarked.

"You might have told me where you were going, my lord," Hannigan said. "Val's been back an hour since, and we were beginning *to* be worried."

"I can take care of myself," Ramsey said easily. "Besides, I had young Julian to keep me safe. He's a fierce little lad—he could scare off anything that might wish to do me harm."

Hannigan snorted in disapproval of his levity. "That's as may be. But next time you might let me know where you're going. You're new to this place, and there might be dangers…"

"We went down to Dead Man's Cove," Ramsey said soothingly. "And if I survived deserts and jungles, I can probably survive a haunted shipwreck."

Hannigan crossed himself, turning pale. "I told you not to go there, my lord."

"Hannigan," Ramsey said in a deceptively gentle voice, "I know you've appointed yourself my keeper, but I intend to go anywhere I damn please. I'm not concerned with ghosts. Neither is Julian. He's not afraid of anything, are you, my boy?"

She'd been listening to this exchange with complete fascination, and it took her a moment to realize she was being addressed. "Not a thing," she said belatedly. "Except snakes."

"I don't blame you, boy," Hannigan said with a shudder. "I don't like snakes either."

"Or haunted coves, obviously," Ramsey remarked. "It wasn't until we came here that I realized you were so superstitious."

"It pays to be careful," Hannigan said righteously. "I've heard stories all my life about that cove. There's unfinished business down there. Lost souls looking for peace."

"Hannigan comes from this part of the world originally," Ramsey confided to Juliette. "He still has family all about. They're probably the ones who filled his head full of ghost stories."

"I know what I know," Hannigan said mysteriously.

"I'm sure you do, old friend. In the meantime, I'm off to see my lady-wife." His voice was deeply ironic. "Unless you have something of import to tell me."

Hannigan glanced at Juliette, who'd made no effort to disguise her interest. "It can keep."

"Come along, lad," Ramsey murmured. "You're probably famished."

Actually, she'd finally eaten enough that day, but she had no intention of telling him so. She scampered after him, uneasily aware of Hannigan's troubled gaze as it followed their progress into the dim, cool exterior of the house.

Ramsey turned and dumped the picnic basket into Juliette's waiting arms. She staggered for a moment beneath the weight of it, and once more was impressed by Ramsey's agile strength. He kept hold of his sketchbook, however, something she considered a great pity. She would have liked to take a closer look at some of his drawings. Particularly the flattering, disturbing one of her.

She'd never considered herself possessed of vanity. Perhaps it was just the enforced nature of her disguise that made her suddenly want to see her image looking lovelier than she'd ever imagined. She needed to control that impulse. That way lay disaster.

"Go on to the kitchen, lad," he told her. "I intend to closet myself with my wife for a good long time."

"Yes, sir," she said, not liking the idea at all. "Are you going to make love to her?" She stopped, horrified at herself for asking what was definitely, troublingly, on her mind.

He gave a shout of laughter. "What an impertinent question," he said. "And I'm certainly not about to answer it. Why do you ask?"

"Beg pardon, sir," she said, feeling the blush mount to her face and this time not hiding it.

"Any more rude questions before I leave you?" he asked, still amused.

She looked at him. He was a very handsome man, though not in the most usual way of it. She'd tended to think of handsome men as blond and broad-shouldered, with full pink lips and blue eyes and too many teeth.

This man was lean and dark and almost menacing on occasion, with a narrow, cynical face, dangerous gray eyes, and a thin, mocking mouth that was unaccountably erotic. She'd been fascinated by him since she'd first set eyes on him, and she imagined she'd remember him long after she made her escape from England.

"Just one," she said, determined not to be cowed.

"Fire away, young Julian," he said pleasantly enough.

"Why did Hannigan refer to you as 'my lord'?"

The shot hit home. Ramsey's face darkened for a moment, and his mouth thinned. "An old joke between the two of us," he said with no hesitation whatsoever. "Hannigan's always been full of himself, and I used to tease him that he ought to be taking care of a royal duke at the very least. In return, he started calling me 'your lordship' from the time I was ten. Indeed, I imagine I was a very lordly little boy."

"Indeed," she said, imagining it herself.

"And now you can answer an impertinent question for me, young Julian," he said, and she recognized the menace in his voice immediately.

She refused to quail. "Of course."

"You can tell me who you're running away from."

# CHAPTER SIX

Sutter's Head was an old building, rambling, with ells and gables and additions every which way. The outbuildings were in sorry repair; only the stable possessed a solid roof. Phelan and Valerian both had rooms on the second floor of the house, overlooking the spit of land that jutted out into the ocean, and Valerian had flung his shuttered windows wide open to enjoy the midsummer dusk.

"Where's your pet spaniel?" he demanded when Phelan let himself into his room without bothering to knock. "According to Hannigan, she's been trotting at your heels since this morning. Do you think that quite wise?"

"You've been wearing skirts too long, Valerian," Phelan observed easily, heading toward the casement window that looked out over the headland. The afternoon had darkened considerably, and the wind had picked up, tossing the waves below. "You sound like a jealous mistress."

"Not likely," Valerian said with a hoot of laughter. "Though you've got it part right. I *have* been wearing skirts too long." He kicked at his long flowing gown in disgust.

"Hard time with the bluestocking, brat?" Phelan kept

the sympathy from his voice. Valerian was in no mood to tolerate it.

"You could say so. If only she weren't so blasted affectionate. She cuddles up to me like a damned cat, and it's all I can do not to shove her down on the nearest piece of furniture."

"Women are like that with each other. They tend to reserve their physical affection for those who would tolerate it," Phelan said.

"You're telling me about the ways of women?" Valerian countered with good-natured outrage. "You, the woman-hater of all time?"

"I'm not in the slightest bit a woman-hater. I just don't happen to be a dedicated lecher like our late father. I reserve my attentions for those who know what's expected. And for those who understand what they'll never get from me in a thousand years."

"Tell me, Phelan, what will no woman get from you in a thousand years?"

Phelan turned from the window to survey his scapegrace of a brother. Valerian had flung himself on the bed, his long legs spread out in front of him, his sturdy calves looking ridiculous beneath the froth of skirts. "Any number of things," he said. "Among them, love, trust, children, or a title."

"You never intend to marry, then?"

"Never," he said flatly. "I have my reasons. One of them being that I've yet to see anything to recommend it." He leaned against the wall. "Have you?"

"You're such a cynic, Phelan. Granted, your parents never set much of an example of family warmth or marital bliss, but my mother's happy enough with her farmer,"

Valerian replied with a diffident air. "I imagine one could do as well."

"If you're willing to marry a farmer. Sophie's not for you, Val. I wish I could tell you otherwise…"

"I know it." Val's smile was wry, accepting.

"If she weren't equipped with a fortune…"

"And if she weren't so wellborn," Val supplied. "And if I weren't a bastard, and if I weren't under suspicion of murder, and if I weren't wearing skirts… That's a prodigious amount of 'ifs,' brother mine. Too many for me to overcome."

"So you're going to do the wise thing? Keep away from temptation?" Phelan asked, knowing the answer full well. "Come with me to the Continent, where you'll be safe until I can figure a way out of this mess."

"I'm going to do exactly what you would under the circumstances," Val replied. "I'm going riding with her tomorrow morning."

"Val, Val," his brother said with mock despair. "Will you never learn?"

"I doubt it." Valerian surged off the bed and strode around the room. "What have you learned about the new member of our household? Any idea why she's dressed as a boy?"

"I asked her point-blank who she was running from. Her response was innocent shock. I doubt I'll get a truthful answer from her until I demand it. And I'm not ready to demand it."

"And why not? At least one of us ought to be having a good time."

"We're not here for a good time."

"That relieves my mind," Val said. "I was beginning to

wonder." He paused at one of the windows, staring out past Phelan. "Why *are* we here? And don't start trying to get me to agree to leave the country. I'm sick of running. This is as far as I go. But you never explained. Why the hell are we in Hampton Regis? Simply on Hannigan's say-so? Why didn't we stay closer to home, where we might be doing something instead of just sitting around on our bums?"

"If you think I'm enjoying this enforced wait," Phelan said silkily, "then you greatly mistake the matter. I hauled you away from Yorkshire before my demented mother and your hot temper could get you hanged, and we were damned lucky Hannigan knew of a place remote enough to suit. If it were up to me, I'd be long gone from this country."

"Then go!" Valerian shot back. "I've told you, I can take care of myself. I don't need you protecting me!"

"Like hell." Phelan controlled his temper with an effort. "If you refuse to leave England, then at least Hampton Regis has several advantages, not counting your amatory interests. For one thing, it's right on the coast. Once you see reason, we can leave for France on the next tide. For another, Hannigan's family absolutely haunts this area of the country. We may never see them, but they're around, looking after us. If anyone comes seeking Valerian Romney, we'll hear about it in time to escape. And then it's off to the Continent and a life of unbridled merriment," he concluded sourly.

"Be still, my heart," Valerian said. "Will you take your little serving lad with us if we have to decamp?"

"No."

"No? You amaze me, Phelan. Why not?"

"Because, like your precious bluestocking, the child is

innocent. I have no idea why she's embarked on this absurd masquerade, but the fact remains that she doesn't need to be seduced and abandoned."

"You don't need to abandon her, Phelan," Val said softly.

"She'll stay behind. I'll have Hannigan's people look after her, if need be. But for the time being, I'll stay put. Unwillingly, I might add. I suppose we're safe enough out here, a country squire and his wife." Phelan's grin was wry. "You can torment yourself with your little bluestocking, I'll torment myself with the serving lad. And we'll hope no one decides to come after us."

"Who do you think really killed him, Phelan?"

It was the one question he didn't want to answer. "A stray thief," he said firmly. "A deranged servant."

"Not a servant," Val said. "And not a thief."

Their eyes, so much alike, met for a long, pregnant moment of understanding. "We may be wrong," Phelan said eventually.

"Even if we aren't, you know I won't let you do anything about it," Val replied. "I've caused her enough harm…"

"You don't need to pay penance with your life. And the harm was caused by our mutual father, not by you. You didn't ask for your existence; you certainly don't need to give it up to please a madwoman." Phelan grimaced. "Besides, we might be wrong. My mother might not have murdered him after all."

There, the words were out in the open, the unspoken suspicion that had rested between the brothers for so long. He ought to feel relieved at finally having spoken the fear that had haunted him. Instead, he felt even more troubled.

Valerian didn't reply for a moment, and the thought hung between them like a dark cloud. "We can leave it," he said finally. "I'm willing to go to France, or Italy, and spend the rest of my life there. After all, it's not as if I'm turning my back on an inheritance. With Lord Harry dead, I'm not welcome at Romney Hall, even if I wasn't suspected of killing him. There's nothing to tie me to England."

"Nothing but your love of the place. I'm the one who'd prefer to spend my days abroad, wandering. You might just as well suggest I confess to the crime. It would make more sense. Then at least you could return home…"

"I wouldn't let you do that for me," Val said fiercely.

"And I wouldn't let you make that sacrifice for my mother. So that leaves us where we started. Waiting. Hoping for some other answer."

"And if we don't find it?" Valerian asked.

"Then we go together." Phelan's voice allowed no disagreement. Valerian was the one human being he'd allowed himself to care for during his life, with the exception of Hannigan. He wouldn't abandon him now.

"You're a stubborn man, Phelan."

"It's a family trait."

There was no mistaking Hannigan's knock on the door, nor the lack of hesitation before he opened it, then stepped forward and closed it before any prying eyes could peer inside. "We're going to have to do something about yon wench," Hannigan said.

"Which one?" Val asked, flopping down into a chair.

"The new one. I can't call her Julian, since it's clear as rain that she wasn't born with a name like that. She's been asking questions."

"Questions?" Phelan echoed.

"About you, your lordship. Seems quite curious about where you came from, what brought you here, how long you've been married. I might almost think she was taken with you."

Phelan found he could still smile. "And what makes you think she isn't?"

"She's too smart for that. She's looking after herself, that one is, and she's not about to get distracted by the likes of you. If it were the young master here, I might have my doubts. He's got a pretty enough face to turn even the wisest woman's head. But it's you she fancies, or I miss my guess. She's watching you, and those brown eyes of hers are clever. And that's not all," he added darkly.

"Enlighten us, Hannigan," Phelan drawled, expecting the worst.

"I caught her outside this door just now. I think she was listening to the two of you."

"A reasonable assumption," Phelan said. "I don't know that she would have heard anything terribly edifying."

"Maybe. Maybe not. It wouldn't do to underestimate the girl. I wouldn't be surprised if she didn't have a good idea what lies beneath Mr. Valerian's skirts."

"Hannigan, you shock me!" Val protested, his voice rich with amusement.

"That's as may be," Hannigan said, still deadly serious. "But I think we should get rid of her."

"And how do you propose to do that, Hannigan? Cosh her over the head and drop her in the sea like the wreckers used to?" Valerian asked lazily.

"That's not a bit funny, young master," Hannigan replied severely. "I come from these parts originally, and the wreckers are nothing to joke about. They've paid for their crimes, paid dearly. Their like will not be seen again."

"A good thing," Phelan murmured. "So what do you

suggest I do with the girl? Send her over to Pinworth? I doubt he'd thank me when he discovers her true identity."

"The way I see it, you've got two choices, your lordship. Either send her on her way, back to where she came from, or take her into your bed. Either way, she'd no longer be a threat to you."

"Hannigan, you amaze me!" Phelan said with a shout of laughter. "How little you know women! The most dangerous thing in the world is to turn a romantic young creature into a bed partner. They fancy themselves in love, they start expecting all sorts of things, and then they grow furious when they realize their tender passion is all one-sided. I'd as like cut my own throat as take her to bed."

"Really?" Valerian intervened with maddening cheer. "If you feel that strongly, I'd be more than happy to volunteer for such a hazardous duty. It's an unpleasant task, but I feel sure I could rise to the occasion."

"You're not too big for me to thrash," Phelan said in a dangerous voice. "No one's putting a hand on her unless it's me. Besides, what about your precious bluestocking?"

"In case you haven't noticed, she thinks I'm a woman," Val replied irritably.

"You could always enlighten her."

"You don't really suggest that?" Valerian demanded.

"No," Phelan admitted. "For the time being, I think we ought to keep on as we are. You in skirts, our new servant in pants. In the meantime, what are we going to do about our inquisitive little friend?"

"I'm sure you'll come up with something to distract her, Phelan. Particularly since she fancies you," Val drawled.

"That's a matter of opinion. I think she covets my purse far more than my body. But I can certainly give her something more immediate to worry about than who and what *you* are. Even supposing she's guessed. Where is she, Hannigan?"

"I sent her to the kitchen, to peel potatoes for Dulcie. I told her to feed and water the horses when she finished there. I imagine you might find her in the stables."

"Excellent," Phelan murmured, feeling unaccountably cheerful. "While she's occupied, why don't you search her room and see if you come up with anything of interest, Hannigan? I'll see what I can do with the girl."

"Changed your mind about Hannigan's advice, brother?" Valerian asked.

"Not particularly. There are other ways to distract a woman."

"Yes, but they're not so pleasant."

"Lecher," Phelan said lazily, and strode from the room in search of his quarry.

She'd left the kitchen, which was just as well. Dulcie was a maternal soul, and she wouldn't care for his tactics, and wouldn't hesitate to tell him so. He wanted Little Miss Incognita alone where he could do his best to terrorize her into maintaining a discreet silence.

She didn't hear him enter the stables. It was a small building, with only half a dozen stalls, and only four of them filled. She was standing in an empty stall next to his brother's gelding, stroking his long chestnut nose and murmuring to him. Phelan stood just within the entrance, listening to her soft voice.

"You're a pretty boy," she crooned, a low, impossibly erotic sound, and Phelan had the absurd wish that she were talking to him. "Much too big a horse for a lady. I bet I could handle you, though." Her strong, small hands stroked the dark neck of Valerian's horse, and Phelan felt his own skin tingle in sympathetic response. "The question is, what's going on with the master and his mistress? And why would a pretty lady like Mrs. Ramsey want a great big beauty like you?"

"Perhaps she prefers a challenge," Phelan said.

She had nerve in abundance, but then, he'd already admired that about her. She didn't jump, even though she'd clearly had no idea he'd been watching her. It was too dark to see whether the telltale color flooded her face, but he imagined that would be the only sign. She simply kept stroking the horse, keeping her voice that same, soothing murmur. "Perhaps," she conceded. She turned and looked across the stable at him, and her warm brown eyes were absolutely fearless. "And perhaps Mrs. Ramsey is stronger than she appears."

"That's always a possibility," he agreed, closing the stable door behind him, shutting them into muted darkness. He started toward her, and while he couldn't see her move, Valerian's gelding responded to the sudden tension in the hand on his neck, lifting his head and making a worrying sound.

"Easy, boy," Phelan murmured, drawing close. She had no escape—he was blocking the only exit to the stall.

She lifted her head. "Are you talking to the horse or to me?" she asked. "Sir," she added, with defiance.

"The horse, obviously."

"Why obviously?"

She was standing very straight and proud in front of him, her shoulders thrown back, her chin at a pugnacious tilt. She probably thought she looked the image of a street urchin, when instead she looked deliciously, irresistibly female.

He moved closer, and she backed away, up against the rough wood wall of the stall. The building was an intoxicating array of smells, of horseflesh and oats, of fresh hay and the sea, of the wild roses that grew outside and the wild rose that stood before him. "Why don't you tell me?" he countered softly, dangerously.

"I… I don't know what you're talking about." The stammer was so slight, anyone else might have missed it. But Phelan was acutely aware of everything about her—the flutter of her pulse at the base of her throat, the faint sheen of perspiration across her broad brow, the nervous little exhalation of breath. He wanted to catch that breath in his mouth, to kiss her. He couldn't remember actively wanting to kiss a woman before. But he wanted to take that rich, defiant mouth with his, and taste her.

"You were eavesdropping," he said, instead of forcing the issue. "Hannigan caught you snooping outside the mistress's door. I was wondering if you found out anything interesting."

"I wasn't eavesdropping!" she protested, and if he hadn't already discovered she was an adept liar, he might have believed her. "I don't know what Hannigan told you, but I'd just been walking by and I thought I heard someone call my name…"

"It won't wash. Your room is at the back of the house, behind the kitchen. You'd have no business being on the upper floors."

She tried another tack. "So I was curious. You can't blame a boy, can you? I'm new here, and how am I to know you're to be trusted any more than that Sir Neville?

It only makes sense, to find out what one can about one's employers."

"No, I can't blame a boy," he said gently, moving closer still. There were only a few inches between them, and he could practically hear her heartbeat pounding against her chest. "I simply wondered what interesting bits of information you might have picked up."

"Nothing," she said, her voice filled with such disgust that he almost believed her. Almost. "The doors are that thick, and you and the missus were talking in very low voices. There's nothing wrong with a bit of curiosity, now, is there?"

"Nothing wrong with curiosity," he agreed. "But I thought I warned you."

"Warned me?"

"Not to mix your accents. And when you get nervous, your voice rises to quite a feminine level."

There was no mistaking the real panic in her face. "I'm still in the midst of my change."

"I don't think you're going to change that much," he said, his voice rich with irony. "What's your real name? Julia?"

"I don't know what—"

"Spare me," he said, coming up against her, putting his hands on either side of the wall behind her head, trapping her there. "You know perfectly well what I'm talking about."

For a moment she stared into his face, defiant to the last. "Damn you," she said. And made the very grave mistake of reaching up and putting her hands against his chest in a futile attempt to shove him away.

It was all he needed to break the tight control he'd been exerting over himself. He caught her wrists, pulling them down, and dragged her body up against his. Her strength was no match for his, and he was inexorable. "Time for a little honesty, Julia," he said low. "The masquerade is over. Don't waste my time trying to convince me you're a boy. You're not."

She tried to yank herself away from him, but he wasn't about to let her escape. "So tell me, my lady," he said, his voice a cool, thin thread, "who are you?"

"Let me go," she said. It was a plea, simply stated, and so surprising in its simplicity that he released her at once, stepping back, no longer touching her, even though his body raged to do so, and watched as she fell against the wall of the stable, trembling, her face white with emotions he couldn't begin to fathom. Unfortunately, he knew that lust wasn't one of them.

Her reaction answered one question immediately. She was running away from a man. A man who'd hurt her in the ways only a man could. He wanted to curse, both that unknown man and himself, for wanting to do the same thing to her.

"All right," he said, bringing his own powerful reactions under control. "Then explain it to me."

"I'm no one," she said. "If you'll just let me leave…"

"I don't think I can do that. I'm afraid you know too much about us already. I can't have you going off and telling people things you shouldn't."

"But don't you want me away from here? After all, I lied to you—I tricked you from the very beginning." She was rapidly losing her impressive calm.

"You may have lied to me," he said, "but quite frankly, you never tricked me. I'm quite adept at seeing through deception. Didn't you wonder that you haven't been asked to do any of the rough work? Not to mention the fact that people have shown an unusual amount of modesty around you. If you'd been thinking, it would have been more than clear. And if you're attempting such an absurd masquerade, you need to be thinking."

"It wasn't absurd!" she protested. "I've fooled people for more than six weeks now, and you're the first one who's seen through my disguise. I should have known," she added bitterly. "You have devil's eyes, just like your wife's. Let me leave here. I really don't know anything that would harm you or your household. I'll move on, to Portsmouth, perhaps, and…"

"You were planning to rob me, weren't you?" he asked. "You were planning to strip my pockets and book the next passage out of England. I think now is the time to answer my question, dear Julia. Who are you running away from, and why?"

"Juliette," she said in a low, resentful voice.

He made the mistake of laughing. "I should have known! Shakespeare had any number of young heroines dressing up as men and thinking they could fool people, though I don't remember Juliet ever being involved in such a masquerade. You have a romantic streak after all."

"It's not funny," she said furiously. "Release me, or I'll tell the magistrate."

"Tell the magistrate what?"

"That you've got something to hide."

"What?" He pursued it, careful not to touch her, even as he longed to.

"I don't know," she said, her voice rich with frustration. "But it has something to do with your wife and your bullying henchman."

Phelan shouted with laughter. "Such a harsh term for such a gentle man as Hannigan. It would wound him deeply to hear you call him such. I'll spare him your opinion. After all, you'll need to get along with him during the next weeks."

"I'm leaving here!" she cried, trying to push past him.

He caught her narrow shoulders in his big, strong hands, marveling at how fragile, how pliant, she felt. "You're not going anywhere," he said. "Not until I'm ready to let you go."

"You can't keep me here."

"Don't be absurd. Of course I can. With the help of my bullying henchman, of course. Not to mention his extended family. You wouldn't get ten feet away from this place if I didn't allow it. Accept your lot in life, fair Juliette. You're staying here."

"Why?"

He stared at her for a moment, nonplussed. "Why?" he echoed. "Because you amuse me, and I'm damned bored."

"If you touch me I'll cut your heart out," she said so fiercely he almost believed her.

"Juliette," he whispered, "I already am touching you." And he splayed his fingers across her thin cambric shirt, caressing her delicate throat.

She shivered, but mixed with the sheer animal terror was something else, something she couldn't quite hide. She might not recognize it herself, but it existed, deep inside, where that other man's touch hadn't reached her.

"Please," she said again, and it was enough to break his heart. If he'd possessed one.

He leaned forward and put his lips against her throat, gently, feathering the delicate skin, tasting the panic that beat against the vein in her neck. She tasted so damned good, he wanted to slide his hands under that damned shirt and push it from her. He wanted to pull her down into the sweet-smelling straw and taste every delicious inch of her.

But her skin felt cold, and he knew it could only be from fear. He raised his head to look down at her, and contemplated several promises.

He made none of them. Only one to himself, one he hoped he could keep.

He would try not to hurt her. He couldn't guarantee that he wouldn't. He couldn't guarantee that he could keep his hands off her, no matter how frightened she was. For some reason, unbeknownst to him, he wanted her, with a fierce, irrational longing that was stronger than any of the passing lust he'd felt in his adventurous life.

He released her, dropping his hands to his sides, and he saw her strong, lithe body turn limp with relief. "Go back to the house," he said in a deceptively mild voice.

"What are you going to do?"

"For the moment, absolutely nothing. I'll discuss the situation with my...wife, and we'll see what we can come up with."

"I could be her lady's maid," she suggested with sudden enthusiasm. "Dulcie is the only other female in the household, and I expect Mrs. Ramsey could do with some assistance."

"I'll pass on your offer," he said wryly. "Go to bed."

"It's early."

"Go to bed," he snapped, "or I'll take you there."

She was wise enough to recognize a reprieve when she heard it. She skirted around him, scampering from the stable without a backward glance.

He watched her go, wondering idly whether she'd try to leave tonight or wait a few days. He'd have to mention it to Hannigan, though his bullying henchman was probably already aware of the situation.

She wouldn't get far, he had no doubt of that. And he expected she'd probably wait a day or two, thinking she'd lull his suspicions.

She had a lot to learn about him. It was going to be a mixed pleasure, teaching her.

# CHAPTER SEVEN

"Damn him, damn him, damn him," Juliette muttered beneath her breath when she finally reached the privacy of her room. "Damn him all to bloody hell." She used the rich English curses with a certain amount of pleasure. Her father had taught her those, and even worse ones, but she avoided the more intense ones. Mark-David had used those words to her, and she didn't want to think about them in context with the man who saw far too much.

She could curse in many languages: French, Italian, Greek, Arabic, and Spanish; but there was nothing like some of the good old Anglo-Saxon phrases to vent one's spleen.

She flung herself down on her narrow bed, staring out the window to the sea and the evening sky beyond. The room was small and simply furnished, but it was hers, something that should have tipped her off. In a household such as this, she would never have been given the luxury of a private room.

He was right: she'd been foolishly blind, hoping no one would see through her disguise. She'd grown complacent, arrogant in her belief that she could fool everyone. No one had relieved himself in front of her; no one had commented on her myriad trips to the necessary, far too many for a boy. No one had stripped off his clothes in front of her, though Ramsey had threatened. He'd done it on purpose, waiting for her reaction. She hadn't given it to him, but that still hadn't managed to allay his suspicions. Damn him, damn him, damn him.

She wouldn't run right now. He'd be watching; he'd probably be expecting her to make a break for it. He knew her too well, a fact which alarmed her even more than his unmasking her. She didn't like any man seeing her so clearly.

She'd wait a couple of days. He wouldn't touch her again—after all, he had a glorious-looking wife, and Juliette knew perfectly well that she herself was small and dark and plain. Lemur had made it more than clear that she was lacking everything needed for a woman, a fact she rejoiced in.

She'd be safe, if she bided her time. She still had to have money if she was to book passage to the Continent, and if Ramsey had seen through her so easily, others might as well. Perhaps she should reconsider her strategy. She'd grown adept at a working-class accent. Maybe she could book passage as a seamstress or a lady's maid, traveling to new employment.

Even to her hopeful frame of mind, that didn't sound terribly likely. A woman alone on a ship, particularly the kind of ship she'd be able to afford, could run into all sorts of danger, the kind of danger that might make Mark-David Lemur seem welcome by comparison. She couldn't quite imagine it, but anything was possible.

She rose from the narrow bed and walked to the window, staring out past the overgrown gardens to the sea beyond.

The night air was filled with the scent of roses mingling with the salt smell of the ocean, and she leaned against the open shutter and sighed. She should run. She should stop making excuses to herself about lulling Ramsey's suspicions, because if she simply faced the truth, she'd know that she didn't want to leave. Didn't want to leave this place, where she'd found the first measure of comfort and safety she'd known since her father had died.

And for some illogical, irrational reason, she didn't want to leave the greatest threat she'd ever known, the man who'd penetrated her disguise with such devastating ease. The man whose touch had terrified and disgusted her, as every man's had, but whose touch had also managed to spark strange longings inside her that she refused to put a name to.

She moved away from the window resolutely, heading for her bed. Lifting the thin mattress, she withdrew all her meager belongings. The thin lace undergarments, made for a lady. The change of linen.

Juliette sat back on her heels, fury and panic whipping through her. The diamond-and-pearl earbobs were gone.

"Interesting," Phelan murmured, glancing at the jewelry Hannigan had placed on the desk. "Not the sort of thing our little stableboy would be likely to have. Did you discover anything else of interest?"

Hannigan shrugged. "She came tearing back a bit too quickly. I can tell you she wears ladies' undergarments beneath the boys' clothes. High quality they were, too."

"Now why don't I like the thought of you pawing through her underclothes?" Phelan inquired in a deceptively tranquil voice.

Hannigan grinned. "I think you know the answer to that better than I do, whether or not you care to admit it. You want me to lock her in? She might decide that now's a good time to run away."

"She's an enterprising girl—she'd probably use the window," Phelan said. "I think I'll simply remove her clothes. She's not likely to wander about without them. Despite all outward appearances, she does have some sense."

"You want me to take care of it?"

Phelan knew Hannigan was teasing him, waiting for his annoyed reaction. "Don't push me. If anyone's going to be traipsing around her bedroom, it will be me."

"I thought you might see it that way," Hannigan said smugly. "I'll leave first thing in the morning."

Phelan almost called him back. That surge of irrational jealousy troubled him. He'd made it his intention never to care too deeply about a woman. As long as he didn't allow himself to get too close, one was as good as another, as long as she knew how he played the game. Years ago he'd given up any interest in a family, a wife, a normal life. His heritage was far too clouded, too unstable ever to consider passing on. As long as he kept his emotions and desires in check, he didn't need to worry.

Juliette was threatening that hard-won self-control. The thought of Hannigan touching her lacy undergarments sent a shaft of anger through him. The thought of entering her bedroom, where she doubtless lay sleeping, made his gut twist with something that should have been simple, uncomplicated lust.

But it wasn't. Lust was direct, easily remedied, if not with one woman, then with another. If he gave in to his irrational longing for her, he'd be on his way to disaster. He couldn't allow himself to care.

He waited until after midnight, when the sounds of the house and its inhabitants had quieted. She'd locked her door, probably barred it as well. Foolish child. Nothing would keep him out if he decided he wanted to get in.

But he wasn't in the mood for violence. He walked outside, skirting the house, the moonlight leading the way. Her ground-floor window looked out over the ocean. It was shuttered against the night air, but a simple push opened it.

She lay stretched out on the bed, a light cover thrown over her. A chair was pushed up against the door as added protection, and her clothes lay across the chair.

It was a simple enough matter to vault silently through the window, landing on his bare feet in the darkness. He scooped up her clothes, turned to leave, and then paused, giving in to temptation.

She was lying on her stomach, and he could see the narrow, graceful line of her back. Her fist was by her mouth, and he could see the streaks of dried tears on her cheek.

It shocked him. Juliette wasn't the sort of woman who would give way to the weakness of tears. But alone in her room, faced with the loss of her earrings and her disguise, she'd given in.

He reached out a hand to smooth her hair away from her face, then stopped himself. If he touched her, he'd kiss her. If he kissed her while she lay naked in the bed, then he would make love to her. And if he made love to her, he'd have to send her away. Before he made the fatal mistake of caring for her.

He didn't want to send her away. Not without knowing the answers to the secrets she kept. He had to content him-

self with one last, longing look. Then he slipped through
the window again, her clothes over his arm. They smelled
of roses, they smelled of the sea, they smelled of her. He
stood in the moonlit garden and put his face against the
rough material, drinking in her scent. And then he shook
himself.

Moon madness. He was getting as daft as Valerian over
his silly bluestocking. Not as daft as his mother.

No, not that. Not yet.

That particular curse still awaited him.

"I'm going for a ride," Valerian announced the next
morning.

Phelan looked up from the breakfast table, his eyes narrowing as he surveyed his brother. Valerian hadn't bothered with his disguise—he was dressed simply in breeches
and a plain white shirt, his golden-blond hair tied back behind his handsome face. He made a lovely woman, Phelan
thought dispassionately. He made an even more handsome
man.

"Do you think that's wise?" he said mildly, sipping his
coffee. Dulcie was a whiz at coffee—she'd perfected the
Arabian style he preferred, though Valerian still insisted he
got the grounds in his teeth. "Despite our fears, our little
Juliette doesn't yet realize our secret. It might do us well
to keep her in the dark."

"Our little Juliette?" Valerian echoed, pouring himself
a cup of coffee. "Does that mean you're willing to share?"

"Don't try my patience, Val," Phelan said, ignoring his
instinctive anger. He'd never been jealous of a female before, and certainly not with his own brother. He was jealous now. "She offered to be your lady's maid."

"Did she, now? I might enjoy that." Val threw himself into a chair, watching to see how Phelan would react.

Phelan didn't gratify him. "I don't think she would. She's not overfond of men."

Val's good humor remained intact. "I expect you'll manage to change her mind."

"Perhaps. If I decide to bother."

"Let me know if you're not interested..."

"Enough!" Phelan thundered, loud enough for the cups to rattle in their saucers, no longer making any effort to disguise his possessiveness. "I thought I made myself clear."

"You have, brother mine. Crystal clear," Val said cheerfully. "It simply amuses me to see you so churlish. I'm not used to having women mean anything to you other than a few hours of entertainment."

"Juliette doesn't mean anything more to me," Phelan said flatly.

"No? Then why aren't you willing to share?"

"Valerian..."

"Pax, brother mine," Val said, holding up his hands in a gesture of peace. "I'm only teasing. She can't hold a candle to my bluestocking, as far as I'm concerned. I'll simply have to resign myself to a stretch of celibacy."

"You could always seduce Neville Pinworth," Phelan suggested lazily.

"Wretch!" Valerian shuddered. "Where is your little heroine at the moment?"

"Still in her room, where she'll stay for the next few hours."

"How do you know that?"

"Because I took her clothes."

Valerian let out an admiring whistle. "What else did you take while you were at it?" he said with a leer.

"She was asleep, brat. She didn't even know I was there. If I decide to have her, I'll do it when she's fully conscious."

"If?" Valerian's blond eyebrows arched.

Phelan ignored him. "She also came possessed of a magnificent set of diamond-and-pearl earbobs. I'm sending Hannigan off with them to see if he can discover anything about them. The obvious explanation is that she stole them, and that's why she's running, but I don't think so. She doesn't strike me as a thief."

"Even though you were convinced she was planning to strip your pockets and take off?"

"That's a different matter. She hates me. She considers me fair game." Phelan leaned back in his chair, contemplating his coffee. "I think the earrings are hers, and I think they have a history. Stones that size are usually recognizable, and Hannigan should be able to provide the answers."

Valerian reached over and took a brioche. Dulcie had also managed to master French pastry, estimable woman that she was. "And why should Hannigan be able to do that?" he asked. "What nefarious talents has a gentleman's gentleman picked up during his travels with you? Not that Hannigan has ever seemed remotely like your average gentleman's gentleman."

"I think he was always possessed of those talents," Phelan said wryly. "And I don't inquire too closely, as long as the job gets done. Suffice it to say he numbers among his vast acquaintance certain individuals who would be knowledgeable about famous diamonds and about recent thefts."

"You're a loyal employer."

"Hannigan has been with us since before I was born.

You know that as well as I do," Phelan said simply. "He would die for us. You or me," he added.

"I believe he would. Let us hope he won't be called upon to do so." Valerian rose, stretching. "I'm off."

"Have a care. This is a deserted bit of land, and it's still early enough, but it wouldn't do to have any witnesses to your riding about. In truth we don't look so alike that any observers would be sure you're me."

"Such a thoughtful, prosaic old bore," Valerian teased.

"I wouldn't like to lose you."

"You're a better brother than I deserve," Valerian said with sudden seriousness.

"True enough. You still can't have Juliette," his brother retorted, defusing the sudden sentiment. "Be off with you. The sooner you go riding, the sooner you'll be safely back in skirts."

"Don't remind me." He groaned. "Why we ever embarked on this hellish masquerade is beyond me."

"If it was good enough for Bonnie Prince Charlie, brat, then it's good enough for you." Phelan kept the sympathy from his voice. Indeed, he could imagine only too easily the frustration Valerian must be feeling, an energetic, woman-loving man trapped in skirts. While going for bruising rides along the strand represented a certain risk, without those rides Valerian might very well explode. "Do me a favor. Wear a hat. That way people might indeed mistake you for me."

"A hat wouldn't stay on, not at the pace I'm intending to set," Val said. "They'll just assume that dainty Mrs. Ramsey is a hoyden after all, who rides astride, wearing men's breeches."

"I doubt it. You ride like a man."

"Thank God for that much. I was afraid I was starting to mince. I wouldn't want to end up another Sir Neville."

"No chance of that. Not as long as you're mooning after the bluestocking."

"Ah, Sophie," Valerian said soulfully. "She'll be the death of me yet."

"Let's hope not, Val. Let's sincerely hope not."

Hannigan appeared at the door, silent as always. Phelan was used to his ways, having traveled to the far ends of the earth with him over the past ten years, both in the army and on his own, but Valerian still jumped nervously.

"I'm off, then," Hannigan announced. "I left the clothes outside her door, but she refused to open it. Told me to go about my business in no uncertain terms."

"Swore at you, did she?" Val asked in amusement.

"In several languages."

"You're going to have your hands full with that one," Valerian said. "Thank God."

"Why 'thank God'?" Phelan demanded. "Why should you wish me ill?"

"I'd wish for anything to alleviate the boredom. As long as she keeps you entertained, you won't keep trying to make me run for it. Besides, I imagine you'll be more than able to hold your own with a little bit of a thing like her."

"I appreciate your confidence, brother mine," Phelan said wryly. "I sincerely hope it's not misplaced."

He bided his time, finishing his breakfast in peace after Hannigan and his brother left. It was a bright summer's day, almost peaceful, and he allowed himself a few moments to savor it before strolling through the kitchen to the back rooms. Her door was at the end of the hallway, and the black clothes still lay piled neatly outside it.

He rapped on the door. "Your clothes await you, fair Juliette. You have five minutes to get dressed."

"Go to hell."

The voice was muffled and furious, but there was no trace of tears, he thought with satisfaction. She wasn't the sort to cry with frustration. She didn't strike him as the sort to cry at all. He detested tears in women. The ones he'd seen last night must have been a rare occurrence.

"Five minutes," he said again, "or I'll come in and dress you myself. I might enjoy that, but I doubt you would."

Her reply was in Arabic, and so obscene that he actually found himself shocked as well as amused.

"You're right," he replied in the same language. "My father was a rutting donkey, but I doubt he feasted on pig droppings. And as far as I know, my mother never consorted with camels."

The shocked silence from beyond the door was answer enough. "Five minutes," he said again, and walked away, whistling.


He spoke Arabic. Better than she did. All she could do was repeat curses she'd learned by rote, but he could actually converse in the language. Why would a country gentleman know Arabic?

She waited, listening carefully as the sound of his footsteps died away, before she went to the door. She'd wedged the chair under the knob, but she had little doubt he could break it down if he decided to. And she had little doubt that five minutes was all she was allotted.

She was growing tired of cursing. It relieved only a certain amount of her frustration, and then it lost its potency. She wasn't going to accomplish a thing as long as she stayed in her room and fumed.

She counted to sixty, then moved the chair, opening the door cautiously, the thin wool blanket wrapped around her. The clothes were piled neatly on the floor, and she grabbed them, slamming the door behind her.

They were boys' clothes. She stared at them in shock and gratification. She'd expected Ramsey would want her to wear dresses at best, and something cheap and red like a doxy's at worst. She'd underestimated him. The clothes were those of a sober schoolboy, black breeches and vests, white shirts. Three changes of clothes, an absolute luxury, complete with white linen underclothing.

There was only one problem. There was no strip of linen to bind her breasts.

She peered inside her shirt at that offending portion of her anatomy. To be sure, they weren't that large, but they were indisputably female. Flat-chested though she considered herself to be, she was still better endowed than Ramsey's golden-blond wife, and she'd heard that men put a great store in women's breasts. She didn't want to do anything to compare with Mrs. Ramsey.

She stripped quickly, keeping her own voluminous shirt over her as she washed, in case her employer decided to make good his threat. In the end, it was a full ten minutes before she opened the door, just in time to meet him.

She had no idea what she looked like; her room, comfortable as it was, did not have a mirror. Nor could she read anything from his expression. Ramsey was adept at keeping his thoughts to himself. It was no wonder she'd been vain enough to think she'd fooled him.

He simply nodded. "You should find those more comfortable," he said.

"Where did you get them?" She didn't bother with the pretense of "sir."

"Hannigan has many talents. I simply have to ask him and he provides. I've discovered it does well not to inquire too closely into the origin of some of his feats."

"How is he with diamond-and-pearl earbobs?"

Ramsey didn't even blink. "I haven't asked him to procure any for me in recent years. Why, did you have a fancy for a pair? I might expect you to earn them."

Juliette considered a few Greek curses, then thought better of it. If the man spoke Arabic, he was likely to be conversant in other languages as well. She wasn't going to get a direct answer from him. Not until he was good and ready. "What do you want from me?"

He leaned against the wall, considering her question. He really was the most unlikely sort of English gentleman, with his casual ways and his sardonic grace. Not like the military types she had met with her father. Not at all like her precise husband.

"That depends," he replied.

"On what?"

"On my mood. And your cooperation. For now, Dulcie needs some help in the kitchen, and I expect a growing lad like you wants some breakfast."

"Did you tell Dulcie…?"

"Dulcie has always known. The entire household has been aware of your masquerade."

"Then why am I wearing these?" She gestured to her trim breeches.

"I thought you'd prefer them. If you'd rather, I can give

you some of Val's dresses, though I expect you'd swim in them."

"These are fine."

His smile was slight, cool. "Besides, the townspeople would be bound to talk, and we prefer to keep to ourselves out here and not cause comment."

"Then why did you bring me back here in the first place? Wouldn't it have been wiser to leave me to the tender mercies of Sir Neville?"

"I don't think Sir Neville would have been particularly tender, or merciful," he replied. "Besides, I was bored. You've been relatively entertaining, and I'm looking forward to more of your fairy stories about your barmaid mother and your sailor father."

"That was a lie."

"And I'm certain your next explanation will be just as fanciful."

She glared at him. She'd been fully prepared to tell him her mother was a seamstress and her father a groom, but she suspected that wouldn't work. "I wouldn't waste my time," she said with great dignity. "You wouldn't believe anything I chose to tell you."

"Probably not," he agreed. "But you could always try me. Who was your father?"

"Don't know," she said promptly. "I don't think my mother did either."

He smiled then, a smile of pure enjoyment, and Juliette felt that treacherous melting once more. "Charming," he murmured. "And who's your mother?"

She considered several possibilities and quickly dismissed them. "Your wife," she said sweetly, hoping to prod him.

His shout of laughter startled her. "That will come as a great surprise to Val," he said. "Off to the kitchens with you, lad, and see if you can come up with something slightly more believable." He turned and walked away from her, disappearing down the narrow hallway as if he'd lost interest in her.

She watched him go out of shuttered eyes. It was just as well, she told herself. He'd given her a major clue to her survival at Sutter's Head. She would simply have to be as boring as possible if she wanted to keep herself safe from any random attentions he might be inclined to bestow. Though she couldn't help but wonder if she was flattering herself.

One thing was certain: she didn't want him to put his hands on her again. The feel was too disturbing, too confusing. And the most logical way to protect herself was to ally herself with his wife. Surely he wouldn't dare interfere with his wife's maid.

If she'd worried about how Dulcie might react to her, she soon found there was nothing to be embarrassed about. Dulcie put a rich breakfast in front of her, then set her to peeling potatoes with the same matter-of-fact good cheer she'd always displayed. Juliette might almost have thought Dulcie didn't know the truth about her, except when she referred to her quite pointedly as Juliette.

"Anything else?" Juliette inquired briskly as she dropped the last potato into the bowl of water.

"Not for now. Take yourself off, lass. Go for a walk, enjoy the fresh air. I imagine the master will be wanting you later on in the day. For now, your time's your own."

Juliette was far from appeased at this offer. She could just imagine the master wanting her later, and she had every intention of forestalling that eventuality. "Where is Mrs. Ramsey at the moment?" she inquired in her most innocent voice.

For a moment even the redoubtable Dulcie looked taken aback. "In her room, I expect," she said after a moment. "She just came back from a ride. If I were you, I'd keep away from her until you've got the master's permission."

"Why?"

Dulcie looked perplexed. "Why?" she echoed. "Because...er...she has the devil's own temper in the morning. Throws things, she does."

Juliette didn't believe her for a moment. "She looks like such a sweet-tempered lady."

"Pretty is as pretty does," Dulcie said firmly. "You keep away from her, miss, if you know what's good for you."

"Of course," Juliette murmured compliantly, deciding then and there that nothing could keep her from Mrs. Ramsey's side. Her husband must have decreed that Juliette be kept at a distance, and his purpose could only be sinister in the extreme. Grabbing an apple, she headed out into the bright summer sunshine, wandering in the direction of the stables.

The moment she was out of sight of the kitchens she sped around the house, climbed over the wide stone wall, and made her way through the rose gardens, which were in such need of weeding that she almost stopped there and then and took pity on the poor choked blossoms. First things first, she reminded herself. She needed to get to Mrs. Ramsey and enlist her aid before her nefarious husband could stop her.

The front door stood open to the sunlight, and not a soul was in sight. Juliette slipped inside and headed up the curving front stairs on silent feet, moving unerringly toward Mrs. Ramsey's room. She knew to her sorrow that the doors and walls were too thick for efficient spying, but at least she could discover whether the lady of the house was alone. Or, perhaps, embarrassingly busy with her husband.

She stopped outside the heavy oak door, pressing her ear against it, listening carefully. There was no sound of voices, just a cheerful whistling that was surprising from such an elegant lady as Mrs. Ramsey, and the sound of water splashing.

Juliette put her hand on the doorknob, testing it silently. It turned beneath her hand, and taking a deep breath, she called out, "Mrs. Ramsey," as she pushed the door open.

The bathtub was in the middle of the room. Mrs. Ramsey had just risen out of it and was in the midst of reaching for a towel when Juliette stepped inside.

Mrs. Ramsey was indisputably *not* Mrs. Ramsey! He immediately sat down hard in the tub, the soapy water splashed violently over the floor, and he gave a strangled shout, halfway between a choke and a laugh.

"You're not a woman!" she gasped.

"Obviously," he replied with a wryness that was uncomfortably similar to that of the man who was supposed to be his husband. "You needn't sound so horrified at the thought," he added. "It's not as if the idea of dressing up as the opposite sex is a complete unknown to you."

"Hell and damnation!" Ramsey appeared in the opposite doorway, his face thunderous. "You were told to keep away from here!"

"Don't be too harsh on the girl, Phelan," the man in the bathtub said easily. "You can't blame her for being curious. And she was bound to find out sooner or later—you knew that when you brought her home with you."

"On my terms," he snapped, glaring at her.

Juliette backed toward the door, away from the two of them, her shock and disbelief wiping all rational thought from her brain. "You...you're worse than Sir Neville!" she gasped, and turned and ran.

"Hell and damnation!" Ramsey said again, and he started after her.

She made it as far as the back stairs, halfway down the first twisting flight, when he caught her wrist and pulled her up against him. "Let go of me, you...you depraved creature!" she shrieked.

"I'm no more depraved than you are. If you think my brother enjoys wearing skirts, then you're jumping to conclusions. He doesn't enjoy them, and neither do I."

"Your brother?"

"You noticed the resemblance already, my boy." His irony was heavy. "He prefers women in his bed," he said, huge and overwhelming in the darkness, "and so do I."

She lashed out at him in sudden panic, but it did no good. He was much larger than she was, much stronger, and the enclosed dimness of the back stairs left her no room to escape. He pulled her into his arms, pressing his hips against hers, and she was in no doubt as to his meaning. He caught her flailing wrists in one hand, used the other to hold her chin still, and put his mouth against hers, hard, pushing her back against the plaster wall.

She heard a terrified whimper and knew it was her own. She despised it. She'd never whimpered with Mark-David, never begged for mercy. She wouldn't with this man either.

She didn't need to. The harshness of his mouth against

hers softened almost immediately. What had started as an assault had been transformed miraculously into a caress, a wooing that slid beneath her terror and defused it. He released her wrists, putting his arm around her waist and pulling her up to him, gently, and she should have used her freedom to run away from him. Instead, she stayed in the circle of his arms, letting his mouth taste hers, letting his hands hold her, letting him sneak beneath her panic and fear to some long-hidden part of her that ached for something she didn't even begin to comprehend.

And then his tongue touched her lips, and she jerked back, horrified.

He let her go. In the murky light his silver eyes glittered, and she could see the rise and fall of his chest, see the unmistakable evidence of his arousal.

She wiped her wrist across her mouth, not bothering to disguise her reaction. He simply looked at her, a dark, unreadable expression in his eyes. "I expect you now understand why you can't be Val's lady's maid. He does far better with Hannigan. I doubt you'd have the strength to tie his laces." The kiss might almost have not existed.

She could play it the same way. "Why is he doing it?"

There was no mistaking the man's cool smile. What had his brother called him? Not Philip. Phelan? "I'll tell you, fair Juliette," he murmured, "if and when I decide to trust you." He reached out and touched her mouth, his fingers gentle, questing, lightly callused.

She jerked away, staring up at him. "At least he won't have to wear skirts in the house anymore," he continued smoothly. "He'll appreciate that."

"Phelan," she said.

His eyes narrowed. "You heard that, did you?"

"Is that your real name?"

"For my sins, yes," he said flatly.

"It's an odd name."

"Distinctive," he agreed. "According to my mother, it means 'the wolf.'"

Juliette's temporary sense of power vanished. He was aptly named. "I think I should leave here."

"I think," said Phelan, "you won't be going anywhere until I say so. And that won't be for a long, long time." He took a step back, away from her. "Come back upstairs. I imagine Valerian is decently clothed now, and the two of you ought to at least make one another's acquaintance."

"I think I've seen more of your brother than I care to," Juliette muttered.

"Most likely," Phelan said wryly. "Nevertheless, you'll do as I say."

"And if I refuse?"

"Then I'll assume you're a schoolroom miss running away from a stern father, and I'll do my best to return you to the bosom of your family."

"I'll come," she said bitterly.

"I rather thought you would."

And Juliette wondered if she had it in her to kill a man. She would certainly enjoy trying.

# CHAPTER EIGHT

If he'd been a graceful, lovely woman, the man she'd surprised in the bathtub was an even more attractive man. Tall, strong, and intensely masculine, despite the beauty of his face and the silken blond hair, he rose when Juliette entered the room, a wry, self-deprecating smile on his mobile mouth.

"I presume there are no secrets between us," he said with a charming smile. "I'm Valerian Romney."

"Romney?" she questioned, putting her small hand in his.

"Valerian!" Phelan cautioned from directly behind her.

His brother shrugged, turning the masculine handshake she'd offered into a gentlemanly kiss on the back of her hand. "She's living with us, Phelan. She's bound to ferret out all our secrets sooner or later. As far as I'm concerned, it's a relief. Do you play chess?"

"Not very well," she admitted.

"All the better," Valerian said. "My brother always beats me mercilessly. Now I can find someone smaller to trounce."

She glanced over her shoulder at the man who now

seemed to be named Phelan Romney, but he simply watched them, no expression in his silver-gray eyes. "It would be my pleasure," she said demurely. "Assuming I'm not needed in the kitchen."

"You aren't going to make her work, are you, Phelan?" his brother beseeched him.

"Why shouldn't I? She was brought here as a serving lad, not a ward of the house," he replied, lounging against the doorway.

"She can be my page," Val declared. "We can get her a velvet suit, and she can carry my vinaigrette wherever I go."

"You want a witness for your rendezvous with the blue-stocking, brat?" Phelan inquired.

Val's smile faded into uncertainty for a moment. "Not particularly," he said. "Though it might be good for me. At least it would keep me in line."

"I'm counting on your own good sense to do that."

"I wouldn't, if I were you. My good sense seems to have flown out the window the moment I let you and Hanni-gan talk me into wearing skirts," Val said, his voice rich with disgust.

"It's a very good disguise," Juliette offered hesitantly. "I never guessed."

Val grinned at her. "That's because you were too busy trying to fool everybody yourself. I admit, though, I seem to have a talent for acting. Perhaps I should go on the stage, Phelan. Assuming we're driven out of England forever."

"Driven out of England?" Juliette echoed.

"Valerian," Phelan said wearily, "whatever happened to your discretion?"

"I've used it all up on everyone else," he said. "I've none to spare for your little spaniel."

"Spaniel?" Juliette said, incensed.

"Because he's had you trailing around after him, in a misguided attempt at keeping an eye on you. Though now that I have a good look at you, you don't resemble a spaniel at all. Perhaps a she-lion. Or a very young wolverine. Not so tame at all."

Of course, he would also know the meaning of Phelan's name, and his choice of animals wasn't random. "Think of me as a lapdog," she said with deceptive affability. "A fat old pug, with an evil disposition and very sharp teeth."

Valerian shouted with laughter. "I like her, Phelan," he said. "I like her very much indeed."

"Do you?" Phelan's voice was cool and noncommittal, and Juliette resisted the impulse to glance at him. She couldn't begin to guess what the older brother thought of her, and she didn't want to. Because then she might start wanting him to think of her in certain ways, and therein lay disaster.

Valerian was another matter. Handsome, charming, and sunny-tempered, he was as different from his dark, brooding brother as night from day. He was no threat to her whatsoever. So why was she drawn to Phelan?

She'd never been terribly pragmatic, and the past weeks must have overset her common sense entirely. The sooner she escaped from this mysterious family, the better off she'd be. She'd learned she could count on no one but herself. She needed to remember that, when seduced by one man's easy smiles and another's wintry charm.

"Speaking of lapdogs," Phelan said, "the fair Juliette may have a good idea there. I like the idea of her keeping a censorious eye on you while you consort with Miss de Quincey. Why don't we get you a yapping little terrier and have young Julian carry it wherever you go?"

"You don't frighten me, Phelan. Find the terrier and we'll take it from there," Valerian said affably. "In the meantime, let me have Juliette. I need someone new to talk to."

"Later, brat. I have need of her right now."

Juliette turned to glance at him, but as usual there was no reading anything in his enigmatic expression. She didn't want to go with him. For one thing, she didn't want to obey any of his random commands. For another, she didn't want to leave the sunny comfort of the one brother for the doubt-less danger of the other. Did she?

She knew she had no choice. She made a low bow. "Yes, my lord and master."

Valerian chuckled. "Better watch it, Phelan. You can't thrash her when she mocks you."

"I wouldn't be too sure of that," Phelan said coolly. "Come along, lad," he ordered, his voice heavy with irony.

Juliette followed in his wake, wondering whether she ought to keep a civil tongue in her head, always a difficult task for her. Or whether she had anything to lose.

She decided she didn't. "I wish you wouldn't do that," she said.

Phelan paused at the top of the stairs, turning to observe her with unsettling calm. "Wouldn't do what?"

"Call me 'lad' with such sarcasm."

"Forgive me," he said without a trace of sincerity. "I am told my cynicism is one of my greatest flaws."

"I doubt that."

His smile lightened his dark face. "Doubtless you think I have many far greater ones," he suggested.

"Doubtless," she said boldly.

"Are you hoping to goad me into sending you on your way? As I've already remarked, you're extremely innocent. If you irritate me enough, I'll simply see that you're locked in your room."

"I could climb out the window."

"I'm aware of that. I used the window to enter your room and remove your clothes. I'll see to it that the window is barred as well."

She could feel her face pale. "You did?"

"Who did you think? Hannigan? Much as I trust him, I wasn't about to let him wander into a sleeping girl's room. He is only a man after all, and subject to the same temptations as anyone."

"But not you."

"I beg your pardon?"

"You weren't subject to any temptations when you entered my room." She pursued it with an irrational disregard of her own well-being.

"On the contrary," he said, and his voice was low, smooth, and evoking extreme warning. "But then, I have an unfair advantage. I already know what I'm planning to do with you."

"Would you care to enlighten me?" She found she could be almost as mocking.

Almost. Phelan Romney was a master. "No."

She stared at him in mute frustration. "To the kitchen, young Julian," he said, dismissing her.

"I've already helped Dulcie..."

"She's in need of more assistance," Phelan said calmly.

"You just want to keep me away from your brother," she said shrewdly.

"Why ever should I?"

She considered it. Jealousy certainly couldn't be a motive. "You need to warn him not to be so frank. Not if you wish to keep any of your secrets, Mr. Romney." She used his real last name with determined emphasis, hoping for a reaction.

She didn't like the one she got. "Wrong name, little one," he murmured with a mocking smile. "But you're right about my brother. I'm about to tie his tongue in knots before I let you near him again. He could take lessons in discretion from you."

For some reason she was inordinately pleased at the vague compliment.

"But it won't do any good," he added.

"What won't?"

"Your discretion. When I want to find out your secrets, I will. For the time being, I'll let you keep them. I have other, more important matters on my mind." He turned from her. "To the kitchen, child," he called over his shoulder.

The term incensed her. "I'm twenty-two years old."

He turned and looked at her, and there was no mistaking his triumphant expression. "So ancient a hag, are you?" he murmured. "I would never have guessed it. And therein lies a lesson. I just tricked you into giving away one piece of information. I can get the rest just as easily."

"Try it," she challenged, still furious, mainly with herself.

He took a step toward her, and she could read the determination in his face. He was going to touch her. And she was horribly afraid she might begin to like it.

"Never mind," she said swiftly. "I believe you." And she turned and fled down the dark, narrow stairs to the kitchen.

Phelan should have been pleased with the way things were working out. Or so he told himself as he sat alone in the library at Sutter's Head, staring out into the late-afternoon sunlight. The past few days had passed in relative peace and harmony. The introduction of Juliette into their lives had at least temporarily restrained some of Valerian's more reckless tendencies. To be sure, he still rode neck or nothing along the beach to burn off some of his restlessness. But the rest of the time he spent with Juliette, playing chess, teasing her, trying, with a complete lack of success, to ferret out her secrets. He'd made no attempt to travel into Hampton Regis and visit the alluringly innocent Miss Sophie de Quincey, and for that Phelan could only be grateful. A few more days, and he might even be able to convince Val of the wonders of Paris.

Phelan knew he ought to be willing to give up his interest in Juliette as a sacrifice to Valerian's well-being. But there was a limit to his brotherly devotion, and that limit had been reached in the person of a small, determined creature who didn't even realize how deliciously feminine she was.

That was probably the secret of her charm. Most women flirted, using every weapon in their arsenal to try to ensnare men, whether they actually wanted them or not. It was probably just a case of keeping their skills sharp.

Phelan had always found it a dead bore. But Juliette Whoever-She-Was was a different matter entirely. She truly didn't want to entice anyone, and her grace and femininity came from somewhere inside her, unconscious and all the more desirable.

He was having a hard time of it, Phelan thought with grim humor. He ought to get rid of her. Failing that, he ought to encourage Valerian to bed her. He could do neither. As far as he could tell, and he'd been watching with jealous intensity, Valerian treated her like a younger brother, like a tame puppy, like a new toy. As long as that continued, he didn't need to make any decisions. And he could control his own urges, no matter how irrationally fierce they seemed to have grown over the past week, ever since the advent of the fair Juliette into their lives.

God, if only they could leave this place! Leave her behind, with her unconscious temptation. Phelan had no home, and he wanted none. On the Continent he felt free, to roam, to discover, to live.

Taking his allowance and buying a commission in the army had been a rash, childish thing to do, back when he was a hotheaded eighteen-year-old. His father had even deemed it mad. But it had been the sanest thing he'd ever done. While none of his fellow officers could understand why an heir to a tidy estate would enter the army, they had accepted him, and he'd learned the kind of friendship that existed between men when lives were at stake. With Hannigan always at his side, he'd discovered a kind of peace within himself, the sort he'd never thought he could find. He'd accepted his lot with a cynical grace, continuing with his travels during the eight years since he'd sold out his commission. If only he hadn't returned to Yorkshire and set the madness in motion once more.

He leaned back in the leather chair, a frown creasing his forehead. It had been years since he'd wasted his time in useless regrets, in longing for what simply could not be. It was best he kept his attention fixed on what he could do. Enough people were already paying the price of the family heritage. He was damned if he'd let Valerian do so as well.

"We've got trouble, your lordship."

Phelan lifted his head, his eyes narrowing as Hannigan strode into the room. He was still dusty from his travels, and his face was grim.

"It looks it," Phelan said. "Wouldn't you like something to quench your thirst before you tell me?"

"Dulcie's bringing me some ale." Hannigan sat heavily in a chair, with the weariness of an old friend, not a servant, and Phelan realized matters were very serious indeed.

Phelan had never been a man to stand on ceremony. He didn't give a damn about social rules, or class order, or any of that absurdity. When long ago he'd learned that the young boy playing in the kitchens was actually his half brother, he'd seen to it that Valerian had joined in his own lessons. Phelan's mother had protested in shrieks of fury, but even at fifteen he'd managed to ignore her, and for once his father had approved of his actions in taking Valerian under his wing.

Phelan had always considered Hannigan to be more of a father than the man who had sired him, and when they were abroad, Hannigan relaxed some of his standards. In England, however, he always stood deferentially, referred to Phelan by title, and seldom held more than the briefest of conversations.

Phelan leaned back in his chair, waiting patiently. Indeed, he was a man who'd learned to school his impulses, and he'd done very well at it. Until he'd met the girl who called herself Julian Smith.

"She's an heiress," Hannigan said, once Dulcie had delivered his mug of ale and then made herself scarce with her usual placid discretion.

Phelan considered the information. "Valerian will be pleased," he said wryly. "He's been looking for one to marry."

"Won't do him any good. She's already married."

Phelan didn't allow a flicker of emotion to pass over his face. "Is she?" he said evenly.

But Hannigan had known him since birth. "I knew you wouldn't like it," he said. "And you won't like who she's married to even more."

"Someone I know?" He didn't deny his reaction. It would have been fruitless. "Why don't you tell me everything you know? I suppose the girl has a name?"

"Juliette MacGowan Lemur. Her husband's Mark-David Lemur. We met him in…"

"In Alexandria," Phelan supplied, immediately putting a face to the man. Immediately hating him. "I don't remember hearing about a wife."

"Wasn't married then. I thought I'd best get back and tell you what I'd found, rather than waste time ferreting out the details. I imagine you can get them from her just as easily. All's I know is they were married in Egypt, traveled back to London by boat, and then she disappeared. He's looking for her."

"I expect he is," Phelan said calmly.

"Those are her earbobs, by the way."

"MacGowan." Phelan repeated the name in a contemplative fashion. "Then her father presumably was Black Jack MacGowan. No wonder she's so unconventional. He was a true original."

"Did we ever meet him?"

Phelan shook his head. "No. And now I'm doubly sorry. I knew he had a child, but I'd always gathered it was a boy. That explains a great deal. He died a few months back. That must be when Lemur stepped in. Very like him."

"You don't care for the man," Hannigan said.

"To put it mildly. So it's a husband she's running away from, not an overbearing father. I would never have guessed it," Phelan murmured, thinking of the fierce, defensive innocence in her eyes, in her mouth the one time he'd given in to temptation and kissed her. "How did you find all this out?"

Hannigan looked uneasy. "I have connections," he said vaguely. "Friends, family."

"Friends and family who'd know about stolen jewels."

Hannigan gave Phelan his most innocent smile. "Your lordship wouldn't want to be bothered with the sordid details. Suffice it to say word's out about the earbobs. There's a reward for them, and when it comes to a choice between loyalty and gold, I don't think there's going to be much difficulty making the decision. Lemur's going to be able to trace the earbobs back here."

"You think so? When the Bow Street runners can't even find us?"

"We've had help in that matter. It weren't a question of money then. My family's been watching out for you and your brother. But runaway heiresses and diamond earbobs can complicate things."

"The Hannigans have kept the runners away?" Phelan asked, momentarily startled.

But obviously Hannigan had already said more than he wanted to, and he simply rose, taking his empty mug with him. "I need to wash the travel dust off me," he said, dismissing the subject, and Phelan knew he'd get no more out of him. Only Hannigan could withstand Phelan's determination. "Where is the girl? In the kitchens?"

"I imagine she's playing chess with Valerian," Phelan answered. "I was hoping to keep the two of them apart, but fate decreed otherwise." He kept his voice cool and noncommittal, with the distant hope he could fool his oldest friend. He didn't put much stock in his ability to do so, but it was worth a try.

"Has he decided he's in love with her yet?" Hannigan asked, knowing Valerian of old.

"I'm not certain. I expect he's still enamored of Sophie de Quincey, though he's trying to resist temptation. Why don't you come along and see what you think?"

"I might at that," Hannigan said. "I don't want her breaking any hearts around here."

"Valerian's heart is very resilient. And we know that I don't have one, at least as far as young women are concerned."

Hannigan didn't say a word. He didn't need to. His derisive expression said it all.

"No, no, no," Val said. "You walk like that damned Pinworth! You've got to stride more. Swing your arms back and forth... Not too much! You'll knock over the furniture."

He was seated on the delicate little settee, his yellow silk skirts flowing about him, a light cashmere shawl disguising the muscle in his arms, as his rather too capable-looking hands did their best with the delicate teapot.

Juliette stopped her measured pacing to survey him critically. "I've been walking around in boys' clothes for six weeks and no one's noticed. I think I've been doing fine. Certainly better than you are at handling that teapot. You're treating it like a bucket of slop. The milk goes first, you fool, then the tea, then the hot water. And don't splash it in, for heaven's sake! A woman your age would have serving tea down pat!"

"A woman my age would have servants pour the tea for her," Valerian shot back.

Juliette raised an eyebrow. "Where were you raised? The servants bring in the tray; the lady of the house pours. Didn't your mother ever make your tea?"

"My mother would brew me a cuppa in the kitchen," Valerian replied. "If I'd had tea with Phelan's mother, she probably would have poisoned it."

"You don't have the same mother?" Juliette questioned, stopping her pacing and sinking down beside her companion with charming, boyish grace.

"I'm the bastard of the family," Val said with unabated good humor. "My mother was a farm girl, my father the lord of the manor."

"Which is why your half brother is now a lord," she said shrewdly. "So that makes you the black sheep?"

"Not me. Phelan has that honor. He follows his own rules, always has. Doesn't half like it that he's inherited the title, but there's nothing he can do about it. He never liked Yorkshire, or the family, for that matter. Not that I can blame him. His mother...well, the less said about her the better. If it were up to Phelan, he'd spend his life wandering the world, discovering new places, not trapped in a manor house in the north of England. But it isn't up to him. He can't bring our father back to life, and I'm not sure he'd want to, even for the sake of his freedom. For reasons I never understood, my father hated him. And wasted no chance in letting him know it."

"How awful," Juliette blurted out, horrified. At least she had the memory of Black Jack MacGowan's unstinting love to see her through the dark times.

Valerian shrugged. "He wouldn't want your pity. He's learned to live a tidy, self-contained life. No one touches him, and he cares for no one."

"Is that a warning?"

Valerian's smile was supremely innocent. "Why should it be? You have no interest in my brother, do you?"

"Only in when I'll see the last of him," Juliette said firmly. She changed the subject. "How did your father die? Was it recently?" She stretched her legs out in front of her, crossing them at the ankles in perfect imitation of Valerian when he was wearing breeches.

"Not bad," he said, surveying her. "But you need to throw your shoulders back a bit. Tilt your chin up, like you're ready to take on the world."

"And you need to simper more."

"I'm sure I do. Problem is, I don't think you know how to simper. You certainly haven't been very forthcoming with helpful hints on the subject."

"I'm afraid I never mastered the art of flirtation," she said in a cool voice.

Valerian laughed. "Maybe I'll have to teach you how to be a woman as well as a man."

"Don't count on it, boy-o," Juliette retorted.

"Make a lovely couple, don't they?" Hannigan's voice broke through their preoccupation.

She glanced up to see him standing in the doorway, with

Phelan directly behind him. In the dim light of the hallway she couldn't read Phelan's expression, but she could sense his reserve, and guess at his disapproval.

"Lovely," he said, an edge to his voice that to a wishful fool might almost sound like jealousy.

"Like brother and sister," Hannigan continued cheerfully. "Only problem is, who's the brother and who's the sister?"

That remark surprised a laugh out of Phelan, one nearly devoid of mockery. "Indeed, it's hard to say who's the prettier of the two."

"Valerian is," Juliette said flatly. "And definitely the more feminine."

"I don't know if I like that," Val protested.

"You're definitely better at applying makeup," she pointed out, concentrating on the one man she felt at ease with.

"That's because I have an incipient beard to cover. You don't. Stripling," he added for effect.

"But at least I beat you at chess," she said sweetly.

"I see what you mean. Perfect siblings," Phelan said, strolling into the room and taking the seat opposite his brother. "Pour me a cup of tea, brat, and show me how well you've taken instruction."

"He's improving," Juliette said, watching with a critical eye and then handing the cup to Phelan, being very careful to keep her hand from brushing his. "He's still a bit clumsy."

"I make a better woman than you do a boy," Val insisted.

"No," she said smugly, "you don't."

"Children, children," Phelan said. "Stop squabbling and tell me what induced you to put your skirts on again. I thought nothing short of imminent exposure could force you to put those things on willingly. Unless you've developed a taste for them."

"Bugger off, Phelan," his brother replied pleasantly, and mentally Juliette added the curse to her multilingual litany. "I'm going on a social call."

"Not to the bluestocking?" Phelan groaned. "I thought you'd given up on her."

"I've tried to resist temptation," Valerian said with a wholly masculine grin. "I swear, I've tried. Juliette's even given me lectures about the unfairness of being in a lady's confidence. I can't help myself. Besides, Sophie and I are friends. I'm afraid if I don't show up sooner or later, she might decide to pay a little visit herself, and that might prove a bit awkward. At least I'm taking Juliette with me this time. I can't do anything indecent with a witness."

"I hate to inform you," Phelan drawled, "but Juliette's not going anywhere. Not for the time being."

"Why not?" she demanded, furious. "You can't keep me here! There's no reason—"

"There's every reason." He overrode her complaints with that insufferable air of his. "And as a matter of fact, I already have been keeping you here, quite easily, and will continue to do so."

"But it was your idea she accompany me," Val protested, sounding very young.

"And I've changed my mind. You can visit your lady love, Val, as long as you remember why you're wearing skirts, and exercise more than your usual caution. But Juliette stays at Sutter's Head."

If she expected Valerian to champion her cause, she accepted the disappointment when he shrugged his broad shoulders, gave her a wry smile, and rose from the settee with a feminine grace that normally would have had Juliette's lips quivering in amusement. At the moment, she found no reason to smile.

"There's no arguing with him when he uses that tone of voice, Juliette," Valerian said. "Best not to waste your breath." He glanced at his brother. "I take it Hannigan discovered something interesting?"

"He did."

"About the little lady, I presume, not our own filthy mess?" he added, pausing by the door and shaking out his skirts with a brisk hand.

"Discretion, Val," Phelan said wearily, leaning back in his seat.

Val grinned. "I'll never learn. Don't hold dinner for me. I intend to talk Miss De Quincey into feeding me. If not with victuals, then with the fruits of her wisdom."

"Behave yourself!" Phelan admonished.

"You, too, big brother."

They were alone. Juliette rose to her feet, but Phelan's sharp voice forestalled her. "Sit down!"

"I don't—"

"Sit down!"

Juliette sat. She glowered at him across the tea table, feeling childish but not caring.

"Are you going to pour me some tea?"

"You already had some."

"With too little milk and too much water. My brother needs to practice."

"He isn't motivated."

"True enough. I do think you're better at your role than he is at his," Phelan said idly. "At least you put your heart and soul into it. He doesn't want to be a woman—he's finding his skirts infuriating. Whereas I think you'd be much happier if you really were a boy. Or at least you think you would."

"You're very perceptive," she said. "Without question I was born into the wrong body."

His eyes met hers for a long, pregnant moment. "I wonder if you really believe that," he said softly. "I might be tempted to find out."

She couldn't hide the panic that flared through her. "It's the truth," she said.

"Perhaps. I wonder, though, whether Mark-David Lemur would agree with you."

There was a sudden roaring in her ears. Deafening, as only the sound of panic can be. She stared at him, and his eyes were dark, merciless holes, and there was no safety, no pity for her. She rose on unsteady feet, hearing the crash of the tea table as she knocked it over. And then she ran from the room, from the man, from the past that he could somehow see with his devil's eyes.

She ran, terrified that he'd follow and capture her. Terrified that he wouldn't.

And terrified, most of all, by the truth that even she couldn't face.

Phelan watched her leave. His first instinct was to go after her. The sheer, blind panic had struck him deeply, making him feel guilty for one of the few times in his life. He'd been toying with her, wanting to see her reaction, and he'd been amply, cruelly rewarded.

He wanted to go to her, to comfort her. To put his arms around her, press her head against his shoulder, and hold her.

But that wasn't all that he wanted to do. He wanted to unfasten the small white bone buttons that ran down the front of that soft cambric shirt. He wanted to slide his hand between the material and cover her small, perfect breast. He wanted to taste her mouth again, this time more completely. He wanted to use his tongue, and he wanted her to kiss him back.

He wanted too many things that she wasn't prepared to give. Things he could take. Things that Mark-David Lemur had already taken from her.

He let her go. He had no choice. He couldn't go after her and not take her. Not at the moment, when his body was taut with desire and his pulses were racing and he felt as randy as the seventeen-year-old boy Juliette MacGowan Lemur was pretending to be.

He needed time. She needed time. He could only hope that a cruel, indifferent fate was going to allow it to them. If the past was anything to go by, he doubted it.

Disaster was lurking around the next corner. And he'd better prepare for it.

# CHAPTER NINE

Valerian had almost forgotten how much he hated this masquerade. Juliette had been such a welcome distraction that he'd been able to put the unpleasantness out of his mind. Until his ridiculous longing for Sophie de Quincey had grown too much to bear, and he'd climbed back into his corset and skirts once more, and found them to have lost even their capacity to amuse.

The choice was obvious. He could stay out at Sutter's Head, playing chess and parlor games with Juliette, under Phelan's watchful, jealous eye. That in itself was an entertaining distraction. Never in his life had he expected to find his emotionally detached older brother the prey to possessiveness, but there was no doubt as to the uneasy emotions prowling under Phelan's mocking surface.

Or he could give in to Phelan's demands and run like a coward to Paris. Running from Yorkshire had been bad enough. He'd been too shocked and confused, both by his father's murder and by Lady Margery's accusations. By the time he was thinking clearly, Phelan, with the help and possibly at the instigation of Hannigan, had brought him to this deserted spot on the south coast, in preparation for an escape to France.

He wouldn't go. There were a thousand reasons, most of them overwhelming, why he should. If the truth, as he and Phelan suspected, was that Lady Margery had killed her husband, then Valerian had no interest in having it known, even if it would clear his name. His presence at Romney Hall, innocent though it was, had been anathema to Lady Margery. Phelan's fraternal affection had been the ultimate betrayal as far as his mother was concerned.

No, he wouldn't accuse the old lady, for her sake as well as for his brother's.

But neither could he turn tail and run. Not yet. Sooner or later he'd have to accept the fact that he'd never see England again. But for just a few brief moments; minutes, hours, days, he intended to glory in a perfect English summer. And a perfect English girl.

And if the runners caught up with him before he made his escape, it would be worth it. Not for just any woman would he put on these absurd clothes and mince his way into town. He was a man who had always liked and appreciated women in all their glorious diversity, appreciated them with a healthy appetite and respect. There were so many of them, each with her own special charm, that he never thought he'd be so besotted with one quiet young lady barely out of the schoolroom. Besotted enough to endanger his safety, and even that of his brother.

Why did she have to be so wealthy, so beautiful, so damned well-bred? Couldn't he have fallen in love with a barmaid, a miller's daughter, an upstairs maid? Why did he have to reach the advanced age of five and twenty, only to fall hopelessly in love with an innocent?

He hadn't been able to rationalize his way out of it. He hadn't listened to his brother's warnings, Hannigan's suggestions, or his own better judgment. All he could listen to was his heart. And his heart was in search of his bluestocking.

It was a shame Phelan had grown so possessive about Juliette. With Juliette along, dressed in her sober boys' clothes, Val might have been able to keep things in better perspective. He'd hardly attempt making love to Sophie with Juliette's wise dark eyes watching.

But he'd been forced to come out alone, and on Phelan's head be the results. Not that he would do anything to jeopardize his own or his brother's safety. But he could indulge in a flirtation so light, so expert, that Miss Sophie de Quincey would never realize she'd been trifled with by a master.

It was the most he could ask for, the most he could hope for, in a doomed relationship. He intended to enjoy every moment of it.

Hampton Regis was a small seaside town, neither too smart nor too shabby, with the Fowl and Feathers its only hostelry. It possessed several small shops, a confectionery, and a lending library, and it was to that establishment that Valerian Romney made his first stop. He'd learned more about the ways of women from the French romances he'd been reading than he'd learned in a lifetime of observing the feminine half of the species, and he considered himself an apt pupil, always eager to learn more. Besides, the delicately phrased love scenes were as close as he was coming nowadays to physical satisfaction. At least he and Sophie were reading the same passages, even if they weren't able to enact them.

For once his luck was with him. Miss de Quincey was on the premises; he could hear her voice from one of the back rooms, raised in warm laughter. He loved her laugh. It sent shivers of desire through his body, torment that he gladly welcomed. At least it reminded him that he was still a man.

He strolled through the library in search of that voice, pausing on his way to respond to the various greetings, flirting archly with old General Montague, allowing Sir Hillary Beckwith to kiss his large, gloved hand. He plastered a suitably languid expression on his face as he stepped into the back room, and it took all his self-control not to let his expression deteriorate into a furious scowl.

Miss Sophie de Quincey was not alone. Beside her, holding her hand, for God's sake, was an absolute Adonis. Not a worthless exquisite like Sir Neville; this was the enemy. A true rival, Valerian decided miserably, from the man's pomaded hair, dressed in the windswept style, to his perfectly tied neckcloth, to his buckskin breeches that molded sturdy legs to his coat that looked like it had come from his father's tailor, the great Weston himself. The man inside those faultless clothes was a paragon, with perfect teeth, a chiseled profile, massive shoulders, and a flat stomach. Valerian paused inside the door, holding his long skirts in one strong hand, and glared.

The man, who'd doubtless been pouring compliments into Sophie's willing ear, looked up first, and his admiring glance was all the more infuriating to Valerian's trampled sensibilities. And then Sophie turned, and her bright blue eyes lit up with such joy that his bad temper vanished, and he crossed the room with a decidedly unfeminine stride to meet her outstretched hands.

She didn't stop there. Miss Sophie de Quincey flung herself into his arms, holding him tightly, and her breathless little gulp was as much tears as laughter. "I've missed you so much!" she whispered in a shaky voice.

He couldn't resist. He stroked the line of her back, careful not to let his errant hand linger past her waist, all the while making soothing, appropriate noises. When she finally released him, her eyes were damp and shining. "Are you all right?" she asked, searching his face. "When you weren't seen in town, I was so worried…"

"A minor indisposition," he said with an airy wave he'd perfected from Juliette's instructions. He had every faith that he did it better than she did. "I'm quite well now."

"Oh, no!" Sophie breathed. "Don't tell me. You didn't… That is… You… I mean…"

He was quite mystified as to what she was struggling to say, and her preening beau didn't help matters. At least the overbuilt wretch had the sense to realize it. "I gather I'm *de trop*," he said. "I'll take myself off now, and look forward to a formal introduction at a later date. Your servant, Miss de Quincey." With a polite bow and one last, lingering, disgustingly soulful glance at Sophie, he left them.

"Who was that popinjay?" Valerian demanded irritably.

Sophie managed a throaty laugh. "Oh, you shouldn't call him that. Captain Melbourne is quite the most-sought-after gentleman in town. I'm very honored to be the subject of his attentions. Or so my friends inform me."

"Fustian," Valerian said, stifling his urge to come up with a term a great deal stronger and not at all ladylike. "He seems very conceited."

"He is. But then, if you were vastly wealthy, wellborn, and a hero besides, you'd probably be conceited as well."

"Since I'm none of those things, I'll remain blessedly humble."

Sophie laughed, and once more he felt that tremor of desire shake his bones. And then her face fell. "But you still haven't told me! Perhaps I shouldn't ask, but I felt... That is, there seemed to be a certain closeness, a certain lack of constraint between us that..."

"You may tell me anything, ask me anything," Valerian said, taking her slender hand in his, hoping she wouldn't notice the disparity as much as he did.

"Did you lose the baby?"

"What?" He couldn't disguise his confusion.

"I knew I shouldn't have said anything!" Sophie said miserably. "But your husband mentioned it to Mowbray, and you know how things get around. I know you didn't admit me to your confidence about the matter, and I understood your delicacy, but when there was no sign of you for days on end, I was so worried..."

"I'm not pregnant," Valerian said flatly, inwardly seething.

"Oh, I'm so sorry," Sophie said, once more flinging her arms around him.

It was torture. It was heaven. Her breasts pressed against his chest, her silky blond hair tickled his nose, she smelled of lavender and lilacs and silk, and he thought if he didn't kiss her he would surely die.

But she was crying. He could feel her hot tears against his neck, feeling her slender body tremble, and he felt more evil than if he'd been the villain who'd plunged the knife into his father's heart.

It took all his stoicism to clasp her arms and gently pull

her away. "There's no need for tears, Sophie," he said in a gruff voice.

"But the baby!" she whispered. "You lost the baby."

Damn his brother's soul to an early and painful hell, Valerian thought savagely. "Let me assure you, dear Sophie, that I was never pregnant. It was all a mistake. Alas," he added for good measure in a suitably sober voice, "it turns out that I'll never be able to bear children."

She looked ready to start sobbing anew, and in desperation Valerian cast around for something to distract her. While the thought of his Sophie weeping over his future was a delight, the cause of that weeping was less than enthralling. "Let's talk about more cheerful things," he said determinedly, tucking his arm through hers. "Tell me about your suitor. Are you going to marry him?" *And am I going to have to kill him?* he thought to himself.

"He wants me to."

Valerian swallowed his growl. "He's offered?"

"Oh, not officially. But he's dropped several hints, just so that I might be prepared for the honor. And my mother had a talk with me." She wrinkled her nose.

"Did she? What did she say?"

"Oh, she explained my duty, and told me I might as well marry Captain Melbourne as anyone else. At least he was pleasant to look at and wouldn't make too many demands."

"You don't want a demanding husband?" Val asked innocently.

"Does any woman? Marriage is a social institution after all, not at all like the books and plays. One marries for security and position."

"And children," he added.

"Oh, Valerie!" she said, ready to dissolve once more.

"Calm yourself, my dear." He patted her hand. "Nevertheless, with the right sort of man, there might be more to marriage than convenience and security."

"What?" she asked, looking up at him.

"Passion?" he suggested.

She considered the notion. "For the man, perhaps. But women don't feel passion. Love, perhaps, in certain lucky circumstances. But not passion."

"You know this from your great experience?" Valerian said gently.

She stopped in the door, staring up at him uncertainly. There was no one within earshot, a lucky thing. "You promised me you would tell me about what really went on between men and women," she said. "Do you mean to keep that promise?"

Valerian closed his eyes for a moment. It had been a rash suggestion, one prompted by his own inner devil and his desire to at least make verbal love to her. If he kept that promise, he'd be the one to pay the price. "Don't you think you should leave that for Captain Melbourne?" he suggested. I'll cut off his balls first, he thought.

Sophie wrinkled her pretty little nose in distaste. "I don't think so. Somehow the idea of procreating with the captain is very…ridiculous. I can't imagine him taking off his perfect Hessians."

"He probably wouldn't," Valerian muttered.

Sophie looked at him in shock. "He wouldn't? But how… But why…?"

"Come with me, my love," Valerian said soothingly, "and I'll tell you all about it."

A combination of fascination and trepidation showed in her wide blue eyes. "Is it as horrid as Mother said?"

He had a momentary longing to throttle Sophie's stern mother as well. "It depends on whether you end up with Captain Melbourne," he said, "or with someone you can't resist."

Sophie giggled. "A man I can't resist? I can't imagine such a thing."

He smoothed his hand over hers, keeping his touch light. "You'd be surprised, dear child. You'd be surprised."

It was a beautiful day. The sun sparkled on the water in the harbor, the sky was a perfect blue, and Sophie de Quincey was by his side as they left the library and ambled down to the shore. A man couldn't ask for much more, Valerian thought. Unless it was to be wearing breeches instead of a bloody day dress!

Sophie was looking out over the sea with a dreamy look in her eye. "Someday," she said, "I'd like to run away from everything. Just get on a ship and sail away, with no one to stop me, no one to ask me questions, no one to lecture me about my duty to society."

"Odd," he said in a deliberately light voice, "I never would have thought you'd be the type with wanderlust."

"Actually, I'm not," she said. "I love the sea, but I'd just as soon see it from the window of a house on solid ground, rather than from a ship. I'm just feeling restless." She gave him an impish smile. "Better now that you're back, though."

"Perhaps you should marry Captain Melbourne after all," he said. "How old are you? Seventeen? Eighteen? There's a reason why women marry so young."

"Because they get restless?" Sophie supplied. "Is that why you married?"

"Let's not talk about me," Val said, sick of spinning lies.

"Let's plan your future instead. Much more exciting. Mine is already set in stone."

"In stone? I wouldn't have thought Mr. Ramsey would be quite so stubborn."

"He is, dear friend, he is," Val said grimly. "So we have Captain Melbourne applying for your hand. He's very handsome, of course, though perhaps a trifle large."

"Not as large as your husband," Sophie pointed out.

"But you're not as large as I am," Val returned. "Other than that, your Captain Melbourne seems a pleasant enough fellow."

"He's not my Captain Melbourne. Not yet, at least," she added truthfully. "He has other advantages. He lives in the Lake District. Far, far away from my parents."

"Always a point in a future husband's favor," Val agreed politely. "Does he hunt?"

"Excessively."

"Oh, dear."

"And he's very fond of his dogs."

"Is that a point for him or against him?" Val inquired.

"I'm not quite sure. He tells me he's a simple man, and I believe that's what I want. I want to live in the country, and have a dozen babies, and put up jellies and jams and count my linens and tend my flowers."

"Sounds idyllic. And Captain Melbourne would give you all those things, and then be so busy hunting he wouldn't bother you," he said, cursing himself for his honesty.

"Yes," she said in a gloomy voice. "But when I conjure up that rosy picture, I simply can't see Captain Melbourne beside me."

"Well, perhaps he'd be amenable to breaking his neck once he got around to fathering those dozen children."

Sophie giggled. "Life is seldom so opportune."

"I suppose not," Val said with a sigh.

"But if it was, perhaps your husband could continue without you on his travels, and you could come and stay with me. The Lake District is quite beautiful, you know."

"I know," Val said mournfully. "But I don't think you can count on life taking such a convenient turn, dear girl. I expect I'll be following Mr. Ramsey into the wilds. And I expect your husband will live to a ripe old age, and probably wear you out with your bearing all those children."

"Nonsense," she said. "I'm young and strong and healthy. I don't intend to become some frail female who gives up the ghost the moment she starts increasing. I have every intention of living to be ancient."

He looked at her fresh young face, her glowing eyes and soft, crushable mouth, and he smiled, feeling ancient himself. "I believe you can do just about anything you choose to do."

"So tell me, dear Valerie," Sophie said with a winning smile, seating herself on a large rock with a careless disregard for her pale muslin dress, "if Captain Melbourne won't do, whom should I marry?"

He glanced at her. He didn't have as many dresses to spare—having gowns tailored to his almost six-foot-tall frame was a difficult matter, and Phelan would likely complain loud and long if he destroyed his current toilette.

The hell with Phelan. He seated himself beside Sophie on the large rock. They were down at the edge of the strand, and all the bustle in town was conveniently distant. People might watch them, but no one would hear what he said to her. He could be as indecent as he dared. And he was in a wild, daring mood.

"I didn't say you shouldn't marry Captain Melbourne," he said with great reasonableness.

"You think I should wait for someone with passion."

"Did I say that?"

"Not in so many words. But I honor myself with thinking that I know you fairly well, even in such a short time, and you think it would be sadly tame of me to take such a poor way out. You probably think a bucolic life such as I described to be utter torment."

"Not at all," he said. "There are times when I'd love nothing more than a quiet farm by a lake, with sheep and cattle and the affairs of nature, not the affairs of man, keeping me busy. Though I tend to prefer Yorkshire to the Lake District."

"I love Yorkshire as well," Sophie exclaimed. "I knew we were well suited."

"Unfortunately, I'm already married," he said wryly.

She laughed, that glorious, warm laugh that was such torment to him. "True," she said. "And you are unequipped to give me children." She blushed slightly at her shocking statement.

At that moment he didn't know which was stronger, his pride or his passion. He wanted to throw caution and sanity to the winds, drag her off someplace private, and show her just how well equipped he was, at that very moment, to give her things she hadn't even dreamed about.

Self-preservation didn't stop him. It was the smiling trust in her blue eyes. No matter how much he wanted her, how much he hated this masquerade, he couldn't make her pay the price. And it might be the same price his mother had paid, twenty-five years ago. He wouldn't do that to the innocent young woman he'd been fool enough to fall in love with.

He had to settle for the dubious satisfaction of grinding his teeth. "I must warn you, dear Sophie, that if you choose the way of passion, life can sometimes be extremely uncomfortable. Perhaps you'd be better off with your captain."

"Perhaps," she murmured doubtfully. "While you were gone I was almost convinced."

He glanced at her. "And now?"

"And now I'm not so certain. Tell me, do you feel passion for Mr. Ramsey?"

Her words startled him into a laugh. "No," he said shortly.

"Then why should I expect to get anything more?"

"Because you deserve more."

"What exactly do I deserve?"

He wanted to tell her. Even more, he wanted to show her. His gloved hands gripped the rock beneath him, and he felt the thin leather split beneath the force. He managed a calm smile. "You deserve to be happy," he said.

"I intend to be," she said, kicking her legs out in front of her, and beneath the muslin gown he could see her ankles, neat, well turned, and unbearably erotic. If he ever had the chance to make love to her, he'd want to start with her ankles. And then work his way up, slowly, deliberately, until by the time he got to the top of her thighs...

He scrambled down from the rock with more haste than grace, stumbling slightly. "Let's walk," he said in a harsh tone that was slightly deeper than the one he usually affected.

"Are you all right?" she asked, sliding down the rock

after him, so that he had no choice but to put out his hands to catch her, to hold her for a brief, torturous moment.

"Perfectly splendid," he said between clenched teeth. "I just had a sudden longing for the sea."

"We'll walk," she said, "and you can tell me what to do with Captain Melbourne."

"I beg your pardon?" It was getting worse and worse, Val thought miserably.

"You're a woman of the world. You understand far more than most people. If my husband is more interested in his dogs and his hunting than he is in me, what should I do about it?"

"If your husband is more interested in his dogs and hunting than in you, then he's a lost cause," Val said flatly. "And you shouldn't marry him in the first place."

She wasn't to be deterred. "I could wear filmy clothes," she mused. "Or perhaps nothing at all, except the baroque pearls my mother gave me on my come-out. They're really too big for me, but they were my great-grandmother's, and they're awfully pretty. Have you seen them?"

"Yes," he said. He'd seen the damned things, all right. Pearls the size of his thumbnail, a matched set of them clasped around her slender neck. She was right—they were too big for her. They overpowered her muslin gowns and demure neckline. With nothing but her creamy skin, she'd be perfect.

He tripped, cursed, and righted himself. "It sounds as if you've made up your mind," he said in a cool voice.

"I have," she said serenely. "I won't marry him."

Relief flooded him. "Why not? I thought you wanted the Lake District and a tolerant husband."

"I want someone who loves me more than his dogs, and I

don't know if I can compete with a water spaniel," she said with a small smile. "I think I'd best wait for your brother."

"I'll kill him," Val muttered.

"You don't want me to marry your twin either?" she asked, nonplussed.

For a moment Val didn't have the faintest idea what she was talking about. And then it sank in. "Oh, my twin. Valerian? You haven't even met him. The two of you might not hit it off."

"Does he look like you?"

"As much as he possibly could, given that he's a man," Val said with complete truthfulness.

"And is he like you in nature?"

"He lies," Val said flatly.

Sophie's face fell. "Truly?"

"Truly," Val said.

"Then I suppose I shan't marry him either. I cannot abide being lied to. It's the one thing I cannot forgive."

Splendid, Val thought grimly. If he'd had any wild hope of a miracle happy ending, that faint possibility was now completely dashed.

"I think I shall be an eccentric," Sophie said calmly. "If I can't find the right man to marry, then I shan't marry at all."

"What about those half-dozen children?"

"Oh, I'll have them anyway," she said with a mischievous smile. "All by different fathers. My mother told me women are slaves to men and there was no reason for it. I can simply be an original."

"Not as original as you might think," Val said. "I thought your mother wanted you to marry Captain Melbourne."

"I think she felt I could handle him. That he wouldn't interfere with my pleasures."

"She's right in that. Most women seek a husband who doesn't interfere with their whims. It always seemed a cold kind of future to me."

"But I thought you and Mr. Ramsey lived separate lives," Sophie said, her pretty brow wrinkled in confusion.

"We do. More's the pity," he said mendaciously. "I think you should hold out for the kind of true love you read about in novels. Where your heart pounds, your pulse races, your stomach churns, and you tremble and shake."

"It sounds like the influenza to me," Sophie said in a caustic tone. "Most unpleasant."

"But worth it, my child. Definitely worth it," he said with a sigh.

"Have you ever been in love, Val? And don't fob me off with some story about Mr. Ramsey, because I won't believe you. If ever there was a marriage of convenience, that one is it. Have you ever really loved someone?"

"Yes," he said, looking at her.

"And it ended badly?" Her voice was soft with sympathy.

"Yes. It was bound to. I knew it was hopeless from the start."

"Why? Love shouldn't be hopeless!" she said with the passion of her eighteen years.

"He was a bastard. Ill-born, running away from a crime, without a penny, without a scrap of a future," he said, watching her carefully to gauge her response.

"Did he ask you to go with him?"

"No, he wouldn't. He had that much honor left to him. He didn't ask. And I didn't offer."

"Then you mustn't have really loved him," she said in sturdy tones.

"You know nothing of the matter," he said stiffly.

She took his big hands in her small ones, clinging tightly, and her expression was very fierce. "You mustn't have really loved each other," she said again, "because if you had, you would have seen it through. Love can conquer anything. I truly believe it."

He looked down at her, at the soft, determined mouth, bright blue eyes, and cloud of golden-blond hair. "I only wish I could," he said. "I only wish you could convince me."

But he was older and wiser. And he knew there was no happy ending for them. No happy ending at all.

# CHAPTER TEN

Sutter's Head was still and silent as Juliette crept from the building. It was just before dawn, that cool, still time of morning, and the birds were singing their hearts out after their night of silence. The tide was coming in; Juliette could hear the rush of it along the sand, and the early morning mist caught in her hair, turning it into a mass of unruly curls.

She was running away. She'd had a stay of execution the day before, though she wasn't quite certain why. She only knew her reprieve wouldn't last long, and the sooner she escaped, the safer she'd be.

Phelan Romney hadn't come near her once she had run from him. The name Mark-David Lemur had been enough to terrorize her, and he hadn't bothered to pursue her, obviously thinking he'd cowed her.

Just the opposite. She'd always known she'd have to escape. The fact that he had learned the truth about her only made the escape more imperative. For all she knew, he'd take her back to her husband, probably pocketing a handsome reward.

No, he'd already claimed his reward. The diamond-

and-pearl earbobs must have led him to her husband. And doubtless Romney would now lead her husband straight to her.

She'd rather die. She'd rather walk straight into the sea and have done with it than return to that man. And she would, if she were left with no other choice.

Everyone at Sutter's Head was still sleeping. Valerian had returned late that night, a dark expression on his usually sunny face, and he'd disappeared into his room, taking a bottle of wine with him, and hadn't been seen again, according to Dulcie.

Phelan had dined in a solitary state, with Hannigan in attendance. Juliette had eaten in the kitchen, content to keep Dulcie company and listen to her prattle. All the while her mind was feverish with worry. When the night grew late and Romney still hadn't demanded her presence, still hadn't come for her, she told herself she should be relieved. Instead, her panic increased.

She hadn't planned to sleep. She hadn't dared, knowing that Phelan Romney had entered her room once before, knowing that locked doors and barred windows wouldn't keep him out. She didn't even make the attempt. It was a warm night, and without the fresh sea air filling the room, she felt stifled, strangled. She lay in her bed in the darkness, waiting for sleep, waiting for the early morning light so she would make her escape, waiting for the confrontation she dreaded. Not certain which she wanted to come first.

Sleep came first, claiming her weary body despite her misgivings. And then came the dreams.

The room was candlelit, haunted with shadows. Lemur usually came to her in darkness, wanting the night to cover his perverse deeds, but tonight was different. She was in bed, watching him, knowing there was no escape. When she tried to run, he hurt her, even more badly, and she knew her best chance lay in being perfectly still and compliant.

She watched him as he crossed the room. He'd always insisted she keep her eyes open so that he could see her hatred.

He was a handsome man. In his prime, without an ounce of extra fat around his middle. His brown hair was unstreaked with gray; his features were even, pleasant; his manner was kindly. He was a monster. She knew what he was going to make her do, and she choked at the thought, shielding the hatred from her eyes. She knew, to her sorrow, that her hatred excited him.

"Turn over," he said in his soft, hushed voice.

She had no choice. He would try, and he would fail again. And then he would hurt her. It had happened so many times, she'd lost count.

She lay on her stomach in the bed, clenching her fists, burying her face in the pillow to keep from crying out, waiting for the touch of his small, cruel hands.

The first feather-light caress was a revelation. Fingers skimmed across her back, gently, shaping her body beneath the thin lawn nightdress. She braced herself, waiting for the assault, waiting for him to rip her clothes from her, climb on top, and try to thrust himself into her unwilling body.

But nothing happened. Just his hands caressing her, patiently, slowly, almost delicately, moving up the center of her back, lifting her hair.

And then his mouth touched the nape of her neck, and a shiver of reaction ran through her entire body, one he must have felt. He'd never kissed her before. The cool, damp touch of his mouth against her vulnerable neck was another revelation, one she hated. She didn't want to learn to like what he did to her. She didn't want pleasure with the pain.

She was having no choice in the matter. There was no pain this night, no degradation. Even as she lay in the bed, her face thrust into the pillow, she couldn't fight her reaction to the deftness of his hands as they slid beneath the nightdress, touching her skin. Even his hands felt different, larger, stronger, callused whereas they'd always been soft and almost feminine. She braced herself, waiting for him to climb on top of her, to hurt her, but he made no move to do so. He simply kept touching her, caressing her. Arousing her.

And then the pressure of his hands was undeniable. He tugged at her shoulders, and she turned, keeping her eyes tightly shut, unwilling to see the triumph in his small, pale eyes.

The touch of his lips against her eyelids was a benediction. He kissed each one, and her eyelashes fluttered against his mouth, helplessly. He kissed her temples, her cheekbones, her ear. And then, for the very first time, he kissed her mouth.

First just a gentle brush of his lips against her tightly compressed ones, a soft wooing that coaxed her into relaxing. Then came the first touch of his tongue, something she knew she should resist. Something she couldn't resist.

She opened her mouth beneath the gentle, insistent pressure and let him kiss her, let his tongue touch hers as his hands pushed her hair back from her face, smoothing it.

He'd never kissed her before, yet she knew his mouth, his taste. In the candlelit darkness she opened her eyes, and the man leaning over her had dark hair, and silver eyes, and a wicked smile. "You knew it was me," he whispered.

And she couldn't deny it. Any more than she could deny her response to him. She lifted her arms, sliding them around his neck, and pulled him back down to her, on top of her, his large, strong body covering hers more completely than Mark-David's ever could.

He lay in the cradle of her thighs, against the bunched-up nightdress. She shifted beneath him, restless, yearning for something, and when he touched her she cried out as a small, hot convulsion shook her.

The sound of her own voice woke her, shockingly. She was alone in the darkness, lying on her bed, covered with a light film of sweat. There was no one at the window; the door was still locked. It had been a dream. A wicked, treacherous dream.

She'd dressed swiftly, her hands still shaking with remembered response. In the end, even her own dreams had betrayed her. She needed to run, far and fast.

She had few regrets, she told herself as she stole down the pathway to the sea, her new clothes wrapped in a kerchief. She was sorry she wouldn't have a chance to say good-bye to Dulcie and Hannigan. Dulcie had been one more in the line of women who wanted to mother her, wanted to feed her, and she'd appreciated every one of them. And there was something about Hannigan she trusted. She understood his priorities—the Romneys and their secrets came first. But her instincts told her that he'd have a care for her as well, and she longed to be able to let someone else watch over her.

She wouldn't have a chance to see Valerian either. He made her laugh. He was the brother she'd never had, and the sister as well, she thought with a wry smile. She would never know what had made him embark on his masquerade, so much more difficult than her own. She could only hope he had more success than she had.

She wouldn't miss Phelan. Not for a minute. Never did she want to feel his silver eyes drifting over her, watching her, measuring her, seeing past her defenses to the part she kept hidden from everyone. Never did she want to feel the touch of his hands on her body. The touch of his mouth against hers.

It had only been a cruel twist of fate that she'd dreamed it. Or perhaps not so cruel after all. Perhaps, long years in the future, there might be a man whose touch wouldn't sicken her. Who might give her babies and tenderness, unlikely as that possibility seemed.

She intended to follow the shoreline away from Hampton Regis, heading west toward Plymouth. She could get lost in the bustle of a larger city, hide until she decided how she could best make her escape. She no longer had her earbobs as security, and she hadn't dared search the house for anything of value. Phelan Romney knew her far too well to leave anything around that would aid her escape.

There was a thick mist just rising off the sea, and she paused for a moment, planning to strip off her shoes and walk barefoot through the surf, when she realized she wasn't alone on the beach.

She held herself still, motionless, peering into the gathering light. She saw the pile of clothes on a rock near the incoming tide. And then she saw the man in the sea.

She'd never had any doubt as to who it would be. One man at Sutter's Head loved the sea, one man would wake up at dawn and swim in it. Phelan Romney.

She should turn and creep back the way she had come, before he saw her standing on the deserted shore. She should run, fast and furious, away from him, away from Hampton Regis and Sutter's Head and temptation that she couldn't even begin to understand. Instead, she stood there, motionless, staring out at him.

He was incredibly graceful, diving through the white-foamed surf like a seal, sleek and powerful and elegant, at home in the sea as no human should be. Juliette found herself remembering the tales told by her old Scottish nanny, about magical creatures that were half of the sea, half of the land. Mermaids and Mermen, silkies and the like. On this mist-shrouded morning she could almost believe in such fairy tales.

And then she realized with utter horror that he was emerging from the sea. Walking straight out, coming toward her, seemingly unaware of her presence. For a moment she couldn't move, staring at him in unabashed wonder.

He was wearing absolutely nothing at all. He was very different from her husband, very different from the children she'd seen playing naked in the native bazaars. He was beautiful, there was no other word for it, and she never thought she'd find a man's body to be so. She stared, shocked and disturbed, until she realized she had no time to escape. All she could do was hide.

There was an outcropping of rocks and trees nearby. She dove behind them, curling up into a ball, holding her breath, praying to a heretofore-unsympathetic God that he hadn't seen her.

She waited. The sound of the surf covered any other noise he might have made, and she could only hope he'd gone back to the house, leaving her time to escape. When the suspense became unbearable, she uncurled herself and lifted her head. Only to stare straight into Phelan Romney's mesmerizing silver-gray eyes.

He'd put on his breeches, a small comfort, but his chest was bare and glistening with seawater, and his black hair sparkled in the early morning sunlight. He squatted down beside her, and it should have made him less threatening. Instead, she felt more vulnerable than ever.

"Running away, fair Juliette?" he asked in a deceptively lazy voice.

She wasn't fooled. She also wasn't prepared to lie, knowing full well it wouldn't do her any good. If she ran now, he would catch her. She could only hope to reason with him. "It seemed the wisest course," she said. "You know too much about me. I imagine you've already sent word to Lemur…"

"Now why should you imagine any such thing?"

"You stole my earrings. You traced me to Lemur. You must know there's a reward for information about me."

He shrugged, the gesture drawing her attention to his shoulders. They were very nice shoulders, broad, well muscled without being overdeveloped. She wondered what his skin would feel like. Soft, like Mark-David's? Or hard?

"There are a great many things of more interest than money," he said.

"I wouldn't be providing them."

"Don't flatter yourself, my girl. I'm not palpitating with uncontrollable lust for you."

She flushed. "All right," she said. "You don't want my body, and you don't want the money you could get by turning me over to Lemur. What do you want from me?"

He sat back on his heels, considering the question. She tried to keep her attention on his face, but his eyes were too disturbing. More disturbing than his body, even. She tried to stare at the sand around them, but she kept getting distracted.

He had a very flat stomach, lean and muscled. And he had hair on his body; she'd glimpsed it before. Dark hair swirled across his chest, trailing down his stomach. It was probably course and scratchy to the touch, she told herself. There was an old scar across his chest, white against the tan. A jagged one that must have come from a knife. She jerked her gaze away.

"What do I want from you?" he mused. "I'm not quite sure. Distraction, perhaps. Your secrets. Even your bad temper."

"I thought you knew my secrets," she said.

"How naive of you. Don't assume anything. I know Mark-David Lemur is looking for you, and I know you're his wife. Beyond that, it's a mystery. And I've been bored recently."

"I would have thought your own mystery would be entertaining enough."

"The little cat still has claws, does she? One's own mysteries are uninteresting if one fails to discover the answers. Whereas you're a relatively simple matter. All I have to do is touch you, and you panic, and tell my anything I want to know." His hand reached out and brushed the hair from her face, and she leapt back, startled.

"You said you didn't want my body," she reminded him, fighting the panic.

His cool smile failed to reassure her. "I never said any such thing. I said I wasn't burdened by uncontrollable lust for you. I'm a man with a very great deal of self-control. Something you would have noticed if you were a little wiser in the ways of the world."

"I'm experienced enough," she said sharply.

No expression of sympathy marked his face. "I imagine you consider yourself to be. Marriage to a man like Lemur can't have been a pleasant experience."

"Why do you say that?"

"Why else would you have run off?" he countered.

"Perhaps he cheated on me. Set up a mistress? Ignored me?" she suggested.

"In that case, you wouldn't be running away, obviously terrified by the touch of a man. You would have simply taken a lover yourself, to pay him back."

"Is that what people do in English society?" she asked.

"It tends to simplify matters."

"I don't like it here," she said flatly, no longer guarding her tongue. Indeed, there didn't seem to be any point to it. Phelan Romney saw through her lies. "It's a country full of trickery and deceit."

"It's *your* country."

"Not anymore," she said firmly. "I'm not sure where I belong, but it's not here."

He stared at her for a long, contemplative moment, and she wished she had even a tiny portion of his success at reading minds. "I imagine you'll find your answers," he said. "If you stop running away."

She didn't move. Her desire to run was stronger than ever, her desire to stay even more overwhelming. She'd told herself she was running from the reappearance of Mark-David Lemur. Told herself she was running back to Egypt, to the exotic lands where she'd felt at home.

But in truth, what had concerned her most was to run from this man who was kneeling too close to her. The man who was watching her with such an intent expression.

"Let me go," she said suddenly, not bothering to disguise the plea in her voice. "Give me back my earrings and let me leave. You'll never see me again, I promise. Sooner or later Mark-David would find me here, and you wouldn't like that. He can be an extremely unpleasant man to cross."

"So can I."

"Please," she begged.

"It would be the wisest thing to do," he said in a contemplative voice. "After all, our own situation is complicated enough. It was quixotic in the extreme for me to bring you back, rescue you from Pinworth, but then, as I said, I was bored. If I had any sense at all, I'd do as you ask. Even advance you a bit of money to ensure you made a safe getaway from this island you hate so much."

She could feel the treacherous hope rising within her heart. "Would you?" she asked in a hushed voice.

He put out his hands, cupping her face, threading his long fingers through her hair, and his eyes were gleaming. "I should," he murmured. "Convince me."

His mouth was cold and wet against hers, and tasted of the sea. She couldn't withdraw—his hands were holding her face still—and she couldn't, wouldn't, struggle. She knelt in the sand, her fists clenched in her lap, and let him kiss her. She told herself she could withstand anything, if only he let her leave.

She was wrong. She could withstand brute force, she could withstand arrogance. She could not withstand the coaxing gentleness of his lips as they nudged hers apart, or the faintly shocking intrusion of his tongue in her mouth.

Mark-David had never kissed her like that. Mark-David had never kissed her at all, except for dutiful social pecks on the cheek when they had witnesses. And suddenly she wanted to be kissed, wanted to know what it was like. She wanted to kiss Phelan back.

Her tongue touched his, shyly. He groaned deep in his throat, and moved his body up against hers. His skin was cool in the morning air, still faintly damp from his swim, and the hair that swirled across his chest was soft, springy beneath Juliette's long fingers as she slid her hands up against him, telling herself it was to push him away, knowing she couldn't even fool herself.

He moved his head, and she expected him to pull back, but instead, he simply angled his head and kissed her again, his tongue thrusting gently, rhythmically, into her mouth, his hips pressed up against hers, his cool flesh turning warm beneath her clenching fingers. There was a soft, moaning sound, one of fear and incipient surrender, and she knew that sound came from her. And the thought terrified her.

She went rigid in panic, jerking herself out of his embrace before he could tighten it, scrambling back against the rock outcropping and staring at him. It was hard to breathe. He'd stolen her mind, her heart, the very breath from her body. She hunched back away from him and shivered.

He didn't move after her. He simply knelt there in the sand, the breath coming deeply in his own chest as he watched her. She didn't want to look at his chest, so her eyes cropped lower, to the hard ridge of flesh beneath the tight black breeches, and her panic increased.

"Change your mind, fair Juliette?" he murmured, not

bothering to disguise the tension in his voice. "I thought you were well on your way to bargaining for your release."

She met his ironic gaze. "What do you mean?"

His smile was mocking, unpleasant. "Simply that you strip off your boys' clothes and earn your freedom, and an extra twenty bob besides. After all, it's nothing that you haven't given Lemur a dozen times over."

She slapped him. Hard. Her hand crossed his face in a blow that shocked both of them with its force and unexpectedness. She stared at him, white with fear, waiting for him to use that tightly leashed strength to hit her back.

He didn't. "It's always possible," he said in a casual voice, "that I deserved that. I would suggest, however, that you don't try it again. My temper can be very uncertain."

Juliette couldn't move. Never in her life had she hit another creature in anger. She'd seen too much of the world's cruelties to take out her frustrations on others, but no one had ever aroused her fury as fully as this man. Her hand still hurt from the force of the blow.

"We'll go back to the house now," he said, rising to his feet, towering over her.

She glared up at him. "You never were going to let me go, were you?" she asked.

"No," he said. "Not yet, at least. I was merely interested in seeing what you were willing to barter for your freedom."

"Would you have given it to me?"

"I can think of a great many things I would have been willing to give you," he said, "but your freedom wasn't among them. Stand up, Juliette. Unless you want me to carry you. I doubt you'd like that idea. I'm quite strong, but even such a light burden as you might prove to be too exhausting, and if we stopped to rest on the way back to the house…"

Juliette surged to her feet. "You're worse than Lemur," she snapped.

He was unmoved by the insult. "Am I? Since you have yet to inform me of the depths of his perfidy, I don't know whether I'm insulted or not. Come along," he said, starting up the winding path to the house.

She stared at his back, the graceful strength of him, and wished with all her might for a sharp knife to plunge into the tanned, strong flesh. She wondered if there was a chance in hell she could outrun him along the sand.

Not likely. She was a bit younger than he was, but his legs were longer, and he was barefoot, while she was encumbered by her ill-fitting shoes. He'd catch her, push her down on the sand, and her nightmare from the previous night would come true. If, indeed, she could truthfully call it a nightmare.

She tried one last appeal to his reason. "It would be far more prudent of you to send me away. Lemur will find me sooner or later, and he's a dangerous man to cross."

He turned to look at her. "I was never known for my prudence. I protect my own. As long as you're here, I won't allow him to hurt you."

"I am not yours," she said fiercely.

"Not yet, perhaps. But you will be."

"And if I refuse? Will you turn me over to him…?"

"Mark-David Lemur won't touch you again," he said flatly. "You have my word on it."

"And what makes you think I'd trust your word?"

He shrugged, unmoved by the blatant insult. "Your instincts, fair Juliette. I think they're very well developed and, given a choice between your husband and me, you're wise enough to pick the man who's at least not a proven villain. You're right about one thing. He'll show up here, sooner or later. If not here, then wherever you run to. He'll catch up with you. You're a great deal better off with Valerian and me to protect you." He held up a hand to forestall her protest. "And don't tell me you can take care of yourself. I've seen your best, and it's not good enough. All you can do is run, and eventually he'll catch you."

She stared at him. He was right; she knew it, deep in her heart of hearts. Nothing could be worse than the things Lemur had done to her, had tried to do to her. If she had to submit to the same sort of things with Phelan Romney, she'd survive, wouldn't she? He could hardly be more brutal. At least she found a certain devastating wonder in his kisses.

Which might make it all the more wretched. Her feelings for Lemur were simple, uncomplicated. She despised him, and wished him dead.

With Romney, fear and longing were all twisted together. And he had the capacity for destroying much more than her body. He could destroy her soul.

"Are you offering me a choice?" she asked, her head held high.

"No. I'm giving you a chance to salvage your pride, to pretend it's your decision. In reality, it's not your decision at all."

Her mouth curved wryly. "At least you're honest," she said.

"In some matters."

"I'll come with you," she said, "on one condition."

"And that is?"

"That you don't touch me again. You don't kiss me, you don't put your hands on me. Is that agreed?"

He crossed the stretch of sand, took her shoulders in his hands, and hauled her up against him. He kissed her hard, a brief, thorough, devastatingly sexual kiss that lasted just until she began to respond. And then he released her.

"Agreed," he said. And he started up the pathway, this time not bothering to see whether she followed.

She rubbed her hand across her mouth, trying to wipe the taste of him away. She took one last, lingering glance at the endless stretch of sand leading to Plymouth, leading to freedom. And then she started after Phelan.

# CHAPTER ELEVEN

Yesterday had been pure hell. It had been torture, of the most extreme variety, and he had deserved every exquisite moment of it, Valerian told himself. Phelan had warned him. Hannigan had warned him. If he'd listened, he would have warned himself. He should have stayed away from Miss Sophie de Quincey. Failing that, he never, ever should have brought up the subject of lovemaking. Particularly when she was such a bright, such a curious young lady.

They'd made their way up the rock-strewn beach to the edge of the de Quincey property, Valerian wondering how he was going to change the very dangerous subject he'd introduced, Sophie strolling beside him, lithe and graceful, her hand in his.

"So explain it to me, dear Valerie," she had said when they'd reached the tiny seaside gazebo at the edge of her mother's garden, continuing their discussion.

He'd allowed her to draw him inside. In the distance he could see the formidable Mrs. de Quincey herself, observing them with guarded approval. The dashing Mrs. Ramsey was a bit fast for a sweet young girl like Sophie, but at least she was harmless. It wasn't as if she were a rapacious young male.

Val threw himself down on the padded seat, stretching his legs out in front of him, forgetting that his overlarge feet were prominently displayed. Sophie, ever tactful, said nothing, simply sitting too damned close to him, practically curled up beside him, tucking her arm through his.

"Tell you what?" The side of his arm was held next to the sweet young swell of her breast, and the tiny gazebo was filled with the scent of Sophie's perfume.

"About it. About men and women, and what they do together, and why it should be worthy of all the fuss."

"I thought your mother explained it to you."

Sophie wrinkled her nose. "She did. In very technical terms. I must say it sounds extremely undignified, and quite messy."

He glanced down at her, stifling a groan. "It is," he said. "If the man who's making love to you is thinking about his dignity, then he isn't thinking about you. And that's no fun for either of you."

"Fun?" She seemed shocked at the very notion. "It's not supposed to be fun."

"Of course it is. Why do you think there are so many babies in the world? Not because people want 'em, Lord love you. Most of those babies are an afterthought. People can't keep their hands off each other, and then it's too late."

"But if people don't want babies, why do they make love?"

"Darling," he drawled, "babies don't come from every lovemaking experience. There are ways to prevent them."

Her eyes widened in shock. "How?" she asked bluntly.

Valerian had kept himself from cursing. "Things men can do," he said evasively.

"You aren't going to tell me?" she demanded. "I wouldn't think you'd be such a poor sport. Maybe I should marry Captain Melbourne and have him tell me."

"If you think that stuffed-up popinjay is going to explain anything to you, you'll be in for a major disappointment. I expect his entire knowledge of lovemaking comes from watching his dogs breed."

"Then you tell me," she said. She released his arm, pulling away from him, and he accepted the respite with relief. Until she turned around and stretched out on the padded bench, putting her head in his lap. Dangerously close to a part of his anatomy that sweet Sophie would have trouble identifying.

Hell and damnation, he thought miserably. "You start," he said, resisting the urge to stroke her golden hair.

She bit her lip, looking adorably serious, as she considered his request. "Well," she said, "I know a man climbs on top of a woman and puts his member inside her. And she lies there until it's over, and afterward she's...damp, and needs to bathe, and use a pad. There'll be pain the first time, and blood, though not as much as your monthly flow. Was it that way with you?"

Valerian remembered the dairyman's plump, friendly daughter, the smell of the hayloft, and the glorious pleasure of his first encounter. She'd been a great deal more experienced than he, and until he met Sophie de Quincey, she was the closest he'd ever come to being in love, despite the fact that she was now happily married with three little ones and a jealous husband, and quite alarmingly stout. "Not exactly," he said.

"My mother says women don't enjoy it much, though they might like the cuddling afterward. Is that what you prefer?" She shifted her head to look at him, and she brushed against his aching body.

He gulped. "The cuddling's nice," he allowed. "Both before and after. But there's more to it than that."

"Is there?"

He gave up then. She wasn't going to be distracted, and he was so damned miserable it couldn't get any worse. "There is," he said, letting his voice become low and beguiling. He took a strand of her golden hair and began playing with it, a surreptitious caress she wouldn't begin to recognize. "For one thing, it's much better if the woman doesn't just lie there. She puts her arms around the man, and her legs around him…"

"Her legs?" Sophie echoed, profoundly shocked.

"And she moves," he said, running the hair between his fingers. He usually wore gloves to disguise the masculine shape of his hands, but he'd ripped his earlier and had discarded them along the way.

Sophie swallowed. "Moves? How?"

"In concert with him."

"*He* moves?" she sounded horrified. "I thought he just lay on top of her until the seed was planted. Rather like a hen laying eggs."

Val grinned, leaning his head back against the wall. "Not exactly. A certain amount of…friction is required for mutual satisfaction. He puts himself inside her. And then he moves back out again."

"Indeed?" Her eyes were wide.

"Indeed. Have you never seen animals mating?"

"Once, a long time ago. But they were doing it differently. One was behind the other, and they were…" Her face turned the most delicious shade of pink.

"It's a different position, one that humans use as well," he said, dropping the lock of hair and soothing it against her head. "But the motions are generally the same."

"And women enjoy it?" she asked.

"Yes, if the man is skilled, and interested in bringing pleasure to his partner as well as to himself. Far too many men are only concerned with their own release."

"Release?"

The thought was murderously sweet. "Release," he said. "Both physical and spiritual. The culmination of lovemaking. The couple keep up the friction, back and forth, in and out, until it builds and bunds into a climax. The French call it *la petite morte*."

"The little death," Sophie said. "It sounds unpleasant."

He grinned. "Far from it. It's quite the most sublime experience in the world. For both of them."

"I find that difficult to believe," she said in a doubtful voice. "Where does the dampness come from? Mother said you only bleed the first time."

If sweet Sophie moved her head just a fraction of an inch, she would find out firsthand. "When the man reaches his climax, he fills the woman with his seed. That's part of it."

"And the rest?"

"Comes from her. When a woman is enjoying herself, she gets hot and damp and moist…" He forced himself to stop, taking a deep, calming breath.

"Fascinating," Sophie breathed. "But messy."

"Undoubtedly messy," Valerian agreed. "When the woman comes…"

"What?" she shrieked, moving her head dangerously close.

He gritted his teeth. "The woman climaxes as well. That is, if the man is expert enough. It's not considered as crucial to the endeavor by some men, but someone who loves you wouldn't think of leaving you unsatisfied. There would be little pleasure for him if he were the only one to climax."

"Really?"

He considered telling her the truth. That most men wouldn't give a damn whether they pleased her; they'd take her luscious young body and use her and leave her, messy and undignified and frustrated, giving her babies and nothing else. He didn't want that to happen to his Sophie. He didn't want anyone but him to touch her, to give her babies, to make her come.

"For a man who loves you," he qualified. "That's why you shouldn't rush into marriage with a man who's more dedicated to his own good looks and his dogs. He's the sort who'll put your pleasure last."

"You don't think Captain Melbourne would make me..." She searched for the word. "Make me climax?"

I can't bloody well stand it, Valerian thought desperately, holding very still. "I think it's unlikely."

She lifted her head off his lap and sat up, a moment before disaster struck. "Then I'm sure I won't marry him," she said serenely. "I don't quite know how I'll explain it to my mother. The truth may not suit." Her mischievous smile nearly undid him.

"If I know your mother, she probably won't have the faintest idea what you're talking about." He disguised his tension in a drawl.

She swung around, tucking her feet beneath her, and delivered the coup de grace. "You know what I wish, Val?"

she said with adorable seriousness. "I wish I could meet a man who was just like you."

After that, she'd been all solicitude as he'd hobbled from the gazebo, attributing his condition to a back problem. He'd accepted Mrs. de Quincey's invitation to dinner, and sat through the interminable meal, being questioned as to his bluestocking proclivities; all the while Sophie added to his torment by kicking him gently under the table, ensuring that his uncomfortable condition never abated entirely. He'd taken his leave at an acceptable hour, suffering the sweet torment of having Sophie fling her arms around his neck and kiss him soundly on what he still profoundly hoped was his smooth-shaven cheek.

"You are my very favorite person in the entire world," she'd whispered in his ear. "Thank you for this afternoon."

He'd thought of the misery he'd endured. "Thank you for what?" he'd countered.

"For your honesty. I value that above all things."

He'd taken the words as a blow to the heart. He'd traveled through town sedately enough, waiting only until he'd turned the corner on the seldom-traveled road to Sutter's Head. And then he'd driven like a madman, trying to race the anger and frustration from him. He'd failed entirely.

When he returned, he finished two bottles of wine, and even that wasn't enough to drive the memory of Sophie's trusting face from his mind. Or the way her delicate hand had rested on his thigh. If she discovered she'd discussed such intimacies with a man, she'd never forgive him. Bloody hell, if she discovered she'd been lied to at all, she'd never forgive him.

The words had been a death knell. She valued honesty above all things, and all he'd ever done was lie to her. Any distant, errant hope he'd had for a miraculous happy ending was now vanished. He might as well join Phelan on his rootless wanderings. Without Sophie, there would be no peace for him at home.

On top of everything, he was pledged to go driving with her the next day. He hadn't been able to resist, any more than he could resist her innocent questions. He had paid the price for it, and tomorrow would be even worse. Just the two of them, driving in his small, open carriage to the ruins of the old Roman fortress. He would have to keep her mind on subjects other than sex. If he didn't, he couldn't be certain that he'd be able to control himself.

The fortress at Kenley was a good twelve miles away. They'd be gone all day, and Sophie's cook would pack them a picnic lunch. It would be heaven, it would be hell, and it would be the last time he allowed himself such a space of unsupervised time alone with her. After tomorrow, he had every intention of keeping his distance. Of ending this damnable stalemate and heading to Paris, and to hell with guilt and cowardice. He couldn't worry about the blot on his name. After all, it had never really been his name in the first place. Not legally.

He only hoped he could carry through with that fine intention. The more distance he put between them, the more likely she was to forgive him if she ever found out the truth. Though the possibility of forgiveness was remote indeed.

There was no sign of Phelan or Juliette the next morning when Valerian awoke with a miserable headache. He bathed in unheated water as penance, and was standing in the middle of the room, wearing petticoats and shaving, when Juliette appeared in the open door to watch him out of critical eyes.

"I didn't know gentlemen shaved themselves," she said.

He truly liked Juliette, with her wry observations and her unselfconscious air. Why couldn't he have fallen in love with someone like her?

Because his surprisingly jealous brother would kill him. He glanced over at Juliette and grinned. "But I'm no gentleman," he said, carefully denuding his chin of stubble.

She laughed. "True enough. I'm not sure what you look like. Maybe some mythical creature, like a centaur."

"I assure you, I'm entirely male."

"I remember," she said, her wry smile at odds with the faint color of embarrassment in her cheeks. It was no wonder Phelan was obsessed with her, Valerian thought.

"What have you been doing this morning?" he asked, working on the other side of his face.

There was no answer, and he glanced at her to see that the color had deepened. So Phelan had moved one step closer. Or perhaps more than that. He wondered where she'd spent the night.

Not in his brother's bed, he decided. If she had, she wouldn't be looking quite so...fresh.

"Out walking," she replied with an airy tone that fooled him for not one moment. Obviously she hadn't been walking alone. Remembering his brother's predilection for early morning swims, he could make an educated guess as to the morning's events. "Good God, what are you doing?" she shrieked.

He grinned at her. "Shaving my chest, dear girl. I have to do it every few days. It would hardly serve for Mrs. Ramsey to have golden hair on her rather nonexistent breasts."

"That's disgusting," she said, shuddering, even as with appalled fascination she watched him apply the razor.

"I tend to agree with you, but I have little choice in the matter. Don't worry—Phelan doesn't shave his chest."

"I know," she said artlessly. And then she blushed deeper still. "I mean, it doesn't matter to me what he does with his body."

"Of course not," Valerian said in a soothing voice, not believing her for a moment. He wiped the rest of the shaving soap from his chest with a resigned sigh. "How strong are you?"

She eyed him warily. "Why do you ask?"

He held up the monstrous whalebone contraption. "I need to reclaim my girlish figure."

"Where did you get that?" Her voice was filled with awe as she stepped into the room "I've never seen one before."

"I believe stout old ladies wear them. Probably stout old men as well." He wrapped it around his torso and presented his back to her. "Just pull the strings as tightly as you can."

"Valerian!" Phelan's voice was as sharp as a cracked whip, and Valerian winced.

He turned and saw his brother glowering at him from the doorway. "I have a bloody headache," he said wearily. "Don't shout at me."

Phelan glowered. "If you have a headache, then it's your fault. You never could hold more than a bottle of wine. Unfortunately, you don't take after our father in that matter."

"Small consolation," Val said gracelessly. Juliette had dropped the strings to the contraption, and her face was now pale with various complicated emotions that Valerian was too weary to interpret.

There was no mistaking Phelan's reaction, however, and

Valerian decided to take pity on her. "If you could procure me some coffee from Dulcie," he said to Juliette, "then I would be your slave for life. Phelan can help me with my toilette."

She escaped without a word, and the moment she was gone Phelan advanced on him with a furious expression. "Phelan will help you with your toilette, all right," he snarled. "Keep your bloody hands off her!"

If his head hadn't ached so much, Valerian would have found the sight of his usually imperturbable older brother amusing. As it was, he simply shook his head. "Look at me, man! Do you think having someone help me dress as a woman is the road to seduction?"

But Phelan wasn't being reasonable. "I don't know what's going on in your mind. I just don't want you touching her."

"I wasn't touching her, damn it. She was tying my bloody corset. Not the most erotic act in the world, I assure you. If you think it is, I'll be glad to lend it to you and you can see if Juliette finds it arousing."

Phelan swung at him. Normally Valerian's reflexes were fine-tuned enough that he would duck, but the aftereffects of too much wine and not enough sleep slowed him just enough. Phelan's fist connected with his face, the force throwing them off-balance, and the two of them tumbled over onto the floor.

"Get off me, you horse!" Valerian said furiously, hampered by his hated skirts.

Phelan scrambled to his feet, holding out his hand to help his brother up. Valerian ignored it. "Damn you," he said. "How the hell am I going to explain this to Sophie?"

"You'll have a bruise, all right," Phelan said in a subdued voice. "She'll just have to think your husband beats you. No doubt you deserve it."

"That's all well and good, but I've been busy extolling the virtues of married life and the pleasures of a good husband." He rose, wandered over to the mirror, and surveyed his reflection with a dubious air.

"Have you really? I can't imagine why. Surely you don't want to encourage her to marry, since she obviously can't marry you."

"Obviously," Valerian growled. He was going to get a bruise, damn it. "And I'm in no hurry for her to marry. I merely want to ensure that when she does, she doesn't settle for less than she deserves."

"Oh, good God, Valerian! What have you been telling her?"

"I've been informing her of the wonders of lovemaking. She was absolutely fascinated."

"I imagine she was. And how very noble of you. It couldn't have been the most comfortable topic of conversation."

"Hardly." And then Valerian laughed at his own inadvertent joke. "If I can't have her, at least I want her to be happy. With the information I gave her, she'll never settle for a stuffed popinjay like Captain Melbourne."

"Who, pray tell, is Captain Melbourne?" Phelan asked, mystified.

"One of her suitors."

There was a long silence. "I'm sorry, Valerian," Phelan said in a somber voice.

"The bruise will fade."

"That's not what I was talking about."

"I know."

Their eyes met for a pregnant moment, and then Valerian shrugged, smiling ruefully. "I'll take what I can get. Which isn't much, more's the pity. We're spending the day together, and then I'm going to absent myself. You'll have your wish, Phelan. I'll run like a whipped cur. I'll go to France with you."

There was silence from his older brother, and Valerian, surprised, stared at him. "I thought you'd be jubilant. You've been trying to get me on a boat ever since we got here. I told you, I'm willing to run."

"Why?"

"Because I've accepted it. Accepted that Sophie isn't for the likes of me. Accepted that the truth about Lord Harry's death won't ever be known. And perhaps that's just as well."

"I'm not certain she did it," Phelan said flatly.

Valerian sat down on the end of the bed and proceeded to don his oversize silk stockings. "It's only natural that you wouldn't want to believe it. You wouldn't want to think your mother murdered your father."

"My mother is unnatural to begin with," Phelan said flatly. "I'd believe her capable of anything. But something about this whole affair simply doesn't feel right. I've learned to rely on my instincts, and my instincts are telling me she didn't do it."

"Then who did?"

"If I had the faintest suspicion, I'd be doing something about it, wouldn't I? I don't know where to start."

"Phelan," Val began, "are you certain we can trust Hannigan? And don't look at me like that! One black eye is enough for a day."

"I've known Hannigan all my life. He's devoted to the family."

"I know he is. I just wondered whether his devotion included an allegiance to the truth. I get the sense he might know more than he's telling us."

"You might have a point," Phelan said slowly. "He's devoted to us, but he also might be a bit too protective." He strode over to the window, looking out at the sea. "Three more days," he said. "They won't make much of a difference. If we can't come up with a single possible suspect by then, we'll decamp for foreign lands and live a life of wondrous adventure."

"I'm not certain I'm all that suited for adventure. I suspect I'm a farmer at heart, just like my mother."

"You would have been good for Romney Hall," Phelan said.

Valerian shrugged. "It's out of our hands. You don't want it and I can't have it."

"I'll tell you what. If we have to become émigrés, we'll kidnap Miss de Quincey and carry her off with us. She strikes me as a romantic young creature—she'll probably love the adventure. You can be married over the anvil once we reach France."

"I doubt it. She might love adventure, but she hates falsehood of any kind," Val said glumly.

"Oh." There wasn't much more Phelan could say.

"Of course, you could always share Juliette with me." Valerian held up his hands in laughing protest. "Don't hit me again, Phelan. I'm only teasing you."

"I don't find it amusing."

"So I noticed. It's the first time you've ever taken a woman seriously. If you have."

"Have what?"

"Taken her."

"I don't intend to."

"Are you mad? We both don't have to be lovesick and miserable," Valerian protested.

"Love has nothing to do with it. I'm not going to take her into my bed, or to the Continent. I won't deny I find her appealing…"

"Just as well, because I wouldn't believe you…"

Phelan glared him into an unrepentant silence. "But I don't need the added complication of bedding a woman who has almost as many troubles as we have."

"What has Hannigan found out about her? Does he know where the diamonds come from? What her name is?"

"He does," Phelan said. "And I'll be more than happy to share that information with you if you decide to be sensible for once and stay home today."

"Being sensible was never my strong point," Valerian said cheerfully. "Tomorrow I'll be as solemn and responsible as anyone can wish. For today, I intend to enjoy my last few hours with Sophie de Quincey to the fullest."

Phelan shook his head in mock disgust. "Then you'll have to leave it to me to decide what's best for Juliette. And what's best for us as well, which doesn't happen to include taking her to the Continent with us. We'll give her shelter here while we remain, and once we leave we'll make certain she's safe. That's the best we can do for her."

"You don't want her, and I can't have her. It doesn't make a hell of a lot of sense."

"I didn't say I didn't want her. I said I wasn't going to take her. And if I catch her alone in your bedroom with you half dressed again, I'll give you more than a black eye."

Valerian whisked a hare's foot full of powder across his face. The bruise was already ripening, and by the end of the day it would doubtless be quite impressive. "You never were obtuse before, Phelan," he said thoughtfully.

"What do you mean?"

"Anyone with eyes in his head can see that she's obsessed with you. She thinks of me as an older brother. Or older sister," he added wryly. "I'm sexless as far as she's concerned. You're a far different matter. When you're around she can't keep her eyes off you. She's almost as smitten with you as you are with her."

"I'm not smitten."

"You're hopeless," Val said. "And so damned jealous you can't see what's in front of your face."

He could see Phelan control his anger with an effort. "It scarcely matters. Now is not the time to complicate matters by...by being foolish."

"By falling in love. Use the word, Phelan. It won't burn your tongue off," Valerian said cheerfully.

"I don't believe in it, brat. And if I did, I'd hardly confide in a scapegrace like you. Concentrate on your own amours, and leave me in peace."

"Agreed," Val said. "Just don't black my eye again when you're suffering a fit of jealousy over someone you don't love."

Phelan just looked at him. "I hope your little bluestocking makes your life a living hell today," he said calmly.

"Don't worry, brother mine," Valerian replied bitterly. "She already has."

# CHAPTER TWELVE

Sophie de Quincey surveyed her reflection in the mirror anxiously, which in itself was an odd occurrence, one she couldn't help but be aware of. She wasn't the sort to primp and posture in front of a looking glass. She knew she was well favored, and her parents were generous enough to see that she was dressed in the latest mode. She wasn't possessed of any particular vanity; she simply accepted what she looked like.

But this morning she was anxious, checking and re-checking her reflection, determined to look her absolute prettiest, and all for the simple pleasure of a day spent with the dashing Mrs. Ramsey.

It puzzled her, and since she had a lively, intelligent mind, Sophie didn't tend to leave puzzles alone. There was something about Valerie Ramsey that touched her deep inside, that drew her to the tall, unconventional woman in ways that were as mysterious as they were intense. Next to her new friend, the appeal of handsome men such as Captain Melbourne, or the attentions of any of the numerous young sprigs who were courting her, paled in comparison. As long as she had the choice, she would always prefer Mrs. Ramsey's company.

She was still unsettled after yesterday's astonishingly frank conversation. She'd done her best to appear to have no more than an intellectual curiosity about the process of mating, when in reality her fascination went much, much deeper. When her mother had instructed her in the technicalities, it had sounded as uninteresting and unpleasant as the phenomenon of her monthly flow.

When Val described it, it had sounded like heaven.

Disturbingly so. She couldn't imagine Captain Melbourne evoking those kinds of feelings within her, and she wasn't sure she wanted him to. To feel so strongly would be to lose a part of oneself. She was already uncomfortably attached to Val. She didn't have much more of herself to spare.

"I might accompany you," her mother announced when Sophie sailed into the front withdrawing room to await her companion.

Sophie did her absolute best to keep the crestfallen expression from her face. If her mother knew how much she cherished the time alone with Mrs. Ramsey, she'd be certain to come along, keeping the conversation on such decorous topics as the rights of women and the deplorable condition of slavery in the Americas. And while Sophie agreed with her mother on both those issues, at the moment she was far more interested in hearing more about sex.

"That would be delightful," she lied, hoping she was convincing.

She wasn't a practiced liar, but Mrs. de Quincey wasn't adept at seeing through her daughter's unexpected perfidy, so she simply shook her head. "However, I suppose I shall be too busy. I have complete faith in Mrs. Ramsey. She may be a bit *dashing*, but I cannot find fault with her. She has a lively, almost masculine mind, and a manner that is open and pleasing. I shouldn't want you to emulate her in everything, but she does have a certain style that wouldn't come amiss in a girl like you."

Sophie cast a worried glance down at her pale rose sarcenet dress, one that she'd always considered her most becoming. "I lack style?"

"Oh, heavens, you have style enough for a young girl in your situation. One would not expect town bronze on a miss just out of the schoolroom. Time enough to acquire polish when you marry Captain Melbourne," her mother said with rare indulgence.

Sophie heard the words with a sinking heart. "He's offered, then?"

"Not in so many words. But I've not hesitated to let him know we would look upon his suit with favor. You could go a lot farther and do a great deal worse, my dear. With Captain Melbourne you would always maintain control of your life. Why, think if you were married to someone like Mr. Ramsey. Dragged all over the globe, never a home to call your own."

"If one's companion was cherished, I imagine it would be acceptable," Sophie said hesitantly.

"It would be most unpleasant," her mother said firmly. "With Captain Melbourne you would have estates worthy of your consequence. You would never have to lift a finger except in the ordering of your servants."

"Wouldn't you consider that a wasteful life?"

"In anyone other than my daughter, I would. However, I know you would spend your time improving your mind, reading tracts of scientific and philosophical interest. You have intelligence, my child. You just need a bit more discipline and a bit fewer romantical notions."

Sophie thought longingly of the jams and jellies she yearned to make, the stacks of linens to mend and count. All given to a servant who wouldn't even enjoy the labor. "You're right, Mother," she said dutifully, thinking about limbs. And dampness. And the little death that Val had described, which was instead the epitome of life.

"There you are, Mrs. Ramsey." Her mother was suddenly all graciousness as their guest was ushered into the room. "My daughter and I have just been having a little talk about the future. I know I can count on you to give her sage advice."

"Of course," Mrs. Ramsey replied promptly in that deep, drawling voice Sophie admired so much. "Come along, child. If we don't have your future well in hand by the time we return, then I would be much surprised."

Mrs. de Quincey beamed at the two of them. "I knew I could rely on you. You've seen enough of this world to be practical."

Sophie controlled her embarrassment with an effort, daring to steal a glance at her tall, stately friend. There was a wry expression in those wonderful gray eyes of hers, so like those of her husband's, an expression of shared amusement, and Sophie felt that treacherous, tingling warmth fill her.

"I'm a great believer in practicality," her friend murmured.

"You're driving all the way to Kenley? Then we shan't expect you home until late." Mrs. de Quincey cast a fond glance at her daughter. "Don't let her prattle bore you, dear

Mrs. Ramsey. Despite my best efforts, she's still a very romantical young girl."

"I find your daughter's conversation to be eminently intelligent."

Mrs. de Quincey preened as Sophie squirmed. "I fancy I may congratulate myself for that. I have ever aimed to improve her childish mind."

Sophie kept her expression purposefully blank. Childish mind, indeed! she fumed inwardly. Her mother *would* accompany them out to the carriage, peering into the bright blue sky with a dubious expression on her face. "I don't trust this weather," she said darkly.

"Mother." Sophie finally let her exasperation break through. "It's a glorious day!"

"Exactly. Things are always brightest before disaster."

"I thought the saying was, 'Things are always darkest before the dawn,'" Mrs. Ramsey said, and Sophie could hear the undercurrent of amusement in that deep voice.

"I never was an optimist, my dear Mrs. Ramsey." Mrs. de Quincey folded her daughter in her embrace, then held her at arm's length, eyeing her critically. "You're too warm, my dear, and your color is pale. I'm uncertain whether I should allow you to go."

It took all of Sophie's self-control not to wrench herself from her mother's sturdy grip. "The fresh air will do wonders for me, Mother," she said with some firmness. "You can trust Mrs. Ramsey to see to me."

"I do, my dear," her mother said. "I do."

Sophie climbed into the light curricle and sat next to Mrs. Ramsey, who took the reins in strong, large hands that weren't quite disguised by the thin leather gloves. Mrs. Ramsey's size and strength were the most impressive things about her, Sophie thought. That and her laughing eyes.

They drove in silence for a few moments, Mrs. Ramsey concentrating on the distractions of town traffic and Sophie concentrating on the embarrassment of a condescending, oversolicitous mother. It wasn't until they were on the road to Kenley that her companion finally spoke.

"She's a formidable woman, your mother," Mrs. Ramsey observed dryly.

"She is, indeed. She thinks I'm an idiot."

"I wouldn't say that, child. I expect she's quite proud of you. It's just that no one can measure up to her own exalted intellect."

Sophie managed to smile. "I have something quite wicked to confess," she said.

"Good," her friend said promptly. "I love wickedness."

"I sometimes wonder if my mother is not quite as brilliant as she imagines herself to be."

Mrs. Ramsey's burst of laughter was low-pitched and warming. "I suspect you may be right. She spends so much time convincing herself and everyone else of her intellectual superiority that I doubt she ever gets to exercise her mind at all."

"Oh, she's very busy," Sophie assured her. "Usually with other people's concerns."

She could sense her companion's curious glance. "I don't suppose you'll be just like her when you get older?" There was almost a hopeful expression in that deep, drawling voice, and Sophie looked at her in surprise.

"Lord, I hope not," she said devoutly. "Actually, I'm considered to take after my aunt Edith, a sadly impractical creature who gave up everything for love. She could have married a duke's son, but instead, she ran off with a curate. She's lived a very happy life with her husband and six children in Somerset, but my mother considers that she's wasted her life."

"And what do you think?"

"I think my aunt is very happy in her life, and doesn't consider it the slightest bit wasted. And neither would I if I had half her blessings," she said firmly.

"I think, dear girl, that you are far wiser than your mother." A large, gloved hand reached over and covered Sophie's, and she felt perfectly, divinely happy. "Let's not think about her, shall we? It's a glorious day, and despite Mrs. de Quincey's misgivings, it is *not* going to rain. If it does, I shall take it as a direct insult."

Sophie giggled. "Now *you* sound like my mother."

"Wretched girl," Mrs. Ramsey said easily, snapping the reins. "Let us enjoy our glorious day. Who knows when we shall see its like again?"

It was a melancholy thought. "Who knows?" Sophie echoed. And tucking her arm through Mrs. Ramsey's strong one, she slid closer on the seat, prepared to wring the last ounce of pleasure from the perfect, cloudless day.

It rained. Valerian had known since his brother had managed to plant him a facer that the day was doomed, and if he'd had any sense he would have sent word to Sophie that the elegant Mrs. Ramsey was once more indisposed. Except that she'd probably decide her dear friend was suffering the pangs of childlessness, and would doubtless appear with hot soup and poultices and that devastating sympathy.

The drive to Kenley was pleasant enough. No, it was more than pleasant, it was sheer heaven, with Sophie curled up beside him, serenely peaceful. They explored the old Roman ruins, and if the rough footing underneath forced Valerian to put a steadying hand under Sophie's elbow, gradually increasing it to an arm around her slender waist, then there was no one around to think it the slightest bit odd.

They ate in the shade: cold chicken and cheese and thick brown bread. They drank lemonade and listened to the lazy sound of the bees, busy in the wild roses that bloomed so freely. And then they both slept.

When Valerian woke he was being pelted by hot, wet raindrops. He sat up quickly, afraid the water might wash away the disguising powder with which he'd covered himself so liberally. His skin was too tanned from years in the sunlight, his beard had a normal tendency to grow, and with the addition of his burgeoning black eye, he needed all the covering he could get. He quickly grabbed the oversize hat and yanked the concealing veil down over his face, just in time to face Sophie.

She looked absolutely adorable. Her blond curls were tousled, her blue eyes sleepy, her soft mouth curved in a welcoming smile. He almost leaned over and kissed that mouth. Instead, he climbed to his feet, holding out his large hand. "It's raining, child," he said, lightening his voice deliberately. "We'd best head back before we get soaked."

"Damn," she said succinctly.

He grinned behind the veil. "Damn?" he echoed. "What would your mother say?"

"Double damn," said Sophie. "My mother would say, 'I told you so.'"

"There are worse things in this life than having your mother say, 'I told you so,'" he said consolingly.

"Name one."

The deluge hit just as they reached the open carriage. Sophie slipped, and Valerian reached underneath and shoved her up into the seat, controlling his real need to let his hands linger. He vaulted up after her, grabbing the whip, and in a moment they were off, careening down the road at a spanking pace.

The summer-dry roads quickly turned to soup, the horses were high-strung creatures, not overfond of thunder and lightning, and his gloves split beneath the strength he was exerting in controlling the team. When he could, he spared a glance at his companion.

She was sitting close beside him, her hat draped soddenly around her head, and he told himself he was about to see his beloved at her absolute worst. He'd yet to meet a woman who could survive a cold, soaking rain in a reasonable humor, and he could only hope the well-bred Miss Sophie de Quincey would indulge in a full-fledged tantrum. It might make his departure easier.

Suddenly she reached up, took the dripping hat from her head, and sent it sailing into the bushes, tilting her face back into the rain and laughing. And Valerian wondered how he was ever going to let her go. Disaster and temptation weren't through with them yet. The rain, instead of abating, only seemed to increase. The horses struggled mightily, Sophie curled up beside him, taking some shelter from his larger body, but eventually he gave up.

"We're stopping?" He could barely hear her question beneath the thundering rain.

"We're at an inn," he shouted back. "We'll have to take shelter until this damned storm breaks."

An hostler appeared out of the rain to take the horses'

heads, and Valerian leapt down with an immodest disregard for his skirts, reaching up for Sophie. She jumped into his arms, laughing in unselfconscious delight, and it took all his willpower to release her, keeping hold of her hand as they made their mad dash into the inn.

The innkeeper appeared, wiping his hands on a thankfully clean apron. "It's wicked weather, my lady. We've got a warm fire and hot tea, if you'd condescend to enter."

"Certainly, my good man," Valerian said from behind his sodden veil. "But first my young friend and I shall need private rooms to mend our toilettes."

"I'm most sorry to tell you, my lady, that I can't oblige. We have only two bedrooms, and one of them is already bespoke."

"Only two bedrooms in an inn this size? Don't be absurd!" Valerian protested.

"We've had a fire, my lady," the man said miserably, wringing his hands. "We haven't yet finished the repairs."

"Show us your room," Sophie said, smiling sweetly. "I'm certain it will be just fine."

"Indeed, ma'am, it's a very comfortable bed."

Valerian controlled himself with an effort. "We weren't planning to spend the night, my good man, but just to wait out the worst of the storm."

"Begging your pardon, my lady, but the road's already flooded between here and Hampton Regis. Even if the rain were to stop right now, the water wouldn't go down till after midnight."

"What an adventure!" Sophie cried, obviously pleased. "Don't worry, Val. Your husband has complete faith in your self-reliance, and so does my mother. I'm certain they won't worry unduly."

Valerian thought of his brother's strictures, and made an unseen grimace. "Mr. Ramsey is more strict than would first appear," he said.

"Well, there's nothing we can do about it. Unless there's another road to Hampton Regis?" She turned her bright, inquisitive eyes to the unhappy landlord.

"There's only one, miss, and it lies even lower than the main road. It floods even more often. I'd advise against trying it."

"Well," said Val in what he hoped was a matter-of-fact voice, "it appears we're stranded, at least for the night. I don't suppose you could come up with dry clothes, my good man?"

"For the young miss, I'm certain we could devise something," he said. "Begging your pardon, my lady, but I doubt we'd have anything to fit you." He looked up at Valerian with awe. "Most of the women around here are built along smaller…er, that is to say…"

There was nothing to do but take it with a sense of humor. Sophie was eyeing him warily, trying to gauge his expression behind the damp veiling. "I know, I know," he said lazily. "I'm gargantuan. I'll just have to sit by the fire and hope I dry off."

"My wife has an extra night rail she could lend you. She's not so tall, but she's good and stout, and I imagine it'll fit," the man said anxiously.

Wearing the clothes of a stout landlady didn't particularly appeal to Valerian, but there wasn't much he could say. "That would be very generous of your wife."

"In the meantime, let me show you to your room, and I'll see about some hot tea."

Valerian was in a very bad mood indeed. "As a matter of fact," he said, "I might prefer a hot rum punch."

Such a request from a lady was unusual, but the innkeeper did his best not to blanch. "Hot rum punch? I could see to that. I was going to make one for our gentleman guest, and I could brew you up some as well. Something a bit weaker."

"By no means. I want it strong and hot and spicy," Valerian said determinedly.

"So would I," Sophie piped up. "Forget about the tea."

"Rum punch?" the landlord echoed, horrified. "For both of you ladies?"

Valerian took Sophie's hand in his. "For both of us ladies," he said. And his voice was dangerously low.

The bedroom under the eaves was small, cozy, and smelled faintly of wet smoke. The bed was tiny, and if anyone thought Valerian would be able to share it with Sophie and not touch her, that person was out of his mind.

Val had a scant few minutes alone as Sophie sought the privacy of the convenience. Time enough to strip off his sodden hat and try to repair his appearance. He ran a worried hand over his strong jaw, but he'd shaved very closely that morning, and the faint stubble was almost indiscernible. At some point he'd have to closet himself and shave again, but he didn't dare attempt it at the moment. Sophie was innocent, but she wasn't stupid, and he could think of no excuse for the dashing Mrs. Ramsey to be shaving.

He had to make do with whisking powder over his face. The black eye was beginning to show through the makeup, and he accepted it reluctantly. At least it might distract her attention from his faintly darkening chin.

He had no skill at all with his hair, and no choice but

to tie it behind his neck with a riband. The effect was too masculine, but fate had taken a hand, and he could only work with what he had. At least he always kept his razor and powder with him, ready for disaster.

When Sophie reentered the room she looked flushed and breathless. She glanced at him shyly as he tried to shake some of the water from his sodden skirts. "You know," she suggested, "you could probably borrow some of the landlord's clothes until yours dry. I know the suggestion is quite shocking, but you must be wretchedly uncomfortable."

He almost choked. "I don't think it would be quite the thing for me to dress up as a man," he said gravely.

"No, I suppose you're right." She had a pale blue dress and a froth of white lace over her arm, and she dropped the clothes on the bed before presenting her narrow, delicious back to him. "Would you unfasten my dress?"

For a moment he didn't move, casting his eyes heavenward in a silent prayer. She glanced over her shoulder at him, and without further hesitation he moved behind her, his usually deft hands clumsy as they began to unfasten the row of tiny buttons.

He'd undressed a great many females in his life. Ladies of fashion, dairymaids, farmers' daughters, and governesses. They'd all been more than willing, and he'd grown quite conversant with the intricacies of women's clothing. Even in the heat of advanced desire, he'd never had so much difficulty with the fastenings.

"Are you all right, Valerie?" Sophie asked when the last button finally parted and the damp dress slid down over her shoulders.

"Splendid," he growled, then coughed to cover the masculine note in his voice. He moved away, turning his back to her, uncertain if he could stand to watch.

"How are your hands?"

He glanced down at them. They were one of the most revealing things about him. They were large, well shaped, used to hard work, and undoubtedly masculine. "Fine," he said, wishing women's dresses came with pockets so that he could hide them.

"Your gloves ripped again, didn't they? I just wanted to make sure you weren't hurt..." The blasted girl came around in front of him and caught his hands in hers. She'd dispensed with her pink dress, and she was wearing her chemise and petticoats. He could see far too much of the swell of her small, perfect breasts, he could see the shape of her legs beneath the damp petticoats, and he almost groaned.

He tried to yank his hands away, but her grip was surprisingly strong. "You go through more gloves than any female I know," she said humorously, running her soft fingers over the calluses on his palm. Her touch was deft, innocently erotic, and he was immediately hard beneath his concealing clothes. A frown creased her brow. "You must have worked hard in your life," she said.

It was now or never. He needed to warn her, needed to drive her away, and the only thing he could think of was more lies. "I'm afraid I have," he said, letting his large hand rest in hers, trying not to stare down her cleavage, not to drink in the lavender scent of her perfume. "I'm afraid I've been living under faintly false pretenses."

"You've been lying to me?" Her voice was still and wary, but, she didn't release his hand. It was a warning.

"No," he said, lying once more. "I just haven't made my

antecedents clear. I'm not quite as wellborn as one would think. I...I married above me. By quite a bit."

"There's nothing wrong with that," she said soothingly.

"I used to work as a seamstress," he said desperately, hoping to give her a disgust of him.

"I'm sure you were very industrious."

"And I worked on a farm," he added, this time truthfully.

"You're so lucky," she said soulfully. "And your hands show honest toil. You shouldn't be ashamed of them." And to his utter horror she leaned forward and put her lips against his palm.

And then she released him, backing away, suddenly startled. "I'm sorry," she said. "That was foolish of me." And she turned her back to him, her beautiful, narrow back, and reached for the clothing on the bed.

He couldn't stay in that room a moment longer, with the feel of her mouth still on his hand, the scent of her perfume on the air, the sight of her creamy skin dazzling his eyes. He practically raced toward the door. "I'll meet you in the parlor," he said in a strangled voice.

She turned, and through the dampness of the thin white material he could see the faint darkness of her nipples, puckered against the cold, wet material. "I might need help dressing," she protested.

Not from me, my girl. One more moment alone with you and you won't have any need for clothing, he thought grimly. "I'll send the maid," he said, escaping.

The landlord met him at the bottom of the stairs, a troubled expression on his cherubic face that Val suspected was habitual. "Begging your pardon, my lady, but there's a bit of a problem. We've only one private parlor, and that's already been bespoke by the gentleman in the other room. I thought it wouldn't be proper asking him to share, seeing as how you two ladies are traveling without male escort, so to speak, so I thought you might condescend to use the taproom. No one's going to come in on a night like this one, and if they do, we'll just send them on their way. You and the young lady will have your privacy, I promise you, and no interference from the gentleman."

"The taproom will be fine," Val said, sailing past him with what he hoped was a certain majesty. He paused, looking back. "Are you certain none of the other bedrooms are available? I don't mind the smell of smoke."

"Certain, my lady. Especially in this weather. We're fixing the roof, but as it is…" He shrugged. "Was there some particular problem, my lady? Most women prefer to share a bed. Gives 'em a bit of company, and while my inn is in every way respectable, another woman would give you some added protection, so to speak."

There was no way Valerian could argue it further. He knew perfectly well that his insistence on a private bedroom was peculiar. Indeed, it would be very odd if he didn't share Sophie's bed to give her companionship and countenance. He was just horribly afraid that wasn't all he'd end up giving her.

"The room will be fine," he said wearily. "I was only thinking of the young lady's comfort. I am a bit large for that particular bed."

The poor landlord could say nothing. To agree would be to insult his guest; to disagree would be even worse. "Perhaps the gentleman might be willing to exchange rooms. His bed is larger and—"

"Heavens, no!" Val said with a perfect trill of laughter he'd perfected several weeks ago, having learned it from

Neville Pinworth. "That would be quite indecent, I assure you. I wouldn't think of asking him to trade. My niece and I will make do. Perhaps if there's a pallet, an extra mattress…?"

The landlord shook his head once more. "Burned, my lady."

Val cursed inwardly. I tried, Lord, I tried, he said silently. "Then I suppose we'll simply have to make do," he said in a dulcet voice. "How is our rum punch coming?"

"I've made some for the gentleman, and I was just about to brew up a fresh batch for you. Something a bit more suited to the ladies."

Sophie had appeared on the stairway, decently clothed in a pale blue dress that had obviously been the height of fashion twenty years ago. The neckline was low, the waist a more natural one, and the dress clung to her curves like a second skin. Valerian didn't know but that it was even more arousing than her skin.

"We want strong punch," she said, descending the stairs. "Mrs. Ramsey and I intend to enjoy our night of freedom, don't we?"

Valerian let his eyes drift over her white shoulders, the pale slope of her breast. "Immensely," he said, consigning his misery to the devil. He would take tonight, take whatever he dared to enjoy, and tomorrow he would willingly pay the price.

The landlord let out a resigned sigh. "Very well," he said. "I've already had the table laid for you two ladies. If you go on into the taproom, I'll bring you some rum punch. But it's very strong, I warn you."

"We're very strong ladies, aren't we, Val?" Sophie said mischievously, tucking her arm through Val's.

"We do our best," he said, savoring the feel, the scent, of her.

"Very well," the man said again. "And I'll tell the gentleman not to intrude on the taproom. Not that he would. Likes his privacy, I can tell, and he's not a man who'd offer a lady an insult."

"Let us sincerely hope not," Val drawled.

"No, I could tell the moment I saw him," the innkeeper said firmly. "Mr. Lemur would never harm a lady."

# CHAPTER THIRTEEN

Phelan Romney was in an exceedingly bad mood. Not only had Valerian failed to return that evening, he'd disappeared with the de Quinceys' virginal daughter, Sophie. While the redoubtable Mrs. de Quincey had no lack of faith in Val's ability to watch over her little hatchling, Phelan was feeling far from sanguine.

He knew his brother very well, knew that despite his reckless, lighthearted attitude, his masquerade was slowly driving him crazy.

And he knew his brother was in love. An odd admission for a man like Phelan, a man who didn't believe in love, but he couldn't ignore the fact. Valerian loved women, and treated them all with the same amount of tenderness and care. But one had only to see his face when he said Sophie's name to know the man was completely moonstruck.

And Phelan, who longed to ride to his younger brother's rescue and right any wrongs, much as he had when they were younger, was helpless. At the worst, Valerian was a fugitive from justice who had lied to his beloved, an exile from his native county with the ugly charge of patricide hanging over his head.

At best, he was a landless bastard, he who loved the land so much, whose existence had driven a well-bred lady to butcher her own husband.

Either way, it wasn't a pretty notion.

And he could hardly blame Valerian for following his reckless desires when he himself wouldn't even listen to his own advice. He'd tried, of course, refusing to admit he didn't have full control of his urges.

He'd tried to distract himself with useless errands. He'd decided to explore, and he'd ridden in search of Hannigan's mysterious family, only to find the tiny village of Hampton Parva peopled solely with Hannigans and no one else. He'd been welcomed, warily, and not a single one of his questions had been answered. Each one was directed back to Hannigan himself, and when Phelan rode back home to discover Valerian missing in the sudden storm, his mood was none too pretty.

He should have taken a page from Valerian's book and retired to his bedroom with a couple of bottles of wine and his own dark thoughts. He should have kept as far away from Juliette MacGowan Lemur as he could. At least until she was ready to tell him the truth.

But he wasn't sure that he could. He was a man who prided himself on his self-control, on his imperviousness to the vagaries of most human weaknesses. But when all was said and done, he was proving to have as little will-power as his impetuous younger brother. And, trapped alone in a storm-swept house on a desolate strip of land, he had all he could do to keep from taking a taste of danger. Just a sip, mind you. Of Juliette's soft, defiant mouth.

* * *

"Master wants you," Hannigan announced tersely, poking his head inside the kitchen.

Dulcie looked up from the stove. "I'll be right there," she said, putting down her ladle.

"Not you, woman. The lass there."

Juliette lifted her head, trying to ignore the little shiver of alarm that swept through her. It had been a relatively peaceful, almost indolent day, spent in the kitchens helping Dulcie. She'd expected it to end the same way, without having to endure the unsettling presence of the master of the house.

She rose, reaching for her jacket. "No need for that, lass," Hannigan said. "He wants you to serve dinner. You'll do fine as you are."

"Serve him dinner?" Dulcie echoed, scandalized. "What does he think she is? I've a notion to teach him his manners."

"He thinks she's a servant," Hannigan said sternly. "Which, at this moment, she is. Until she tells him otherwise. Come along with you, lass."

Juliette hesitated. "Who else is there?"

Hannigan's mouth curved in a wry smile. "You'll need to learn that such questions are none of a good servant's business," he said. "As a matter of fact, the master dines alone tonight."

"Then why does he need someone to serve him?" she countered.

"Ask him yourself, if you dare," Hannigan suggested.

It was probably just another salvo in the battle waging between them. She refused to let it reach her. She would serve his dinner with calm efficiency. And she'd resist the impulse to fling the plate at his head.

The formal dining room at Sutter's Head was small, elegant, and candlelit. Phelan sat at one end of the table, holding a glass of wine in one long-fingered, graceful hand, and his dark hair was rumpled over his high forehead. He was wearing dark breeches and a white shirt open at the neck, informal wear for a private evening at home. She made her way carefully down the length of the room, bearing the tray in her hands, and she was acutely aware of his eyes on her, watching her every movement.

She worked with calm competence, serving the delicious dinner Dulcie had made, her movements deft and precise as she opened the second bottle of wine, shook out the heavy linen napkin and draped it in his lap, brushed an imaginary crumb off the table.

"Was there anything else, sir?" she asked in a deferential tone that was only faintly mocking.

He didn't bother to glance up at her, concentrating instead on the dinner. "Sit down," he said shortly.

"I'd rather return to the kitchen, sir."

"Sit down."

Juliette sat. He began to eat, slowly, with a complete lack of self-consciousness that in another time Juliette might have found admirable. She hated having people watch her when she ate—if there were servants in the room, she usually dismissed them. She stared stonily ahead, only allowing herself an occasional glance in his direction, waiting for him to speak to her. He ate as he did everything, with a kind of offhand, negligent grace.

"I'm trying to decide what to do with you," he said, and it took her a moment to realize he'd even spoken.

"You don't need to do a thing with me. You can return my earbobs and let me leave. Surely that would be the prudent course."

"I have little interest in prudence." He leaned back in his chair and looked at her, and she realized he'd been drinking more heavily than usual. Not enough so that it really showed, just enough to put a dangerous glitter in his eyes.

A moment or two passed before she realized he had snapped his fingers in her direction. "Yes, sir?"

"You may refill my wine."

The wine bottle was next to his hand. Gritting her teeth, she rose from her seat, reaching for the bottle. In her temper she spilled a drop, and Phelan shook his head in disapproval. "You need experience, young Julian, if you're to continue as a servant," he murmured. "Perhaps I'll have you serve all my meals. After all, if you intend to make a career of this, you'd best learn a certain amount of proficiency. It's the least I can do to help you."

"I'm very proficient," she said between her teeth.

"And you need to remember not to talk back to your betters," he drawled, obviously enjoying himself.

"I'll endeavor to do so, sir," she said. "If ever I'm in the presence of one." She started to move away, but his hand shot out and caught her wrist.

"You really have no idea how very dangerous your behavior is, do you?" His voice was silken.

She looked down at him, at the hand on her wrist. She was tanned from her years beneath the blazing tropical sun, but his skin was just as burnished. Sprawled there in his loose white shirt, he looked like no English gentleman. He looked like a pirate, a marauder, a very threatening man indeed. So why did she persist in thinking he could save her from Lemur?

"Why is it dangerous?" she asked, her voice deceptively steady. Even though he held her, there was no pain in her wrist. Instead, his thumb was stroking the skin, absently.

She wondered what would happen if she tried to pull away. She wondered why she wasn't interested in trying.

"Because I'm a man," he said. "I've been celibate for longer than I've ever been since I turned sixteen, and I'm getting to the point where anything would attract me. Including a child who can't decide if she's a boy or a girl."

She did jerk her hand away then, and he let her go, surveying her out of assessing eyes. "I'm going to bed," she said, stalking toward the door.

"You're my servant." His voice followed her, lightly mocking. "At least for the time being. And I haven't dismissed you."

"Go to hell," she said succinctly. And slammed the door behind her. And the sound of his laughter echoed down the hall after her.

She went straight to her room, locking the door behind her. It was hot and stifling inside, but the rain was coming down so heavily she didn't dare open the window. She sat there, alone in the darkness, and wondered what in God's name was going to become of her.

She must have slept. When she awoke the house was silent, only the noise of the rain against the window disturbing the unearthly quiet. She was hot, suffocating, trapped in that room, in those clothes, in a life that was not of her own choosing. Silently she unlocked the door and stepped into the deserted hallway.

The kitchen was still and dark. Hannigan and Dulcie must have gone off to their rooms in the cozy little outbuilding by the stable. She could only hope Valerian had finally made it home through the storm. Otherwise she was alone in the house with a man she found far too disturbing.

She opened the kitchen door a crack, feeling the swirl of rain and wind slap against her face. It felt wonderful, cool and harsh and cleansing. Without a moment's hesitation she slipped outside, into the deluge, closing the door behind her.

She was instantly soaked to the skin, her white shirt plastered against her body. She could barely see two feet in front of her, and the wind whipped her hair into her face. If she had any sense at all, she'd turn and run back to her room. But she was feeling far from sensible.

The wildness in the storm called to a wildness in her heart, and she had to answer. She'd left her shoes in her room, and she took off through the flooded courtyard, zigzagging around the house to the gardens. She glanced back at the house, but she could see nothing but darkness through the driving rain. Phelan must have retired long ago, lulled to sleep by the rain and the wine. He wouldn't disturb her this night.

She should try once more to run. No one would notice she'd gone until the morning, if then, and the rain would wipe any trace of her away with the dawn. If she had any sense at all, she would take this chance while she had it. She might not get another opportunity.

His arguments had been persuasive. She'd been no match for Lemur herself. Perhaps Phelan could protect her. But would he? Or would he sell her for the price of the diamond-and-pearl earbobs, and more besides?

She didn't trust him. She didn't trust any man. It was past time she remembered that fact.

She would need her shoes, her clothes, and money. She would need every last moment she could steal. And she could hesitate no longer.

She knew where he kept his money. Indeed, he'd made no effort to hide it from her. There was a stack of gold coins and paper in the top drawer of his desk. She wouldn't take all of it. He'd be more likely to realize she was missing if he came downstairs and found his desk pilfered. Besides, Valerian might need that money even more than she did, and he had been kind to her. Unlike his mocking, cynical older brother.

She moved silently back through the house, pausing in her room to gather up her shoes and clothing before heading down the hallway to the library. A lamp was burning low on the hall table, and she picked it up, moving into the library. It provided minimal illumination, but she headed toward the desk unerringly.

It was unlocked. Setting the lamp down, she reached for the money, prepared to tuck most of it inside her shirt and start back out into the rain, when she thought better of it.

Phelan's watch lay on the desk. It was gold, and probably worth a great deal, and she'd seen him hold it in his hand more than once. She reached out to touch it, telling herself she ought to take it in payment for her missing earbobs. It felt warm to her damp hands, and she found she was caressing it, as a woman might touch the skin of a lover.

The room smelled of rain, of leather, of smoke, and wine. It reminded her of things she couldn't have, things she didn't want to have. She needed to run, she reminded herself desperately, picking up the watch.

It felt alive to her, part of him. The steady tick was like a heartbeat, the bright gold was warm in her hands, and she knew she couldn't steal it. Couldn't steal his money. Couldn't run, no matter how much she knew she should.

She replaced the watch carefully. She slid the desk drawer silently shut, the money safe within. And then she turned to leave.

"That was a wise decision on your part," Phelan Romney said, and Juliette let out a muffled shriek of panic, dropping her shoes and clothing on the floor. The coins that Mowbray had handed her spilled through the kerchief, rolling onto the floor with a noisy clatter.

He was sitting in the winged armchair in the dark, watching her. The bottle on the table next to him was empty, and there was a dark, ominous glitter in his eyes.

"I didn't know you were there," she said stupidly.

"Of course you didn't. You're not adept at stealth, fair Juliette. I heard you coming a mile away, and I simply extinguished the lamp. I wanted to see what you were going to do. You surprised me."

"You were surprised that I decided to run?"

He shook his head, rising slowly, lazily, with a grace that barely showed the amount of wine he'd drunk that night. "Surprised that you changed your mind."

"I haven't changed my mind about running. I just decided not to rob you. You told me you'd beat me if I did, and I decided you were ruthless enough to do just that."

"Of course you did," he said, moving slowly across the room. During the hot, muggy night he'd unfastened his shirt, and it hung loosely around his bronzed torso. She thought absently of Valerian's shaved chest, and a little frisson of emotion ran through her, one she refused to examine. "I've been such a damned brute so far, haven't I?" he said.

She almost agreed, until she realized that once more he was being ironic. He probably thought he'd been the soul of restraint. And perhaps, in comparison, he had been. She only knew that each time he looked at her, she reacted as strongly as if he'd put his hands on her.

"You can keep the earbobs," she said nervously, taking a step backward, prepared to run.

"Noble of you. I don't care for them, though."

"Give them to Valerian. They'll look charming on him."

His mouth curved in a grin, and Juliette could no more deny her reaction than she could fly to the moon. That was the reason she had to run; she knew it full well. Not from the harm he might do, but from his rare, devastating smile.

"I'd rather see them on you," he said.

"They don't suit me."

"The diamond-and-pearl earbobs," he said in a dreamy voice that made her realize how very drunk he really was. "And nothing else." And he reached for her.

She almost went to him. For one brief, mad moment she swayed toward him, wanting the dangerous comfort of his arms, his body against hers. But the sudden streak and fizzle of lightning saved her, followed almost immediately by a crack of thunder.

She ran, barefoot, half mad with fear and longing, out into the stormy night in wild disregard of nature's fury. He caught her by the edge of the garden, the rain pouring down on them, soaking them. "I'm getting damned tired," he said in a thick voice, "of having you run away."

She was no match for his strength. She didn't wish to be. She went into his arms this time, hidden within the curtain of rain, and tilted her face up to his. Letting the rain pour down on her, letting his kisses pour down on her, and she slid her arms around his waist beneath the damp, flapping white shirt, the violence of the storm and her own wild, confused feelings sweeping her away.

His hands were rough as he held her. His mouth was hard, demanding, and when he pushed her down into the wet grass she went, no longer fighting it. His body covered hers, his mouth settled across hers, and the rain surrounding them was a benediction and a torture.

He reached between them and yanked at her shirt and the buttons popped, the wet material ripped, and she was bared to the waist. The cool dampness of the air was a shock against her skin; the hot dampness of his mouth was even more astonishing. Pushing her shoulders back into the drenched earth, he put his mouth over her breast, teasing the hard peak with his tongue, the hot, sucking pressure sending streaks of desire spearing through her body, centering between her legs. She felt panic sweep through her, a dark fear that was so very different from the terror of her nights with Lemur. This wasn't the fear of a man's cruelty, the fear of pain. It was the fear of her own weakness, and of longing.

His hand slid down between her legs, cupping her through the wet material of her breeches, and the heel of his palm rubbed against her, slowly, enticingly, so that her hips arched against him, seemingly out of instinct.

He lifted his head, and the cold night air on her breast made her shiver. He looked down at her, a dark, searching expression on his face, and she closed her eyes, letting the rain pelt her cheeks, her eyelids, afraid to let him look too closely.

He was resting against her hips, and she could feel the hard ridge of flesh pressing against her. She waited, holding herself still for his next move, prepared for the worst.

He gave it to her. He kissed her eyelids, feathering them gently. His mouth moved down to brush hers lightly, nibbling at her lips slowly, delicately, until she had no choice but to cling to him, reaching up for him, unable to deny the fact that she wanted this, she wanted him. Until his hand reached down between them, and he began to unfasten the row of buttons on her breeches.

Panic swept through her again, and she began to struggle. She was fighting so forcefully she couldn't hear him, couldn't see him, and it wasn't until she was spread-eagled, immobilized, that his voice penetrated the mists of her terror.

"Calm down," he said, clearly not for the first time. "I won't hurt you."

Her eyes focused on his dark face, and a shiver ran through her body. He was still hard against her, she recognized that much, and she knew that she couldn't stop him from taking her. His effortless control of her body left no question in her mind that he could take her, and it would be worse, far worse, than anything that Lemur had tried to do to her. Because some wretched, evil part of her wanted it. Wanted him.

"Stop struggling," he said, "and I'll release you."

She hadn't even realized she was still fighting him. She tried to calm herself, but she couldn't. If she relaxed, even for a moment, the darkness would descend, and she couldn't bear it.

"Stop it," he said again, his voice sharp and furious, and his anger finally penetrated the black cloud that had descended over her. She froze, staring up at him as he loomed over her in the rain-swept darkness, blinking as the water splashed into her eyes.

"That's better," he said in a milder voice. "I've never raped a woman, and I'm not about to. I can't imagine there'd be much sport in it. I prefer my women warm and willing, lying in a soft, dry bed, not rutting in a garden in the dead of night in a thunderstorm." His words were mocking, bitter, and she wasn't sure if that contempt was directed at her or at himself.

He rose abruptly, hauling her up with him. "Next time," he said, "I might not let you go."

For a moment neither of them moved. And then she realized her shirt, like his, hung open, exposing her small breasts to the night air and his piercing regard. She yanked the torn ends together, covering herself, and stumbled toward the house.

"Too late, Juliette." His voice followed her, cool and dark as the night air. "I've seen you, I've touched you, I've tasted you. Sooner or later I'm going to have you. It doesn't matter to me that Lemur was first. He only hurt you."

"You'd hurt me, too." She paused by the door, and her voice was no more than a thread of sound.

"Never."

She closed her eyes for a moment. "Let me leave," she begged.

"Never."

He stood alone in the garden, long after she'd left him. He needed the dubious comfort of the cold rain. He'd had too much to drink; he'd had too much to dream. He had been thinking about her, fantasizing about her, when he'd heard her surreptitious footsteps in the hall, and it had been a simple enough matter to reach over and plunge the room into darkness.

The sheer force of the fury that had rocketed through him when he saw her delving through his desk drawer had set the actions in motion. He'd told himself he was going to be cool, distant, toying with her. He'd watched her pick up the watch that represented the one fond memory he had of a father who'd despised him, and he'd wanted to vent that fury on a body that aroused him far too much for his own good.

He'd used the first excuse. Even her obvious better judgment hadn't stopped him from going after her. She wouldn't have gotten far in this storm without shoes or money. She would have been back in her room by morning, and they both could have pretended it had never happened.

But he'd been looking for a reason to touch her. And he would have taken her, coupling with her in the grass and mud like a rutting boar, ignoring her obvious shyness, her obvious panic, if something hadn't penetrated his lust-driven daze.

He'd told himself he could take her. It wasn't as if she were unused to it. She'd been married to Lemur, and her husband's reputation was none too savory. Doubtless rolling in the mud would have been pleasurable by comparison.

But he'd felt her panic, and while it hadn't diminished his desire, it had brought back his sanity. She was small, and cold, and frightened. Frightened of him, of his strength, of his lust, of his anger. And for the first time in years, he felt ashamed.

If he thought there was any chance of maintaining his self-control, he'd go to her, wrap her in his arms, and kiss away the tears. Comfort and warm her, croon to her all the stupid, lovesick things women liked to hear. He'd never wanted to say those things before. He wanted to say them now.

But he didn't trust himself. His idea of comfort could rapidly turn into the same passion that had almost overwhelmed him. And if he took her now, against her will, when she was lost and frightened, she would never forgive him. And he would never forgive himself.

He knew he should send her away, to some place safe

from people like Mark-David Lemur. Safe from people like Phelan Romney. And he knew he wasn't ready to do it. Not until he'd managed to get Valerian on a boat bound for France.

If it were up to him, they'd be gone. But he couldn't leave Valerian behind, and his brother refused to run. They were at a miserable, frustrating impasse, and Phelan didn't know who would explode first. Or who would survive that explosion.

Time was running out. No mysterious suspect had yet to appear, no logical alternative to the wretched likelihood that Lady Margery had finally taken a knife to her bullying husband. And the longer the brothers stayed in England, at Sutter's Head, the more precarious their situation became.

Sooner or later someone would unmask Valerian. Sooner or later they had to make the decision—to accept their sacrifice and leave the country, or to tell the truth. If they didn't, that decision would be taken out of their hands.

Once they were in Europe, Phelan could get hold of the substantial income he'd inherited from an aunt and uncle who had died just around the time he was born. He wasn't accused of a crime—it was only the need to keep their whereabouts secret that stopped him from touching his inheritance. Once he had access to it, he could send Juliette far away from her marauding husband, send her somewhere safe.

Or he could take her with him. The thought came, unbidden and tempting. He could protect her, keep her with him, by his side, in his bed...

But he couldn't have that, no matter how much he wanted Juliette. He'd already accepted his fate long ago. There would be no woman in his life, no permanent one. Sooner or later they all started fussing about marriage, and babies, and staying home, and Phelan couldn't stand staying in one place. And he was never going to father babies. Never going to pass on the madness he'd seen in his mother's eyes.

Of course, Juliette wouldn't fuss about marriage. She was already legally tied to another man. And she wouldn't long for babies when she was terrified by his touch, although he had every intention of teaching her how to like it. He'd already made great strides in the endeavor, and he had no doubt as to his eventual triumph.

She might not even complain about travel. She'd spent most of her life following her notorious father through countries most Englishwomen had never seen, and she seemed more than eager to depart this demi-paradise, this England.

And then reality hit him. He was standing in a midnight garden in the pouring rain, his body still rock-hard with frustrated lust, weaving fantasies about a happy ending with a runaway wife.

Clearly he was going mad.

He was going to send her away, with her diamond-and-pearl earbobs, with every cent he could spare, with the bloody watch his father had given him if need be. He was going to send her away, tomorrow morning, at first light.

Before he couldn't bear to let her go.

# CHAPTER FOURTEEN

The rain continued, unabated, pounding against the windows of the old inn, thundering against the rooftops. The wind rattled against the doors, sending gusts of smoke down the chimneys, but inside, the fire was warm, the hot rum punch delicious, and their mysterious fellow guest kept his distance, safe in the private parlor. In all, Valerian was content. Or he would have been if the memory of that too-small bed didn't lurk at the back of his mind.

It would be easy enough, he told himself. He must simply pretend that he really was a woman. Think of himself as his elderly nanny, the one he'd shared with Lord Harry's one true son. Nana had been plump, comfortable, and about as conversant about sex as an elm tree. She'd cozy up in bed with a young lady, even offer a soft shoulder as a pillow, and no one would think twice.

But even contemplating that was too great a leap for Valerian's imagination. He wasn't going to be able to do it—he knew he couldn't. He sat in front of the fire, half an hour after a yawning Sophie had taken herself upstairs, and he knew he'd be spending the night in a chair there.

He propped his long legs out on the settle, sipping meditatively at his punch. His clothes had finally dried, the damned corset was digging into his ribs, and his huge slippers smelled of wet leather. He wanted to curse the fate which had brought him to this decidedly uncomfortable pass. But he couldn't curse a fate which had brought him to Sophie de Quincey, no matter for how short a time.

He leaned back, contemplating just who their fellow guest, the unseen Mr. Lemur, was. Mine host had suggested he came recently from foreign climes, and he was rather a mysterious gentleman, though well mannered for all that. For a moment Val wondered whether Phelan might have had the ill luck to meet the man during his lengthy travels, but he discarded the notion as unlikely in the extreme. No, odds were that they had nothing to fear from the foreign-traveling Mr. Lemur.

He toyed with the idea of convincing himself that the man was a villain, that he should go up and join Sophie in bed to protect her from the marauding male sex inhabiting this inn. Except that he knew perfectly well he was the most marauding of them all.

She'd be asleep by now. She'd been exhausted, her eyes overbright, and he'd made certain she'd downed enough rum punch to ensure a good night's rest. She would never know he hadn't spent the night at her side.

For that matter, if she were to sleep so soundly, why couldn't he spend the night in bed with her, watching her? It would be his only chance, and surely after all the torment he'd endured, he deserved that much...

He'd had too much rum himself, to be thinking that way. Another mug of it, and he'd start thinking she wouldn't notice if he touched her. If he kissed her. If he slid his hands underneath her thin white undergarments and caressed her warm, creamy flesh…

The sound of footsteps on the stairs was muted, discreet, surreptitious. Valerian flipped his skirts back down over his large feet and sat up, listening. Was that damned villain thinking he could sneak up on a helpless female? Val would cut the man's heart out if he touched her.

He heard the quiet footsteps outside the taproom door. He'd just begun to search around him for a possible weapon when the door opened noiselessly, revealing Sophie standing there in the firelight.

For a moment Valerian didn't move, didn't breathe. Indeed, he couldn't. Sophie was wearing a thin cotton nightdress, and he could see the silhouette of her body in excruciating detail. She'd brushed her long hair and braided it loosely, she'd scrubbed her face, and she looked so damnably young it broke his heart.

"Aren't you coming to bed, Val?" she asked.

"I thought you'd be asleep by now."

"I was waiting for you. I…don't like to sleep in strange beds. It makes me nervous. And the rain is so noisy." She crossed the room, and he saw that her feet were bare. She had beautiful toes.

He stared at her, trying to think of an excuse, so dazed by his longing for her that his brain wasn't working properly. "I'm afraid I snore," he said.

She smiled. "That's all right. I probably do, too."

"I'd take up most of that tiny bed."

"I don't need much room."

*I want to make love to you*, he thought, but didn't say the words out loud. There was no escape, and he should have known it from the beginning. One more fitting piece to his punishment, and he hadn't even done anything so terribly wrong.

He stood up then, admitting defeat. "I'll come upstairs," he said. "But don't expect me to sleep. I'll just sit in the chair and keep you company until you fall asleep..."

"There is no chair." She reached out and took his hand in hers, and there was no missing the wicked expression in her eyes. "It's all right, Val. I know your secret. I promise not to tell a soul."

For a moment he stared at her, shocked. "What secret?" he demanded, his voice unnaturally hoarse. He wondered how he could have given himself away.

"For all that everyone thinks you're such a bold female, I know the truth."

"The truth?" he repeated stupidly.

"You're actually quite modest, aren't you? I saw how uncomfortable you were in helping me to undress. Why, you couldn't even look at me," she said with gentle amusement. "I cannot imagine how a woman with your healthy attitude about the process of mating could suddenly turn so shy. After all, there's not such a great difference in our bodies."

"That's what you think," he said gruffly.

"To be sure, you're quite tall and strong, and in comparison I'm just a little dab of a thing," she admitted. "But we're both female, despite the fact that you're a great deal older and more experienced."

"Actually," he confessed, "I am a bit more comfortable with male bodies. I don't know why..."

"You may undress in the darkness, dear Val," she said with a naughty smile. "I promise not to peek. But please, come to bed. It's cold and lonely up there, and the wind howls around the eaves and frightens me."

He couldn't resist her. He put his arm around her, a major mistake, considering that she was wearing absolutely nothing beneath the thin white cotton, and he could feel the warmth and resiliency of her flesh. He wanted to push her away, feeling burned, but there was no alternative. "I'll come up if you really want," he said in a low, resigned voice. "I am rather tired."

She smiled up at him, winningly. "Thank you, dear Val. I knew I might rely on you."

The bedroom was pitch-black, the rain too intense to allow for a trace of starlight. When he closed the door behind them, it took him a moment to get used to the inky darkness. He could see Sophie flit ghostlike across the room, hear the enticing creak of the bed, and he had to stifle his groan.

"Do you want me to light a candle?" she asked. "There's a nightdress across the foot of the bed that the landlord brought for you."

"No," he said in a strangled voice. He kicked off the damp leather slippers. "I can find it myself," he said more normally.

He encountered her foot first when he groped for the nightdress. Granted, it was beneath a pile of covers, but it still shocked him, and he wondered how he was going to survive a night lying next to her.

He pulled the voluminous nightgown over his head. Fortunately, it was the size of a tent, and he had no difficulty reaching underneath to unfasten the back of his clothes. They were cunningly designed so that he should have little trouble divesting himself of them. One of Hannigan's myriad unseen relatives had crafted them, and not for the first time he thanked that unknown benefactress. He could even unfasten his corset beneath the huge white nightgown. Retying it in the morning would prove quite beyond his capabilities, and he could hardly ask Sophie to assist him. He'd have to hope nobody searched too closely for a willowy waist.

He draped his clothes across the table, hoping the night would remove the last trace of clammy dampness from them, and then turned toward the bed.

"I didn't want to mention it before," Sophie said cheerfully, "but I have excellent night vision."

"Wretch," he said, wondering if the darkness would aid his disguise. Or unmask him.

"I don't know what you're making such a fuss about, Valerie. People share beds with each other all the time. I promise you, I don't have lice."

He laughed despite his tension. "You're a ridiculous child."

"I'm eighteen. About to become engaged," she said, her voice suddenly hollow.

He walked over to the bed, staring down at her in the darkness. "He's made an offer, then," he said resignedly. "That's what your mother was talking about."

"Not yet. But he's going to. Mother's already informed him how pleased we would be."

"She might have asked you."

"Mother doesn't ask people their opinions. She informs them, and expects all and sundry to follow suit." She looked up at Val, and her face was beseeching. "I don't want to marry him."

"Then you shan't," Val said, giving in and climbing into bed beside her. The sheets were fine linen, and warm. From her body, he realized.

"Tell that to my mother."

"I will. The moment we return."

Sophie shifted in the bed, looking at him. "It won't do any good," she said despairingly. "Mother's made up her mind, and there's no moving her once that happens."

"Then we'll have to change Captain Melbourne's." He'd had too much rum punch, he knew that. He'd had too much proximity to temptation, and the entire bed smelled like lavender.

"But how can we do that?"

"We can always ruin you," he said recklessly.

She giggled. "I'm afraid, dear Val, that you lack the necessary equipment to ruin me."

Her artless statement didn't improve his temper. He neither confirmed nor denied it. "We can always say someone else ruined you."

"Who?"

"The mysterious Mr. Lemur. Or my husband. Or Sir Neville Pinworth."

"He's about as likely a candidate as you are, dear Val," she said with a burst of laughter.

"Less likely," he allowed himself to say.

"You're probably right. Well, then, once I'm ruined, what happens next?"

"You come with us to the Continent. We'll visit all the great cities: Paris, Vienna, Florence. We'll live a life of unbridled dissipation."

"I thought we'd need a man for unbridled dissipation. And I'm afraid your husband won't do. He frightens me."

"Phe—Philip?" he countered, genuinely surprised. "Why?"

"He's so dark, and cold, and cynical. He must be a very uncomfortable person to be around."

Valerian thought of his blackened eye. "On occasion," he said wryly. "And I wasn't suggesting you have an affair with him."

"Perhaps we can find me a very handsome lover," Sophie said sleepily, sliding down in the bed, "since you insist that the pleasures of the flesh are worth sampling. I'll count on you to pick the right man for me."

Valerian lay back beside her, arms folded across his chest, stiff in more ways than one. "Describe to me your requirements," he said, "and I'll see what I can do."

"I'd like him to be tall," she said in a dreamy voice, "but not too tall. I do have a partiality for blond hair, and I'd like him to be strong, but not too muscular."

"Not overbuilt like Captain Melbourne?"

"Exactly. Someone a bit leaner. It would be nice if he were handsome, but it's not strictly necessary. I wouldn't want a man who was more interested in his reflection than in me."

Valerian almost laughed. He'd spent an inordinate amount of time staring into a mirror in the past few weeks, out of necessity, not fascination, and he'd yet to find his reflection nearly as interesting as the woman lying too bloody close to him. "Handsome, but not conceited," he noted. "What else?"

"I'd like him to be kind," she said. "And to love the countryside, and to be gentle, and to care about pleasing a woman. I'd want him to love me."

He almost reached for her. She might as well be describing him. Surely there was hope...

"And I'd want him to be honest, and faithful, and never lie to me," she added.

It took him a moment to regain his voice. "A tall order," he said.

"I know. But since I don't intend to marry, it can't hurt to dream, can it?"

"It can. It can hurt very much indeed," he said dolefully.

A streak of lightning illuminated the room for a brief moment, followed by a clap of thunder. Sophie shrieked, and scuttled across the small space he'd kept between them, flinging herself against his shoulder. Instinctively he put his arms around her, knowing he was playing with fire. She settled against him with a contented sigh, her head nestled perfectly against the hollow of his shoulder, and her golden-blond curls were like silk against his stubbled chin. "Do you mind?" she whispered, yawning.

"Not in the slightest, child," he lied, clenching his fists to keep from touching her. He could do this for her. He could hold her and comfort her in the dark and the storm, no matter how tormenting it was for him. He owed her that much for the lies he'd spun her, for the joy she'd given him. He could survive the night. Couldn't he?

It was a close thing. The night was endless, and far too short. She made little noises in her sleep, soft, seductive little sighs and murmurs. He'd expected, and almost hoped, that she'd move away from him once she was solidly asleep. She never did. She clung to him, rubbing her face against his arm like a contented kitten, and there was nothing he could do but lie there in torment, in an odd kind of glory, and hope the morning would come soon. Or not at all.

When he finally slept it wasn't for long, and he awoke as the first rays of dawn were streaking across the darkened bedroom. She still slept in his arms, trustingly, her hand resting on his flat chest, against his skin, inside the voluminous nightdress.

He moved very, very carefully, taking her hand and placing it beside her on the bed, slipping away from her. She roused for a moment, peering at him sleepily through the early dawn light, and he hoped to God she couldn't see clearly. "Are you getting up?"

He *was* up, he thought miserably. "I was always an early riser," he said lightly, wanting nothing more than to join her back in the too-soft, too-small bed. "You sleep some more. We won't be able to leave for several hours at least."

She needed no convincing, snuggling down in the covers with a blissful sigh. He stood there for a moment, watching her. It would be like this if life were different, if he'd been better born, if he'd been able to court her, marry her. He'd wake up every morning and look down at her, sleeping.

As it was, this one morning would have to suffice for the rest of his life.

He didn't know how long he stood there staring at her, drinking in every detail of her rose-flushed cheeks, her softly parted lips, the faint blue veins in her eyelids. And then he turned his back on her, deliberately, and began the arduous task of his toilette.

When he finally emerged from beneath the tentlike folds of the landlady's nightgown, he knew he was in trouble. He'd only managed to fasten the corset around his waist, not use it to manufacture a female figure. The dress was stiff and wrinkled, and no woman in his experience would be caught dead in such an atrocity, and the hat had shrunk. He tiptoed over to the small mirror the inn provided, and his worst fears were confirmed.

It had been almost twenty-four hours since he'd shaved, and no one could miss the light brown stubble on his angular jaw. His eye was quite magnificent, with dark purple bruises almost distracting the gaze from Mrs. Ramsey's incipient beard. Almost, but not quite. His hair hung limply around his face, and despite the bedraggled female clothes, he looked entirely male.

He could think of no way to avail himself of the straight razor he carried in his reticule, not without drawing unwanted attention to himself, and even dusting powder across his face wouldn't provide much disguise. He grabbed his hat, yanked it on his head, and pulled down the veil.

He had a blessed hour alone in the taproom. The landlord himself brought him coffee and then made himself scarce, and he sat there, staring at the dying embers of the fire, and considered the cruelty of life.

The rain had stopped at some point during the night, and the sun was shining weakly through the wet leaves. Valerian lifted his veil to take a better look, then yanked it down again as he heard someone enter the taproom.

"I beg your pardon, I thought the room deserted." The gentleman about to make a hasty retreat could only be the mysterious Mr. Lemur.

"As you can see, it is not," Valerian said in a suitably frosty voice. The man was obviously harmless, and well enough looking for all that. A bit past his first youth, he was neatly dressed, and his brown hair was combed close to his scalp. He had colorless eyes, a pleasant expression, and small hands, and in retrospect there seemed nothing the slightest bit mysterious about him. Just an ordinary gentleman on a trip to Hampton Regis.

"There you are, sir." The innkeeper appeared at the door with his habitual worried expression on his face. "Begging your pardon, my lady, but the private parlor sustained some damage last night. The roof's worse than I thought. Would you condescend to allow this gentleman to share the taproom with you?"

"It is really quite extraordinary," Valerian began the protest, not in the mood for any company, when Sophie's sweet young voice interrupted.

"Of course we wouldn't mind. There can surely be no impropriety, since Mrs. Ramsey and I have each other to lend us countenance. You're welcome to join us, Mr....?"

"Lemur," he said, with a correctness that contained not a trace of unctuousness. So why did Valerian's hackles rise? "Mark-David Lemur, at your service."

"I am Miss de Quincey, and this is Mrs. Ramsey." She'd put her own dress on again, and she looked adorably bedraggled in it. She crossed the room to Valerian, pausing to stare at him, her lips compressed as she struggled not to laugh. And then she couldn't help it. A soft burble of laughter escaped her. "Val! Why in heaven's name are you wearing a veil this morning?"

"You think I look absurd, you should see beneath the veil," he said grimly. "Allow me this tiny bit of vanity, if you please."

"I'm sure you look charming." Sophie sat down beside him, pouring herself a cup of coffee with an ease Valerian had never managed. "Would you care for some, Mr. Lemur?"

"With pleasure, Miss de Quincey," he said promptly, taking a chair opposite them.

Valerian leaned back, watching them with a sour expression concealed by his veil. She was charming Lemur with the same effortless grace with which she'd poured the coffee. It was a social talent, it meant nothing at all, and he was eaten alive by jealousy.

"Are you new to this area, Mr. Lemur?"

"I am. I was on my way to a small coastal village called Hampton Regis when the weather waylaid me."

"That's our home," Sophie said brightly.

"Then perhaps you might have news of the person I'm seeking. A young lad named Julian Smith."

Thank God for the veil, Valerian thought. He didn't have to hide his reaction.

Sophie shook her head. "I'm afraid I don't know him. He can't have lived in Hampton Regis for long, or I'm certain I'd have heard of him…"

"I imagine he's been in town only for a week or so. He's a bond servant of mine, one who stole from me and ran off. I've heard that he was seen in this area, and I hope to catch up with him."

"A distressing tale," Val said in a silken voice. "What did the wretch steal?"

Lemur looked at him with calm, trustworthy eyes. "A pair of diamond-and-pearl earbobs belonging to my wife."

"Shocking," Val breathed. "Yet I wonder why you're in search of the lad yourself. Why not send the Bow Street runners after him?"

"I have a fondness for the boy. He's made a mistake, but I have no doubt that with proper discipline he can be made to see the error of his ways." Lemur smiled, and Val felt a frisson of horror slide down his spine. He'd spent so little time at Sutter's Head recently that he had no idea if

Phelan knew what had sent Juliette into boys' clothes. The answer lay in the pleasant-faced creature in front of him.

Val stretched out a hand for his coffee, hoping the seemingly placid Mr. Lemur wouldn't notice its size. "Now that you mention it," he murmured, "there was a young lad working at the Fowl and Feathers who was newly come to town. I don't remember the boy's name, but he was a well-turned-out lad. Small, brown hair, brown eyes, almost girlish-looking?"

Lemur couldn't disguise his eagerness. "That's him. Where did you say he was? The Fowl and Feathers?"

"Not anymore," Val said sadly. "I gather he ran off more than a week past with half the landlord's silver. Someone said he was seen heading north."

Sophie turned amazed eyes toward him, but she said nothing.

"North? I've just come that way," Lemur said, for a moment letting his placid demeanor slip. "If you ladies will excuse me, I'd best be going."

Valerian could afford to play with him now. "Oh, do stay and have some more coffee," he said affably. "Perhaps the roads are flooded to the north as well. You wouldn't want to get too early a start."

"Thank you, no," Lemur said hastily. "The roads I traveled on traversed higher ground. Even if they are underwater, I'll simply wait. Your servant, ma'am. Miss de Quincey." He almost bowled over the landlord in his speed.

"Has something happened, my lady?" the innkeeper inquired anxiously.

"Nothing at all, my good man," Val said lazily. "Mr. Lemur simply discovered a pressing engagement back the way he had come."

"And I just wanted to inform you all that the road to Hampton Regis is now clear."

"Your timing is excellent. Any sooner, and our friend might have taken off on a wild-goose chase. Would you see to it that the horses are put to the carriage? Miss de Quincey and I should be on our way as well."

The innkeeper pronounced himself more than happy to do the lady's bidding, and quickly absented himself. There was a moment of silence, and then Val cast a glance at Sophie's disapproving expression.

"You lied to him, didn't you?"

She was far too observant, his darling Sophie was. "What do you mean?"

"I remember now—that young boy at the Fowl and Feathers went home with your husband. He didn't steal anything, and he didn't go back north at all, did he?"

"Since you've already told me you despise liars, I'll tell you the truth. Julian Smith is safely lodged at Sutter's Head, and we intend to keep him as far away from Mr. Lemur as we can. I don't believe the lad stole a thing. He's been the subject of cruel treatment, and we're not about to hand him back to a master who abuses him."

"Even though it's the law?" she asked, and he couldn't sense whether she approved or not.

"Even though it's the law," he said firmly. "People should come before the law."

She smiled at him. "You are truly a wonderful woman," she said.

Val controlled his urge to snarl. "Why? Because I take pity on helpless creatures?"

"Yes. And because you don't mind risking your own well-being to help them."

"Don't be ready to grant me sainthood, Sophie. I'm not as kind or noble as you think. I have hidden flaws you would find quite unacceptable."

"I doubt it," she said, her eyes shining. "I think you are truly the most wonderful, kind, honorable human being I have ever known." And she leaned over and kissed him through the veil.

Her aim was far too good. Her mouth touched his through the thin, filmy stuff, and her lips clung to his for one incredible, earth-shattering moment. And then she pulled away, a startled expression on her face.

"Well," she said breathlessly, "if we're going to leave shortly, I'd best see to…er… That is… I'll need a few moments…" She was babbling as she backed out of the room, and her face was pale with confusion.

He watched her go, unmoving, his expression hidden behind the concealing veil. And when he was alone in the room, he began to curse in a quiet, steady voice.

But the sound of his voice brought him no comfort. And he suspected nothing would. Nothing ever would again.

# CHAPTER FIFTEEN

The sun shone fitfully through the damp leaves as Valerian whipped the horses along the muddy road. He was driving too fast, he knew that full well, but he didn't slow down. He needed to get Sophie back to the formidable bosom of her mama. He needed to warn Phelan about the sudden appearance of Mark-David Lemur. Most of all, he needed to shave.

The wind was whipping his veil past his stubbled chin, but Sophie had curled up against him, her eyes closed, her cheeks flushed, and he could only pray she wouldn't notice. Driving at a sedate pace was beyond him at this point. He needed to get home before disaster struck.

He had no idea who Mark-David Lemur was, but he expected Phelan knew full well. Phelan knew just about everything. He would need to be warned. Whatever Lemur's connection to Juliette was, he didn't mean well by her. And neither of the Romneys was going to stand by and let him take her.

He glanced down at the woman curled up beside him. She felt warm, her eyes were overbright, and she complained haltingly of the headache. He suspected yesterday's drenching hadn't done her any good, and he wanted her home, in bed, with hot tea and a posset.

Actually, he wanted her home, in bed, with him, but that wasn't a possibility. He'd already spent the one night he'd ever have with her, and his body was still in torment from it. He probably wouldn't survive another one. Could a man die of frustration? Could his member get so hard for so long that it simply stopped working?

He was going to have a chance to find out, he through wryly, slowing the horses as they approached the outskirts of Hampton Regis. As a medical experiment, it lacked a certain charm. He thought he might possibly prefer death.

Sophie lifted her head when he stopped the carriage outside her parents' house. It was late morning, the sun shone brightly overhead, and her beautiful blue eyes were dazed and feverish.

"Where are we?" she asked, looking up at him with undisguised adoration.

It just about killed him. "Home, love," he murmured.

"That's good. I'm afraid I feel a bit...unwell," she said as the front door opened and her mother appeared.

"Sophie!" There was no denying the passionate concern in her mother's voice as she raced to the carriage. "What has happened? We heard the road was flooded, but we had every faith in Mrs. Ramsey..."

"She's feeling unwell," Valerian said tersely, jumping down from the carriage with a complete disregard for ladylike decorum. By that time Mrs. de Quincey, her tiny, ineffectual husband, and several members of her staff had surrounded the carriage, with the matriarch issuing orders in a stentorian voice. Valerian ignored her, scooping

Sophie's light body up in his strong arms and starting toward the door.

"My dear Mrs. Ramsey!" Mrs. de Quincey gasped. "Let one of the servants carry her. It is quite unseemly…"

He ignored her, striding through the open door and heading for the broad front stairs. "Tell me where her room is."

"I really don't think—"

"Tell me where her room is," he said again, in a voice reminiscent of his brother, and the formidable Mrs. de Quincey nervously complied.

"Is she all right?" she chattered, racing along beside them, the small army of servants thundering in their wake. "Was there an accident, has she been hurt…?"

"I told you, she's feeling unwell. Too much rain, and she caught a chill. A few days in bed and she'll be fine." He sounded graceless, but Mrs. de Quincey was so caught up in her daughter's well-being that she didn't notice.

Sophie's bedroom was the stuff dreams are made of. At least, his dreams. Her bed was large, high, and piled with soft white linens, and he laid her down carefully.

"She needs a hot bath," her mother announced. "She needs a mustard poultice for her chest, and I shall brew an herbal posset for her that will put her in good heart. Mrs. Ramsey, we cannot thank you enough. We'll put a room in order for you immediately—you will not wish to be seen in public until you can secure a change of clothes. We'll send someone out to Sutter's Head to reassure your husband. Mr. de Quincey, see to it. Walker, tell the cook to make some chicken soup. Mary, accompany me…" She disappeared, issuing orders, taking her crowd of servants and her husband with her. Leaving Valerian alone with Sophie.

It would last only for a moment. Her maid would reappear, once she'd absorbed all of her mistress's commands, and he would be effectively banished. He stared down at Sophie, and he told himself this would have to be the last time he saw her. He couldn't trust himself otherwise.

She was asleep, or nearly so, her cheeks flushed, her breathing rapid. And then her eyes opened, and she looked up at him, and smiled.

"You look an absolute quiz," she said softly.

"Flatterer," he replied in not much more than a whisper. "Your mother's rallying the forces, and I'm getting out of here. Good-bye, dear girl."

Distress crossed her face. "You'll be back."

He'd lied so much, he didn't want to lie again. "I'm not certain. Mr. Ramsey has talked about leaving for the Continent, and a wife's duty is to follow her husband."

"You never struck me as particularly dutiful."

"There's a great deal about me that might surprise you," he said wryly, giving in to temptation and stroking her cheek.

She turned and pressed her lips against his hand. "Promise me," she whispered. "Promise me you won't leave without saying good-bye."

"Good-bye," he said, leaning down to kiss her cheek.

At the wrong moment she turned. He'd lifted the hem of his veil, just enough to let his lips brush against her face, but instead, his mouth landed on hers. Hot and wet and open.

He wanted to use his tongue. He wanted to climb onto the bed, push her down, and make love to her. He groaned, deep in his throat, and pulled away before he could do worse than simply give her the beginnings of a man's kiss.

She was staring at him, white with shock. The crumpled

veil obscured his face, and God only knew if she'd felt the stubble on his chin. He didn't think so, but he couldn't stay around long enough to find out.

"Good-bye," he said again. And he turned and left her, without a backward glance.

Phelan Romney's mood had gone from bad to worse. His uncertain temper wasn't improved when his brother strode into the library just before noon, taking his bedraggled hat off his head and throwing it into the fireplace. On a warm summer's day no fire was burning, but the gesture still retained force.

"Good God," Phelan said faintly, surveying his sibling. "Did you drive through town looking like that?"

Valerian threw himself into a chair. His black eye was magnificent in coloration, he needed a shave, and he looked as if he wanted to hit someone. Phelan wondered idly whether he was to have that honor.

"I had no bloody choice. We were stranded ten miles away from Hampton Regis and forced to spend the night in an inn."

Phelan sat up in alarm. "Val, you didn't…"

"No, I damned well didn't. I spent the whole bloody night in her bloody bed with her bloody head on my bloody shoulder and I never touched her!"

"Good for you," Phelan said faintly.

Valerian surged out of the chair and stalked across the room, leaning over the desk with a pugnacious expression on his face. One that was particularly comic, given his limp, ruffled apparel. "Good for me," he mimicked. "I'll tell you what's good for me. We're getting out of here. I'm sick and tired of waiting for Hannigan to come up with a happy solution, I'm sick and tired of sitting around on my bum doing nothing, and if I see Sophie de Quincey again, I'm going to—" He stopped, belated gentlemanly restraint keeping him from informing his brother exactly what he longed to do to his bluestocking.

"I can imagine," Phelan said wryly.

"I won't fight you anymore," Valerian said. "You've got your wish. We're getting out of here, and we're taking Juliette with us."

Phelan froze. "No! I've told you, she's staying. You're not going to get rid of your sexual frustrations on her."

"Do you think I'm that kind of man? I ought to black your eye," Valerian said dangerously.

Phelan barely managed a wry smile. "You're looking for an excuse to hit me, and doubtless I deserve it. I might enjoy a good mill as well—I haven't been any too satisfied myself recently, but it would be a waste of time. Thank God you're finally willing to get out of here, but we're leaving Juliette behind."

"To the tender mercies of the man looking for her?"

Phelan grew very still. "I didn't tell you about him," he said with great surety.

"No, you didn't. We ran into him in the inn. A seemingly pleasant fellow named Lemur, who said he was looking for his runaway bond servant. A boy named Julian Smith."

"Bloody hell."

"Oh, don't worry, brother mine. I told him she'd taken off north with half the contents of the town, and he raced off after her. But I don't know how long that will wash. Sooner or later he'll come back. And I'm not about to hand her over to him."

"No," said Phelan. "Neither am I."

"She isn't his bond servant, is she?"

"She's his wife."

Valerian let out a low whistle. "Then we'd better get out of here," he said. "And fast."

"Are you traveling like that?"

"This will be the last time I climb into these damned skirts," he warned.

"Don't be any too hasty. It might take a day or two to book passage. In the meantime, keep away from your bluestocking."

"Oh, I intend to. But I wouldn't take my time. I may have put Lemur off the scent, but it was a temporary thing. He'll be here sooner or later, and I expect it will be sooner."

Phelan considered the notion. There would be nothing he'd like better than to vent some of his frustration on that little worm. He'd hurt Juliette, hurt her quite badly, and for that he wanted to kill him.

Unbidden, the train of thought continued. If he killed him, as Lemur no doubt deserved, then Juliette would be a widow.

Why the hell should her marital status matter to him? He simply wanted to see her safe. As far away from her husband as Valerian's bluestocking.

"We'll leave," he said. "In the meantime, keep out of town. You must have caused enough comment already."

Valerian glared at him. "You aren't going to give me a chance to hit you, are you?"

Phelan laughed bitterly. "Not this time. When we reach France you can do your damnedest to pummel me. Then it won't matter if you have a second black eye."

"You think so, do you?"

"I'm bigger than you, little brother. I always could out-box you."

"I'm madder than you, big brother. And a hell of a lot more frustrated."

Phelan thought back to his encounter with Juliette in the rain-soaked garden. "I wouldn't count on it," he said wryly.

In the end, they had far less time than Phelan would have hoped. He rode into Hampton Regis that afternoon, with the ostensible purpose of calling on the de Quinceys to make certain their daughter had suffered no ill effects from her sojourn on the road. In reality, he had two goals. One, to make sure that Valerian hadn't given himself away. And two, to book passage on the next boat, ship, or raft bound for France. Or anywhere away from England.

He failed in both those endeavors. Mrs. de Quincey received him, but she was distraught, distracted, and barely civil. Sophie was decidedly unwell, the doctor had been called, and she would be unable to receive visitors for any length of time. Phelan had politely taken his leave, wondering whether Sophie's indisposition had any emotional component.

The search for passage to the Continent was even less fruitful. The one ship in the small harbor had sustained damage during the heavy rains, and none of the smaller boats could be hired for love or money. The best he could come away with was a promise for three days hence. He had the uneasy feeling that might be too late.

He wanted to get back to the house. He hadn't seen Juliette since their midnight encounter in the rain, telling himself he didn't care, knowing he was lying. He forced himself to stop by the Fowl and Feathers, strolling into the taproom with a negligent air, intent on proving to the world that Mr.

Ramsey had nothing to hide. Seeing Sir Neville Pinworth in the corner, deep in conversation with another man, didn't improve his mood, and he almost turned and left.

"There he is!" Sir Neville announced in his high, mincing voice, after lifting his head and espying Phelan. "What luck! Philip, join us. You'll never guess who this gentleman has come in search of."

Bloody hell! Phelan didn't move, couldn't move, as Mark-David Lemur turned to face him, a placid expression on his blandly handsome face. And then his colorless eyes narrowed as he looked into Phelan's face.

They'd met only once, several years ago in Alexandria. They'd shared a bottle of wine and enough desultory conversation for Phelan to recognize that Lemur was a strange soul, then had separated. Another man might not even recognize him.

"We've already met." Lemur rose. "It's been a long time, Romney."

"Indeed, it has," Sir Neville said with a giggle. "You've even forgotten his name. It's Ramsey, Philip Ramsey."

"Of course it is," Lemur said smoothly, a pleasant smile on his face. "Forgive my *gaucherie*."

"There's nothing to forgive," Phelan murmured, knowing he had no choice but to brazen this through. "It's good to see you again, Lemur. What is it you're in search of? I'd be more than happy to be of assistance."

"It's the boy," Sir Neville crowed.

Phelan arched an eyebrow. "The boy? I haven't the faintest idea what you're talking about."

"Don't be deliberately obtuse. The serving lad who was working here. You spirited him away from under my nose, and if he isn't still happily ensconced at Sutter's Head, I would have heard about it. I made it my business to enquire after his well-being." Pinworth's predatory smile exposed yellow teeth. "I have a kindness for young boys in need of a helping hand."

"I think I may have met your wife," Lemur said smoothly. "At a small inn not ten miles north of here. I look forward to making her acquaintance again. And to finding my nephew."

"Your nephew?" Phelan could be just as smooth. "I hardly think the young man who's been working in the stables at Sutter's Head could be your nephew."

"Working in the stables!" Pinworth exclaimed. "What a waste!"

"He seems to enjoy himself. He's good with the horses."

"He always was," Lemur said. "But I'm afraid his little adventure is over. I intend to take him back to London with me as soon as may be. I'll accompany you out to your house, if I may."

There was nothing Phelan could say. "What made the boy run off in the first place?"

"A misunderstanding. He considered me too harsh a guardian, but, of course, children sometimes see things that way. I intend to convince him of my love and devotion the moment we're reunited."

Phelan wanted to kill him. He'd killed before, in the army, when his own life had been threatened. He didn't consider himself a particularly violent man, but right then the notion of cold-blooded murder had a definite appeal.

"My wife is very fond of young Julian," Phelan said. "I think I'd best prepare her for your arrival."

"I imagine she's already prepared," Lemur said politely. "She was full of helpful information when I met her. I'm afraid she thought I meant the poor boy ill. You can set her mind at ease."

"I don't think—"

"Come now, Romney!" Pinworth protested, obviously enjoying himself immensely. "You can't keep a man away from his nephew. Particularly when he's the boy's guardian. Accept it, man; you're going to have to lose him. Might as well put a good face on it."

Phelan wondered idly whether he might kill Sir Neville as well. It would be a waste of energy, he decided. He had no choice but to take Lemur back to Sutter's Head with him. He'd find his way out there sooner or later, and Phelan preferred keeping an eye on him.

"I still think it would be better to warn my wife," he said. "But if you're determined, we might as well leave now. It's getting dark—you'll accept our hospitality for the night, won't you, Lemur?"

"With pleasure." It was all so damned polite, Phelan thought. If he weren't so suspicious, if he hadn't known the truth about Juliette, felt her shiver in his arms, he might believe in the bland surface Lemur presented to the world. Except for the rumors he'd heard in Egypt. About the Cairo girl scarred for life. And the missing maidservant.

Neither of them said a word as they rode out of town along the westerly road. The path followed the line of cliffs, and beneath it the sea was still stormy, precluding a midnight escape. Phelan kept his face remote, his thoughts to himself, until Lemur drew abreast of him.

"I didn't realize you had a nephew," Phelan murmured.

"And I didn't know you had married, Romney. Beg pardon, I mean Ramsey," Lemur corrected himself in a mild tone that belied his malicious intent. "I am desolate to take my nephew away, but he's a rebellious lad."

"And you tried to beat submission into him?" Phelan asked the question lightly, waiting for a response.

The one he received was subtle and sickening. Just a flash of unholy excitement in Lemur's pale eyes before he shook his head. "Of course not," he murmured. "I've tried to shower the boy with love. It does seem odd that you'd lure him back to your home. Were you in need of servants, or did you suspect my nephew wasn't quite what he seemed?"

Phelan smiled blandly, almost enjoying the verbal battle. "I could tell he was obviously better bred than he wanted anyone to believe. As for luring him to my home, we viewed it more in the light of a rescue."

"Indeed?" Lemur was just as good at dissembling. "How so?"

"You've met Pinworth. He took a fancy to the boy, and my wife and I decided your nephew was too young to judge the danger an experienced roué like Sir Neville could offer him. At least at Sutter's Head he was safe."

"As he is with me, of course."

"Of course," Phelan murmured.

"And how are your dear parents?" Lemur asked.

Phelan's hands tightened on the reins as he urged his horse forward. "You've never met them," he pointed out with less than his usual grace.

"True," said Lemur. "But I've heard so much about them in the past few weeks. Your half brother as well."

Phelan glanced over at the cliffs. He was a larger man than Lemur, taller, and perhaps ten years younger. But Lemur had a bull-like torso and very strong arms, and he was on his guard. It would be no simple matter to entice him to the cliffs and then push him over. Particularly when Phelan wasn't certain the man deserved to die, much as it might convenience him.

"They are all doing splendidly," Phelan said coolly.

"So glad to hear it."

It was close to evening when they rode up to Sutter's Head. There was no sign of Valerian, and Phelan could only hope he wouldn't come galloping up, dressed in his own clothes, while Lemur was watching. He still wasn't quite sure what he was going to do about the uninvited guest. Clearly Lemur knew about his father's murder, knew that his brother was the chief suspect. He had only to drop a word or two in the right ear and Valerian would be hauled off to jail.

But the alternative was unacceptable. Phelan wasn't going to let Lemur take Juliette away. The notion of having the man bound and gagged and sent far away from England in the hold of a ship held a certain merit, even if it didn't contain quite the visceral satisfaction that cold-blooded murder did. Whatever happened, Phelan Romney could take care of his own. His younger brother. And Juliette MacGowan, who had somehow, unexpectedly, become his as well. Even if neither of them would accept it as yet.

"We'll be having a guest for the night, Hannigan," Phelan said easily as he slid off his horse.

Hannigan was eyeing Lemur with his bland servant's expression, one that hid his devious mind. "Shall I be informing Mrs. Ramsey? She saw your approach from the window and I imagine she'll be down directly."

"That will be time enough. Come along, Lemur," he said. "We can open a bottle of claret before my wife joins us. She's a sad romp, and greatly addicted to her vanity, so it might take her a while."

"I did think the veil she was wearing was a bit odd," Lemur remarked.

"She'd been through a distressing night, and she had neither a maid nor a hair-dresser to assist her. Not to mention fresh clothes."

"The lady did, however, have another young lady with her."

"A most charming young lady," Phelan agreed. "She and my wife are close friends."

Lemur simply nodded. He was good, Phelan had to admit that. He had no idea whether Lemur recognized the identity of his putative wife or not, and nothing short of a flat-out question would avail him of the answer. He wasn't ready to be frank. Lemur would be just as uncertain as to whether Phelan knew the identity of his so-called nephew, and Phelan preferred to keep it that way. It was a small enough weapon in their war of wits.

"I'd like to see my nephew," Lemur announced, following him into the library.

"There's no hurry, is there? After all, he has nothing to be afraid of, does he?"

"Of course not. But you know children. They can dream up the most extreme fantasies." He settled himself in Phelan's favorite chair, his movements small and precise. "I wouldn't want you to warn him."

"Why should I do that?"

"Out of a misguided concern for his well-being, perhaps?" Lemur suggested. "Your wife lied to me about him. She was foolish enough to tell me he'd taken off to the north. I hadn't gone but a few miles before I decided to continue to Hampton Regis after all. My nephew might have run in the first place, but he'd have no reason to do so again. I don't hold it against your wife, of course. We don't know each other that well—I had even forgotten your name. You might assume I was in reality a dastardly villain. Believe me, I have no interest in harming young boys."

Their eyes met, and there was a flash of cold, murderous understanding. "I'm certain you don't," Phelan said. "I'll go in search of him."

Lemur moved, blocking the exit. It was absurd, given that he was shorter and older, but Phelan wasn't ready to wrestle him out of the way. "Send for him," Lemur said.

Hannigan, bless his heart, appeared at the door. "Could I be getting you something, Mr. Ramsey?"

"A bottle of claret and two glasses," Phelan said. "And have the young boy bring them. Julian, I believe his name is."

Hannigan didn't even blink, but Phelan had no doubt the message was received. "Very good, sir. I'll see if I can scare up the lad."

"He's not here?" Lemur demanded sharply.

"I've not seen him for several hours. He was going for a walk, seeing as how he wasn't needed. I imagine he'll be getting home soon. It's nearly time for supper, and you know how young lads are when it comes to food. Shall I send him in?"

"Yes," Lemur said, the polite pretense slipping for a moment.

"See to it, Hannigan. Our guest grows impatient." Phelan took another chair, stretching his legs out in a casual gesture that belied the fury in his heart. "The boy means a great deal to you, Lemur."

"More than you can imagine." He'd once more regained control of his facade. "There is nothing more important than the bonds of family, is there? The love of a brother for a brother, for instance. You have a brother, don't you? A half brother somewhere?"

The message was clear. Lemur had heard the rumors, and if he guessed the identity of Phelan's putative wife, they'd be facing disaster.

That disaster wasn't yet upon them. Phelan smiled sardonically. "Unfortunately, my brother is traveling abroad. But I understand your meaning. It will be my pleasure to reunite you with your nephew."

"I knew you would see it my way," Lemur murmured.


"Find Juliette at once," Valerian hissed. "Forget about me."

"I've been trying, Lord love you," Hannigan snapped back, yanking on the corset strings. "Half my family is out looking for her. She must have wandered off down the strand."

"You don't suppose she's run away, do you?" Valerian mused, sucking in his breath as Hannigan pulled. "She's attempted it before."

"I doubt it. Her clothes are still in her room, and your brother still has her earbobs. She wouldn't get far without any money. I imagine she's just forgotten the time."

"She's going to walk right in on that bastard," Valerian fumed, pulling a yellow sarcenet day dress over his head with a muffled curse. "Damn, I thought I wouldn't have to wear these things again."

"It's for Miss Juliette's sake," Hannigan said, handing him the powder pot.

"Can't you just do something about the man, Hannigan? Have some member of your limitless family drop him down a well or a deserted mine or something?"

"This isn't mining country," Hannigan said reprovingly.

"Well, do something about him. I can't imagine why Phelan would have brought him home, but obviously he had no choice."

"Obviously. He already knows the man."

Valerian accepted that information in momentary silence. "Then we'll have to kill him," he said flatly. "Might as well, since I'm being hunted for a murder I didn't commit. They're going to catch me sooner or later, and probably hang me. I might as well do something decent to deserve it."

"Don't talk that way, young master," Hannigan said in a disapproving voice. "There's a way out of this tangle, I'm sure of it."

"I've yet to see it. We're running out of possibilities, Hannigan. For all of us."

"We still have time," said Hannigan. "Which is more than I can say for the man downstairs. If he's threatening his lordship, he'll have me to deal with."

Valerian shoved his feet into an oversize pair of slippers, tossed back his hair, and laughed. "A harmless, oversize bear like you, Hannigan?" he hooted. "Better leave the dirty work to me. At least I'll earn my keep."

"Flirt with the man," Hannigan said. "I'll go out after Miss Juliette. I don't want her to see him without being warned. There's no telling what she might say or do."

"Look after her," Valerian said. "For my brother's sake, if not for hers."

"Lord love you, do you think I didn't notice?" Hannigan said, incensed. "Don't you worry, young master. I'll keep her safe for his lordship if I can. You just take a care for yourself. I don't trust that man."

And Valerian, remembering Lemur's pale eyes and soft, cruel smile, nodded. "Neither do I," he said. And departed the room in a cloud of perfume, ready to do battle.

# CHAPTER SIXTEEN

Juliette had given up running away. It was a wasted effort, a lost cause. She wasn't going to get away from Phelan Romney until he was good and ready to let her go, and that moment didn't seem imminent. The best she could do was accept her fate with good grace.

She just wished she didn't feel so dratted cheerful about it.

The aftermath of the storm had a beneficial effect on the land, giving everything a hazy, freshly washed look. She couldn't say whether it had as beneficial an effect on her. She felt edgy, restless, disturbed, with a longing to see Phelan, to be alone with him, that was quite irrational.

Fortunately for her, he left the house early. Dulcie shooed her out of the kitchen, Hannigan sent her from the stables, and she was left with a fine day on her hands and nothing to do with it. She ended up hiking down to the old wreck, going barefoot on the rain-slick trail, unencumbered by anything more than a kerchief wrapped around an apple, a hunk of bread, and a bit of cheese. There was something about the place that called to her. The eerie skeleton of the old ship with its toppled masts framed against the post-storm sky was hardly the most cheerful sight in the world, but then, Juliette wasn't in the most cheerful of moods. She wanted a quiet place, to think, to plan, to reflect. And the somber beauty of Dead Man's Cove was the answer.

She lost track of time. Sitting barefoot on the beach, her legs drawn up in the circle of her arms, she watched the sea crash against the ruined hull of the ship. The violence of the surf matched the violence of her emotions, and for some reason she found the remnants of nature's rampage soothing. Disaster was coming, lurking, though she couldn't say how she knew.

By the time she realized she ought to be getting back, the sun was sinking low behind the headland. She made her way slowly back up the path, wondering whether Phelan would think she'd tried to run off again. When at last she reached the boundaries of Sutter's Head, a mist had closed in, obscuring everything.

The large kitchen was deserted, despite the food cooking in the huge ovens. There was no sign of the servants in the yard, or anywhere about.

She considered going to her room and staying put. She heard the distant sound of voices from the library— Valerian's husky, feminine drawl, Phelan's deeper voice. If she had any sense, she'd keep away, but she'd already proved she had no brains at all when it came to the master of the house. She hadn't seen Phelan since those brief, wild moments in the rain-soaked garden, and she couldn't keep away from him. She hadn't been able to think of much else but him, the feel of his hands on her bare breasts, the touch of his mouth on hers. She needed to see him, to prove to herself that it was all midnight madness. That in the cool, clear light of day she was invulnerable.

But it wasn't daylight; it wasn't cool or clear. It was foggy, warm, and dark, and her emotions were still rampant. She should keep away from him. But she couldn't.

The door to the library stood ajar. She pushed it open, hesitating, as the three inhabitants of the room turned to stare at her. Valerian was frowning at her quite fiercely, and he looked absurd in yellow frills. Phelan stood in the background, his expression unreadable as always. And then her gaze fell on the third man, and terror swept through her, so intense that she couldn't move, couldn't run, couldn't even speak. She simply looked into the pale, blank eyes of her husband in shock.

"Nephew!" he said, rising from his chair and crossing the room to her. "How long I've waited for this reunion!"

Juliette tried to back away, but the door came up behind her, and there was nowhere she could go. Lemur flung his arms around her, clasping her against his body, and his fingers dug into the sensitive skin of her upper arms with painful urgency.

She made no sound of distress, as he'd taught her, and when he released her there was a look of smug satisfaction on his bland face.

Through her panic she could feel Phelan's eyes on her, watching her reaction. He'd brought Lemur back to Sutter's Head, obviously willing to hand her over. Lemur must have met the price Romney had insisted didn't exist.

And then Valerian insinuated himself between them, his full skirts an effective barrier, and his large hands on Juliette's were gentle. "Naughty boy," he crooned, his eyes dark with worry. "Not to tell us about your uncle. Here we thought you were a poor orphan, cast adrift upon the world, when in actuality you had a guardian who clearly loves you deeply." He squeezed her hands reassuringly. "Such a happy reunion."

"Yes," Juliette whispered.

Lemur tried to move closer, but Valerian was a great deal larger, and he managed to block the older man, much to Lemur's obvious frustration. In another time, another place, Juliette might have found the byplay amusing. Right now she was simply sick with dread.

"We'll be leaving now, Ramsey," Lemur announced. "No need to trespass on your hospitality a moment further."

"Nonsense," Valerian said. He turned his back on Juliette and began advancing on Lemur. "We wouldn't think of letting you leave, would we, Philip?"

"We wouldn't think of it," Phelan echoed in a cool voice.

"It's been a while since you've seen your dear nephew," Valerian continued, "and obviously you parted on not the best of terms. We insist you stay here for a few days to get reacquainted."

"I wish to take Julian back to London immediately," Lemur stated. "I've been away from my affairs for too long as it is."

"Feel free to go," Phelan said affably. "We'll bring Julian up to join you in a week or so."

"I'm not leaving without him."

"Then you'll simply have to stay for a few days, won't you, Lemur?" Phelan murmured. "Don't try to fight it— you know how women are when they make up their minds, and my wife's as stubborn as a goat. Tell me, old man, are you married?"

Juliette felt sick inside. Lemur was watching her, and

his blank expression terrified her. "As a matter of fact, I am," he said. "To a spoiled, willful creature who's much in need of discipline."

"Rather like your nephew, Mr. Lemur?" Valerian asked archly. "I might venture to give you a hint. It's a great deal easier to secure cooperation if you use a gentle hand."

Lemur seemed to collect himself. "Dear lady," he purred, "I am the soul of gentleness. I seek only to renew my acquaintance and very real affection for my nephew."

"And what better place but here, Mr. Lemur?" Valerian countered. "Your room is already made up, and we won't take 'no' for an answer. Will we, Philip?"

"We won't," Phelan said.

Lemur's smile was a tight one, and it boded ill for the future. He was going to hurt her, Juliette thought. Before, he had hurt her for no reason; now he had what many might consider justification. Valerian's attempts at protecting her would probably only make it worse.

It didn't matter. She felt numb with fear and betrayal. Phelan had brought Lemur here. Phelan had sold her out. She should have known that no man could be trusted. She'd never considered herself particularly dull-witted; why hadn't she learned such a simple lesson?

"We'll leave in the morning," Lemur said, and his light voice was implacable.

But Valerian was in full force, playing his role to the hilt, and he batted his naturally long eyelashes at Juliette's stony-faced husband and tucked his arm through Lemur's. "If you insist," he cooed. "But I intend to see whether I can persuade you to extend your stay just a little bit longer. I have to make up for my little prevarication at the inn. How was I to know what a charming man you were?

After all, you spun me some faradiddle about Julian being a thieving bond servant, and I knew that couldn't be true. We've grown very fond of the boy, and we're not ready to part with him. Besides, I would adore the chance to get to know you better. My husband is a frightful bore, and an attractive new man is a gift from heaven."

Juliette was too sick inside to be amused, but Lemur actually preened, allowing himself to be flattered. "Dear lady," he said unctuously, "there is nothing I'd like better than to spend time here, but my business needs are pressing."

"And your wife must miss you dreadfully," Valerian murmured sweetly.

"Dreadfully," Lemur echoed, his colorless eyes meeting Juliette's, and she shivered.

"We'll deal with tomorrow when it arrives," Phelan said. "In the meantime, Julian hasn't eaten, and most of the staff are out scouring the woods for him. Got to the kitchen, lad, and find yourself something to eat. Then you can retire for the night while we discuss your future with your uncle."

She looked at him for a long, silent moment, the sense of betrayal clear in her eyes. "Don't you want me to serve dinner, sir?" she said.

It might have been wishful thinking on her part, or sheer imagination. It might have been the ungovernable tension of the moment. But Phelan Romney looked guilty at the reminder of how he'd tried to humiliate her the previous night.

"Go to bed," he snapped, making no effort to be pleasant. "We'll deal with you in the morning."

For the moment, Valerian had managed to captivate Mark-David Lemur, and the two of them were seemingly unaware. Juliette's eyes locked on Phelan's, and for a brief moment she let her emotions run free, no longer hiding her reactions. And then she turned and left, closing the door silently behind her.

Phelan stood very still, oblivious to his brother's arch efforts to flirt with Lemur. Juliette's expression burned in his mind, his belly, what passed for his heart. Betrayal and loss had shadowed her eyes. She thought he'd handed her over to Lemur.

He ought to be angry with her for doubting his word. Instead, he felt an odd gratification. For with that betrayal and loss was a longing that she no longer bothered to hide. She wanted him, perhaps not as much as he wanted her, but the need was there, buried beneath her fear and hurt. If he could just get rid of Lemur, he could have her.

There was never any question that he'd get rid of Lemur. He wouldn't turn a dog over to that brute—he'd hardly let him get his hands on Juliette. But the situation had to be handled delicately. Despite his murderous impulses, he couldn't really kill Lemur. He simply needed to make sure he never came near Juliette again.

Phelan had to admire his brother. Valerian had thrown himself into his role with wholehearted abandon, taunting and teasing Lemur with a malicious glee that his victim missed entirely. Once Phelan managed to squash the irrational pangs of jealousy over Juliette, he could admit that Valerian had a very innocent fondness for the girl, and his urge to punish Lemur was possibly as great as his own.

He watched them over the dinner table, saying little, his mind busy with various plots. While he'd recognized the panic in Juliette's face when she'd seen Lemur, he had also recognized the hopelessness and defeat. As terrified as she was, she wouldn't run. She'd given up hope.

It was up to him to rescue her, a task he viewed with pleasure. He hadn't had the chance to play knight-errant before, and for once the notion appealed to him, particularly when he intended to claim his reward.

Though it wouldn't do to underestimate Lemur. The man had a certain cunning, and while Valerian was enjoying himself, it would be foolish to assume he'd manage to make Lemur forget his reason for being at Sutter's Head.

Phelan left the two of them alone, flirting archly, as he stepped out into the garden, ostensibly to avail himself of a cheroot. He didn't actually intend to smoke, but he wanted a few moments of privacy. When he returned, Valerian was alone, a disgusted expression on his face.

"That man's a menace," he said flatly.

Phelan smiled sourly. "What did he do, pinch you?"

"As a matter of fact, he did. Hard enough to raise a bruise," he replied. "I wasn't sure I'd be able to fob him off. Lord, but I would have liked to pound the little worm."

"You were promising a great deal. I suspect he, unlike Pinworth, wouldn't be any too happy to discover what lies beneath your skirts."

"Put a sock in it," Valerian growled. "I wouldn't exert myself for just anyone. Did you see the expression on Juliette's face when she saw Lemur? I thought she was going to throw up. We're not going to let him have her."

"Of course we're not. I'm simply not certain how far we'll have to go to keep him from getting her." Phelan frowned. "He has gone directly to his room, hasn't he?"

"I escorted him there myself, much to the sorrow of

my poor, abused backside," Valerian snarled. "The man's a beast."

"I suspect that may be putting it mildly. I think I'll make certain our guest is safely settled for the night. It wouldn't do to underestimate the man."

Valerian shuddered, and there was nothing delicate or feminine about the gesture. "He's an evil man, Phelan."

Phelan's uneasiness grew. "I know," he said. And he started for the door.

"There you are, my love." Mark-David's soft, oily voice slid over Juliette like rancid grease as he stood in her open doorway, a key in one hand. He surveyed her with a pleasant smile that made her blood run cold.

She didn't move. She knew from past experience that it would do no good. He was blocking the only exit, and if she tried to scramble off the bed, to run away, he would have an excuse to hurt her. She simply watched him.

"I'd forgotten you had a taste for playing the boy," he continued in a meditative voice. "I shouldn't have indulged you earlier. It's no wonder you failed to excite me sufficiently in the past. You need to be taught who and what you are. A mere woman, and my possession."

She had to try. "Leave me be, Mark-David," she pleaded. "I'll disappear; no one need ever hear from me again. You can keep my money…"

"Don't be absurd, child," he said. "I'll keep your money anyway. A husband has sole rights to his wife's inheritance under English law. Surely you're bright enough to realize that. As for your disappearing—you've already tried. And I've scoured the country, looking for you. Now that

I've found you," he said dreamily, reaching out his hand to touch her, "I have no intention of letting you go."

She flinched, but he wasn't about to allow her to escape. He stroked the side of her face, the caress a mockery. "I haven't yet decided which of the Romneys you're enamored of—Phelan or his long meg of a wife. It won't do you any good, you know. Once Romney realizes you're a girl, he'll be quite disgusted. And I fancy his wife is more interested in the opposite sex than her own."

A faint ray of hope penetrated Juliette's despair. So Lemur wasn't quite as clever as he thought he was. He assumed Phelan accepted her as a boy; he hadn't realized Valerian was embarked on the same masquerade. If Lemur could make two mistakes, he could make more.

"We'll leave in the morning," he said in a dreamy voice. "I intend to take you to Chichester—we need privacy to continue our honeymoon." He smiled faintly. "And don't think that Romney will save you."

His use of Phelan's real name suddenly penetrated her fear. "Ramsey," she said in a rusty voice.

"That's what he's told you. But he lied. His name is Phelan Romney, and he and his brother murdered their father."

"They couldn't have!" Juliette protested, shocked.

"Oh, but I'm afraid they did. At least one of them, but since they both ran off, it doesn't really matter which one did it. Not that I care. He can slaughter his entire family if he chooses to, as long as he leaves me and mine alone." Lemur's smile was chilling. "No one has the faintest idea where he is, you know. Except me." He took a step back. "I wouldn't hesitate to let the authorities know where they might find him. And doubtless he'd have to tell where his brother is as well."

"You wouldn't!"

"There's no need to. Not as long as you come with me. You need to convince Romney and his wife that you're very happy to return with me. Or I won't answer for the consequences."

"He wouldn't try to stop you. He brought you out here."

"Against his will. There wasn't much he could do to keep me from accompanying him, once that pansy Pinworth told me where to find you. Romney has a certain fondness for you, Juliette. I wonder if he shares Pinworth's tastes."

It took a moment for Mark-David's malicious words to sink in. "He didn't want to bring you?"

"I was half expecting him to try to push me off a cliff. But I'm far too clever for the likes of him."

"Far too clever," Juliette murmured dazedly.

Lemur let his hand trail down her throat, using his fingernails against her delicate skin. "I've waited too long for you, Juliette," he said in a hoarse voice. "I won't wait much longer." And his hand tightened against her throat.

"Lemur."

Phelan's voice was quietly reasonable, yet Lemur withdrew his hand, stepping back swiftly from the bed. He glanced at his dark host as he stood in the doorway. "I was just discussing our future plans with my nephew," he said, and there was only a faint tremor in his voice.

"Tomorrow's time enough for that, don't you think?" It was said in the mildest of voices, but Lemur wasn't fool enough to think that he had any choice in the matter.

"Of course. Till tomorrow, Julian." Lemur moved into

the hallway. Juliette lifted her head to look at Phelan, knowing she had no reason to hope, but hoping anyway.

"I didn't want to bring him," he said in a voice that carried only to her ears.

"I know."

"You're not going anywhere with him."

Ah, but she was. This time she had no choice. Lemur would do as he said and more. If she begged Phelan for help, he'd give it to her, but he and Valerian would be destroyed, and she couldn't let that happen.

She could take care of herself. She had wits, she had courage. She'd survived Lemur before; she would do so again. As long as she got him away from the Romneys, she could deal with anything.

She didn't answer Phelan, and he didn't seem to expect her to. He closed the door behind him, and she heard the polite murmur of voices as he escorted Lemur away from her room. Juliette got out of bed and went over to the door, leaning her head against it and shivering. This was her last night.

Her last night of freedom, her very last night when she could call her body her own. Tomorrow Lemur would take her away from here, no matter what the Romney's did to stop him. Tomorrow Lemur would take her body, and he would undoubtedly finish what he'd tried to do so many times before. He would hurt her, and debase her, and in the end, he might very well kill her. She could only hope he did.

But tonight was her own, to do with as she pleased. And she wasn't going to spend that night locked away in her room, quaking like a scared rabbit. She was going to wait until it was dark, seek out Phelan Romney, and give him what Lemur had been unable to take.

She was going to make love with Phelan Romney, and deprive Lemur of his final triumph.

Phelan was alone in his room when he heard the quiet footsteps in the hallway. Lemur was at the far end, trapped, though he didn't realize it. Hannigan was keeping an eye on his door, and if he tried to leave, he'd be politely, efficiently stopped.

Those weren't Hannigan's footsteps, or Valerian's. Despite his brother's efforts, he simply hadn't managed a feminine glide. No blind person would ever mistake Valerian's approach for that of a woman.

Dulcie had a heavy tread, and she wouldn't be wandering around the upper story in the middle of the night. There could be only one person moving quietly outside his room.

Phelan was lying stretched out on his bed, fully clothed, his shirt undone, a glass of brandy in his hand. He'd left the window open. It was a cool night, but the damp summer air soothed him. It was well after midnight—Valerian had retired hours earlier, but Phelan sat up, waiting.

He wasn't certain what he was waiting for, but now he knew. Juliette MacGowan wasn't the sort of woman who allowed herself to be backed into a corner. Despite her very obvious terror, she wasn't about to give up, not so easily. She was out roaming, looking for help.

The question was, whom was she going to ask?

Was she moving silently toward Valerian's room? He would be the obvious choice—he'd been far kinder to her than Phelan had ever been. If she had any sense at all, she'd throw herself at Valerian, and Valerian, ever the gentle-man, would catch her.

The footsteps continued past Valerian's room, pausing outside his own door. Phelan waited, still and silent, hold-ing his breath, as the door slowly opened.

There was a three-quarter moon that night, shedding a silvery glow. He could see her face, and he almost wanted to laugh. She looked pale, determined, like a child forced to taste some particularly nasty medicine. And Phelan had the unflattering notion that he was that medicine.

He didn't move, lowering his eyelids so that he appeared asleep, and he watched her as she closed the door behind her and turned the key. The girl had wicked plans, that was for certain, but she didn't seem very happy about them.

He lay perfectly still, regulating his breathing as she tiptoed over to him. It was child's play to guess her mo-tive. She planned to offer her body to him in exchange for protection from her husband.

The question was, would he accept that noble sacrifice?

He'd have a hard time refusing it. He'd been in an ado-lescent quiver of lust since he'd first set eyes on her, and the thought of her offering herself almost made him dizzy with desire. She didn't seem too excited about the prospect, but he had enough confidence to assume he could eventu-ally guarantee her enthusiasm in the project.

He could take what she offered. He deserved it, didn't he? He was ready to endanger his own and his brother's welfare for the girl's sake. Wasn't he due some sort of pay-ment? In advance, for services rendered?

She was standing so close he could feel her body heat, smell that faint trace of flowers that seemed to cling to her.

All he had to do was reach out his hand, and she'd come to him, willingly paying the price for his protection.

He opened his eyes, watching her in the shadowed darkness. She was biting her lower lip, and the expression on her face was hardly conducive to passion. She was trying to work up her nerve to touch him, and if he weren't so damnably aroused, he might think it funny.

"Yes?" he said in a bored voice.

She jumped, emitting a startled squeak that she silenced almost immediately by clapping her hands over her mouth. Her huge eyes were accusing. "You're awake," she said finally in an angry whisper.

"I am. I'm a light sleeper. I heard you clumping through the hallway and I wondered where you were going."

"Here," she said.

That gave him pause. "So I noticed." He sat up, surveying her dispassionately. "I wondered why."

The question annoyed her. "Isn't it obvious?" she said.

"Not particularly. Why don't you enlighten me?"

She looked as if she wanted to hit him. With a visible effort she controlled herself, trying to put a conciliatory smile on her face. She merely looked irritated.

"I came for you," she said.

"To do what?" He was beginning to enjoy himself. If he couldn't take her, and his damnable conscience was giving him a hard time about that, then at least he could amuse himself by baiting her.

"To take me to bed." She spat out the words like nails.

"You were already in bed," he pointed out with great practicality.

"To make love to me," she said furiously.

"Oh," he said with an air of great surprise, glad that the

shifting moon shadows were disguising his more normal reaction to her words. "Any particular reason for this sudden surge of uncontrollable passion on your part?"

She glared at him. "I thought you wanted me," she said in a tight voice.

"Oh, I do," he murmured. "Most definitely. I'm merely questioning your motives."

"Why should you care about my motives?"

"I'm funny that way. Somehow I suspect you're here for reasons other than overwhelming desire. Am I right?"

"No," she said.

"No?" he echoed. "Prove it."

She stared at him blankly. "What do you mean?"

"I mean, dear Juliette, that if you've suddenly decided that you're possessed of an overpowering lust for me, than you need to climb up on the bed and demonstrate. You're a married woman. It shouldn't be too difficult for you."

She almost left him. She started to turn, and he wasn't sure what he would have done if she'd really stalked from the room as she obviously longed to do. If he were a decent man he'd let her go.

But he knew he'd reach the door ahead of her, barring her escape.

She didn't force him to make that choice. She turned back, and even in the moonlight he could see the color in her cheeks, the determination in her soft, pale mouth.

"All right," she said, game as ever. And she started to climb up on the high bed beside him.

# CHAPTER SEVENTEEN

The bed was soft beneath Juliette when she scrambled up, seductively so. She'd been in other beds, too many, with her husband, and none of them had felt so treacherously comfortable. She hadn't wanted to be in those beds. For some obscure reason, she wanted to be in this one.

No, she didn't, she reminded herself. This was an act of vengeance, the only one she could take. It certainly wasn't a matter of her own choice.

Phelan was still lying there, stretched out, watching her out of hooded eyes. For all that the blasted man said he wanted her, he probably would have let her go. Just as he'd let her go with her husband in the morning, for all his protests.

She knelt on the bed, uncertain what to do next. He hadn't moved, and if she had any sense of self-preservation, she'd climb down off that bed and run. But Lemur's threats lingered in her mind, and she knew there was nowhere to run to.

She took a deep breath. She could do this. He was the most attractive man she'd ever seen. Surely that would make the experience less awful.

To some people Lemur might be considered a well-enough-looking man, past his first youth, but handsome enough. And there was no question that Valerian was astonishingly beautiful, both as a man and as a woman.

But Phelan Romney was something else entirely. His dark hair framed his saturnine face; his eyes watched her; his thin, wide mouth was curved in a faintly mocking smile. His shirt was unfastened around his tanned chest, and his long, long legs were clad in snug black breeches. She even found his bare feet beautiful. And there was no question but that he had the most wondrous hands in the world.

But those hands weren't moving. He hadn't done a thing except lie there and wait.

"Well?" she said, unable to keep the irritation out of her voice.

"Well?" he said, and she couldn't miss the amusement in his.

She almost left then, only the memory of Lemur keeping her there in his bed. He was still making no move to touch her, and his very stillness goaded her.

She flopped down on the big bed beside him, on her back, staring at the canopy above her head. "Go ahead," she said between gritted teeth. "Do it."

Finally he moved, rolling on his side to lean over her. Her hair had fallen in her face, and with a gentle hand he picked up the strand and moved it. "Such a gracious offer almost unmans me," he murmured. "Almost."

She cast a worried glance up at him. Surely he wasn't supposed to be lighthearted about this endeavor. And yet he sounded so.

"Do you want me to take off my clothes?" she asked, determined to get on with it.

"It usually works better if you do."

"What do you want me to leave on?" She was reaching for the buttons at the throat of her white shirt.

"Nothing."

"Nothing?" The thought shocked her.

"Absolutely nothing," he said again.

She watched him warily. "You are going to do this, aren't you?" she asked suspiciously. "You aren't just playing a game with me?"

That faint smile faded. "Oh, I'm most definitely going to do this," he murmured. "Even if I know I shouldn't."

"Why shouldn't you?"

"Because you don't really want it. I haven't quite fathomed why you've come to my bed, ready to offer yourself like a virgin sacrifice, and if I were a decent human being I'd send you on your way. But I suppose I'm not really a decent human being after all, and I want you more than I want my self-respect."

She could feel the color mounting in her cheeks. Virgin sacrifice was a bit too appropriate, but she had no intention of telling him that. "Does it matter why?" she asked.

"It should. I'm not in the habit of taking women for anything other than mutual pleasure, but I'm afraid I consider you irresistible. I suppose you think by sleeping with me you'll be more likely to have me protect you from Lemur. I've already told you it's not necessary. I won't let him take you away from here."

"That's not it," she said, knowing she should stay silent.

"Then why?"

She hesitated for a moment longer, then blurted it out. "Revenge."

He laughed. "How erotic," he said, his voice sardonic. He moved her hand away from her throat, and his long fingers began unfastening the small buttons. "I would think sending him away without you would be the best revenge. You don't need to cuckold him as well."

She tried to sit up, but his hand was at her chest, holding her down. "If you don't want to do this…" she said.

He smiled, and there was something unnerving about his expression. It was predatory. Aroused. And oddly tender. "I just want to make sure you do as well."

"I'm here, aren't I?" she said in a tight little voice.

"Yes," he said. "You most assuredly are." And he leaned down and brushed his lips across hers.

She could taste the brandy on his breath, and she held her own, tensing. But he seemed content with just the soft feathering of his lips against hers, not seeking to deepen the kiss, and she forced herself to relax. Until she realized that he'd undone all the buttons on her shirt, and the cool night air was dancing against her skin.

She shivered then, unable to help herself, and he lifted his head to look down at her. "Are you having second thoughts?" he murmured. "Or are you just cold?"

"No second thoughts," she lied.

"All right." And he rolled on top of her, covering her with his larger, stronger body, his hard chest against her soft breasts, and his skin was warm, almost fiery hot. He threaded his fingers through her hair and held her still, and she looked up at him with what she hoped was fearlessness.

"Is this going to take a long time?" she asked, allowing a trace of asperity to creep into her voice.

"Were you in a particular hurry?" His voice was lazy.

She thought of Lemur, somewhere in the house. What if he decided to come and find her again? What if he decided to leave in the middle of the night? She needed to get on with this unpleasant task so she could return safely to her room.

"I just thought we should get it over with."

"Rather like a trip to the tooth-drawer?" he mocked, and his long thumbs were soothing the sides of her face.

"It isn't supposed to take that long," she said stubbornly, trying to ignore the insidious effect his hands were having on her. Trying to ignore the feel of him, cradled against her. He was far readier than her husband had ever been; she had enough experience to know that much.

"It can take as long as we want," he said, kissing one eyelid and then the other. "We can do it fast and hard"—and he punctuated his words with a brief thrust of his hips against hers—"or we can take our time. There's much to be said for both ways."

"I'd rather you did it quickly," she said in a stony voice.

"Would you, now?" he said, not bothering to climb off her. "But then, I like taking my time. There's more pleasure that way. For me. And particularly for you."

She couldn't hide her look of contemptuous disbelief. "Don't worry about me," she said tartly. "I'm not expecting to enjoy it."

He dropped his head down on her shoulder, and she could feel a faint tremor ripple through his body. She realized he was laughing at her. "I see," he said gravely. "Are you certain you want to do it?"

"You've asked me that before. If you aren't interested…"

Once more he bumped his hips against her, leaving her

in no doubt as to his interest. "Would you mind terribly if you did enjoy it?" he inquired politely. "Just a little bit?"

"I suppose not," she said ungraciously. "But could we just do it and stop talking about it?"

"I suppose so."

"Well?"

"Well?" he countered again, that unholy amusement in his silver eyes.

"Well," she said fiercely, "climb off me and I'll take off my clothes and turn over."

All amusement fled. "Why?"

She was rapidly losing her patience. "Because that's the way it's done, isn't it? I thought you had experience in these matters."

"Apparently more than you," he said. "Is that the way Lemur did it?"

She didn't want to meet his searching gaze. "I thought we were going to stop talking about it."

He was silent for a moment. "More and more reason to send you back to your room," he said, half to himself.

Sudden panic swept through her. "You aren't going to, are you?"

"And deprive you of your revenge? That would be extremely unkind of me, wouldn't it?"

"Extremely unkind," she agreed in a whisper.

"To answer your previous question," he said, "that is the way it is done on occasion, when one wants a change of pace. I prefer it this way. Where I can watch you when you climax."

She blinked. "I don't have the faintest idea what you're talking about."

"I know. But you will, fair Juliette. You will." He'd been

bracing himself above her, his hips resting lightly against hers, but now he settled down against her, his hands coming up to cover her bare breasts. "We'll do it, as you requested, and we won't talk about it. Unless you change your mind."

His hands were hard against the softness of her breasts, hot against the coolness of her flesh, and she squirmed, wanting to push his hands away. "Can I?"

"Yes," he said.

She put her hands over his. And then she let them drop onto the mattress, steeling herself. "I won't change my mind," she said.

"You know, my love," he murmured, brushing his lips against hers temptingly, "you would have made a very nice early Christian martyr. You wear that long-suffering look so well." He increased the pressure against her mouth, just slightly, and she felt the damp, questing tip of his tongue. She opened her mouth, more by instinct than by volition, and he deepened the kiss, slanting his lips across hers, pushing his tongue past her teeth to taste the darkness of her mouth.

Her first instinct was to fight. And then she remembered she'd liked his kisses, even as they'd frightened her. She tilted her head back, closing her eyes, and let him kiss her, telling herself that at least it might hurry things along a bit.

She tried to concentrate on the sound of the surf outside the window, the feel of the damp night air. She tried to concentrate on the feel of the linen sheet beneath her fingers, the softness of the mattress. But her hands had left the mattress, sliding up under Phelan's loose shirt to touch his back, and she found she couldn't concentrate on anything but what he was doing to her mouth.

His back was smooth, muscled beneath her fingertips, and she could feel the tension beneath his heated skin. She slid her hands down, to the waistband of his breeches, then up again, to the width of his back. She liked the feel of him.

He groaned, deep in the back of his throat, and rolled to one side, taking her with him. He released her mouth, and she took in great gulping breaths of air, not even realizing she'd been holding her breath. And then she sucked it in again as his mouth traveled down her throat, to taste the heavy beat of her pulse at the base of her neck.

Her nipples were hardening beneath his deft hands, and the heat flowed down between her thighs. She tried to clamp them together, but he put his knee between her legs, pushing against the pulsing core of her, and she felt an odd little thrill of something she told herself was fear but felt a great deal more like desire.

His hands moved away from her breasts, and her shock of disappointment was followed by an even greater shock as his mouth followed, covering her breast, sucking it hotly, while he pushed the shirt from her shoulders and down her arms. She thought vaguely that she should protest, that she shouldn't be lying there in only the tight breeches, but she didn't know quite what she could say. Particularly when the sensation was so astonishingly delightful.

He moved his mouth between her breasts, tasting, nibbling, sliding down her rib cage. "You went swimming today," he murmured against her skin. "You taste like the sea."

She wanted to say something pragmatic, but his lips were having the most debilitating effect on her. Particularly when he moved down, leaning over her, and put his mouth between her legs, against the rough black material of her breeches.

She could feel the heat of his breath through her clothing, and she arched against him as his hands cupped her hips. He bit her gently through the layers of clothing, and an astonishing heat and dampness seemed to flow from her.

Her breath was coming rapidly now, and she closed her eyes in the darkness. Only to open them again when he moved back up to take her hand and place it against the solid ridge of flesh at the front of his breeches.

"No," she said.

"No?" He didn't release her hand, simply rubbed his hand over hers, pressing it against him. "You've changed your mind?" There was a thread of desperate tension in his cool voice, but no rage.

She shook her head. "I haven't changed my mind," she said. "But it's not going to work."

"Why not?"

She wasn't about to tell him, and have him laugh at her. He was the experienced one; if he didn't know, then she wasn't about to tell him.

He, however, wasn't about to let her keep silent. He moved up her body, kissing her lightly as he traveled. "Why not?" he asked again, kissing her mouth, and his hand moved between her legs where his mouth had been.

She wasn't sure if the dampness had come from his mouth or from her. The very thought was disturbing, but he didn't seem to mind. He was stroking her, gently, tracing random, almost idle patterns with almost no pressure, and she told herself she didn't need to worry.

"Why not?" he asked, increasing the pressure of his hand on her, increasing the pressure of her hand on him.

"Because you're...much too big," she said finally, knowing she was blushing furiously.

He did laugh, damn it, a soft, coaxing sound. "It's always worked before."

"Then there must be something wrong with me," she said stiffly, "because Lemur is much smaller, and yet he couldn't... I mean, he had great difficulty..." The words trailed off beneath Phelan's suddenly intent gaze.

"You need to finish your sentence," he said calmly. "Did Lemur have great difficulty, or couldn't he?"

She knew what would happen if she told him the truth. For all he mocked his honor, he would never take her, knowing she was still technically a virgin.

And she wanted it. Not for some hazy notion of revenge. That excuse had faded into the night, leaving only the truth that she hadn't wanted to face. She wanted him, his body, taking hers. Before she had to leave forever.

She did the only thing she could think of. She let her fingers curl around him, caressing him. And she put her mouth against his, touching his lips with her tongue.

She was astonished at his reaction. With a low groan of desire, he pulled her against him, trapping her hand between their bodies as he kissed her back. And suddenly she wanted to get closer still, to sink into his very skin, to merge with him. She kissed him, her tongue meeting his quite shamelessly, and she writhed beneath him, wanting things she didn't begin to understand.

He reached down and stripped the breeches off her, clumsily. And then he unfastened his own, freeing himself, and she tried to pull away from him, suddenly shy.

"Don't stop now," he groaned. "You were just developing an appreciation for the sport."

"Sport?" she echoed in outrage. "You call this—" His mouth silenced her, with a deep, thrusting kiss that wiped her protest out of her mind. And he put her hand back, over his throbbing male flesh no longer shielded by his clothing, keeping it there, until her initial panic began to fade and an odd, sensual curiosity took over.

He was smooth, silken, and damp. She told herself she should be disgusted, but her fingers slid, fascinated, around the width of him, circling him, measuring him, delighting in his strangled groan of reaction.

His hand moved between her legs, and she stilled, waiting for the pain. There was none. His long fingers parted her, stroking her, and she felt an unfamiliar burgeoning warmth, one she could neither control nor deny. She arched her hips against his hand, and she heard his low murmur of approval as he deepened the pressure, sliding into the unexplained dampness of her, arousing her when she was certain nothing could.

She could feel the tendrils of delight build, spiraling upward. She knew it wouldn't last, that it would turn to pain and fear, but it was already so much more than she'd ever dreamed that she wasn't willing to settle for less.

"Promise me," she said, and her voice was a gasping thread of sound.

He didn't halt the insidiously delightful movement of his fingers; instead, he slid even deeper into her, and she could barely control her moan of pleasure.

"Anything," he said.

She forced her eyes to open, to look deep into his in the moonlit room. The silver gray had darkened to a midnight black, and the passionate wildness in his expression should have frightened her. Instead, it simply deepened her pleasure and her resolve.

"Don't stop," she said. "Even if I beg you, don't let me stop you."

His stillness was unnerving. "I can't…" he began.

"Don't stop," she said again. "Promise me. Even if I grow frightened, uneasy, even if I beg, you have to do it. I know what I want."

"And what do you want? Revenge?"

It had been as good an excuse as any. But now wasn't the time for excuses. "No," she said. "I want you."

He cursed then, her words unleashing the last of his self-restraint. He pushed her back against the bed, holding her shoulders down against the soft mattress as he knelt between her legs. She could feel him against her, heat and hardness against her, and she shivered in sudden, undeniable longing as he hesitated.

"Promise me," she whispered again. "Don't stop."

"I promise." The words were muffled as he pushed against her, sliding into her heated dampness with a sure, hard thrust. Only to come up against the evidence of her virginity.

He was rigid in her arms, impaling her, but not quite. "Open your eyes, damn it," he said in a fierce voice.

She didn't want to, but she had no choice except to comply. She looked up into his eyes, waiting.

"You're a virgin," he said in a low, bitter voice.

"Yes."

"He never touched you."

"He tried. He couldn't." She wanted to cry. Emotions were rocketing through her body, feelings she couldn't even begin to define. She was certain he was going to pull away from her, leave her. "Phelan," she said in an imploring voice.

"I thought I told you I don't need a virgin sacrifice," he said, and his wintry voice was at odds with the heat of his body.

"You promised me," she said furiously, clutching him. "You said you wouldn't stop, even if I begged."

He just looked at her for a long moment. "I'm not going to stop," he said. "You're mine. The bonds of marriage are worthless, they're a sham. I'm the one who makes you come alive, and you belong to me." His voice was fierce and possessive, and she gloried in it. "And I intend to take you." And before she realized what he was doing, he'd thrust deep inside her, breaking past her maidenhead to rest at the very entrance to her womb.

She let out a small shriek, more of surprise than of pain, and he quickly covered her mouth with his. They stayed motionless for a moment as her body grew accustomed to his, and then he began to move, rocking against her, pulling away and then pushing back in, filling her ever more deeply. He reached down and caught her legs, wrapping them around his hips, and she dug her fingers into his shoulders, holding on, telling herself she was doing this for him, for the sheer, once-in-a-lifetime pleasure of belonging, when her body began to tremble once more beneath his embrace.

Something was building inside her, a panic, a confusion, a longing she couldn't begin to understand. She clung more tightly, her fingers scraping against his sweat-damp flesh, and each time he surged against her she raised her hips to meet him. She wanted more, she wanted something she had never had, and she couldn't even find the words to ask for it.

She didn't need to. He slid his hand between their bodies and touched her. He clapped his hand over her mouth just as she screamed, and her body convulsed around his, in a shimmer of magic and madness. It took forever for the moment to pass, an endless, velvet eternity. When she could finally open her eyes, she saw him looking down at her, his body still rigid in hers.

"That's what you meant when you said you wanted to see me climax," she said in a raw whisper.

"Yes." And he surged against her, deeply, each thrust sending new shivers of delight through her flesh. She wanted to beg him to stop, to tell him she couldn't stand any more, but the pace of his thrusts increased, and she found herself warming, melting once more beneath him, and she wrapped her arms tightly around him, trying to draw him in deeper, deeper, as his body pushed her against the bed, his hands clenched around her shoulders, and suddenly he went rigid in her arms, a strangled cry on his lips, as he flooded her with his seed.

She took it all, folding him against her, clinging to him with a fierceness that knew no boundaries. For these few short hours he was hers, hers alone, and she was his. All too soon she would leave, for his sake as much as for hers, and she'd become nothing more than a curious memory. For now, she had a small, brief glimpse of eternity.

Because she'd heard the word, his strangled gasp as he'd given himself to her completely. And that word had been "love."

She was damp and sticky when she slid from the bed. There was blood on the white linen sheets, indisputable proof of her virginity, and she felt sore and stretched between her legs. She looked down at the man sleeping there so peacefully in the predawn light, and she felt her heart break.

Damn him. Why had he gone and broken past her defenses, into her heart? She hadn't even recognized his insidious effect on her, except to know that he infuriated her as much as his touch had aroused her. She should have known better than to come to his bed. If she hadn't, she might have continued her life in happy ignorance of what she was missing, and never thought of Phelan Romney again.

No, she couldn't convince herself of that. Perhaps she would have thought of him with distant affection and lingering regret.

No, not that either. She'd fallen in love with the man, and she knew exactly when. Not when he'd taken her body and shown her the wondrous things humans were capable of, in stark contrast to the pain and bestiality of Lemur's attentions.

Not when he'd kissed her in the rain-soaked garden, or even when he'd rescued her from Neville Pinworth on a whim, though all those things added to it.

It was when she'd glanced at his sketchbook and seen that drawing of herself asleep on the beach. The sullen, vulnerable woman-child, with defiance, an unlikely beauty, and a stern vulnerability she'd never admit to. When she saw how well he knew her, and still had made her beautiful, she'd known she could love him.

She pulled on her clothes, promising herself a thorough wash when she reached her room. No longer did she want to fling her revenge in Mark-David Lemur's face. If he was ever able to finally take her, he'd find out for himself that someone had been there first. And she had no intention of telling him who.

But first she had one stop to make. She was going to go by way of Phelan's study, find his sketchbook, and take that drawing with her.

So that never again, in whatever became of her life, would she ever forget love.

# CHAPTER EIGHTEEN

Damned if he didn't have a romantic streak in his body after all, Phelan thought several hours later as he dressed. He wanted to strip the bloody sheets from the bed and fling them at Mark-David Lemur. The little worm hadn't even had it in him to take his bride. All he'd done was frighten and hurt her.

Of course, Phelan could bring himself to feel grateful. He was the first and, damn it, the only man who would ever have Juliette MacGowan. He could finally admit to the fierce possessiveness that filled him whenever he thought of her. He wasn't going to go any further with it, to define the reasons for that possessiveness. It existed, and she belonged to him. Forever.

There was only one slight drawback to his satisfaction. The knowledge, unbidden, that he belonged to her as well, he who'd never allowed himself to care about anyone other than his younger brother.

He wasn't going to worry about it, he told himself as he shaved. There would be time enough to sift through his conflicting emotions when he took her away from here. Back to the places he loved so well.

He was actually humming beneath his breath when he bounded downstairs. Hannigan met him coming up, and his expression was ludicrous. "You're singing?" he said in astonishment. "In all the years I've been with you, I've never heard you sing."

"I'm feeling very much in charity with the world," Phelan announced, continuing down the stairs.

"Well, you won't be."

Phelan stopped in the middle of the stairs. He turned to stare at Hannigan, and he could feel the ice flow through his veins. "What do you mean?"

"I mean she's gone. Left with her husband at the crack of dawn, and there weren't nothing I could do to stop them," Hannigan said in a lugubrious voice.

"Damn you," Phelan cursed, pushing past him. "Why didn't you stop him—"

"She wanted to go," Hannigan broke in. "I'm sorry for it, but that's the truth. He wasn't forcing her to do a thing."

Phelan had started back down the stairs at a run. "I'm going after them," he said, but Hannigan was as quick-footed as ever, racing ahead to stop him.

"She wanted to go," Hannigan said again. "If she hadn't, do you think I'd have let him take her? She was calm, and smiling, and damned if she wasn't wearing those diamond-and-pearl earbobs you had locked up in the library. She was glad to be going back with him."

"The hell she was! Tell Valerian I've gone—"

Hannigan caught his arm in a bearlike grip. "She left you a note, lad. In the library."

Phelan pulled away, wanting to shout his fury and denial in Hannigan's face. "I'm going after her," he said in a still, deadly voice. "I don't give a damn what she said in her note—Lemur would have made her write it."

"Lemur wasn't with her when she left it."

"Damn it," Phelan said furiously, "I won't believe it."

"Read the note, lad. If you're still wanting to go after her, I'll go with you."

The library was still and dark, cold and dead. His desk drawer lay open, and the earbobs were gone. He'd meant to give them back to her these past several days. Obviously she'd taken them herself.

The note lay in the middle of his desk. He'd never seen her handwriting before, and he stared at it, avoiding the inevitable, concentrating on the feminine curlicues and sweeps. He would have thought her handwriting would have reflected the real Juliette—direct and fearless.

He picked up the paper and broke the seal. "Direct" was the word for Juliette after all.

"My lord," she wrote, "I am leaving with my husband. Please do not attempt to come after me. Upon due consideration, I realize that my life belongs with him. At heart I am a conventional creature after all, and this adventure has run its course. I cannot see spending my life as the mistress of a murderer when I could live a life of respect and comfort as Mrs. Lemur. And I find, for all the novelty of last night, that I would prefer a less taxing existence, and a husband whose physical demands are few. With every good wish for your future, I remain, Juliette MacGowan Lemur."

He had no idea how long he stood there, staring at the cool, polite words, disbelieving. She had to have been coerced. They had to be lies. But Hannigan said she was alone when she left the note. And it was nothing more than he would have expected from the female of the species.

Lady Margery, the one woman who had ever professed to love him, would be capable of this and more. Denying the truth of it was the rash, foolish act of a lovesick fool, a slave to his emotions. And Phelan had never been anyone's fool, particularly not some snip of a girl's.

"Do you want me to saddle your horse?" Hannigan's voice broke through his bleak abstraction.

He lifted his head, feeling the icy composure cover him, pushing away pain and regret and doubt, leaving nothing but an eerie calm. He'd crumpled the letter in one strong hand, and he let it fall to the floor. "I won't be needing him," he said in a bored tone of voice that might, or might not, have fooled Hannigan. "Did she leave any other word?"

"For Valerian, my lord. Just a note to say goodbye."

Phelan flicked an imaginary speck of dust off his dark coat. "Well," he drawled, "that makes things a great deal easier all around, doesn't it? I was expecting we were going to have to get into some foul to-do with Lemur over her, but if she's chosen to go back where she belongs, it keeps everything much simpler."

"Much simpler, my lord."

"Bring me my coffee, Hannigan," he said with an elaborate yawn. "I've got my work cut out for me if we're to leave for France within the next few days."

"Yes, sir. Are you certain you don't mind?"

"Mind about what?"

"About the girl, my lord. I hadn't thought she was anything special."

Phelan smiled bitterly. "Nothing special at all, Hannigan."

He closed the door behind him, silently. She'd made a

fool of him, she with her innocence and her masquerade. She'd played Lemur for a fool as well. Doubtless the poor cuckold was simply a possessive, incompetent husband, not some paragon of evil. She'd had her revenge on Lemur, she'd made no bones about it, and Phelan had been a besotted moonling to think the hours spent in his bed had any meaning for her.

He was well rid of her, well rid of a temporary weakness, a momentary obsession, a brief interlude that went well on its way to convincing him that he really might inherit his mother's madness. She was gone, and he should thank the heavens for it. He was free of her, blissfully free, and he need never think of her again.

And with that, he slammed his fist into the heavy oak door, full force.


It was an unseasonably cold morning. Juliette couldn't keep from shivering, even wrapped in an enveloping cloak. She hadn't been warm since she'd left the dangerous shelter of Phelan's arms, and somehow she doubted she would ever be warm again.

Lemur had been waiting for her when she crept back into her room. The look on his face should have terrified her, but during the past few hours she'd lost her capacity to fear. It no longer mattered what he might do to her. She had tasted love, and that memory would sustain her.

Not for a moment did she consider running to Phelan for help, protection. He would have two choices, and two choices only. One, he would have had to let Lemur leave, and her husband would have returned with the Bow Street runners to take him in for questioning, and the truth about

Valerian would be bound to come out. Or two, Phelan would have to kill her husband.

And while Juliette had no doubt that Lemur deserved to die, she didn't want it to be for her sake. And she didn't want his blood to be on Phelan's hands.

It was the one gift of love she could give him, one he would never know he'd received. But the gift was in the giving, and the knowledge could almost warm her.

She'd wept when she'd written the note, but had been careful not to let any tears mar the smooth handwriting. She'd taken great pains with it, and when she remembered the neat, wicked words, they made her sick inside. She had retrieved the earbobs, to ensure that he would think the worst of her. She hadn't been able to resist taking the sketch. She deserved that much, to keep her strong through the coming weeks and months and years…without Phelan.

It was a dark, blustery day, better suited to October than to midsummer, but it suited Juliette's mood. She rode in silence, for the first time regretting her freedom in riding astride. After the previous night's encounter, she might have preferred sidesaddle for a few days.

She smiled to herself at the notion, the memory a small thing she could treasure, when Lemur's sharp voice turned her to stone.

"Don't make the mistake of thinking I forgive you," he said in a soft, sly voice. "Just because you came willingly doesn't mean you've absolved yourself of your crimes."

She glanced at him, gripping the pommel tightly. "Crimes, Mark-David? I wasn't aware I'd committed any."

"Running away from your husband, to begin with," he said. "Taking my diamonds—"

"*My* diamonds," she interrupted, not really caring. She'd

never been one for jewels; the MacGowan diamonds were simply a way to help her escape. The earrings hung heavily on her ears, and she was half tempted to rip them off and throw them into the sea.

"Not anymore. When you married me, your possessions became mine. You've had far too lax an upbringing, I've told you that before. Your father gave you too much freedom; he never had the sense to beat some deference into you."

"You haven't had much luck trying."

"Don't goad me, girl. I will have my justice, and I doubt you'll like it much."

"Do your worst," she said coolly. "I really don't care."

"Not about yourself, perhaps. You never put much stock in your own well-being. But I fancy you won't like seeing your lover and his wife brought up on charges, will you? Humiliated, degraded, thrown in jail…"

"You promised you'd leave them alone," she said furiously.

Lemur's smile would have done an archbishop proud. "And you believed me. I never truly considered it. After all, Romney did me a great injury by shielding you. And I'm not convinced he didn't suspect you were a woman. To be sure, you're scarcely feminine, even in dresses, but one shouldn't assume anything."

She said nothing for a moment, biting her lip. It felt tender, swollen, and she knew it was from the delicious, insistent pressure of Phelan's mouth. "He hadn't any idea," she said. "He thought I was a boy. There's no need to have anything more to do with the man. Leave him be."

"Since you ask so sweetly, how can I possibly refuse?" Lemur said in a dulcet voice that didn't fool her for a moment. "Just answer me one thing. Where were you this morning, while I waited for you in your room?"

She wanted to tell him the truth. She wanted to fling her defiance in his face, but the only way she could protect Phelan was to lie.

"In the library," she said with a certain amount of truth. "I was looking for something to steal." And stolen it she had. The sketch Phelan had drawn of her now lay folded against her skin.

"Still thinking you could get away from me? I trust you've learned otherwise."

"Indeed. I've accepted my fate," she said, hoping she sounded conciliatory.

"That pleases me. I only hope you can accept Phelan Romney's fate as well."

She stifled her protest. She'd already revealed too much of her feelings, and if there was one thing to be said for Mark-David Lemur, he was not a stupid man. "His fate is none of my concern," she said with a shrug of her shoulders.

"You didn't think him handsome, my lady wife? Such a tall, dark man. Most women would find him quite attractive, though I gather his brother is even more glorious."

"I am not interested in the attractions of men," she said coolly. "Nor women either. The pleasures of the flesh escape me entirely." And she shifted in the saddle, the better to accommodate the throbbing between her legs that still lingered from Phelan's touch.

"I'm glad you feel that way. A decent woman isn't supposed to enjoy her husband's attentions. She must simply submit." Lemur rode his horse closer to her, his leg brushing against hers, and she jerked away, unable to control her distaste. He reached over and put his hand across her gloved one, pressing her fingers into the hard leather of the saddle with painful intensity. "I've bespoken rooms in a small inn a few miles north of here. It seemed wisest to avoid Hampton Regis entirely. Romney might not accept your departure as wisely as you have, and I haven't had time to alert the authorities to his presence."

"Does it matter?" she managed to ask in a disinterested voice.

"Only to you, my love," he said, the endearment a cruel joke. "Only to you."

The ride was endless. A cold, light mist began to fall sometime in late morning, and the cloak Lemur had brought with him had no hood. The rain matted Juliette's hair and slid down the collar of her jacket. She could only hope it wouldn't reach the piece of paper she had tucked inside her shirt. It was all she had left of Phelan; for some reason, she knew if she lost it she would lose everything worth living for.

They reached the inn by late afternoon. Juliette was almost faint with cold and hunger, and her entire body was a mass of aches. Miles back, she'd lost the ability to bless each and every one of those tender aches, and while she wanted to suffer nobly, she felt remarkably querulous. She was beyond terror—if Lemur was going to rape her, beat her, kill her, she simply hoped he'd get on with it. Otherwise she wanted a good meal, and a hot bath, and a warm bed.

The inn was not devoid of company. An elderly lady had bespoken private rooms as well, and the landlord was hard pressed to take proper care of both of his exalted guests, particularly when Lemur was so demanding. No sooner had they been settled in a parlor than mine host disappeared, leaving Lemur fuming.

"I don't see why some old lady deserves better treatment than we do," he said irritably.

Juliette was standing by the fire, stripping the wet cloak from her chilled body, and she made no reply. But the serving maid, with astonishing temerity, ventured to speak up. "It's 'cause she's a lady," the girl said, obviously in awe of that fact. "We've never had someone with a title staying here, and Mr. 'Awkins is that impressed. Meaning no disrespect to you, sir," she added hastily, having finally realized that Lemur was enraged.

"Obviously we have made a mistake in choosing such a low-class inn," he said bitingly. "I'm used to places where even royalty is well served. Put your cloak on, Julian. We'll find another inn."

She almost fainted at the notion, but it wouldn't do to show her misery to Lemur—he'd simply feed on it. She'd pulled the cape back over her shoulders, shivering beneath the damp wool, when the door opened and the landlord bustled back in, all apologies and cringing deference. In the end, however, it took only one item to change Lemur's mind about dragging her out into the rain once more.

The elderly lady's name: Lady Margery Romney, of Romney Hall, Yorkshire.

"What the hell do you mean, she's gone?" Valerian thundered.

Phelan refused to meet his gaze, toying with his cup of coffee, and Valerian felt his fury grow, "As I said," Phelan murmured. "She decided to leave with Lemur, and I could hardly prevent her from going, could I?"

"Damn it!" Valerian stalked across the room, throwing himself into the leather chair. "She was terrified of that creature, and rightly so. You can't make me believe she would have left us for that—that monster."

If Phelan had the slightest regret about her disappearance, he wasn't exhibiting it to his brother. "I wouldn't call him a monster," he said calmly. "Not the most pleasant of gentlemen, but they were legally married. Obviously he and Juliette must have come to an understanding. I gather she wrote you a note." He didn't sound in the least bit curious.

"Saying absolutely nothing," Val fumed. "Just thanking me for everything and wishing me well. What did yours say?"

Phelan's smile was almost a grimace. "That she'd rather live a life of comfort as a respectable wife than tie in her lot with a bunch of suspected murderers."

For a moment Valerian didn't move. "I don't believe it. And what's more, you're a fool if you do. What did you do to her, Phelan?" he demanded. "Terrify her so much that even her wretched husband was preferable? Did you touch her, injure her in any way…?" His voice trailed off in the face of his brother's fury.

"I might remind you," Phelan said casually, despite the dark rage in his eyes, "that you still have a black eye. I'd be more than happy to black the other one."

"Damn it, why would she leave?"

"Why do you find it so hard to accept her reasoning? Once she realized her choice was with her lawful husband or a pair of gentlemen fleeing a murder, she made the only practical decision. And women are very practical creatures, you understand."

"You're wrong," Valerian said flatly. "Juliette wasn't like that."

"You knew her so well?" Phelan said in a silky voice that held a thread of warning.

"Obviously better than you did. I wasn't blinded by lust for her."

"I didn't lust after her."

"You could have fooled me. You couldn't keep your eyes off her. I know you, brother, better than you imagine. She was driving you mad, and I suspect your chilly attitude drove her away."

Phelan's mouth curved in a mocking smile, the one that Valerian had always particularly hated. "I assure you, Valerian, our last encounter was far from chilly."

It was the last straw. Valerian hurled himself across the room, lunging for Phelan's smug face. He sprawled across the desk, scattering papers and notebooks everywhere as he caught the front of Phelan's shirt and yanked. "Damn you, Phelan," he spat, "she wasn't that kind of girl!"

Phelan simply stared at him, unmoved. "They're all that kind of girl. Haven't you realized that by now?"

Val hit him. It wasn't nearly as good a punch as Phelan had landed a few days earlier, but it was satisfying enough, sending Phelan over backward in the chair, with Valerian following him down. The next few minutes were exceedingly enjoyable, punctuated by grunts, curses, and the occasional gasp. When it was over, Phelan lay against the wall, bleeding from a split lip, while Valerian was stretched out beside him on the floor, trying to catch his breath.

"You're getting stronger," Phelan said, panting. "I would have thought your time in skirts would turn you into a weakling. If I hadn't hurt my hand, you wouldn't be feeling so chipper."

"How'd you hurt your hand?" Valerian wheezed.

"None of your damned business."

"Damn it, Phelan, how could you have done that? No wonder she ran away."

"As a matter of fact, it wasn't my idea. Though it's no concern of yours, she came to me."

Dead silence filled the room. "Well," Valerian said eventually, "I would have thought you'd do a better job at it. I've never heard the women complain before. Maybe true love made you clumsy."

Phelan kicked him, hard. "True love has nothing to do with it," he said grimly. "We spent a mutually enjoyable night together. The next morning she was gone, entirely of her own accord. It's that simple."

"I don't think so. Did you tell her you loved her?"

"I told you before, love hasn't anything to do with it."

"She was in love with you."

"I must have hit you too hard. Your brains are addled."

"Deny it all you want. I've learned a great deal about women in the past few weeks, and I could see it in her eyes."

"It's that," Phelan mused to himself, "or the insidious effect of the bluestocking. I've been told love makes a man a simpering idiot, and you're proving that to be true."

Valerian sat up and swung around, staring at his brother in disbelief. "You bedded her, and then just let her go, and now you're denying the existence of love?"

"I'm not denying the existence of love, though I've yet to see solid proof of it. I'm simply saying it had nothing to do with what went on between Juliette Lemur and me."

"Does that mean you won't do anything to get her back?"

Phelan's eyes narrowed. "That's exactly what it means. She wanted to go, and her husband happens to know far too much about the Romney fortunes. He's not a stupid man— he was just so besotted by his wife that he failed to look at you closely. She seems to have that effect on men; God knows why. If he sees you again, he's bound to realize."

"Do you think I could put my safety before hers?" Valerian countered.

"Don't be absurd. Of course she's safe. She'd hardly have gone with him if she wasn't. Even so, it would be wise if you learned to think of yourself first. This is a cruel, harsh world, and we're about to embark on exploring a large part of it. If you continue to be noble and self-sacrificing, you won't last the year," Phelan said cynically.

"Perhaps I don't want to live like that." Valerian rose, staring down at his brother. "Maybe it's time to head back to Yorkshire."

The cool mockery fled from Phelan's face as he surged upward. "Don't be an idiot. They'll hang you, and you know it. You can't sacrifice yourself for an old woman's craziness."

"I was a part and parcel of what drove her mad. Having to live with the evidence of her beloved husband's unfaithfulness right before her eyes…"

"Bullshit," Phelan said inelegantly. "She never loved him, never expected him to be faithful, and she was half mad long before you were born. Just ask Hannigan."

Valerian stared at him, stricken. "Good God," he said in a hushed voice. "I never thought…" He let his voice trail off.

"Never thought what?"

"You're descended from that line."

"So I am," Phelan acknowledged coolly. "The strain of tainted blood runs through my veins as well as it does my mother's. Does it worry you? Do you think I'll come into your room and strangle you while you sleep? Perhaps it was my hand that plunged the knife into our father's heart."

"Don't be ridiculous," Valerian said. "You may be stupid, but you're not crazy."

"Stupid?" Phelan echoed, finally insulted. "What the hell do you mean by that?"

"Only a mental defective would have let Juliette go with her husband. Only a village idiot would think he was going to inherit his mother's madness."

"Dear boy," Phelan said wearily, "the madness has already been passed through the generations. It would be extremely optimistic to assume I'm going to miss the taint, and even if I did, my children would doubtless be afflicted. Children are tedious enough as it is—I certainly don't want to father some poor little maniac."

"Phelan," Valerian said earnestly, but his brother held up a restraining hand, and he saw the swollen, bloody streaks that hadn't come from hitting him.

"Enough," Phelan said. "You may break your heart over my doomed future, or my stupidity, or whatever you like. If anyone is going to go to the gallows for a murder he didn't commit, it might as well be me. After all, I don't intend to have children, and I haven't even a bluestocking to lust after."

"You have Juliette. If you only realized it."

"Juliette has gone with her husband," Phelan said, stooping down and picking up the scattered papers that had sailed off the desk during their tussle. "She'll probably have a parcel of children by the time we return to England."

"Will we return?"

"Eventually, I would think. Lady Margery can't live forever, and Lord Harry wasn't a well-loved man. In ten or fifteen years we might venture back. By then, however, you may find you've lost your taste for this place, and acquired an appreciation of foreign climates."

Valerian shook his head. "Never. This is my home. Sooner or later I'll have to—" He stopped. "What's wrong?"

Phelan was staring at the disordered pages of his sketchbook, his brow knitted with confusion. And then he looked up, shaking his head. "Nothing," he said, shuffling them together without another glance.

"You know, Phelan, you're an impossible bugger at times."

Phelan shuffled the papers together once more. "I know," he said absently. "I know."

"You must be tired, my dear," Lemur said in a soft, chilling voice. "Don't let me keep you up."

Juliette huddled deeper in the chair. It was after nine, and she was exhausted, both in body and in spirit. She hadn't slept at all the night before, and today's ride through the rain had been almost as draining. She knew what awaited her upstairs, however. Lemur would have no qualms about coming to her—he'd taught her not to make any protest, even a faint whimper of pain.

She couldn't bear the thought. She wanted one night, just one, when she still belonged to Phelan. By tomorrow she would accept her fate; for now, she still clung to a foolish memory. "I'm not really tired," she said, stifling her yawn.

Lemur's colorless eyes gleamed with amusement. "Nonsense. You look about to drop. Go on up now, and don't wait up for me. I might be a while."

A faint ray of hope penetrated her bleakness. She knew better than to ask, however, so she remained silent, waiting, knowing that he would have to expand on his own cleverness sooner or later.

"I've sent my card in to Lady Romney," he informed her, too pleased with himself to make her wait. "I thought she might be interested in finding out what her son and his wife have been doing."

"You aren't planning to say anything!" Juliette said, horrified.

"Of course I am. I'm not about to let an opportunity like this one pass me by. Don't look so horrified—we're no more than twenty-five miles from Hampton Regis. She must be on her way to visit them. I just wonder what she'll think of you."

"Why should she think anything of me?" she asked faintly.

"Why, because I have every intention of telling her that you are her son's inamorata. That you left your husband's bed for his, committing adultery under the same roof as his charming wife," Lemur hissed. "You think I didn't know what you were doing?"

Juliette felt sick inside. There would be no respite for her tonight. "Why do you think she'd care?"

"Oh, I don't imagine she would. But her family name is already so plagued with scandal, I rather thought she might appreciate a chance to hush this one up. And I imagine she'd rather it not be bruited about where her son is hiding."

"You're going to blackmail her?"

"Such a harsh word. Merely ensuring our future financial security."

"You'll keep quiet about the Romneys? For money?" She couldn't keep the hope from her voice.

Lemur smiled, and his sharp, pointed teeth looked like tiny fangs in the firelight. "No. But I'll convince Phelan Romney's elderly mother that I will, and that should suffice. You married a clever man, dear Juliette. A devious, careful, clever man. You didn't realize that, did you? You thought you were fulfilling your father's deathbed request, and that you were finding another father to indulge you. But I've surprised you, haven't I? I have depths you wouldn't begin to guess at."

"You surprised me," she said faintly. "You would have surprised my father as well. He thought he was taking care of me."

"Not exactly. You see, I told him we had formed an attachment, but that you were too shy to talk about it."

"He wouldn't believe that!" she said furiously.

"You forget, he was dying. Half delirious. He still didn't like the idea of your marrying me, so I added the coup de grace. I told him you were carrying my child."

"You monster," she whispered.

His eyes narrowed. "Go on up to bed and wait for me, Juliette. My interview with Lady Romney shouldn't take long." He smiled, a faint, evil smile. "Don't bother getting undressed. I'm going to enjoy taking you in boys' clothes."

And Juliette rose, smooth and graceful, the sharp table knife hidden in the folds of her jacket as she started up the stairs.

# CHAPTER NINETEEN

Juliette wouldn't have believed she could sleep. The room she was to share with her husband was small and ill-furnished, the better quarters obviously going to Lady Romney. Their room consisted of a straight chair and a sagging bed, and it would have done her no good to think she could delay matters by curling up in the chair. She lay down on top of the covers and closed her eyes, keeping her hands at her sides, the knife tucked beneath her. There was no way she could prevent the inevitable, short of flinging herself from a window, and she would never take the coward's way out. She had little left but her pride, and she would have sacrificed even that to save Phelan. But it wouldn't do any good. Her best chance was to keep her husband distracted enough so that he forgot about revenge. If the knife failed her, then she'd do anything else she could.

She was so very tired. It seemed a century since she'd slept, and she would have given anything to have a few hours' rest. But she had to remain vigilant; she had to remain awake. There was no telling what Lemur might do to her. Consciousness was the only defense she had, weak though it was.

She could hear the noises of the old inn, the sound of voices carrying in the darkness, the whistle of the wind through the trees overhead, the rattle of the windows. Somewhere in the night she heard a muffled shout, a choking gasp that died away almost as quickly as it had come, and then nothing more to disturb her. And she slept, dreaming of Phelan, only to awaken to the cold gray light of dawn, and look into the face of death.

She didn't move, frozen in time. The eyes that stared down at her were black, small, and indisputably mad. The woman was very old, and she looked like no one Juliette had ever seen before. Yet she knew without question that this was Phelan's mother staring down at her.

"Had your beauty sleep, my little pretty?" Lady Margery crooned. "I've been sitting here waiting for you to open your eyes. You sleep soundly. That can be a dangerous thing. I could have slit your throat while you slept, and you never would have known. Your blood would have drained away, and no one would ever know. It's not precisely neat," she said, running a gnarled finger against the blade of a dark-stained knife, "but it has the advantage of being swift and silent and relatively fast. Your husband barely made a sound."

She was sitting on the foot of the bed, a thin, scarecrow-like figure. Juliette held herself very still as horror swept over her. There was one other person on the bed, one who no longer breathed. She turned her head, an infinitesimal amount, to see the body of her husband, his cut throat like a second smiling mouth beneath his own, dead in a welter of his own blood.

Juliette scrambled off the bed, rolling to the floor in a desperate effort to get away. The old woman was blocking the exit, an eerily placid expression on her lined face. "You won't escape," she said cheerfully. "You needn't think you can. I'm quite strong. It was a simple enough matter to kill your husband and drag his body in here. He never suspected that a sweet old lady like me could be so dangerous."

"What do you want from me?"

Lady Margery's smile was chillingly sweet. "I would think you'd be grateful. You needn't look for that knife you were clutching beneath your coat—I removed it. I simply did the deed for you. And I must say I enjoyed it," she mused. "I've never killed a man before. And he clearly deserved it. Thinking he could blackmail *me*!" She was clearly outraged by the notion.

The room smelled of death, and of madness. "What do you want from me?" Juliette asked again.

"Your husband was very informative before he died. He told me that you and my son were lovers. I can't have that. No one can have Phelan. I did my best to get rid of his brother, and so far I've failed, but I've come to finish the job. I won't allow a female to come between a mother and her child."

"I wouldn't come between you. My husband lied. Phelan thinks I'm…"

"Phelan?" Lady Margery echoed silkily. "You call him Phelan?" She shook her head. "You're coming with me, child."

"Why?"

The old woman seemed to consider it for a moment. "I imagine I'll kill you, sooner or later. In the meantime, I'll need your help. I had to hurt Barbe in order to go after your husband, and I'm afraid I might have hit her too hard. Hannigans are a tough breed, but even they have their frailties. I'm afraid you'll need to take her place as my servant."

"Hannigans?" Juliette said.

"Ah, yes, the Hannigans. A quite remarkable family. I don't know what I would have done without them. I owe them more than I can say. That's where we're going, by the way. Not to Hampton Regis or Sutter's Head. You see, I know perfectly well where my son and his bastard kin are hiding. We're going to a tiny village a few miles inland until I decide what to do. The Hannigans live there, and no one else. They'll make us welcome."

Juliette thought of Hannigan, with his kindly, bearlike demeanor and his protective stance, and she felt a faint ray of hope. "All right," she said. "I'll go with you."

"My dear," said Lady Margery, fondling the bloody knife, "you really have no choice."

Valerian had spent a more wretched time than the next two days, he was sure of it. He simply couldn't remember when. Phelan had declared the town off-limits until they could book passage out of the country, and Valerian had no interest in arguing with him. He was so damned sick of his skirts that it would have taken force to get him in them. Force, or the knowledge that Sophie needed him.

He had no idea what Sophie needed, what she was thinking, how she was faring. She'd been ill when he'd brought her home, but not desperately so. Mrs. de Quincey was an alarmist, the sort who tucked her only child in bed with tisanes and mustard plasters for nothing more than a cold. She should have been recovered by now, and that knowledge ate away at him.

For all he knew, Sophie had gone into a decline after the horror of his inadvertent kiss. Lord, the girl was innocent, but even she must have guessed that there was something wrong with an openmouthed kiss between women.

Or had she felt his beard? Had she finally guessed? The fact that she'd never even suspected his sex was simply another wound to his self-esteem. Surely she should have felt the sheer force of his attraction to her…

He was lucky she hadn't. It would only confuse matters for her, and endanger him. He and Phelan were coming to the end of their stay here, and the Continent beckoned. He could fight it no longer. It would be years before they were back in England, if ever. Sophie was much better off remembering her eccentric friend than a man who loved her.

Phelan stayed closeted in the library, a forbidding expression on his face. He refused to mention Juliette's name, and in a belated understanding, Valerian kept his peace. She was gone, disappeared beyond their reach, and he had no choice but to believe she'd gone willingly. Even if his brother refused to admit that it tore him apart.

Valerian rode fast and hard along the shore, the salt wind whipping against him, riding as if the hounds of hell were after him. When they got to the Continent, he was going to lop off his overlong blond hair, he was never going to shave, he was going to be filthy and disreputable and as grossly male as he could. He intended to drink and brawl and womanize, just to remind himself that he was a man.

The problem was, he'd never been in doubt of that. And the measure of a man wasn't in his ability to outdrink, outfight, and outwench anyone else. The measure of a man was in his own worth. And in his ability to love.

It was late morning on the third day since Juliette had left. Valerian rode back up to the house. Both he and the horse were sweating from their furious run across the strand, and he pulled off his shirt and tossed it at Hanni-

gan as he wandered in through the kitchen. "Where's my
brother?" he asked Dulcie, grabbing a fresh raspberry tart
on his way.

"In the library, brooding as always," Dulcie said, smack-
ing his hand with calm affection. "Are you going to walk
around the place half naked?"

"No, love," he said with a faint attempt at a grin, "I'm
going to strip off my breeches and walk around bare-
arsed." And he reached for the buttons.

"Off with you!" Dulcie shrieked. "This is a decent
household, you wretch."

Laughing, he grabbed another tart and sauntered up the
back stairs to his room.

But his grin faded by the time he was out of Dulcie's
sight. Another day, another endless, waiting day. Thinking
of Sophie, at home in that delectably feminine bedroom,
lying in her bed. If only he hadn't seen it. His fantasies
had been bad enough. Now he could actually envision her
stretched out, pink and rosy, amid the soft white sheets,
and the vision was sheer torment.

His windows overlooked the sea, and he'd left them
open to the early morning air. He paused, staring out into
bright sunlight when the sound of voices penetrated his
brooding abstraction. And he realized with sudden horror that it was the voice he most wanted, and dreaded, to
hear. Sophie de Quincey's.

Quickly he yanked the shutters closed, plunging the
room into darkness. He sprinted for the door, and he could
hear their voices quite plainly, Phelan arguing with that
damned supercilious tone, Sophie, *his* Sophie, being ada-
mant right back.

"If she's ill, all the more reason to see her," Sophie was saying stubbornly. "We parted on...confusing terms."

"She really doesn't want to see anyone," Phelan argued, but their voices were coming damnably closer. "She has the headache..."

"She'll see me," Sophie said flatly, and Valerian could tell by the proximity of her voice that she'd reached the top of the stairs. The only way Phelan could stop her would be to forcibly remove her, and Phelan wouldn't do that. Particularly since he knew Valerian would explode out of his bedroom and flatten him if he dared to touch her.

He had no choice. He shut his door, as silently as possible, and dove for the bed, pulling the covers over his bare chest. The chamber was very dark, only a faint crack of light filtering through, and as long as she stayed at the far end of the room, he would get away with it. Indeed, short of locking the door, he had no choice. And his beloved was a stubborn female—she'd find a way in sooner or later. He might as well face the inevitable.

"Valerie?" Her voice was soft, sweet, troubled, and the door opened a crack, letting in a dangerous amount of light.

He released a convincing moan. "It's too bright," he said, and she quickly scooted into the room, closing the door behind her. Smack in Phelan's face.

He could see her silhouette in the shadowed room, the faint glint of her golden curls, the tilt of her chin as she started toward the bed. "Dear Val," she said. "Are you all right? I was so worried..."

"Of course, child," he said faintly, trying to sink farther back into the pillows. "Just one of my miserable headaches. I do get plagued with them, and then nothing will do but for me to have darkness and complete quiet."

"And I'm disturbing you," she said miserably. "I'll leave…"

"No," he said, unable to resist. It would be the last time he saw her. Surely he could indulge himself just for a brief moment. "Sit and talk to me. My…husband told me you were ill, and receiving no visitors."

"That was my mother," she replied with some asperity. "I've told you what a fuss she makes. I had a slight cold, and I was…troubled."

"Troubled, Sophie?" he echoed, troubled himself. "What about?"

She moved across the room, much too close to him. Instead of taking the overstuffed chair that was set at some distance, she perched herself on the foot of the bed, dangerously near his booted feet, which lay hidden under the covers.

"About you, Val," she said in a voice that left no doubt that she had steeled herself to start this conversation. "About me. About us."

Saints preserve us, Valerian thought miserably. "Dear child," he said faintly, "I don't quite understand."

"Neither do I," she said, her voice rich and miserable. "You must know that I feel closer to you than I ever have to any other living being. There's a bond between us, one that I've never felt before, and I find it very confusing. It's not as if I don't have good friends, and a mother who's devoted to me. But you're different. I want to spend all my time with you, to talk with you, to laugh with you. I'm drawn to you in ways I can't begin to understand."

Valerian stopped cursing himself long enough to respond. "My dear," he said gently, "I'm really very flattered."

"I don't want you to be flattered!" she shot back. "You're

a woman of the world. You understand these things far better than I do. Explain it to me. Explain why I'm far more interested in spending the rest of my life with you than with Captain Melbourne. Explain to me why when I touch you I feel hot and cold inside, and my stomach hurts, and my pulses race, and my heart beats too strongly."

"You once told me it sounded like the flu," he said.

"Don't laugh at me," she said. "No, on second thought, *do* laugh at me. It's absurd, isn't it?"

"Absurd," he said faintly.

"I want to go with you."

"What?" She'd managed to shock him.

"You said your husband was getting ready to leave, to travel. I want to come with you."

"Your mother would never allow it," he said flatly.

"I know. So I thought we wouldn't ask her. Really, she'd have no cause to fuss. After all, you'd provide a perfect chaperone for me, and it would give me a chance to see the world. No one would think it the slightest bit odd."

"Everyone would think it very odd indeed," he said in a biting tone of voice. "You aren't running away from home."

"Perhaps if you asked, Mama might be reasonable."

"I'm not about to ask. I don't want you coming with us."

He heard her swift intake of breath, and knew that he'd hurt her. He cursed himself, even knowing that he'd had to do it.

"I thought… Forgive me," she said in a small, miserable voice. "I thought you felt some…affection for me as well."

"I do. Which is why I won't drag you around the Continent, trailing after my husband. We're vagabonds, child. Rootless wanderers, with no proper home to call our own. I wouldn't ask you to share that kind of life."

"But, Val, I have a very great deal of money," she said eagerly. "We could set up house here, and your husband could continue his travels. I confess, I don't really want to leave England, but I want to be with you."

"Sophie," he said gently, "it really won't do."

"Why not?"

"We'd be ostracized by society."

"Why?"

Lord, the child was an innocent! "Because," he said brutally, "we wouldn't be sharing a house as two friends. We'd be sharing it as lovers."

He'd finally managed to shock her. And then she delivered the killing blow. "If that's what you want," she said humbly, "I'm willing."

It took all his self-control not to reach for her. He took a deep, calming breath. She didn't even realize what she was offering, didn't understand either the ramifications or the logistics of such a suggestion. He knew full well that she didn't desire women. She desired him. Enough to risk everything she had.

"I'm not," he said. He gave her a moment to absorb the blow. "My dear Sophie, you're very young. I'm experienced, sophisticated, and you find that attractive." He was damned if he'd refer to himself as a woman again. "But you need a husband, babies, a life of your own. And I prefer my unfettered way of living. And I'm not interested in the romantic attentions of my own sex."

"Oh," she said, her voice small and mortified. "I didn't mean, that is, I thought…" Her words trailed off in a flurry of embarrassment. "I'd better leave." And she started to rise from the bed.

He couldn't bear it. Humiliating her was even worse

than lying to her. But telling her the truth simply wasn't possible.

"Forgive me, Sophie," he said, his voice naturally deep. "I didn't mean to hurt you."

"Oh, Val," she said with a muffled sob. And she flung herself across the bed, weeping, against him.

His arms came around her small body, almost of their own volition, when he should have pushed her away. He stroked her hair, kissing the flower-scented sweetness of it. He murmured soft, soothing words as she sobbed in his arms, her fingers clutching him. And she suddenly grew still, and he knew it was too late.

Her hands slid up his bare, muscled arms to his stubbled chin, and his hard, flat chest was beneath her tear-streaked face, and she froze. Then, abruptly, she pushed herself away from him, scrambling off the bed, and a moment later she'd crossed the room to fling open the shutters, letting in streams of bright, damning sunlight.

She stared at him, and her face was white with shock. The sheet lay at his waist, and he sat there in bed, indisputably masculine. Indisputably guilty.

"You bastard," she said low, her voice full of misery.

"As a matter of fact, yes," he said. He kicked off the sheets, rising from the bed.

"You lied to me. Tricked me."

"Yes," he said again.

"And all the time you were laughing at me. At the stupid little provincial, ready to throw everything away in her passion for another woman."

"I never laughed. I was…touched."

"Damn you," she said fiercely.

"Yes."

She slammed the door as she left. He made no move to stop her. There was nothing he could say, no excuse that would make his lies more acceptable. He'd known there was no future for the two of them. He'd just hoped he could have salvaged a tender memory.

The door slammed open again, but this time it was Phelan. "What the hell happened?"

"Can't you guess?" Val said wearily, turning from the window. "She offered to run away with me. I declined the offer. She told me she loved me. I told her she should wait for a man. She flung herself into my arms, and then the entire question became academic. She hates liars."

"Did you try to explain our reasons?"

"No."

There was a moment of silence. "Just as well," Phelan said finally, ever practical. "The fewer people who know about us, the better."

"We've got to get out of here, Phelan. Once the people of Hampton Regis find out…"

"She's not going to tell anyone. It would only reflect poorly on her. After all, everyone knows she's been living in your pocket for the past few weeks. Not to mention the fact that she spent the night alone with you in an inn. If it's discovered you're a man, then she's well and truly ruined."

"She might not realize it. She's absurdly innocent…"

"Innocent, yes. Stupid, no. She won't tell anyone. And not for her own sake. Once she calms down enough, she'll realize you must have had a good reason for lying to her. She might not understand that reason, but I'm willing to wager our safety that she'll keep quiet in deference to it."

"I've got to get out of here, Phelan. If worse comes to worst, I'll swim for France."

"Tomorrow."

"What?"

"There's a small boat leaving for France tomorrow. I've booked passage for the three of us. You, me, and Hannigan."

"What about Dulcie?"

"She stays behind. She has family nearby—she has no interest in wandering the globe with us."

"Tomorrow," Valerian said glumly, telling himself he should be relieved.

"Cheer up, Val. By the time we're in Paris, you'll have forgotten all about her," Phelan murmured.

He glanced up, meeting his brother's eyes. "Just as you've forgotten Juliette?"

"Juliette? Who, pray tell, is that?" Phelan countered.

"Just someone who loved you."

And Phelan stamped from the room, no longer making any attempt to hide his temper.


Sophie de Quincey was sick, angry, and shaking inside. If she hadn't made the journey out to Sutter's Head in the old trap, pulled by an ancient and much-beloved mare, she would have raced homeward in a frenzy. But Buttercup was too dear and too old to be whipped into accumulating some speed, and Sophie had to content herself with plodding slowly back to town, tears of rage and hurt streaming down her face.

How could she have lied to her? Or rather, how could *he* have lied to her? Valerie Ramsey, the bawdy, elegant, sophisticated lady of her acquaintance, was no lady at all, but a man.

And such a man. She'd never seen a man without a shirt

on before, and the sight had been dazzling. He had all that
bronzed, muscled skin. And it was so warm and resilient
beneath her hands.

He hadn't shaved. The stubble across his chin only made
him more attractive, and those beautiful gray eyes with
their absurdly long lashes no longer seemed the slightest
bit feminine. How could she have been so gullible?

He was so tall, looming over her in the bright light of
the bedroom. He'd never seemed that tall before. But suddenly, shorn of his disguise, he'd been large, and masculine, and absolutely devastating,

And a liar, Sophie reminded herself. What a fool she'd
been, ready to throw everything away for him. She hadn't
even understood herself what she'd been offering; she only
knew that a future without Valerie Ramsey had seemed
bleak indeed.

It would have been heaven, compared to this devastating betrayal. Better for her to have gone through life thinking she'd been moved by a female. *Aroused* was the word,
much as she'd shied away from it. Fallen in love. There
it was, for her unwilling mind to accept. She'd fallen in
love with another woman. Only to find out he was a man.

Suddenly the absurdity of it struck her, and she wanted
to laugh out loud. Until she remembered stripping off her
clothes in front of him. Beseeching him to tell her about
what men and women did together. Lying in the gazebo,
her head in his lap, while he told her about the strange
and wonderful things that went on between a man and a
woman.

She could feel the heat suffuse her entire body. She'd
talked about things she wouldn't even discuss with her

mother, or with her closest friend. She'd allowed her curiosity full rein, and he'd satisfied it. Damn him.

If he'd been any gentleman at all, he would have steered the conversation to more acceptable topics. He would have kept away from her, not encouraged her. He would have...

He would have told her the truth. It was the one thing she needed in her life. Honesty, no matter how brutal.

It wasn't until she was almost at the outskirts of Hampton Regis, her tears dried on her cheeks, that she thought to consider exactly why he'd lied to her. She hadn't bothered to ask, and he hadn't offered an explanation. But he must have had a very good reason.

And who was the man calling himself Val's husband? A relative, obviously, and Sophie guessed they were probably brothers. But why were they embarked on such an absurd masquerade?

She was half tempted to turn around and drive back to Sutter's Head. Her mother would have a fit of the vapors when she realized her daughter had taken the trap out alone, though at least she'd assume Sophie had gone calling on a female friend, an act which was completely acceptable. If her mother ever found out she'd been alone in a bedroom with a half-clad male...

Come to think of it, she'd spent the night in bed with that same male. If anyone were to find out, she'd be thoroughly ruined.

The thought didn't even begin to disturb her. She wasn't interested in the opinion of society, her mother's disapproval, or even Captain Melbourne's offer.

She was only interested in whether Val's reason for lying was justification for his acts. And whether she could ever forgive him.

# CHAPTER TWENTY

Juliette sat in the corner of the tiny cottage and tried not to stare at the woman across from her, concentrating instead on the arcane intricacies of pastry dough. Lady Margery had seldom left her alone in the past few days. Juliette had become maid, driver, and cook, taking the place of the mysterious Barbe. She allowed herself to wonder what had happened to the woman who'd accompanied Lady Margery as far as the inn. Was she as dead as Mark-David Lemur, or perhaps only wounded? Lady Margery seemed to have no interest in her servant's fate, and Juliette hadn't dared to ask. She'd simply done as she was ordered, stripping out of the boys' clothes that had gotten soaked with blood, dressing in skirts that were too long for her slender body. It was the first time she'd worn women's clothes in more than a month, and she hadn't missed them at all.

"I can't imagine what my son would have seen in you," Lady Margery had said with a critical glance. "I would have thought he'd have better taste. I brought him up to be more fastidious."

"He didn't see anything in me," Juliette had replied, and received a stinging slap across the mouth for her troubles. Despite her elderly appearance, Lady Margery was far from weak. But then, Juliette had guessed as much. It would have taken a certain amount of strength to cut Lemur's throat, then drag his body up onto the bed beside her.

"Don't ever lie to me, child," the old woman said, her eyes glinting with madness. "I don't care for it. If you had decent clothes you might not be bad-looking, but no one is worthy of my son. He belongs to me, and me alone. Anyone who interferes between a mother and a child deserves to be punished. Don't you agree?"

She had had little choice. If she'd said yes, she might be signing her own death warrant. If she'd argued, the result could be the same. She'd said nothing, learning that silence was her safest course.

Lady Margery needed not much more than a servant and an audience, and Juliette performed those roles admirably. She had no difficulty handling the small carriage, and they arrived at the tiny village of Hampton Parva by midafternoon the next day. But all of Juliette's hopes for assistance against a murderous madwoman were in vain.

The village was small, shabby, not much more than a settlement. A few ramshackle cottages, a straggly garden or two, and pigs and chickens roaming the narrow streets like vermin. There were less than two dozen people there, and they all regarded her with unfriendly curiosity. And they all looked vaguely familiar.

"Hannigans," Lady Margery announced, answering her unasked question. The hovel they'd taken over was just as decrepit as the others, the thatched roof undoubtedly leaked, and Juliette could hear the rustle of rats as they nested in the corners. The vermin frightened her far less than Lady Margery. "Everyone in Hampton Parva is a

Hannigan. They've inbred quite a bit, and it's no wonder. Decent people won't have them around."

Juliette wanted to ask questions, but she kept silent, waiting, pounding on the pastry dough that simply seemed to get tougher. She couldn't cook, but Lady Margery was too mad to notice. She ate what Juliette put in front of her, and Juliette found herself wondering if she might find some rat poison in this benighted town.

Hannigans. The suspicious-looking villagers were a far cry from the Hannigan she knew, with his protective mien and friendly nature, but there was a definite physical resemblance.

"They've been at Romney Hall for close to forty years now," the old woman continued. "Not that they're there now. No, Hannigan ran off with my son, and Dulcie went with them. And Barbe—I wonder where she is," she said, her mind beginning to fade a bit. "She came with me to the inn."

"Did you hurt her?" Juliette asked.

"Hurt Barbe? Why should I do that? She's been with me since Phelan was born. Since Catherine died."

"Catherine? Who was Catherine?"

"None of your business," the old lady snapped, furious. "You concentrate on the cooking." She smiled with sudden cunning. "I remember what happened to Barbe. I hit her."

"Did you kill her?"

Lady Margery shrugged her thin shoulders. "I don't know. I hardly think it matters—you never met her. There are enough Hannigans in this world, and doubtless no one would blame me. Not any more than they'll blame me for killing your husband. A worthless bully."

"Will they blame you if you kill me?" Juliette asked carefully, laying the thick, cracked dough in a pie tin.

"Certainly not," she said with great dignity. "They'll trust my judgment. After all, I'm Lady Romney of Romney Hall. I'm not a nameless little nobody like Catherine Morgan."

"Who was Catherine?" Juliette asked again, no longer worrying how Lady Margery might react.

"Catherine doesn't matter. She's been dead for more than…thirty-four years."

"If she doesn't matter, why do you keep talking about her?"

"I don't keep talking about her, you do," the old lady shot back in a querulous voice.

Juliette kept silent for a moment, waiting for the woman's garrulousness to get the better of her. It didn't take long.

"She was very pretty, Catherine was," she said in a dreamy voice. "Too pretty. Harry wanted her, of course, but he didn't dare touch her. Not when she was married to his younger brother. Back then he had a few standards. Keeping faithful to me wouldn't have entered into it, but he wouldn't have taken his brother's wife."

"What happened to her?"

"She died."

"How sad," Juliette said gently.

"Not in the slightest," Lady Margery snapped. "Her husband had been killed in a carriage wreck several months before, and she had nothing to live for. It was a blessing, even if Barbe and Hannigan didn't see it that way."

"Why wouldn't they?"

"They were her servants, you see. Hannigans are a

strange breed, wildly loyal to those they choose to serve, completely amoral where others are concerned." She didn't seem to think it the slightest bit odd that she pass strictures on someone else's morality.

"But they transferred their loyalty to you, once she died," Juliette said.

"They transferred their loyalty to my son. But I keep them under control. I know their secrets," Lady Margery said craftily. "Just as they know mine. We cannot hurt each other, as long as we know so much."

"Secrets?" Juliette asked idly, tossing chunks of onion into the pie crust. She hadn't managed to get all the papery skin off them, but she didn't think it would matter. "What secrets?"

"If I told, they wouldn't be a secret anymore, now would they?"

"Who would I tell?"

The old lady smiled, exposing large, yellowed teeth. "True enough. You won't have a chance to tell, will you? I won't tell you my secrets. I'll carry those to the grave. But I can tell you one thing about the Hannigans."

Juliette couldn't care less about the Hannigans, but she decided any information might come in handy if she was going to get out of this mess alive. "What about the Hannigans?"

"Don't you wonder why they're forced to live out here, far away from civilization? Why no one will have them around, why they're considered the dregs of the earth?"

"I hadn't realized they were," Juliette said mildly.

"They're murderers."

Juliette thought of her husband's body, lying lifeless in the bed next to her. "Really?" she said politely to his killer.

"That's their family business, girl, for generations."

"They don't look particularly lethal to me," she said. But then, neither did Lady Margery.

"Oh, they don't ply their trade anymore. Most of their lot was hanged more than fifty years ago, and since then they've had to turn to more peaceful ways of earning a living. They're terrible farmers, but they make good servants. They're very loyal."

Juliette glanced at Lady Margery, wondering if this was one more mad fantasy. It had the eerie ring of truth. "Why did they kill people?" she asked, pouring semi-congealed pig fat over the potatoes and onions and trying to keep from shuddering.

"Why do most people kill? For money. Have you ever been to a place called Dead Man's Cove?"

"I've heard of it," she said carefully, thinking of Phelan's long, deft hands, and the sketch that she still managed to keep hidden from Lady Margery's sharp, crazed eyes.

"The Hannigans were wreckers. They lured ships to their doom, and then they clubbed the survivors to death, leaving them in the water after they stripped them of their valuables. They thrived for hundreds of years, until the government sent in the militia to put a stop to, it, and they hanged every Hannigan they could find, be it man, woman, or child."

"How horrible."

Lady Margery shrugged, clearly unmoved by her gruesome tale. "The children were just as savage as their elders. A few of them ran into the woods to hide, and they stay here to this day. They leave people alone, and in return they're not hunted like the monsters they are."

"Why did you come here? Why did you bring me here?"

"It's the best place to keep an eye on Phelan. Why do you suppose Hannigan talked them into coming here? So his family could make sure they were safe. He didn't realize I would guess where they were hiding, or that I'd force Barbe to come with me. Where is Barbe?" she added in a fretful voice.

Early on, Juliette thought that querulous vagueness signaled an opportunity for escape. It hadn't. Lady Margery grew even more dangerous when her confusion reined, and Juliette had a knife slash on her wrist to prove it.

"She'll probably be here sooner or later," Juliette said gently.

"I hope so. Once I take care of you, I'll need someone to help me. I don't like to be alone. Too many ghosts. Harry comes to me at night. Never did when he was alive," she added with a cackle. "But he comes to me now. And Catherine. So reproachful. It's not my fault. I've done my best, better than she ever would have. She was weak, weak-blooded, weak-minded. I was strong. It was only right what I did. Only right."

"What did you do?"

Lady Margery gave a sly smile. "I'll tell you," she said, "just before I kill you."

"A shame about your friends, dear," Sophie's mother said across the dinner table.

Sophie listlessly stabbed her sturgeon with a fork. Her mother's conversation always tended to be arch, and Sophie had learned to ignore the majority of it.

"Which friends are those, Rosalind?" Percival de Quincey, Sophie's kindly, slightly befuddled-looking father, asked dutifully.

"That odd Mrs. Ramsey and her husband. I must say I always found her a bit...dashing for my taste, but certainly there was no harm in her. Nevertheless, I'll be happy when my precious concentrates on friends her own age. After all, it won't be long before she's a married woman, and these gay, happy summer days will be long gone."

Sophie ignored her mother's ridiculous phrase to concentrate on what mattered. "What has happened to the Ramseys?" she demanded, dropping her fork.

"Why, I assumed you would be the first to know," said her mother, clearly assuming no such thing. "After all, you paid a courtesy call on the woman this morning."

"We didn't have much of a discussion," Sophie said. "She was feeling unwell."

"This climate doesn't agree with her," Mrs. de Quincey said archly. "If they'd asked me, I could have recommended an herbal concoction that would have made a new woman out of her."

Sophie couldn't help it, she found she could laugh. "I'm not certain it would have been appreciated."

"Perhaps not," her mother said in a judicious tone of voice. "Acts of Christian charity seldom are. Still, I imagine you'll miss her."

"Miss her?" Sudden, overwhelming dread filled Sophie's heart.

"Her husband has booked passage on the *Sea Horse* for the next tide tomorrow. I don't imagine you'll see them again."

"The next tide," Sophie's father announced, "is at eleven fifty-two in the morning." He beamed, obviously pleased with himself.

"Yes, dear," his wife said, dismissing him. "I'm certain

Sophie doesn't care when the tide is. She has more important things to consider."

"On the contrary," Sophie said breathlessly. "I'm fascinated by the tides."

"That's a new one," her mother said critically. "At least
you're showing a trace of scientific interest, instead of
being so abysmally concerned with household matters."

"Nothing wrong with household matters, m'dear," Mr.
De Quincey dared to remark. "She's a little earth mother,
is our Sophie."

"No daughter of mine," said Rosalind de Quincey in
a chilling voice, "is an earth mother." She made it sound
like something completely indecent. "She has an excellent mind, and I'm certain Captain Melbourne will give
her ample opportunity to use it."

It hit Sophie like a bolt of lightning, the sudden, joyous
realization, and she laughed out loud, startling her father
into dropping his soup spoon. "I'm not going to marry
Captain Melbourne," she announced firmly.

Her mother looked at her as if she'd suddenly grown
horns. "Don't be ridiculous, child," she said flatly. "Of
course you are. It's a daughter's duty to be guided by her
parents in matters such as these, and your father and I decided—"

"As a matter of fact, *I* haven't decided," her father said
abruptly. "I don't care for the fellow above half. Dashed
dull stick, if you ask me."

"Nobody asked you," Mrs. de Quincey said in frosty
tones.

"Yes, my love." He subsided quickly.

Mrs. de Quincey turned her steely blue gaze back to her

recalcitrant daughter. "As I was saying, you will— Where are you going?"

Sophie had already fled the table, racing toward the door on dancing feet. "I'm off to see Mrs. Ramsey," she called back over her shoulder, her voice a bubble of laughter.

"Stop her, Percival," Mrs. de Quincey demanded. "She can't run off at this time of night."

"I imagine she just wants to wish her Godspeed." Sophie's father, as always, was trying to be reasonable. "No harm in that, my love."

Sophie paused at the door. "No," she said. "I most definitely do not." And she ran out of the room before her parents could come up with one more halfhearted protest.

She grabbed her dark blue cloak as she went, against the dampness of the night air, but she didn't bother to change her slippers. A moment later she was out in the gathering darkness, walking swiftly down to the shore.

She had no intention of driving the trap. Buttercup was too slow, the road too narrow in the dark. She was going to take the shortcut through the woods, following the beach to Sutter's Head. She would be there in no more than half an hour, less if she hurried, and indeed, it felt as if her feet were flying.

How could she have been so foolish? All she'd thought about were his lies, his deception. It had taken till now to realize the wondrous joy of it all. He was a man. A man who cared about her; she knew it as well as she knew her own name. A man who could give her love, babies, everything she had ever dreamed of and more. If she was brave enough to ask.

By the time her parents realized she'd gone on foot, it would be too late. With luck they wouldn't notice—for all her mother's prosing, she trusted dear Mrs. Ramsey completely.

As did Sophie. Whatever his reasons for lying, they had to be good ones. That was all she needed to know. She needed to see him, talk to him, touch him. Lord, she didn't even know his name!

By the time she reached the other side of the woods, her slippers were soaked. She paused in the shadows, taking them off, pulling off her silk stockings as well, before she stepped out onto the sand. The moon had risen, a full, ghostly moon, and she shivered for a moment, remembering the old tales of wreckers, and dead men floating in the cove. But that was miles away from here. This stretch of beach had never known violent, ugly death. It was serene, beautiful, a place to dance in the moonlight…

She heard the sound of the horse from out of nowhere, and superstitious terror filled her. She saw the rider loom up on the edge of the strand, riding so quickly that he no sooner appeared than he was upon her, his huge dark horse from hell pounding down on her.

She stood mesmerized for a moment, unable to move as the horse bore down on her. And then at the last minute she threw herself to one side, just as the rider finally saw her.

She twisted her ankle as she fell, and she lay there in a heap, watching with remote horror as the monstrous animal reared from the force of the rider's hands, and a moment later they went down with a flashing of hooves. The horse lay there, kicking, squealing in fright, and the rider was on his back in the sand, spread-eagled and motionless beneath the moonlight.

He was dead, she knew it. And then he moved, gingerly, and began to curse, loud and long, and she realized with tearful relief that it was the man she'd known as Mrs. Ramsey.

He surged to his feet and stalked over to his horse, kneeling down and checking the animal for injury. "Whoever the hell you are," he said bitterly, "you should know better than to go flitting around like a ghost, scaring a poor animal. He could have taken a great injury."

"So could I," Sophie said.

He was in the midst of pulling his mount onto unsteady feet, but at the sound of her voice he whirled around. "Sophie?"

"Flitting around like a ghost," she acknowledged wryly.

The horse scampered off down the beach, bored by human conversation and obviously unhurt, as the man crossed the sand slowly to stand over her.

The moon was behind him, leaving his face in shadows, and she felt suddenly, miserably, shy. Perhaps she'd imagined too much. Perhaps all the feeling had been on her side.

And then he knelt down beside her, taking her hand in his, and said, "God, Sophie, don't torment me."

And she knew she was loved.

Sophie de Quincey was the last person Valerian expected to see that night as he took Hellfire out for a final, desperate ride along the strand. He'd accepted Phelan's pronouncement with gratitude, more than ready to leave this miserable place. His only objection was that the ship left in broad daylight.

"I'm not putting skirts on again," he'd thundered as he'd vaulted onto Hellfire's back.

Phelan stood in the courtyard, watching him. "One last time, Valerian. We've come this far..."

"I'd rather hang," he said mutinously.

"I'm certain you would. However, think how it would reflect on your precious Sophie."

Valerian knew when he was beaten. "Once we leave the harbor," he said in a dangerous voice, "I'm going to strip off those clothes and throw them overboard."

"I wouldn't if I were you," Phelan drawled. "You know what they say about sailors. I'm afraid they'd find the spectacle far too fascinating."

"I'm counting on you to protect me," Val growled.

"Valerian," Phelan said, suddenly serious. "I'm sorry. I know you cared about her."

His brother smiled wryly. "Not as sorry as I am for you, old man. At least I can admit it."

And he'd taken off into the night before Phelan could reply.

He might have killed her. She lay in the sand, looking up at him out of her beguiling blue eyes, and he realized she was no longer furious. His heart, which had just begun to calm after the spill, started speeding up again, and he felt the blood heat and pool in his veins.

"What are you doing here?" He tried to sound remote, but he was still holding her chilled hand, still kneeling over her in the moonlight, and his solicitude ruined the effect of his disgruntled words.

"They told me you were leaving."

He didn't deny it. "Tomorrow morning. It's for the best."

"Take me with you."

He dropped her hand, but he couldn't move away. "Don't be ridiculous. It was bad enough when I was supposed to be a woman. You certainly can't go off with two unmarried men."

"Then marry me." She sat up, looking at him defiantly. "There, I've shocked you, haven't I? My mother may be a ridiculous person, but she taught me to go after what I want. And I want you."

"You don't know what you're talking about," he said, trying to back away, but she reached out and caught his hand, pulling him toward her.

"Yes, I do. You explained it to me, quite nicely, in the gazebo that day. I want to marry you and make love with you and have your babies."

"It's quite impossible."

"No, it's not. You're not Valerie Ramsey at all. You're…" Her forehead creased in sudden confusion. "I don't even know what your name is."

"Valerian," he said. "And I don't have an honest last name. I'm a bastard, with no family, no money, no prospects."

"I have money and prospects enough for both of us."

"I'm wanted for murder," he said desperately. She looked too damned beautiful sitting there in the moonlight, beseeching him.

He expected her to pull away, to run from him as she had earlier. Instead, her mouth curved in a dazzling smile of relief. "I knew you had to have a good reason for lying to me," she said. "It doesn't matter."

"Don't you even want to know whether I did it or not?"

"No," she said. "If you did, you would have had an excellent reason. If you didn't, it needn't concern me."

"I won't marry you, Sophie."

She considered this for a moment. "Very well." she said. "We'll live in sin. My mother makes noises about free love—we'll give her a chance to prove her convictions."

"Sophie, Sophie, you don't know what you're talking about," he said miserably. "I won't do this to you. You need to find some worthy man and marry him, have his babies…"

"Like Captain Melbourne? No, thank you, Valerian. I want you."

He stared at her in mute frustration, his determination almost at the breaking point. "Get up," he said flatly. "I'm taking you home to your mother."

"I can't."

"Why not?" he demanded.

"Because I turned my ankle when I jumped out of the way of your horse," she said simply.

Remorse flooded him. "God, Sophie, why didn't you say something?" He flipped back the hem of her skirts with unconscious concern as he took her slender ankle in his. "Does it hurt?" he asked.

"A bit. But not that one. The other," she said with a faint tremor in her voice. One that could have been pain. Or something else.

He picked up her other foot, more gently this time. She was barefoot, and she had the most beautiful ankles he'd ever seen in his life. The right one was faintly bruised from her tumble, and he gave in to temptation, telling himself it would be just once. He leaned forward and put his mouth on her ankle, and she let out a squeak, one he knew damned well wasn't of pain.

Might as well be hanged for a sheep as a lamb, he thought, kissing her other ankle. This time the squeak was closer to a sigh, and the sound of it made the blood burn in his veins, pooling in his groin with such blatant sexuality that he ought to be ashamed of himself. But he couldn't be. He'd wanted her too desperately, for too long.

He kissed her calf, moving up the faint swell of it until he reached her knee. He kissed the back of her knee, using his tongue, and her skirts frothed back against her hips, and she shuddered with pleasure.

He groaned, deep in the back of his throat, fighting the urge to push her into the sand. Her cloak lay spread out beneath her, and he wanted to throw her skirts up to her shoulders and push himself between her long white legs. He was shaking with need, and he made one last attempt to stop himself.

"No, Sophie," he said, his voice tight with tension. "I can't do this to you.'

"Valerian," she said gently, "you can't help yourself." And she reached her arms up to him, offering herself, to him and to the moonlit night.

It was too much for him to resist. "You're right," he said. "Even though I'll be damned for doing it." And he caught her arms, pulling her up to him, and set his mouth on hers.

# CHAPTER TWENTY-ONE

It was the kiss he'd always longed to give her. His mouth opened against hers, wet and warm and seeking. He used his tongue, his teeth, kissing her so thoroughly he was dazed with the wonder of it. And the knowledge that she was kissing him back, clinging to his shirt with surprising strength, parting her lips beneath his forceful pressure, tilting her head back to better receive him, only added to the glory of it. He groaned, telling himself he was every inch the bastard to do this to her. Knowing it was too late to stop.

His arms were around her, and he could feel the fastenings of her dress. He was far more familiar with women's clothing than he had ever been before, and he knew how to unfasten the dress. Despite his shaking hands, he could do it in a trice, and it would fall down to her shoulders and beyond, baring her to the night air and his hungry gaze.

Maybe if he stopped kissing her he could keep from unfastening the dress. But he couldn't stop kissing her. And his hands were deft, busy, untying the ribbons, slipping the thin muslin down her shoulders, her arms, and then they were no longer deft, they were shaking, and he tried to pull away.

She wasn't letting him go. She clung to him, and her lips were damp and beestung, and the dress fell to her waist. She was wearing a thin cotton chemise, similar to the one she'd worn at the inn, and while he couldn't see the dusky color of her nipples in the moonlight, he could see their shape, distended against the thin cloth. He bent down and covered her breast with his mouth, suckling it through the thin cloth, his tongue swirling against the hard nub, and once more she shrieked, digging her hands into his shoulders in reaction.

He was beyond rational thought. He pushed her down, and she went willingly, pulling him with her. The cloak was a blanket beneath them, cushioning the sand, turning it into a bed. He sank between her legs, pressing against her, and she felt hot and damp and ready for him.

He'd never bedded a virgin in his life. He needed to be gentle, go slow, when everything in his rigid body was telling him to hurry, hurry. He cupped her face, kissing her mouth, her neck, her breasts, tugging the thin chemise down so that he could taste her flesh. She made a breathless little sound, one that might have been desire, or just as easily might have been fear, and he tried to pull back.

She wouldn't let him. She lifted her hips against his, cradling him. "Show me, Valerian," she whispered. She took his hand and put it between her legs, to the heated center of her. "You told me I'd be damp and ready for you. Show me, Valerian. Teach me."

He could no sooner stop than he could have forced his heart to stop beating. She was moist, and hot, and wanting him, and there was no way he was going to deny them both. His hands were clumsy as they unfastened his breeches over his swollen manhood, freeing himself, and he sank between her legs, resting against her, keeping his weight on his arms, feeling his chest press against her breasts. They were damp from his mouth, hard from arousal and the night air, and their tightness against him was one more level of burning that threatened to push him over the edge.

"I don't want to hurt you," he said in a strained voice, trying to hold back.

"It will only hurt the first time," she said, reassuring him. "I can stand it if you can."

He laughed, a strangled sound as he began to sink into her hot, milking depths. When he reached the barrier he halted, wishing there were some way he could make it easier for her, some way to keep that haze of confused desire in her passion-dark eyes.

He put his hand between their bodies and threaded his fingers through the damp tangle of hair, just above their joining. She jerked, startled, as he pressed hard, rubbing against her, and then he felt her begin to shiver and shake, her breath coming in strangled rasps, the tight wet clasp of her drawing him in deeper, deeper, until she shattered, and he pushed all the way into her, breaking through the barrier with no more than a slight force, neither of them even noticing that hurdle had been breached.

She was panting in his ear as stray tremors racked her body. "Oh, Valerian," she whispered in a voice strained with awe. "That was wonderful. Even better than you told me."

"Yes," he said, trying to control his need to thrust madly into her. He was going to explode, he knew it, but he wanted to give her time to get used to him, not fall on her like a rutting beast.

"We aren't finished, are we?" she asked sweetly. She lifted her legs, encircling his hips, drawing him in deeper still. "There's more, isn't there?"

"I don't want to hurt you," he said through gritted teeth, trying to pull away from her.

"The worst is already over," she said practically. "And the worst was splendid. Show me the rest."

He thrust back into her then, a deep, sure thrust, one she met with welcoming gladness, and he was lost. He surged against her, gone into some lost, dark place of his own making, and she was with him, wrapped tightly around him, as he rocked her against the sand, holding her hips with his big hands, thrusting again and again, and her body was trembling and shivering and shattering around him as he went rigid in her arms, spilling his seed inside her in a glorious wave of love and desire.

He collapsed against her, breathless, panting, trying desperately to regain even an ounce of sanity, enough to make certain she was all right. There were tears streaking her face, her eyes were tightly shut, and her mouth trembled, and he knew he'd been a brute, a monstrous, rapacious brute, and he wanted to kill himself. He wanted to walk into the sea and never come out again. He wanted...

She opened her eyes and smiled at him, a tearful, blissful expression on her face. "That was quite awe-inspiring," she said in a hushed voice.

He wanted to make a joke, but he couldn't. "Yes," he said. "It was."

"Is it usually like that?" she asked, her voice soft and breathless. "You made it sound delightful, but you hadn't described it in quite such glowing detail."

"No, it's not usually like that. As a matter of fact, it's never been that good," he said, looking down at her.

She smiled at him again. "That's because we're in love."

He rolled off her, afraid that if he didn't he might never leave her body. "Sophie..."

She wasn't about to hear his attempts at common sense. She glanced down at her body. "Goodness," she murmured. "You didn't even take my dress off."

He couldn't resist. "I wasn't wearing it," he said.

She laughed, a sound of pure joy dancing on the night air, and she pulled the dress off her, following with the chemise, so that she knelt there on her cloak, naked and beautiful, her virgin's blood staining her white thighs, her breasts high and full and tempting. "I'm going swimming," she announced. "And then I want you to show me more."

She was running off into the surf before he could stop her. He watched her go, guilt and desire coursing through his body. And then he stripped off the rest of his clothes and followed her into the cold, dark sea.

He was used to the icy York waters. The chilly Atlantic made no difference to his need—he was already hungry for her again, and the dead of winter wouldn't have lessened his desire. She flung herself against him, cold and wet and laughing, and her hair was plastered against her white body, wrapping around them both. "We can't do this," he said as she slid her body around his, and her mouth was cool and delicious against his, tasting of the sea. "I don't want to leave you with a bastard, like my mother was left. I should have been more careful, but I won't take another chance…"

"Too late," she said cheerfully. "You know a great deal about making love, but I know more about women's bodies. Women are most likely to conceive when they're right in between their monthly flows, and we've timed it perfectly. I imagine in nine months' time we'll be happy parents."

"Sophie!" he said.

"And he's not going to be a bastard. You're going to marry me, and we're going to live happily ever after."

He was standing in the surf, holding her, her legs wrapped around his waist, her hands cupping his face as she stared at him fiercely. "Do you hear me?" she demanded, over the roar of the surf. "Happily ever after, damn it."

He gave up then. "How can I fight it?" he asked the heavens. And before she even realized what he was doing, he'd shifted her, pulling her down on his iron-hard arousal, sinking deep into her, and within moments she was clutching his back, clawing him, shattering around him, and he was following her, dissolving into her body, falling into the surf with his body still tight within hers.

He carried her up to the house, wrapped tightly in her cloak. He was wearing his breeches and nothing else, her clothes had been tossed to the four winds, and she was naked, wet, and blissfully happy. The house at Sutter's Head was dark and silent, everyone long since in bed, as he bore her through the hallways to the room where she'd first discovered the truth.

He set her down on the bed, following her down, his warm, strong body covering hers, and she nestled against him. "Where will we go?" she asked sleepily.

He'd given up fighting her, at least for now. "I'm leaving it up to Phelan. He's spent most of his adult life abroad—this is one of the few times I've been out of Yorkshire."

"I love Yorkshire," Sophie said. "My aunt Beatrice has a farm up there, on Robin Hood's Bay. She's always said she'll leave it to me."

"Romney Hall is very near there. If you run away with me, you'll never see it," he warned.

"I imagine France is just as lovely," she said bravely, dismissing Yorkshire with only a pang.

"I don't think so," he said, stroking her sea-damp hair

as he held her close. "I think I'd be taking you away from everything you'd ever loved, and you'd grow to hate me."

"The only reason I'd hate you," she said fiercely, "is if you left me behind. You can't seduce and abandon me, Valerian. We belong together."

"You'll hate me," he said again, "but I can't let you go."

"Wise decision," she murmured sleepily, rubbing her face against his chest. "You have such smooth skin."

"Not usually. I had to shave my chest."

"You aren't going to do that anymore, are you?" she asked, suddenly worried. "Or wear skirts?"

"Only if you beg me," he murmured against her ear.

She slapped at him, sleepily.

"Are you sure you won't miss your dreams of an English country farm? Of dairies and preserves and closets full of white linen?" he asked her.

"No more than you'll miss fields of sheep and cattle," she said. "Truly. I'm certain I'll learn to be very adventurous and love foreign lands. That dream was just a girl's fantasy. I'm sure I would have grown dreadfully bored."

"Dreadfully," he echoed dryly.

"Besides, as long as I'm with you, I'll be perfectly happy." She snuggled closer. "You still haven't said it, you know."

"Said what?"

"That you love me. You do, you know. I have no doubt of it whatsoever."

"Then why do you need to hear the words?"

She pulled herself out of his arms to stare at him. "I don't need to hear the words," she said sternly. "*You* need to say them."

He cupped her face, looking down into her eyes, and

the expression on his beautiful face was bleak. "Not yet," he said. "Not until I deserve to."

"Valerian!" she protested, but he silenced her mouth with his. And then there was no more need for words.

"Wake up, slut." The voice was hissing in her ear, and Juliette struggled out of sleep. She was lying on a thin pallet on the dirt floor of the shack, and Lady Margery was looming over her in the darkness, her eyes gleaming in the moonlight that shone through the broken window.

"What...?"

"Don't ask questions. I'll tell you what you need to know. Barbe has come after me, and she'll tell on me, I know she will. They'll try to stop me, and I can't have that. We must hurry, before they come back."

"Who? Why must we hurry?"

"Don't ask questions," she said again, hauling Juliette to her feet with superhuman strength. "They'll tell Phelan the truth, and he won't understand. He'll think I'm wrong, and he won't let me do what needs to be done. Come along now, don't dawdle."

"Where are we going?"

"Dead Man's Cove. I've been thinking about it for a few days, and it seems the logical spot."

"The logical spot for what?"

"Why, to kill you, my dear. What else?"

Phelan sat alone in the darkness, listening to the night. No one would bother him. Everyone had steered clear of him during the past three days, unwilling to be exposed to the lash of his vicious temper. Even Valerian had been hard put to be around him.

All of which suited Phelan perfectly. He didn't want to see anyone, talk to anyone, deal with anyone. All he wanted was to leave this damnable place and never come back again.

He'd never let someone make a fool of him before. He'd been ready to trust her, ready to give her his heart, something he hadn't been sure he even possessed. And she'd run away from him, gone off to a life of security and boredom.

It made no difference that she'd done the acceptable thing by going with her lawful husband. He didn't give a damn about what was proper or not, and he hadn't thought she did either. He thought she would follow her heart. Perhaps she had.

Never before had he any doubts as to what he wanted, what he needed, who and what he was. One small slip of a creature, one who wasn't sure if she was a boy or a girl, had disordered his life completely, turning it upside down with far more effectiveness than something as shocking as his father's murder and his mother's obvious culpability.

And the more he fought against it, the worse it grew. He sat back in his chair, crossed his arms over his chest, and listened to the night while he made one last attempt to talk some sense into his willful brain.

He heard Valerian return, heard the whisper of voices, the rhythmic creak of the bed overhead. A short while later he heard Val's horse wander back into the courtyard, obviously having been abandoned for better companionship, and he almost rose to take care of the animal, then thought better of it. Hannigan would be out and about—it was his time of night. He'd see to Hellfire, sooner or later.

Phelan heard Hannigan leave for one of his frequent visits to the tiny village of Hampton Parva. He'd be back by dawn as always. But this dawn would be different. This would be the beginning of their last day in England.

He flung open the windows, watching the night sky, the clouds scudding past the full moon. A lover's moon, mocking him, he thought as he wandered over to his desk to begin packing up his papers.

His sketch pad lay there, still disarranged from his tussle with Valerian. He'd avoided looking at it for days, unwilling to see her image, but suddenly he wanted to; he had to look at her. To convince himself that she didn't matter.

It took him endless moments of flipping through the sketchbook before he realized the picture was gone.

There was only one person who'd seen that sketch, one person who could have taken it. When Juliette had left his bed and his life, she'd taken the sketch with her.

He stared at the sketch pad for a moment, then let it drop down on the desk.

She'd lied to him, and he'd been too caught up in his own fury and confusion to think straight. She hadn't turned her back on him for a life of respectability and comfort. Whatever her reasons for going with Lemur, they would have nothing to do with her own wants.

He was going after her, as he should have three days ago. He didn't give a damn about the strictures of society or what idiotic sacrifice Juliette thought she was making. He was going to find her, and he was never going to let her go.

He bounded up the stairs two at a time, crashing into Valerian's room without bothering to knock. They were asleep, his brother and the little bluestocking, but they woke up at his presumptuous entrance, the girl diving under the covers with a shriek of embarrassment, Valerian looking ready for another bout of fisticuffs.

"I'm not going," Phelan said flatly.

"Just as well," Valerian said. "Neither am I."

"I've got to find Juliette."

Valerian's thunderous expression vanished. "It's about bloody time," he said.

"Yes," said Phelan. "It is." He started toward the door, then paused, turning back to see his brother bending over the lump hidden under the bedclothes, his voice a coaxing murmur. "By the way, brother."

"What?" Val growled, his temper back.

"You'd better find a way to marry the girl."

Val laughed then, flipping back the covers to expose a tangle of golden-blond hair and a bright red face. "I intend to. Assuming they don't hang me first."

Hannigan was waiting for him when Phelan strode into the darkened kitchen. One lamp was burning on the table, illuminating his face. "You're looking a bit lively for this early in the morning, your lordship," he said heavily. "You've finally gotten over the girl?"

"I'm going after her," Phelan said. "We're not sailing today. We might not sail at all. It's time we knew the truth, Hannigan. Even if it's not what we want to hear."

Hannigan stared at him for a long moment. "What is it you're wanting?" he said slowly, his tone caustic. "The truth, or the girl?"

"Both. Juliette first. They've got a three-day start— Lemur's probably taken her to Chichester by now."

"Lemur's in Somerset."

Phelan stared at him in disbelief. "What are you talking about? How the hell would you know where he is?"

"I know what I need to know," Hannigan said. "He's

deep in Somerset. About four feet under. I put him there myself."

The man Phelan had known all his life, the man who had been almost another father to him, was suddenly a stranger. "Did you kill him?"

Hannigan shook his head. "Not me, lad. I was hoping I wouldn't have to tell you. You'd gotten rid of the girl; she was no longer our concern. But things have been moving too fast, out of my control, and you're going to find out sooner or later. It was just damned bad luck that Lemur took her to that inn."

"She did it, didn't she?" Phelan demanded. "He tried to touch her again, and she killed her own husband. Damn it, if only I'd gone after her!"

"Not her, lad," said Hannigan. "Though if I hadn't helped Barbe get rid of the body, that's doubtless what they'd believe."

Phelan's horror deepened. "Barbe? She was in Yorkshire, watching over Lady Margery."

"She was in Somerset, watching over Lady Margery," Hannigan said heavily. "Your mother killed Lemur. With the same knife she used on your father. And she's going to kill the girl."

It was a cold, misty day, the sun barely rising, as the two women scrambled down the path to Dead Man's Cove. Lady Margery was pushing Juliette ahead, one hand clasped like a talon around her wrist, the other holding the knife. She was clever, all right. If she'd gone first down the steep, winding path, Juliette could have given her a shove, taken the chance that she'd be dragged down as well. If she pulled the murderous old woman down on top of her, it would mean certain death, and Juliette wasn't quite ready to face it.

She wasn't sure why. She'd been living with death for the past three days, ever since Lemur had taken her away from Phelan. She should have begun to accept it.

But oddly enough, the moment she'd woken up to find Lemur dead beside her, she'd known hope. And nothing had been able to take it from her.

The woman behind her stumbled on a loose rock, shrieked, and Juliette tensed, ready to pull away from the steely grip if it should loosen.

It didn't. Lady Margery righted herself with a demonic cackle. "Like a mountain goat," she said, more to herself. "And they won't come after us. Don't you be thinking anyone will come to your rescue. They're too scared."

"Who is?" Juliette asked breathlessly when they reached the sand. It looked different in the early morning light, the full moon still hanging in the sky. Eerie, ghost-ridden. Not the place where she'd lain in the sand and watched Phelan. Not the place she'd returned to, and dreamed. It was well named, a place of death.

"The Hannigans. None of them will come down here. The ghosts of their victims haunt this place, haunt them. It's their penance. Barbe explained it all to me. They must stay nearby so that they may never forget the crimes of their ancestors. But they never venture any closer."

"That's ridiculous."

"No, it's not. It's a place of death and it's where you're going. Come along." She started dragging her across the sand.

Juliette no longer bothered to argue. Who could reason with a madwoman? She stumbled into the surf, moving through the waist-deep water toward the beached wreck, her long skirts trailing in the water, slapping against her legs.

The wrecked ship was sturdier than she would have guessed. Lady Margery clambered up the side, dragging Juliette after her, crawling over blackened timbers with a spiderlike agility unhampered by the butcher knife. "They say drowning's easy," she said, panting, climbing onto the slanted deck. It was pitted with holes, but Lady Margery navigated them like the mountain goat she professed to be.

"That's a blessing," Juliette murmured uneasily, wondering whether the corpses of long-dead sailors still lay in the rotting hull, or just their ghosts.

"Not for you, love. I'm going to cut your throat before I toss you over. That way the fishes can feed on you while you bleed to death."

Juliette shivered in horror at the gruesome words. It was going to be a beautiful day, she thought, in contrast to her desperate situation. The sun would burn off the early morning haze and shine brightly down on this cove of death. And Juliette had every intention of staying alive to see it. Of staying alive to get back to Phelan.

She looked to the cliffs. She could see the Hannigans lined up on the edge, watching the ship from a distance, none of them making any move to descend the path and come to her aid. They looked like ghosts in the faint light, silent, eerie, a witness to one more death.

She yanked herself away from Lady Margery and raced across the scarred deck toward the far end of the ship. "Help me!" she screamed, but the line of people didn't move, and her foot caught in the splintered deck, sending her sprawling.

Lady Margery scuttled toward Juliette, a cunning smile

on her face. "It won't do you any good," she crooned. "They're afraid. If they try to help you, the ghosts of the sea will rise up and drown them."

Juliette rolled onto her back, staring up at the old woman with undisguised hatred. "The ghosts of the sea will rise up and kill *you*," she said. "They'll pull you under the sea and the fishes will feed on *you*."

Lady Margery's laugh was bright and silvery. "Don't be ridiculous, child. Do you think I'm crazy?"

The question was absurd enough to make Juliette weep. Instead, she scrambled to her feet, the long wet skirts hampering her as she edged away from her mad captor. "I'm not going to let you do this," she said. "I'm going to fight."

"There's nowhere you can go," the old woman said smugly. "You can't dive overboard. If you didn't hit the rocks, you'd drown. There's a murderous riptide that will carry you out to sea. No one would ever even find your body."

"I'm going to escape," Juliette said firmly. The masts had fallen, one over the other, making a crisscross against the deck, and the ropes hung crazily in the soft breeze. Juliette started to climb, scrambling up the rotted timber. "I'm going to get away from you, and I'm going back to Phelan."

"No!" Lady Margery shrieked in rage. "He's mine. You can't have him."

Juliette didn't bother to look behind as she scrambled higher and higher. Lady Margery couldn't come after her with the knife in her hand, and without it they were more evenly matched, despite the older woman's greater strength and madness. Higher still Juliette went, her skirts catching on the rotted wood, and when she reached the heights, she could see the Hannigans clearly, watching her.

Lady Margery was far below, clambering after her, the knife held awkwardly in her hand glinting in the early morning sunlight. In the distance two figures had started down the winding path, and Juliette knew, with no doubt whatsoever, that one of them was Phelan.

"No," she said triumphantly, her voice ringing out in the morning air, carrying on the wind. "Phelan's mine."

And Lady Margery let out a shriek of fury as the knife skittered away to the deck far below them.

# CHAPTER TWENTY-TWO

Phelan had no idea how he made it down the steep pathway to the cove. He was only distantly aware of two things—the roughness of the path beneath his feet and the row of silent Hannigans, sentinels at the edge of the cliff, who made no effort to descend and come to Juliette's aid. Hannigan, his own Hannigan, was behind him, fast on his heels, and Valerian had appeared out of nowhere, barefoot, half dressed, racing along after them.

But Phelan's attention was riveted to the rotting hull of the old ship and to the two women, climbing higher, ever higher on the broken masts, their damp skirts flapping in the strong morning breeze.

He ran into the surf and climbed up onto the side of the ship, ignoring the pain in his hands as splinters dug deep. He vaulted onto the deck and had started after the women when Hannigan's hand clamped down on his shoulder.

He whirled around in fury. "Damn you, you knew she had her!" he shouted, enraged. "Why didn't you tell me sooner? Why didn't you try to stop her?"

Hannigan's face was dead white and sweating, and if Phelan hadn't known better, he would have though the man was in the grip of a powerful terror. "I was hoping... I was hoping I could make things work out. Get Lady Margery back to Yorkshire before she could do any more harm."

Phelan grabbed Hannigan by his shirtfront and slammed him against the side of the ship. "She's killed two men, Hannigan. How many more must she kill before we stop her?"

Valerian had reached the deck as well by that time, moving past them to stand directly beneath the tangled masts. "Lady Margery!" he called up.

The old woman stumbled, falling against the mast, and she glared down at the men on the deck. "You!" she shrieked. "I should have killed you years ago! I tried, you know. When you were just a child, I almost smothered you. But I couldn't. I was afraid. Afraid for my soul. But killing's easy, bastard! The first murder was a pleasure I'm looking forward to repeating."

"Then come down and try it," Valerian taunted, picking up the fallen knife and holding it in his hand. "I'll leave this for you, give you a fair shot at me. I'd be much more satisfying than the girl. What harm has she done?"

"She loves him," Lady Margery spat. "No one can have him but me. He's mine, do you hear me, mine!"

Phelan shoved Hannigan away from him in disgust, pushing past Valerian to clamber up the half-rotted timbers after the women. His added weight was almost more than the ancient wood could support, and it creaked beneath them. "Let Juliette go," he called to Lady Margery, his voice low and soothing. "Come back down here. It's dangerous up there. She doesn't matter, let her be."

The old woman stared down at him, her long gray hair whipping in the breeze, and for a moment he thought he'd convinced her. And then she smiled, a strange, savage smile. "You never call me Mother," she said in a mournful voice. "Unnatural child. When I think of all I've done for you, all I've sacrificed for you."

"Come down," he said, climbing higher. Juliette was overhead, staring down at him, her face white and still. "I'll call you Mother. Just leave her be."

She laughed, a mad, wicked sound on the cool morning air. "I know what's best for you. She needs to die. You think you love her, but you don't. You don't love anyone but me."

"Of course not," he murmured. He could feel the extra weight on the mast as Valerian started after him, and he wanted to shout a warning. He didn't dare. As long as he managed to distract Lady Margery from her goal, Juliette had a chance.

"You're my son," she shrieked, scuttling upward, one clawlike hand catching the hem of Juliette's skirt. "My flesh and blood. No one else can have you…"

"Enough!" Hannigan's voice thundered. "Enough of your mad stories! It's time for the truth."

Phelan was astonished at Lady Margery's reaction. She let out a scream of horror, and for a moment her grip faltered on the mast and she hung out over the deck, her long skinny legs kicking. He held his breath, waiting to see her fall, but her hold tightened on Juliette's skirt, and she hauled herself upward, dangerously close to her.

"Lies," Lady Margery babbled. "Nothing but lies! He's my son. Don't listen to him, Phelan. He's trying to turn you against me. I bore you, this body bore you. Catherine died in childbirth, and her babe with her. We buried her in

Italy, and I brought you back. My own dear son. You had silver eyes, just like your father."

Phelan's grip tightened on the splintery wood as he hauled himself upward. "My father had blue eyes," he said.

"But Catherine's husband, your real father, had silver eyes," Hannigan said heavily. "She died, leaving behind you, her child. And Lady Margery claimed you. We promised Catherine, Barbe and I, on her deathbed that we'd watch out for you. You'd be a lord, you'd have parents, rather than be a poor relation. It was a sensible thing to do, and there was no reasoning with her ladyship."

"Lies!" Margery shrieked again. "Don't listen to him!"

Phelan looked up at her, the murderous woman who'd been such a twisted force in his life. She was no blood kin of his—the dark heritage was none of his own. "Come down," he said gently. "You've already killed two men. Don't hurt anyone else."

She laughed again, with that lightning shift of madness. "You love the girl, Phelan?"

He knew he should lie. The truth might drive her over the edge. But he couldn't deny it when they might be the last words Juliette ever heard. "Yes," he said, unable to keep the astonishment from his voice as he realized the truth. "I love her."

The panic fled Juliette's face by magic. She reached down for him, and the rotting mast shifted ominously. "Phelan," she breathed, her eyes alight with joy, and her voice was so soft only he could hear it. He looked up at her, high overhead, and it was all he could do to keep from climbing up after her, pushing the old woman to one side, and endangering both of them.

He had no choice but to hold still, halfway up the broken

mast, as Lady Margery's cackle floated downward. "Ungrateful fool! You're wrong about one thing. I killed only one man, Phelan," she said. "The girl's husband. Consider it a wedding present. A final gift from mother to son." Her mad laugh rang out over the sea. "You wonder who killed Lord Harry? You were both gullible fools, so ready to believe the obvious."

"If you didn't kill him, who did?"

"He deserved to die, and it was only right that I should blame his bastard. But the authorities didn't believe me. Did you know that? You ran for no reason. They thought I was a crazy old woman intent on revenge, and if I hadn't left, they might have blamed me." She glared down at Valerian. "Not that I care. My husband finally knew the truth about you, Phelan. He was going to disinherit you and put Valerian in your place. I would have done anything to protect you. But there was someone who'd been looking out after you far better than I had."

Phelan kept inching upward. As long as Lady Margery continued with her babble, she was distracted, unaware that he was almost within reach of Juliette. "Who killed him?"

"He'll tell you it was an accident, that they were struggling for the knife, and you might believe him. It might even be true. But the fact remains that Hannigan killed my husband."

Phelan felt the wood shift again, the mast begin to splinter with a dreadful grinding sound. Juliette shrieked as she lost her hold and began to plummet downward, only to be brought up short as her long skirts caught on a spar of wood.

"No," Lady Margery screeched, clambering after her on the collapsing masts. "You won't live. I won't let you have him." She reached out a clawlike hand toward Juliette, and her precarious balance shifted. Screaming, she went flying through the air, flapping black skirts and long gray hair. Her body crashed against the railing of the ship, breaking through, and she went over the side, into the turbulent ocean.

"Don't move," Phelan called to Juliette, edging carefully along the sagging timbers, trying not to look down as the body of the woman he'd always thought was his mother was pulled out into the hungry sea. "I'm coming to get you."

"No," she cried. "Get down. You'll fall."

"Nonsense," he said, ignoring his surge of panic. Not for his own safety, but for hers. "I'm not about to let that happen."

He was almost there, his hand within inches of her arm, when the wood holding her skirts gave way. She screamed, reaching for him, and then she went plunging downward, downward, into the roiling sea.

The cold black water closed over her head, and she sank into the darkness, her skirts dragging at her, her shoes weighing her down. She kicked, trying to push upward, but the current was murderously strong, pulling at her as she struggled toward the light. Her lungs were about to burst when finally she shot through into the morning air. Only to find herself being pulled along by the merciless tide, almost out of sight of the old shipwreck and Dead Man's Cove.

She opened her mouth to scream for help, but she promptly sank, swallowing water. By the time she surfaced again she was spinning wildly out of the inlet, and there was no one to watch her go but those silent, useless sentinels on the edge of the cliff.

And then even they were out of sight, as she was swept away. Her stupid women's clothes were dragging her down, and she realized that, for the moment, she had to stop thinking about Phelan and concentrate on surviving. She managed to kick off the heavy leather shoes; then she began struggling with the waistband of her skirt, sinking beneath the surface as she did so.

Ancient though the material was, it proved almost impossible to rip. She finally succeeded, shredding the wet cloth, and when she rose again she was being carried past a stretch of coast she'd never seen before, the murderous tide clutching her like a jealous lover.

She knew it would be useless to try to swim against the current. Instead, she concentrated on keeping afloat, staying alive, as the water swirled and eddied around her, carrying her far, far away.

Just as suddenly as the death swell had caught her, it released her, and she was drifting along the coast, slowly, as the sun beat down overhead.

It took her a moment to realize she was free. She struck out for shore, ignoring the weariness in her arms and legs, determined not to give in. By the time she made it onto the narrow stretch of white beach, she was exhausted, and she collapsed, closing her eyes and lying very still as she tried to catch her breath.

She had no idea how long she lay there. It was minutes, or hours, before she could drag herself into a sitting position, to survey her surroundings with unavoidable dismay.

The cliffs behind her were white, chalky, and impossibly steep. The stretch of sand was narrow and temporary—

she could see by the line at the base of the rocks that during high tide this small beach would be underwater. She couldn't afford to take her time.

She staggered to her feet, staring down at her clothes. She was wearing a shredded petticoat that clung to her body. The upper portion of the dress barely remained, the sleeves having been torn off. In all, she looked like a scantily clad gypsy.

But gypsies could walk as well as swim. Phelan would be searching for her, but he might not know which way the tide had taken her. She needed to get moving, get back to him. There was so much she needed to tell him.

She reached inside the ruins of her dress and pulled out the waterlogged sketch, unfolding it carefully. There was no longer any recognizable shape to it—the salt water had blurred and destroyed the ink, turning it into a black smear. She ought to leave it.

But she couldn't. It had been her one comfort ever since she'd left Phelan. He'd said he loved her, had told the madwoman that quite brazenly. But she needed to hear him say it to her alone, in the dark, in the quiet, before she could really believe it. Before she could let herself love him.

Not that she was having much luck stopping herself. She started down the strip of sand, her bare feet digging deep. She wouldn't worry about love, or the future, or even sketches. She'd worry about finding Phelan again. She needed to find a way off this beach, either back in the ocean or up the cliffs, if she couldn't find a path. The rest would take care of itself.

Valerian walked slowly through the harbor of Hampton Regis early that evening, thankful that no one stared at him, no one recognized the dashing Mrs. Ramsey in the blond young man who strode along so calmly. And they never would, God willing. Not that he intended to spend much time in Hampton Regis in the future. But since his future in-laws lived there, he'd be bound to make an occasional visit when Sophie insisted.

In all, the de Quinceys had proved to be surprisingly amenable to the notion of their precious daughter's imminent marriage to a nameless bastard. Of course, they didn't realize that Valerian Romney had any connection with their daughter's dear friend, and Sophie had been wonderfully adept at giving her parents an ultimatum. Either they accepted a baseborn son-in-law and proved their freethinking principles, or they would never see their daughter again.

He could find any number of flaws in his beloved's argument, but her parents were not as clearheaded. The knowledge that Sophie's handsome young man had a decent competence settled on him by his natural father in years past went a ways toward soothing their alarm, and the fact that he was in charge of his half brother's estates was equally soothing. The casual information that a grandchild might be on the way seemed particularly pleasing to Mrs. de Quincey, once she had recovered from her swoon.

He had no right to be happy, no right at all. During his weeks in hiding, dressed in those damned skirts, his name had been cleared. With Lady Margery dead, the truth had died with her.

Phelan was leaving. Hannigan had disappeared into the forest once there was no hope for Juliette. No one would be able to find him, and in truth, no one cared. Whether Lord Harry's death had been self-defense or murder, an accident or deliberate, it was done, and while Valerian mourned the selfish old man who'd brought such misery into the world, he knew it was time to let him rest in peace.

So Valerian had his unexpected happy ending. But there was no happy ending for him as long as Phelan was in torment.

Phelan had almost drowned himself, diving for Juliette's body. It had finally taken all Valerian's strength to haul him from the sea. "She's dead, man!" he'd shouted. "She's gone."

And Phelan had made one last attempt at flattening him. Only to collapse on the sand, staring up at the bright sunshine, an expression so bleak and deathly on his face that it had broken Valerian's heart.

Phelan had barely said a word since then. They'd made their way back to the house at Sutter's Head, slowly, in silence, and then Phelan had disappeared into his rooms. An hour later he had reappeared, dressed for travel.

"I'm leaving," he said in his cool, emotionless voice. "Romney Hall is yours to do with as you please. I've left a statement saying as much—you shouldn't have any trouble. You can tell everyone that Lady Margery died of the ague while she was visiting us. No one will doubt you, and no one will care. You are a great deal better liked than she ever was."

"You can't go, Phelan," Valerian said desperately. "You can't just—"

"I can. I wish you joy of your little bluestocking," he said. "Make me lots of nieces and nephews."

"Cousins," Valerian said.

For a moment a spark of life glimmered in Phelan's bleak

gray eyes. "So they would be," he murmured in belated surprise. "I hadn't realized that."

"You're still the heir, you know," Valerian said. "Since Lord Harry had no legal child, you're still the next to inherit."

"No," Phelan said. "I never existed. I died in childbirth with my mother, Catherine, and I expect Lady Margery was never pregnant at all. That leaves you, brat. With my blessing."

"But, Phelan..." Val protested.

"I hate the place. I hate this whole bloody country," he said savagely. "I wish you joy of it. I'm leaving, and I don't expect to be back for a very long time."

"You can't spend the rest of your life alone."

"I don't believe I will. Hannigan will catch up with me sooner or later. After a lifetime of watching over me, he's not about to let go now."

"Phelan, he's a murderer. He killed Lord Harry, he knew that Juliette was in danger, and he said nothing. He's a criminal, from a family of criminals."

Phelan shrugged. "The loss of Lord Harry is no great disaster," he said. "As for the other, we'll have a reckoning. Sooner or later. In the meantime, I'm not going to let the sun rise over me on English soil, ever again."

"But Juliette..." The words froze in Valerian's mouth as he looked into Phelan's face, and he knew there was nothing he could say. He was looking into the face of hell, and the memory would haunt him for the rest of his life.

And then Phelan put his arms around him, hugging him tightly. "Have a happy life, cousin," he said.

"Brother," Valerian corrected gruffly.

Phelan pulled back to look at him, and there wasn't a glimmer of life in his eyes. "Brother," he agreed.

Valerian wasn't making any final effort now to talk him out of leaving. He was simply going to watch the ship sail, taking Phelan away from England, back to the places he loved so well. Maybe he'd find some sort of peace there. Valerian could only pray he would.

"Valerian!" A harsh whisper sounded from an alleyway.

He halted, turning to peer into the gathering gloom. He couldn't see a soul, but once more the voice came, insistent, and he realized with shock that there was only one human being in this part of the world who knew his name.

He dove into the alleyway, colliding with Juliette's small figure, flinging his arms around her, and hugging her so tightly she almost choked.

"Let go of me, you ox," she cried. "Where in God's name have you been?"

He held himself away, looking at her in surprise that finally brought the first trace of humor he'd felt in what seemed like a century. "Good God, Juliette! What have you got on?"

"One of your old dresses," she snapped in return. "Why do you suppose I've been skulking around in alleyways? You didn't leave a thing behind at Sutter's Head. I was lucky I found this in the stable, revealing though it is."

"The Hannigans must have cleared everything out. The Ramseys have disappeared forever. Juliette, we thought you were dead."

"For heaven's sake, why? I can swim," she said crossly.

"Most women can't."

"I'm not most women." She shivered in the cool evening air. "Where's Phelan?" A sudden, horrifying thought crossed her mind. "He doesn't think I drowned, does he?"

"What else could he think? You were gone, there was no trace of you," Valerian said. "He's on board a ship sailing for France."

"Damn him, couldn't he have waited to bury me?" she fumed. "Has he sailed yet?"

"In the next hour. You've got to go to him, Juliette."

"Like this?"

He stared at her. To be sure, the outfit was indecent on her. On his strapping figure, the dress had an elegant décolleté. On her, the neckline sagged almost to her waist, and she only managed to retain a speck of modesty by clutching the loose folds in her hands. The yellow skirts pooled around her ankles, and if she tried to board the *Sea Horse* in that getup, she wouldn't even get up the gangplank.

He looked at her, and knew what she was going to say before she even opened her mouth. "No," said Valerian flatly. "I won't do it. Never again."

Juliette just looked at him. "I nearly drowned today," she said sternly. "I've been kidnapped and almost murdered by a crazy old lady, and now I've been abandoned by the man who said he loved me right in front of everyone, and you have a few qualms about doing something you've done a thousand times before."

"Hell and damnation," Valerian said wearily, unbuttoning his shirt. "You'd better name your first child after me."

Phelan sat alone in the darkness. They were about to weigh anchor, but for the first time in his life he felt no sense of adventure. He wanted the darkness, the numbness, and nothing else.

The cabin was large, but he'd barely noticed it. He sat on the bed, listening to the creak of the timbers, the splash of the sea against the sides of the ship as it moved into the harbor, the snap of the sails overhead, and there was no excitement in his heart. No life at all.

He did have a heart after all. He knew it now, accepted it. Cursed it.

He was starting to feel again. He'd ordered brandy, and the first mate had promised two bottles would arrive at his cabin the moment they left the harbor. Two bottles would be a start.

He heard the quiet rap on his door. He moved his head, looking out the porthole, watching as the lights of the town faded into the distance. "Leave it outside."

The rap came again, more insistent, and he cursed. He'd locked the door, and he had no intention of opening it and facing anyone for a long, long time.

The sailor had the gall to jiggle the locked handle. Phelan surged off the bed, happy for the chance to hit someone, and he yanked open the door. "I told you—" he began, and then he broke off abruptly.

She was standing there, wearing Valerian's male clothes. Her hair was stiff and matted from the salt water, and the huge clothes hung on her small body, but she was there, she was real, she was alive.

He didn't dare move, staring at her in disbelief. "You lied to me," he said, his voice harsh.

"Any number of times," she agreed, watching him warily. "Which time were you referring to?"

"The note you left."

"I didn't want you to follow me."

"Why not?"

"Because I loved you. And I thought I'd destroy you."

"You're an idiot," he said.

"So are you," she said, and her eyes were dark with fury. "I can swim, damn it."

He hauled her into his arms, slamming the door shut behind them, pushing her up against the wall as his hands cupped her dear, lost face. "Of course you can," he murmured dazedly. "I should have realized you can do anything." And he laughed, kissing her wildly, holding her so tightly that she gave a breathless little squeak.

She put her hands up to touch his face, and he knew her fingers were wet with his tears. "Why, Phelan," she said in wonder, "you're human after all. You really do love me."

And he proceeded to demonstrate just how much, as the *Sea Horse* bore them away from this demi-paradise, to a heaven all their own.

\* \* \* \* \*